ALSO BY APRIL REYNOLDS

Knee-Deep in Wonder

THE SHAPE OF DREAMS

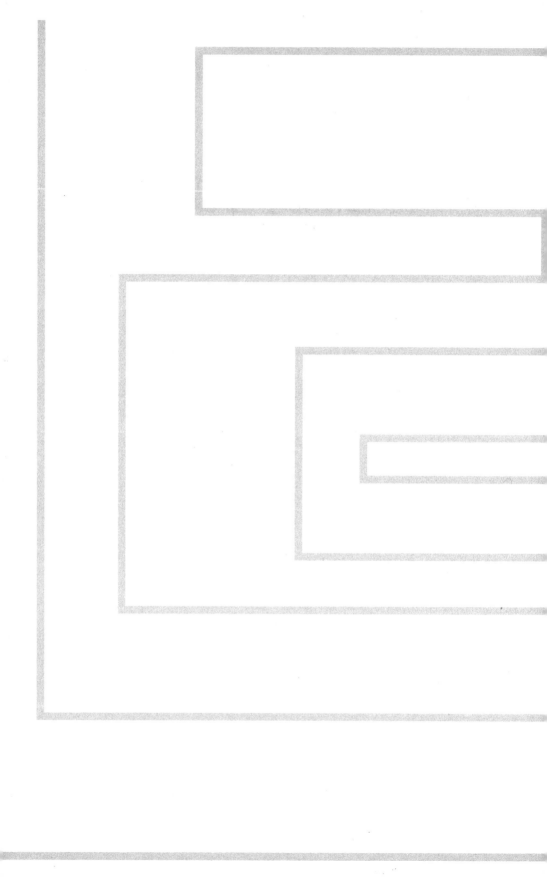

THE SHAPE OF DREAMS

APRIL REYNOLDS

 ALFRED A. KNOPF   2026

A BORZOI BOOK
FIRST HARDCOVER EDITION
PUBLISHED BY ALFRED A. KNOPF 2026

Published by Alfred A. Knopf, a division of Penguin Random House LLC,
1745 Broadway, New York, NY 10019.

Knopf, Borzoi Books, and the colophon are registered trademarks of
Penguin Random House LLC.

Library of Congress Cataloging-in-Publication Data
Names: Reynolds, April, author.
Title: The shape of dreams : a novel / April Reynolds.
Description: First hardcover edition. | New York, NY : Alfred A Knopf, 2026.
Identifiers: LCCN 2025008292 (print) | LCCN 2025008293 (ebook) |
ISBN 9780593316863 (hardcover) | ISBN 9780593316870 (ebook)
Subjects: Classification: LCC PS3618.E588 S53 2026 (print) | LCC PS3618.E588 (ebook) |
DDC 813/.6—dc23/eng/20250311
LC record available at https://lccn.loc.gov/2025008292
LC ebook record available at https://lccn.loc.gov/2025008293

penguinrandomhouse.com | aaknopf.com

Printed in the United States of America
1st Printing

The authorized representative in the EU for product safety and compliance
is Penguin Random House Ireland, Morrison Chambers, 32 Nassau Street,
Dublin D02 YH68, Ireland, https://eu-contact.penguin.ie.

For Michael Davis

THE SHAPE OF DREAMS

PRELUDE

It's easier than she thought it would be. Wanda breaks what looks like stone onto a square of aluminum foil and then feeds the crumbles into a fragile vial that inexplicably has a plastic rose curled at its bottom. "Come close," Wanda whispers. Anita bows her head but does not take her eyes off the vial's bulbous curve that holds the red flower. When small white stones clink and join the scarlet blossom, Anita lets herself believe that she and Wanda are doing a curious kind of gardening. Something will grow from this; she will find Tyrone, she thinks.

Wanda tilts the pipe toward Anita's mouth like a baby's bottle. Anita is ready to suck and suck. She is hungry.

Flame springs from Wanda's hand. Bone-white smoke plumes and crawls along Anita's face. Starving, she takes a deep breath. She expects to cough and choke. She doesn't. The time she burned a roast chicken bothered her more than this. Then bliss. Quiet. She sees her son's face, full of welcome and shy smiles. He is found, finally. Looking at Tyrone doesn't hurt one bit.

Wanda takes her turn, and then both women gradually curl into each other. The pipe slips from Wanda's hand and rolls to the floor. It doesn't break. It rocks back and forth as if it hears a lullaby. Wanda's hands crawl into Anita's lap and rest. Her head finds her friend's shoulder. How wonderful this is, Anita thinks. She tries to think of the last time she'd been touched. Tyrone leaps to mind, but Anita moves away from the thought. No. No. The funeral? No. The last time someone touched her were those seven ladies with caressing sad eyes. They touched her hands, her shoulders, her knees. Compared to that Wanda's hands are lovely.

PART ONE

CHAPTER 1

October 1985

It was not a pretty neighborhood. There was too much hunger and lack for gorgeous architecture to take hold. Rich people were never interested in building block after stately block of brownstones. So the good people of East Harlem gussied up where they lived with what they had. Saint Agnes and Saint Thomas peeked out windows, surrounded by dumb cane and Chinese evergreen. Puerto Rican flags provided both curtains and declarations. This neighborhood was not as grand as Harlem proper, but everyone who hung their hat here knew its allure. One hundred forty-one blocks crowded in Germans, Scandinavians, the Jews, the Irish, Italians, blacks, Puerto Ricans, Cubans, Dominicans, and Mexicans who wanted to make this patch of Manhattan their first stop on the island. As folks came and went, the neighborhood changed its name to fit the times—East Harlem, then Italian Harlem, then El Barrio or Spanish Harlem for those who couldn't roll their *r*'s. The Italians fought and lost to Robert Moses's wrecking whims; Puerto Ricans who could fled to Jersey for the privilege of a backyard. But black folks stayed.

When East Harlem was farm country, black people picked crops; when shantytowns sprang up, they moved in and worked the stockyards. They worshipped in storefront churches, ate arroz con pollo, and bought whiting from the fish market for breakfast. Washington, Lincoln, and Jefferson housing projects were built and black folks settled in, dreaming of moving in with their better-off cousins who lived near Lenox Avenue. And every once in a while, some black family scraped together what they could, got a loan from Grandmomma, told an Uncle Willie Boy he could have the top floor if he pitched in, and bought a building that in the seventies no one else wanted.

Twin Johnson lived in one of those buildings. Instead of an Uncle Willie Boy, she had an Uncle Manuel, and instead of being at home and in bed—it was well before dawn—Twin crouched on the sidewalk, watching her neighborhood reveal a murderous secret.

Sitting on her fat haunches and surrounded by a week's worth of city garbage, Twin wanted to spit. Instead, she swallowed hard. Twice. The smell of Modelo beer bottles overflowing with pee filled her nose, but so did the stink of the dead boy she had just found. She could only see his face's profile and an arm. The rest of him was concealed, tucked under corded cardboard and trash bags. Small black flies marched along his unbearably long lashes.

Their constant movement made it seem as if he were winking. Twin rummaged her memory. Did she know him? This kid wasn't one of her cousin's lookout boys or some little man making a score for his momma. He wasn't one of the neighborhood's young who dared each other to walk up to her and ask her to let him hold ten dollars for a couple of days. Twin touched his elbow and thought, Naw, he's just one more dead black boy on Second Avenue between 109th and 110th hidden beneath garbage on a Wednesday. She ought to have been grateful that the building and its trash out front weren't hers, but she couldn't get the emotion off the ground.

Twin looked down the avenue to make sure no one was coming. With dawn hours away El Barrio was still dark. Its sidewalk empty. Gaylord White, Lehman, Wilson housing projects created high square mountains; the avenue made the valley; trash bags cluttered together looked like out-of-place shrubbery. Like always the East Harlem skyline took her breath away. This scenery—bodegas, funeral parlors, pizza shops—was the only kind of nature Twin knew and loved. And since she wasn't being watched for her well-known antics as the neighborhood crazy, she peered at the kid's half-opened mouth (he really was beautiful) and murmured what was on her heart: "Oh, sweet baby."

What Twin wouldn't give right now for her own hands to be her mother's or a preacher's. On her knees, the older woman massaged her scalp then rubbed her elbows. His eyelids still moved as if he dreamt. Back and forth. Her skin erupted in goose bumps, and Twin told herself it was because of the weather. She hung her head. She had earned her place as a bitch you don't fuck with in El Barrio, or at least on 117th Street. But her thickened skin, along with her toughened reputation, felt supple now. This was the third dead body she had seen this year. The second one she had touched. It was only October. Not even cold yet.

In February she had found an old white woman, freckled and soft, folded into a piece of luggage. Maybe you got limber, she had thought, when you get that little and old. Twin was glad for once that she was a big woman. Otherwise some asshole could put her whole person inside a suitcase meant for weekend travel. Naked as a newborn the dead old lady was smiling, so Twin had zipped her back up and left her in the abandoned community garden underneath the tire where she had found her. Twin didn't shake a bit when she told her uncle all about it over rice and peas. That was winter, 1985. Then at the start of spring she had walked around some Puerto Rican guy in a black-and-green tracksuit and a torn wifebeater, murdered on the footbridge at 103rd that connected Manhattan to Wards Island. Shot a bunch of times in the stomach, twice in the head, stabbed in the arm. Whatever he had done, the fucker who did him wanted to make sure he was good and dead. Twin had lifted a leg, pointed a toe, and stepped over him, careful not to step into the puddle of blood.

Stranger danger, baby girl. Those two bodies, she thought, had been the price she paid for being a roaming soul. Since she was twelve, she had a body that woke hours before dawn and wanted to be outside. Her momma had told her, "Stranger danger, baby girl. The Lord only looks after the good and the innocent, and you ain't neither one." But the warning never stopped her from shoving her size eleven feet in slippers, in sneakers, in combat boots, longing for outside, craving to breathe in the four a.m. chill. Fifty years later her uncle Manuel, who bossed her, her cousin, and his drug enterprise, still asked, "What you do out there, girl?" when she trudged back home with hefty bags full of odds and odder.

"Roam."

Sometimes she would tilt her head and marvel at the only things that soared in El Barrio: the housing projects. Twin looked down the rare building alleys, stuck her hand in sandboxes, found combs with missing teeth, unopened letters from Child Services. She'd stuff them all inside her black plastic bag. It was a good way to mark the time.

In her fifty-seven years of wandering, nobody had messed with her. Twin, almost six feet tall if you included her picked-out Jheri curl, a kiss away from three hundred pounds, walked El Barrio all times of night, sober as a church, mean as a drunk. Most of her neighbors crossed the street when they saw her coming. The hustlers and the homeless nodded when she passed by. Her uncle and cousin dealt weed and crack out of a Jamaican botanical shop on 110th and Second Avenue; they had made a trap in the basement of the tenement building where they all lived. They owned the place; they thought they owned the block. "We the ones who keep you safe." Twin would nod her head as she emptied out her private treasure from a trash bag. There was no harm in nodding. She never told her family what she really thought—that every now and again when she found a preacher and a church that would have her, it was the congregation that kept her safe and whole, even when she wasn't sitting in the pews. Her uncle would never believe that folks would be worried they might be fucking with a follower of the Lord God, Jesus Christ Our Savior. As it was, Twin managed to smile when Uncle Manuel would warn her, "Well, keep at it and you gone find some shit you wish you didn't." Ain't that the truth, she thought, looking at the curve of this beautiful dead boy's cheek.

Twin should have stood up and left. She knew this. Calling the cops would get her nothing but a night or three in the Tombs. If she walked to a phone booth and called for help, her cousin Junior and uncle would lose it. "Don't step in mess" was the family mantra.

She shuffled closer to the body. Twin wasn't really moving her arm; all by itself it traveled over to the dead boy. She herself didn't want to see his haircut; it was her hand that was interested. Maybe somebody during morning rush would stop if they saw him sprawled on the sidewalk. He's not old or Puerto Rican; he's one of mine. Maybe. Twin lifted three bags of trash off the kid and took a hard look. His sneakers broke her heart. Red-and-black British Knights. Every kid in the hood wanted a pair.

She wished she knew the phone number of the preacher of the last church she attended. Carl's name perched on the tip of her tongue. Their church had burned down. He was kind and good and sometimes fierce. She should call him now and ask his advice. What am I supposed to do? How am I supposed to be, when I know some momma put a week's salary on this kid's feet? Some family ate a month's worth of canned beans just so this boy could strut to school in these sneakers. The laces weren't even dirty.

Until right now Matilda "Twin" Johnson had lived her adult life both as a nighttime roamer and as a daylight commentator. In Spanish Harlem there was always a clutter of folk standing on the sidewalk, watching and paying witness to days filled with mayhem.

Stay out on an East Harlem sidewalk long enough and you could see it all: cops only came out when the coast was clear. The men in blue looked at nothing and wrote their stories in notepads. But the sidewalk commentators had stories too, riddled with escape, survival, triumph. They were shot, yes, but somehow they managed to pluck out the bullets. They were drug heads okay, but after two nights on their mothers' couches, they were again sober. If their story was especially heartbreaking, if their fellow teller hadn't had the time to get cleaned up and change clothes, if they had to stand before neighborhood witnesses clutching a tattered shirt together, their friends, the sidewalk commentators held off. "Look at you," they whispered.

"Okay now. It's okay." Neighbors rocked victims in their arms.

Twin was one of their number. She was the one who heard hurt for what it really was, then laughed the loudest. She was the one who had the gall to curse at the violence of gangsters, whose spoken wisdom was so sharp that after her sentences you could see the bone. For almost fifty years she had listened to the story of every slap and punch that happened from 125th to 96th Streets east of Central Park. But never had she been on the other side—the somebody swaying in tatters, the chump running for their life. If she could just wait for daylight and the morning commute, some good citizen in the hood would do the right thing, call in about the body. Right? Twin looked at the pay phone, then down at the dead boy. She heaved herself to her feet and rummaged in her pockets for change.

It took fifty-five minutes for an ambulance to arrive, and then the police showed up ten minutes after that. The hood-wise Twin knew it would take forever for the cops to get there—it always took forever for the police to show up—but still she was surprised at how angry she got from waiting. Twice she almost left. But the dead kid's eyes held her to the corner of 110th. When the paramedics finally showed, looking fully caffeinated yet bored, she learned two lessons. One, she couldn't tell who was the Irish cop or the Italian one when they all wore the same uniform, and two, there's a difference between telling a story after the fact and living within one. The paramedics put on gloves and face masks, and Twin's heart lurched when they lifted the boy from the sidewalk. She expected the body to be a cardboard of rigor mortis. But that didn't happen. His body was as limber as laundry.

The morning commuters arrived and parked themselves in front of the police tape. "Yo, that's a kid, man."

"He dead? For real?" The bystanders grew in number. Six people, then a dozen more joined them. "What's up? What's happening?" While the paramedics tried to decide whether to walk around or step over the stinking trash, a neighborhood's shock began to bloat. Forty neighbors found themselves asking the same questions: "How long this little boy been out here? Who done this? Who is he?" The ambulance moved to the corner so the paramedics didn't have to climb over the heaps of garbage. The three cops who showed up weaved through the crowd trying to find the somebody who made the phone call. Twin waved at them, and finally the police spotted her hiding in plain sight, standing beside her neighbors. "Here they come, Twin," a guy said.

"Ma'am, you found the body?" The police hadn't surrounded her, not with Twin's back against the police tape, but it felt like it. The mustached cop stood on her left. She turned her head, her normally sleepy big eyes wide-awake, and looked him in the eye. "Ma'am, what time did you find the body?"

The truth burped out of her mouth, "I don't know. Morning. Early." Her heart fluttered.

"Your name."

"Twin."

"Your real name."

Twin felt a sharp humiliation. Hadn't she scolded men, women, and children who stumbled over their own names when saying it aloud to some authority figure? Hadn't she admonished those who had aw-shucked the police that *she* would never cower? Where was that dreamt-up woman? Twin could hear her neighbors grousing but unable to swallow their anger and spit out her own. "Y'all can't throw a sheet over that little man?" she said.

"What's your real name?"

She hadn't known this would happen, how her heart would tilt and her stomach and bladder join in on the fun. Her mouth was so dry. "Twin. Matilda 'Twin' Johnson," Twin said. The cops took a step too close. The one in front of her, the one without the mustache, reached out to touch her elbow and for no reason at all stopped himself. His arrested move gave Twin courage.

"Step back," she said.

"Excuse me?"

"You heard me."

"I think you need to come over to the precinct. Answer some questions."

"Naw, man. I ain't doing that."

The cop in front of her touched her wrist, the mustached one clamped a hand on her shoulder, and the one to her right grabbed her sleeve.

"Yo, don't touch me. I mean it." Twin hoped her neighbors would have her back, but it was clear their attention was fractured. Dressed for work—janitor jumpers, nurse's aide tunics, checkered chef pants—their jobs beckoned to them to get going, but most of them were still looking at the dead boy who still hadn't been covered with a sheet, whose new shoes in the morning sun look like their hard work. "You don't got to handle him like that," she said.

"Yo, respect the little man," one in the cluster said.

"Throw a sheet over him."

"How long he been out here?"

"Yo, who did this to the little man?"

The crowd's questions and comments began to get loud, and all at once they realized nothing held them back but flimsy yellow tape.

"Let's get back to the house," the mustached cop said and pushed down on Twin's shoulder, pulling her toward the police car. She wanted to ask a question of her own, one that she had wondered about before the paramedics, the police, or even her neighbors came. A question that would answer a neighborhood's anger.

Nothing came to mind.

CHAPTER 2

Anita missed Tyrone before she knew he was gone. His school had let out at three forty-five, and by five o'clock Anita Jackson was anxious. Not enough to call the cops or anything, but by the time she finished work at the post office, she surprised herself by whispering, "That boy," on the way home. She had told her mother that while standing outside in October afternoon sunshine she had staggered, her knees suddenly weak, and she had had to brace herself against the brick wall of a building. "Mama, I just knew then. I knew it." When they found him, or rather when she was brought in to identify his body, her soft thought sharpened and transformed.

All of it—from the murmured "That boy" to the right now—was just four days ago. She had viewed her son, staged a wake, and begun to call Southern relatives to come to the funeral by Sunday, but all the while her mind was crowded with the clarity of the October day when her son vanished and mixed in with it was the man coming from the army saying, "Your husband, Mrs. Jackson." She remembered the warm, calming smell of envelopes at work as they shot through the sorter at the post office. Like any other workday Anita had walked out of the Hellgate Post Office into Spanish Harlem's city roar in the weak afternoon sunlight. In her memory the piss and rot floating out from the 110th Street subway station was no different than usual, was tolerable, and the ripe scent of bananas heaped on a fruit stand called good evening as she watched for downtown traffic when she crossed Third Avenue.

Like everyone else who lived in this neighborhood, Anita didn't look up from the sidewalk, but if she had, mercy. Every kind of life spilled out of apartment windows. Houseplants turned jungle snaked around the window frames; kids and parents parked their elbows on the sills and watched the shenanigans on the street as if they were a tennis match. "There he goes." "No, he didn't." "Look out, look out, oh!" Twenty-story housing projects carved into the skyline, while too few public schools dominated city blocks, their majesty muted by barred windows. Even the churches mushed on either side by tenements hadn't forgotten their command to astonish. Copper spires rose higher and higher, their cherries on top the shapes of the cross. But no one in East Harlem looked up to see Christ arisen, perched atop architectural feats. Certainly not Anita Jackson. Her church had burned down eight months ago, and navigating her way home demanded too much attention.

The sidewalk was crowded with her neighbors: schoolchildren, commuters, gangsters, the homeless. Lined along the curb were burnt-out cars, weeks' and weeks' worth of trash, tricked-out Cadillacs. Anita had left work early; the school bell had rung; scores of children with backpacks clapping a rhythm shouted back and forth to each other, "Hey! Hey! Hola! Hola!" as if they hadn't spent the entire day together. Children dared each other to climb atop piles of refuse or abandoned car shells and shout victory. Anita stepped quickly around them.

A couple of kids who recognized her post office uniform shouted hello. "Ms. Anita, my mommy says you gone give us a discount on the money order." And Anita, who knew they mimicked their parents' wishes, nodded and kept walking. Her slim glide swept through the children, past the abandoned Cutlasses and Chevettes, and around the brisk business of the Game Room, where drugged customers staggered out into sunlight. Young men stood and guarded what they were brewing; women with unnaturally blond hair draped themselves in muscular arms and preened. Anita's almond eyes, surrounded by thick baby lashes, took it all in: idle men sitting against buildings, applauding with their thighs as pretty girls paraded by; the John Johns and the Los Tres Unidos posses aching to fight, but autumn sunlight kept knives and stolen guns pocketed and banked gangster violence. Young men, brown and black, held boom boxes and yelled over the songs to be heard. Hey, hey, hey, hey. *Solista Pero No Solo* and "Rock the Bells" drew swords and fought for dominance. Boom, boom, boom. The music's thump instructed: Stick em, get em. No, nigga, let the beats battle. Hands high-fived. Shoulders bumped. Later for you, ése.

Across the street only the old men who were gathered at a table on the corner graced her with a smile. She had no idea that under the shadow of their panama hats, old men's mouths watered as she passed by them, because Anita smelled lick-able: cocoa butter and hints of strawberry and apples and grapes begging to burst floated out from her skin. And then underneath the smell of fruit, old men breathed in the unmistakable scent of tender meat. She remembered giving a modest nod to the tight group of dominoes players on the corner of Third Avenue. Funny. She never had before. Or since.

And then the school. PS 083 was completely emptied, as she knew it would be. Not a kid or a teacher or even a janitor in sight, even though the final bell had rung only thirty minutes before. That's when she'd said, "That boy." And as if they had heard her, a flock of seagulls on the cement playground lifted into the sky, one of them as big as a television. Her steps, she was convinced, had frightened them into flight.

But had that really happened? Even retelling, reimagining, rethinking the moment when her son was probably killed, she knew that those big awkward birds had only seen her in the mornings, had only witnessed her morning commute for the past seven years. She never saw them on the way home. But this one time there they were at four fifteen in the afternoon, suddenly aloft. Their unusual appearance had also made her think of her son. That boy. Where he at? Later as she told her mother all about the police station and how Tyrone should have been home when she got there and the all-night worry, she turned that soft musing into the epitome of a mother's intuition. But truthfully—and Anita always tried to tell the truth—those big birds rising, tilting with the wind just prompted a craving to tell her son about an odd afternoon sight, a four-o'clock phenomenon to share with someone who would listen. Her boy was good at that. He would pay attention to her even if the plot of her story found nobody strangled or an I-don't-know-who-that-was in the bed.

Her Tyrone, with his neat short Afro and his big feet that were clearly waiting for the rest of him to catch up, was so, so good at hearing a story that never came to an end. Tyrone, her private, forever interested ear. Which was why she was just the teeniest bit angry as she called out his name at the apartment front door and didn't receive an answer. She looked for him in his tiny bedroom that had space for nothing more than a twin bed and a chest of drawers. Anita thought about his absence as she took off her post office uniform and put on her old gray sweats and a T-shirt. It embarrassed her, but Anita knew she had spent the last two years basking in a son's love that sometimes felt so heavy she wanted to throw it off. Her plump mouth screwed up, annoyed, as she walked down her short hallway headed to the kitchen to add a final heap of olives to the Crock-Pot of black beans. She wanted to tell Tyrone about the seagulls while he hummed over dinner. That wasn't too much to ask, was it? But ain't it the way? Back when she had wanted just fifteen minutes of quiet, she couldn't touch her hip because Tyrone was always attached to it. But now when she craved his presence, when her black beans were acting right and weren't just a kettle of rocks, where was he? Not at the kitchen table, that's for sure. Six o'clock showed but not Tyrone. Anita hissed at paper napkins and gleaming bowls set at the table, then called his friend Kendall's apartment at the Washington projects.

"Hey, girl. Put Tyrone on the phone." But Shelia, the mother and her friend, could only account for her son's whereabouts, not Tyrone's. Bean stew simmered as she called her son's other friend Lucy, and got the same answer. Anita. Anita, calm down. He's somewhere.

She didn't dare call the cops. Who knew what would happen if you sent the police searching for a lost black boy? Instead she wasted almost three hours trying to track him down without leaving her apartment, because what if Tyrone showed up just after she left? His school was closed, but she called there anyway. She looked up the names of his homeroom teacher, the school counselor, and the vice principal in the telephone book and had short, pleasant conversations with strangers who had no idea where Tyrone was. In between all of it she finally broke down and started to phone her local police precinct every twenty minutes and got a busy signal every time. Jesus. She paced the kitchen, its narrow galley three steps long, then the living room, around the couch, around the coffee table, to the window and back, looking in at her bed dressed in its newly laundered sheets, opening and closing Tyrone's bedroom door for no reason at all. Michael Jackson from his *Thriller* poster peered back, and Anita cursed herself blue and headed back to the kitchen. "Where are you?" she asked her empty apartment. She turned off the beans, put up the bowls, forgot about telling the story of the birds, and made herself mad enough to call the one place he had better not be: with Daryl at his crazy momma Wanda's apartment.

Anita had been friends with Wanda because Tyrone was friendly with Wanda's son Daryl. But that didn't mean she liked the woman. She thought Wanda had trifling, high-siding ways. All her clothes were a size too small; she changed her hairstyle from cornrows to Jheri curls to press and set and back to Jheri curls; her hair color changed with the seasons; she came to church late when they had a church and still tried to get a good seat. Both women clucked over their children, but Anita thought Wanda's concern was just talk. Daryl roamed and picked up every kind of trouble. But most damning, at least in Anita's eyes, was when Wanda walked down the street, her round ass in neon spandex turning heads, her bosom on display for ogling. She returned the appreciative stares she received, showing off her dimples on either cheek. Tyrone bet not answer this phone, Anita thought. He didn't.

Wanda talked nonstop. The phone call was ten minutes too long as soon as she said hello. Wanda immediately started in on her lack of employment, how she had just asked her momma for grocery money, and how her on-again, off-again boyfriend Tony was just laid up, expecting her to somehow make all ends meet, and "Anita, can't you help a sister out?"

The sharpening worry for Tyrone made room for the irritation Anita felt when talking to Wanda. "I *did* help you out, and you showed up drunk for the interview, Wanda."

"See. Now see, that ain't right. I was mildly lick—liquored, Anita."

"Sure."

"I was, girl. You know how Tony is in the morning." That they were talking at all about Anita's failed attempt to sponsor Wanda for the union shocked Anita back to the topic she had called about in the first place.

"Wanda. I'm not calling about the post office job. I'm looking for Tyrone. Is he there?"

"Girl, it's ten o'clock at night. You don't know where he at?"

"That's why I'm calling."

"Listen, just a minute, kay?"

Wanda's hand muffled the receiver, but Anita heard her snigger: listen here, there was always a lowest to get to. Normally Wanda kept her dark chuckle swirling around her own woeful stories—like when she told everybody how her son Daryl had been in and out of juvey for the last eight months, accused of burning down the church where both she and Anita had been congregants for more than four years. "He didn't do it; he was home with me. Like that matters." With every telling—whether on the playground, in the beauty shop, or at the checkout line in the grocery—Wanda's stories swam in a cackle that Wanda now tried to cover with her hand over the phone's receiver.

Anyone who heard Wanda's laugh immediately knew there was trouble. No one ever heard its sympathetic undercurrent or its almost silent advice: Just laugh or you'll start crying, and then you'll never quit. Everyone just heard its warning.

Now she said, "Girl, go to the police."

Not bothering to say goodbye, Anita slammed down the phone,

and panicked steps took her out the door so fast she forgot to lock up the apartment. If there were a race all the way to the Twenty-Third Precinct on 102nd, Anita would have won.

She struggled to calm her breathing as she cleared the doors and approached the desk.

"I'd like—"

"Yes?"

"I'd like to—"

"Why don't you take a minute?" The question managed to sound at once kindly and cool.

Anita stopped, counting her breaths until they calmed, but the self-assessing minute proved shocking. She realized gone was the respectable chin-length relaxed hair. Her kitchen had nappied with sweat; her hairline had reverted back to baby. The hum of her breathing honed into a name: Tyrone, Tyrone. "Okay."

"Are you all right?" The matronly white cop at the desk looked both at the windblown woman and the small group of three police officers just beyond Anita's left shoulder. Nothing had happened, but the skinny black woman in the gray sweats had that I'll-do-anything look. It was an expression and stance that compelled an officer of the law to think a Colt revolver, a billy club, and a pair handcuffs (all three to be used frequently and without provocation) were the only things to save you from early retirement and a gimpy knee. New York's finest saw it all most days, when some perfectly normal citizen came in telling a tragedy so outrageous, one was browbeaten into believing in God. Mothers were turning on children; sisters and brothers were doing nasty things together; even four-year-olds weren't left to be innocent. Then collectively bowing under the enormity of those sins, an entire neighborhood, one by one darkened the doors of the closest precinct and confessed things that made the faithful clutch rosaries or find quiet places for prayer. The desk sergeant had tried to explain "the look" to her husband for the past five years and had failed just as long.

"M okay. Okay," Anita panted, noting the desk sergeant's contemptuous expression. Anita realized she had forgotten her hat, her coat, and also her purse. Maybe I should go back home. "I think my son is missing."

Out came a sheaf of papers, then a pen clacked open. "When did you realize he was missing?"

"Well . . ." Just now, when Wanda, the stupidest woman in the world, suggested I do what I should have done by the time the beans had cooled. "I think . . ."

"Ma'am?" The desk sergeant's cold, judgmental green-eyed stare took in Anita's sweat-drenched forehead, the run-down yellow flip-flops, her raggedy gray long-sleeved shirt that had holes in both elbows and under her right arm. The clothes smelled, and so did she after a seven-block run. That with the combination of no purse and her breathlessness, and suddenly Anita wished she hadn't changed out of her work clothes. How many times had she given the exact same flat eye when some I-can't-believe-you-left-the-house-like-that woman stood in line at the post office with some snot-nosed crybaby clutched on one hip and a six-year-old on the other. Anita recalled her own disapproving look as some rattled mother didn't realize that, yes, there was a fee to purchase a thirty-dollar money order.

Being on the receiving end of such a stare, a fully dressed Anita felt naked. Policeman, post office clerk, security guard, subway conductor—no matter the uniform those properly clad never had to declare the obvious: I work, pay bills and taxes, and more often than not vote. Standing in front of the desk sergeant without her pale blue button-down shirt and darker blue pants, she was without citizenship or intelligence or benign purpose.

"Ma'am. Ma'am. Excuse me, ma'am, could you tell me when he went missing?" The bored officer raised the question again, though the tight grip on her pen made it clear this latest asking was the fourth time.

"Sorry. Sorry. Right. I don't know, maybe right after school? Or a little after that?"

Anita's doubtful voice embarrassed them both.

"What was he wearing the last time you saw him?"

But that too proved difficult to conjure. Anita bit her lip. "I don't know. You know, jacket, jeans, shirt ..." Anita's voice trailed away while she gave the question hard thought. What was Tyrone wearing this morning? Suddenly she wished her son were six again, the age when his father was still alive and she was his ideal wife and also the perfect mother who laid out clothes on the bed the night before and checked to see if her son's socks matched. Oh God, she hadn't done that in forever. But now, at twelve years old and in sixth grade? If his clothes smelled clean when he left for school, it was a triumph. Didn't this green-eyed white woman know that? What kind of children did she have?

Anita rummaged around in her head for an accurate description—did he put on that black shirt or the blue one with the hole under the armpit that she hated so much? The gray jeans that couldn't figure out if they wanted to be a pair of shorts or pants? Or the acid-washed ones whose cuffs had apparently just decided they'd rip themselves off and vanish? I just can't remember ... But then her memory seized on her son's sneakers, which Tyrone had begged her to buy. Clunky, with large faux leather swaths of black-and-red tennis shoes. He wanted them so badly he actually cried when he asked her for them. Too old for it, for months he had stood on the cusp of a tantrum; then he humiliated himself into pleading and finally bargaining. "Whatever you want, Momma. Come on, please."

"Whatever I want, huh?"

"I'll take out the trash. Clean my room and the kitchen and everything." Whimper, whimper; snot, snot. "And help with dinner and stuff."

She had finally submitted to his begging and bought the sneakers after he convinced Kendall, Lucy, and that little troublemaker Daryl to go with him to the public library to check out books every Saturday.

What were those damn sneakers called? British Guards? Tyrone's look of overwhelming joy when he tore away the gift-wrapping paper flooded her memory. British Soldiers? British Knights! "Oh, I know. He was wearing a pair of British Knights, red and blacks. He's had them for a week now." With those shoes she had rewarded a straight-A student who had done a civic duty.

"O-kay." The sergeant need not lift a brow; the shape of her mouth said it all. You live in this neighborhood; you don't even know when your boy went lost; you can't remember the clothes he wore this morning; but look at you, happy as all get-out that you bought your freaking kid a pair of shoes that probably cost as much as your rent. Huh. And you got the gall to smile about it? "Good for you. New pair of sneakers. Tell me all about them."

Tempted as she was to scream, *How dare you?*, the white cop's "Good for you" held for Anita such curiosity she wasn't sure which emotion to jump to. A heated reply? A haughty one? He's been an A student for more than three years! Those shoes made him think of people besides himself! He's going to the library and spreading the news that it's fun, like a politician or a judge. Anita opened her mouth, angry, but nothing came out. She was sharply aware of her unmanicured nails, unplucked brows. Where were Tyrone's birth certificate and insurance card? Not in her hands. Where were her pictures of Tyrone at age four at the circus, age five and inquisitive at the zoo, eight years old at Macy's Christmas windows, his fourth-grade photo at ten? Proof that she not only had dressed him in a bow tie for picture day but that she knew how to tie one. Where was her driver's license or Tyrone's New York State ID card? Her checkbook and most recent utility bill? Jesus, God, why had she left home without her folder full of documents that organized and legitimized everything about the two of them?

Tyrone had never left the city, never mind the country, but Anita had still gotten him a passport. And when her friends laughed, she laughed back, thinking you never know. You never know what you'll need. Who was this foolish, coatless woman she'd become? Wanda and that stupid, dumbass laugh. A telephone conversation had pushed her and said, Girl, listen; hurry, hurry. And she had, tracking down Third Avenue without taking a moment to dig into her nightstand and pull out her Trapper Keeper that held every certified moment of Tyrone's life. Now that the fourteen-hundred-yard dash was over, with nothing but her racing heart to tell the tale, she wondered and worried that without her family's stack of information would anyone even bother to listen. Certainly not this cop. Tyrone, where are you? Shivering inside a police precinct on an October evening without socks or a scarf, she hadn't felt this out of place since she entered middle school. Okay, okay.

"Okay, what?" the desk sergeant asked. And what if, while she was here, Tyrone was twisting open their front door that for the first time in his life wasn't locked, filling the apartment with plaintive, panicked cries of Momma? He wouldn't know she put the beans in the refrigerator. She had put the dishes up, so he'd think she'd never been home at all. Had she even raised him well enough that he would turn on the television, watch *Star Search*, and just wait?

She wished her son were an honest-to-God latchkey kid, one of those children who could let themselves in, make themselves an afternoon snack, settle down and do their homework on their own. But no. Not in her house. That's not how I raised him. In the last eight months Tyrone may have learned how to open the door by himself, but before he could even think of trouble, Anita had sailed home not twenty minutes afterward. When their church had burned down eight months ago and that had meant no more after-school programs, she hadn't had the time to find something else to fill the two hours before she got home. The last half a year had been spent explaining to her managing supervisor daily why she needed to leave over an hour early. Oh, baby. Not only did she have to agonize about Tyrone's disappearance, but she found herself biting her lip over what he would do with himself after stepping inside their unoccupied apartment at eleven o'clock at night. Anita fought hard to shut down the worry and remember his Social Security number.

"Do you have a recent photo you can give us?"

"I . . . left that at home."

"Okay, well, we're going to need that," the officer sighed. What time would he normally get home? Have you contacted his school? Did he seem all right—angry, depressed—the last time you saw him? Is he involved in any gang activity or drugs?

Anita sputtered, "He's twelve," but the pointed stare of the officer anchored the indignation Anita tried to float.

"Go home, Ms. Jackson. He might be there, waiting for you." The cop held up a silencing hand. "Come back in the morning with a photo, and we'll make copies. You know kids nowadays."

This officer didn't know how innocent her Tyrone was. His life was shaped by a mountain of literature—*The Outsiders,* Tolkien, Dickens—provided by the local library and manners to match. Anita's closed mouth transformed into a scowl. It was her clothes. It was her ashy feet shoved into yellow flip-flops. She knew she looked almost homeless, but she also remembered when she could beat anybody in a footrace and could pick up the corner of her couch with one hand, when she could buy her clothes at Filene's Basement and didn't bother looking at the price tag. Two years of being a widow had whittled her down. But still. Where was her Tyrone?

The desk sergeant lifted a dismissive chin, and her left hand furtively beckoned to the officers just behind Anita. "I'll bet you he's at home right now."

Anita didn't turn around, but she felt the trio of police move toward her. Her back crawled as she felt them creep steps closer. Who's breathing like that? Girl, that's you. Now she understood what that poor black woman in front of her at the post office, asking for a money order, had been going through.

"Come back in the morning, huh?"

It hadn't been a bad upbringing; it was an articulation of desperation. Every I'm-out-of-patience woman was simply waiting frantically for her turn. And for help. In all the time Anita had talked some mother through the intricacies of priority mail, she had never once heard their keening, I'm here and so are you; so why isn't this working? That's what I never heard, she thought. Shame on me. Her embarrassment about her hair, her clothes, her widowhood, her sweat, her possible—oh, just admit it—her certain stink, her skinniness, her blackness, her predicament fell away like a dropped coat. And what was left was hopping mad.

"Y'all s'pose to help people! And you sit there with your glazed doughnuts and coffee ..." Anita pointed an accusatory finger at a large desk clear of pastries, and the angry crescendo tapered shut.

Standing in between the desk sergeant and the three cops, she noticed the growing silence. Typewriters shushed; folks stopped walking; even the incessant ringing of telephones stuttered. In that collective quiet Anita knew she had the anger but not its cutting language.

She backed away from the desk, refusing to give the three cops the satisfaction of turning on them, and walked blind in the general direction of the double doors of the squad house. She had done nothing right all day, but providence took pity on her. When her arm flew behind her, it easily found the exit rod and pressed it open. Night air, cool, almost baptismal. Her next words had no reasoning to anchor them, but out they came, "I'm union, you know! I work at the post office!" Her hands pushed the door further. And when Anita found herself dwelling on this moment weeks, months later, she still didn't know why it felt appropriate to say, "My husband was a soldier, and I vote!"

CHAPTER 3

And then she ran.

She ran like she never had as a kid—ran like those children at Marcus Garvey Park, up and down sharp hills at a leggy gallop that held nothing back, arms flailing, knees chest-high. Sharp crests of trash along the avenue created a tableau as Anita fled by the stench. Even when she had seen the 6 train pull away from the platform or the city bus hiss up and crawl away from the curb, she had never run like this, fleeing her anger and embarrassment. One block, then two, then three, all uptown. How could she have talked to me like that? And then trying to sic those cops on me like I was up to something. Four blocks later, and Anita was still so mad she couldn't figure out how to pace herself. Fleeing the sneer of a desk sergeant and a three-cop posse, Anita was running and winning. She left behind their contempt and her own.

She fell. No wonder, since the entire time she was just a stumble waiting to happen. Her hands, thrown up at the last minute, just barely protected her face. A top layer of skin graffitied the concrete.

Anita could feel her pain. Everything hurt: her knees, her forehead, her chin, her pride. Thank God nobody saw her pick herself up. Thank you, Jesus, that there's no music to soundtrack the embarrassment. But her self-soothing thought was quickly scuttled by something she hadn't heard since she was sixteen and visiting her grandmother in Eastman, Georgia: quiet. It was a silence so heavy it seemed edible. No salsa or rap beat. No loudmouthed boy shouting. Where was everybody? Nobody was out here, which meant possibly everyone was. Man, woman, and toddler knew that where there was city quiet there was trouble.

She had heard stories from her mother and visiting relatives about just how peaceful it was down there in the South, in deep country. Nothing around for miles, you know? Real nice. You could hear a bird coo in the next county. But Anita had a hard time romancing the dark. When she had listened to girlfriends and coworkers, their stories backed up her quite reasonable fear. Every somebody she knew who had been mugged or clobbered began the telling in the same way: "I was out late on _____ all alone, and then WHAM!" City silence just meant there was a bunch of bad guys lying in wait, eager for prey to casually look the other way; then they could pounce. And well, look here, there she was out in the middle of all that quiet at eleven fifteen at night. Crouched on all fours on the sidewalk on her skinned knees no less. Just a mark. Run. Girl, run. Anita lifted her head and listened for something, anything. She heard nothing at all. Run.

She got off her knees, still crouching, and above her she heard the canned applause of a turned-up television sitcom. She checked and winced at her skinned palms. She clapped her hands together, more for the company of some sort of noise than for cleanliness. Her beating heart slowed; a pounding right in the center of her head slid down to her throat. She glanced up at the traffic lights and allowed herself to think, Safe, safe at last, when her eyes saw a quartet of men, each of them strangely keeping their backs to her. Hadn't they heard that agonizing cry she tried but failed to muffle? Maybe not. Her gaze traveled twenty feet across the sidewalk and spied yet another cluster of men. She could only see a collection of almost disembodied heads with high-top fades and neatly shorn ponytails. Is this what happened at night? When the decent and law-abiding were in bed, groups of men—three, four, sometimes seven large—just stood and looked around, with their hands in their pockets and waiting. But for what? Anita squinted to get a better look, but the two crowds of men stood beyond the bright puddles of streetlights.

Anita forgot her skinned knees and elbows and tried to move ever so softly into standing. She couldn't shake her mother's cautionary voice. "Stranger danger, baby." How many times had she herself said that very thing to Tyrone whenever he left the house. "You get back in the house before streetlights. Stranger danger, hear me?" She had had the talk: "Say 'yes, sir' and 'no, sir' when the police stop you; keep your hands where they can see them," a litany of do this, do that, which would protect her son from a cop's violent whimsy. Yet here she was, all by herself, those men just across the street.

Two men from one group raised their heads and turned to her. Men. No, not yet. Boys, big boys. Who were they? If she didn't know any better, she would have sworn that one was Sam. Was it? Was that Sam or Darren or Tyreck? Juan or Jesús? Was that Jesús? She knew one of the boys' head shape. Were they the same young men she let carry her groceries to her door, but at midnight they were different? Anita Jackson—afraid to just stand there but even more afraid to break out into a run lest they follow her. Before she could decide to book or scream, the young men who stood in a loose circle turned their faces to the Franklin Court projects. Anita could see boys as young as Tyrone and younger standing in the hallways. Their noses and mouths were hidden behind red-and-black handkerchiefs. Each kid held a baseball bat. Anita saw youngsters on the top floor taking off in a run and smashing the nearest light bulb with their bats. Darkness raced toward the window. Floor by floor, the projects went dark. She followed the descent. When her eyes reached the bottom, Anita looked around for the group of men. They were gone. Her heart snatched tight.

Motherhood, all its weight, all its advice: stranger danger; in by streetlights; watch out now; sit down; cut out all that running; stranger danger, stranger danger. What in the hell was she even doing outside this time of night? This time Anita didn't run. She opted for a commuter's stride.

The steady rumble of Sysco delivery trucks that had bracketed her sleep on countless nights greeted her as she rounded the 110th Street corner on Second Avenue. Downtown needed every foodstuff and luxury, and trucks began their journey at the tip of 125th Street and Second. All the crazy that happened at eleven o'clock at night on Third Avenue felt like a town away. Landscape she had watched her entire adult life turned unfamiliar. And that didn't make any sense to Anita since the Franklin Court projects loomed over both avenues. She glanced up at her building, longing to see just one face peeking. Just a neighbor would help. Hers was the lone light on in the building. He's home. She opened her door, her heart thumping. "Tyrone?" Along with her purse, her coat, her socks, her son's photo, and her dignity, she had also forgotten to turn off the lights when she left for the police station hours ago.

She knew he wasn't there, but still she looked for her son the way she would have searched for her keys: from the front door to the kitchen and then the bathroom behind it she retraced her steps, scanned the living room, going down the short hall to check his bedroom, check hers, and take another look at the bathroom because it had a second door. Her stinging hands sang at every doorknob she turned. And while she knew there was Campho-Phenique in the medicine cabinet, she was too tired to go back to the bathroom and get it. She didn't start thinking awful thoughts until she turned off all the lights in the apartment, settled onto her couch (because to take to bed would have meant she had given up), and pressed a cushion against her stomach. The television could have helped, but she didn't have enough wherewithal to turn it on, her mind stuffed to the rafters with green-eyed police. Anita clutched the couch cushion harder, bending it in two. She began to miss him in earnest. Not only her son but her husband.

Reginald would have known what to do. Reginald would have been able to bank her panic, because he had known her since ninth grade and his six-foot-four frame always soothed. Sweethearts. That's what they were and how her heart felt when she had been around him. When he had signed up for ROTC and enlisted in the army at eighteen, it was the perfect punctuation of their relationship. Reginald liked plans, and he'd had one before he was nineteen: "Army's gone pay for college, baby. We'll have savings in no time." Anita missed his certainty.

He would have thought of something brave but organized, and even if it didn't fix anything, while they were in the middle of whatever plan he had, it would have felt like it could work. He would have told her to get off the phone with Wanda or better, don't even bother calling her. Just put on your work clothes and I'll throw on my fatigues and we'll go *together* down to the police. And then *together* they would have stepped through those double doors and the desk sergeant would have stood up and shook their hands, and the cops behind them would have saluted, and all the people who had stopped talking and typing would have come out of the offices and conference rooms she could not see and sung "The Star-Spangled Banner," because there was something about her late husband that made you want to get on tiptoe and stay there.

But then her husband Reginald went off to Grenada and did what his mother accused him of, "went down there and got himself killed." That so few died during Operation Urgent Fury, that where they invaded was so small, that the theater of war warranted just two minutes on ABC's seven-o'clock *Eyewitness News,* that what we were standing for or fighting against felt so ephemeral, made her ten-year-old son sidle closer still. "What does jungle look like, Momma? Who was we fighting?" "Your daddy died fighting for an idea, baby," answered nothing and everything.

South America, communism, homework, his latest pants size—whatever was on Tyrone's mind the last two years—Anita had to be all the answers. Her widowhood meant ten-year-old Tyrone fled back into her arms. Indifference, feigned or real, didn't have a prayer in her apartment. Middle-of-the-night visits, "I love you" said for no reason at all, and the stroking of her elbow while she did the dishes soothed her son's fatherless nightmares that flourished both in the dark and with a night-light. After Reginald was returned to her in three distinct pieces, nobody was better than Tyrone's momma. Nobody was funnier or made better mac and cheese. Nobody had a softer arm to stroke or a laugh more contagious. If a killed-in-action husband hadn't instigated it all, 1983 would have been a banner year.

Tyrone's acute, unflagging attention had acted as a balm to her loneliness. And now what? She wished Victor, her husband's casualty assistance officer, and Keith were here. If not Reginald, then at least them. God bless the military. Victor, who she couldn't help but think of as the short little man with a Santa Claus stomach, gave her the killing news about her husband and stuck around for five months to sort it all out, helping her decide whether to travel to Dover, lending a hand with the funeral arrangements, and standing with her when she had to tell Reginald's mother the news.

Sitting on the couch now, she told herself to stop. Just stop it. She didn't want to become one of those women who boo-hooed over something she couldn't ever have. And she couldn't have Reginald. He was gone. Buried in Arlington. So maybe she could at least have Keith, a member of his unit, or better Victor. Someone who could be the lookout and hover over a black woman's life. Somebody who could point out a path and say, Do this. Anita needed someone like that now. Doing her best not to break into tears, she knew she had no idea what her next step should be. Despite the city's instructions and directions—NO LOITERING, NO STANDING, ONE WAY—the city was full of lost children. A slippery hand, a turned head (just to check out the tomatoes), and blip, where did a little boy go? Where was Tyrone? It was past midnight. You don't just call people in the middle of the night.

So, pray. Anita let go of the pillow and slid off the couch. Even though she knew she had fallen, she was still surprised at her pain as her knees touched the shag rug. She had gone to church just like everybody else, added to the collection plate, felt the giddy relief when she dropped Tyrone off at Sunday school. But that was over eight months ago. She had tried to find another church after hers had burned down, but nothing fit, not the holler of Holy Rollers or the meekness of Catholics. The Ethiopian United Federated Church of Christ had given her and others a soothing combination of structured disorganization for almost six years. Even when she was burying her husband, she hadn't prayed alone. And that was with reason. Careful with asking God for things you knew He couldn't deliver. She had wanted Reginald to be alive.

"Dear Heavenly Father who art in Heaven." Without the shoulder-to-shoulder comfort of a congregation, she could hear the redundancy in the beginning of the prayer. "Dear Heavenly . . . in Heaven"? Am I really praying? Anita started again. All she wanted was the swoon, the long endless dive of grace. A prayer that was unmindful of its language, that could only caw out its need. "Heaven. Lord Jesus, help me." In a congregation there was melody in that spoken desire; it was symphonic. But in a two-bedroom apartment in Spanish Harlem? This place was too small for an echo. Kneeling on a needed-to-be-vacuumed beige shag rug, buttressed by a bamboo-cane-and-glass coffee table and a brown-gray couch that needed replacing, she searched for Him. "Because the thing is, I really love him. I need him. I didn't say one thing when You took Reggie. He put himself in harm's way. I know that. But if You could just . . . I don't know. Please. Please? I don't know what You need me to do, but I'll do it. If you bring Tyrone home, I'll . . . Please. Don't have me here by myself. Don't do that to me."

Anita knew why she hadn't called anyone after she got back from the police station, why she needed Wanda to push her to go to the cops: telling would have meant admitting Tyrone had never been late getting home. Not once.

"In Jesus's name. Amen."

CHAPTER 4

"Hey, girl, you up?" Anita's question was rhetorical; nobody was up at five thirty in the morning. Awake, yes. Up, no.

"Okay, right. Listen, yeah," Wanda mumbled.

"He didn't come home."

"Girl." Oh, Wanda was up now. And worse, her friend was quiet—no string of laughter or commiserate cursing or fast-talking advice—just silence on the telephone. Anita heard rustling in the background on Wanda's end. The small sound did nothing to cover the heartache seeping into the hush. Wanda sighed. "Girl, listen—"

"Stop."

"Just listen. Tony told me when—" Wanda paused to cough the sleep out of her throat, but she wasn't prepared for an Anita who had spent the first night in twelve years without her son.

"Stop."

"Kay."

"Where's Carl?"

"Carl?"

"Reverend Carl."

"That place burned down."

"I'm not talking about the church; I'm talking about him. He's living, right?"

"Yeah, but the deacons run it now."

"I'm not asking who runs the Ethiopian. Where's Carl?"

"Listen; let me think." Anita heard the creak of a bed.

"You there?"

"Yeah. He's on 125th and First. Big yellow sign; can't miss it."

"Thanks, Wanda."

"You want me to come with?"

"I gotta go now." Anita hung up, convinced that sooner rather than later Wanda would shake out of a sleepy stupor and begin to tell her stories of Tony and Daryl and unemployment.

Anita was dressed—tan A-line skirt, navy-blue blouse, penny loafers, and stockings—determined and standing out on 116th Street before she realized that at six o'clock on a Tuesday morning nobody would be at Carl's place to open the door. Missing Tyrone and feeling prepared had carried her all this way, but the thought of facing SORRY, WE'RE CLOSED stalled her steps. Right there on the street in front of God and everybody, she was about to break into tears when she felt a gentle tap on the shoulder that made her arch like a cat. "Oh, I guess you was just gone to leave a bitch." Anita's shiny eyes took in her friend's crooked smile.

"You didn't have to come out here"—but Anita couldn't hide her relief. She saw her friend's sacrifice in her hairdo: half of Wanda's hair was still rolled in pick curlers, which meant Wanda had left her apartment ready to offer herself to ridicule and teeth sucking. That's a friend. I need to be nicer to Wanda, Anita thought, because Wanda had done what Anita wasn't sure she could have: dropped her friend's previous curtness where it belonged—in the forget-it bin—and gone out to find her. Now more than any time she could remember Anita needed Wanda's sly advice and dark chuckle. It would calm Anita with its familiarity and help her walk the rest of the way to Carl's.

"Girl, of course he's there; he owns the shop. Let's stop at Luis's and get coffee. One for him too." Wanda took out the rest of her curlers and put them in her purse as they walked uptown. "Black, lots of sugar. Like the women I see him looking at." Wanda's small giggle showered over their steps. She seemed to know everyone. "Hey. Cómo estás? Hey there. See you. ¡Buenos días! See you, man." Wanda said morning to folks she knew and those she liked the look of. "Hey, girl." She didn't miss a beat as she finger combed her hair. Bold for a woman of thirty-seven to do. Bold and dangerous. Even with a Tuesday morning sunrise to light the way, in the eighties daylight didn't protect a thing. "Morning, brother. Anita, girl, look at who's coming." Six fifteen in the morning and workers whose jobs were to roll up security gates and haul in cardboard boxes full of merchandise, people whose sole occupation was to get ready for customers and their managers' arrival at nine gave both women shy waves as they walked to subway stops and bus stations.

Coming and going, El Barrio's sidewalks teemed with Anita and Wanda's neighbors. Puerto Ricans who had spent nights kneading dough for bakeries or stacking the *Daily News*, *The New York Times*, and *El Diario*, bundling them to smack against bodega walls, were trudging home while the rest of the employed in the neighborhood were heading out to ready the city. If your mouth was set for it, if you could afford it or were brave enough to steal it, those living north of Ninety-Sixth Street and south of 125th on the east side of the city primed, prepared, fluffed, and dusted off your desire. The city is ready. Open for business first thing in the morning. And while Wanda gave bold nods and "see you"s to every store owner north of 116th Street, her hands constantly rubbed Anita's back and shoulder, gliding up and down her friend's skinny arm. Wanda posed questions to which Anita could only answer yes. "You call your job? You lock up the apartment? Brush your teeth?" It was only when the two women were half a block away from Carl's storefront that the mild, almost one-sided conversation faltered, and Anita couldn't force herself to move another step.

"What if he's not there?" Anita stood shivering, her mouth dry as toilet paper.

"Girl, he will be. I told you."

"Okay, but—"

"Listen—"

"No. Wait, Wanda. I'm asking you what are we going to do if he isn't there? Like do you have a backup plan or something?" Wanda stuck out her chest when she heard Anita's "we."

"I got three. This don't work, I still got it, okay? But I ain't gone stand here and tell you all my behind-the-scenes doings and plans cause he's going to be there. Listen, okay? Ain't nothing up here but highway and the bus depot. Nigger couldn't even step out for coffee if he wanted to." Wanda saw tears gather in the corners of Anita's eyes. "Promise. Promise he's there. Watch and see. He gone be waiting for us; he know we coming."

Reverend Carl met them at the door of his storefront community center as if they had made an appointment. His smile made Anita calmer. Carl made family with his sentences, and everything she should have said to the police she didn't have to say to Carl. "Wanda called me and said Tyrone went lost," Reverend Carl said. He knew this sister and her son. They had been a part of his flock when he was the pastor of the Ethiopian.

"Yeah?" Anita glanced at Wanda, startled.

"Sister Anita, we'll find him. We'll find Tyrone." Carl had already made a flyer on the copy machine with Tyrone's photo. It was a good picture: Anita's arm was thrown around her son; he looked happy, his smile filled with teeth too big for his mouth.

Wanda leaned over and touched Anita's shoulder. "Who took that?" Anita shrugged, too embarrassed to admit she had been thinking the same thing. "Girl, you look good."

Every small question he asked led to a big file of answers. But even better, her answers seemed to be just what he was looking for. His "Right. Right. Good job, Sister" was the punctuation to all her comments. If Wanda's small jokes peppered the conversation, then everything Anita supplied was its salt. The three of them leaned over the contents of Anita's colored files, putting certified papers in certain piles, shoving aside for now what was truly important but untimely. As he spoke, she realized she was being treated with the one thing she feared she no longer possessed, that the police precinct had robbed her of or perhaps she had lost while kneeling on her living room floor: respect. Sure, Carl had questions and advice, but her word was heeded and final. Every comment he uttered seemed to say, You know best. I know who led Sunday school for the five-year-olds and I respect that. Let's listen to the mother on this one, and nothing but Anita's brisk, competent nod allowed them to continue.

Wanda let the reverend work his magic, piping up now and then to ask her friend, "What you think?" and "Is that all right by you?" With the exception of those two questions, she stayed quiet. "Is that all right by you, Anita?" Wanda asked her friend again, in some perverse hope of delaying what she knew was coming: the fearful submission of putting all your trust in someone else's hands. It felt like finding Christ for the first time. Wanda knew exactly what that felt like. A while back she'd had her own come-to-Jesus moment with the reverend.

Two years ago Daryl had gotten into his first real trouble, stealing a backpack full of toys from Macy's. Hot rods and G.I. Joes and Lord knew what all. And instead of somebody calling her or some kind stranger whipping Daryl's tail for shoplifting, instead of some manager giving her son a hard lecture about the sin of thievery, the department store had called the police.

Looking at the sweet relief on Anita's face that did nothing to hide the implacable fear, Wanda didn't have to imagine how Anita had spent the night and the early morning. She knew how it felt when life decided to teach you its greatest lesson: that all the well-crafted safety you draped around your children was merely a coat of luck in disguise. All that time it was just luck that protected what you loved with all your might. And when what you held most dear was snatched away and thrown into a cell with grown men, when you and your child were threatened with almost a decade of incarceration at Spofford, that was just life telling you your threadbare luck had run out. You had two choices: One, laugh. Laugh at life's cruelty, laugh at your previous certainty that you had controlled anything at all. And once you were done laughing, two, go and get help. Oh how Wanda had needed help then. Not the teeth-sucking, empty-handed sort she was used to, but real help, the kind with a plan and purpose to brace it. Carl's help.

This small little man drinking their bad coffee and feeding them bagels in return seemed to be the only person with authority who knew black folk still needed a hand. Wanda remembered how she had scampered toward his protection. How she had waited with head bowed as he conjured the Spirit and asked his congregation to join. How hard it was that Sunday to hear his sermon along with the rolling call-and-response that fell over her like a wave. Her reverend wanted her to be good, but he wouldn't withhold his help if she weren't. Carl's voice had been a shout, but the wooden walls of the Ethiopian United Federated Church of Christ had reduced his yell to conversational. Somewhere in the middle of his talk the neighborhood nut had caught the Spirit and done what Wanda had ached to do: stand on a pew and crow her misery. The sermon was about Job and how God had put Satan in his path to prove a point. And God took all Job's luck away to see if he still loved Him. Will you still love Me? "And God made Job sick as a dog and took away his riches, took away his luck, and when He did, even Job's friends turned on him. You hear me, brothers and sisters? They asked him, 'Well, what you do to make God treat you like this?' These his best friends, people. Amen, Jesus.

"Everybody reads Job and thinks there's a man of faith being tested by the Lord. But I always wondered if a different kind of test was happening. Maybe those friends of his were being put to the test. Them best friends never said, 'Now, Job, why don't you come on over to my house and let me help you. Let me lend you some money to tide you over.' No, brothers and sisters, they just looked at him and said, 'Must be your fault.'"

Leaning forward on the pew to catch every word, Wanda had been sure Carl spoke to her directly. She was a Job whose friends were eager to judge and who had withheld a helping hand. But Carl was different. And he wanted his congregation to be different too. Don't be like the rest of the country, point to the meager pile of good tidings, and say that's good enough. Brothers and sisters, don't be like those with power and fail to notice the mountain of trouble that surrounds the Anitas and Wandas of the world. Wanda looked at her friend and saw her own face from two years ago: a mixture of hurt and hope and determination.

God bless Carl. He was reminding Anita of her place in the neighborhood, and Wanda's "What you think?" deference jogged Anita's memory. She *was* one of the respectable ones, wasn't she? Yes, she paid all her bills on time. She voted. Even during the off years when she couldn't have pointed out the face of the congressman or a judge, she had chosen. And she was a member of the PTA. She worked at the post office. Almost ten years in fact. Her husband had died in the war. Bravely. Gloriously. And yes it was a lovely service, wasn't it? Tyrone was missing, but that didn't mean she was a bad mother; you can have a lost son and be a good mother at the same time. Anita found herself feeling almost at ease as Wanda's face hovered just a hair's breadth away from her cheek and Carl stroked her thumb. Thank God I thought to find you. She almost said as much aloud. Thank you, God.

"And let's call that police department and get them to take this seriously!" His practical righteousness felt like her own. That's why I needed you, Anita thought. Shame on me for not wanting to make a decision without a living Reginald. After four years of attending the Ethiopian under his leadership, Carl's God was hers. Not a loving God—a deity that brought you to the pant of desire, that in a time of crisis could embarrass you with His wisdom. No, Carl's God, her God, knew where she ended and He began; whether palm close or a bridge away there was always a distance and He hated it. Anita's god was a god who knew what she had hid away and still smiled at her mysteries. That's why Anita needed to find Carl and was glad Wanda had helped. Because in the four years he was the supreme reverend at the Ethiopian United Federated Church of Christ, Carl had let them in on a little secret.

God was friendly. A real ham, if you got the joke. And God was close. Like a good neighbor or a favorite uncle. Forget the distance, Carl taught his congregants. If you would just idle by, God would love to know how you took your coffee, if you liked your bagel with butter or a smear, or if you liked to be whispered to in a movie theater or left alone. That was Carl's God. This God was touchable. More. Knowable. And well, there's mystery to Him, but ain't that the way with everybody? How many times you done sat around thinking, and I thought I knew my momma? So yes God was unknowable and surprising, but closer than you think. He was more like your best friend who you took for granted from time to time when life gets in the way. And when you hadn't called in a month or forgot a birthday, He didn't make you feel bad about it—He knew how hard you were trying to pull it all together. You didn't have to put on airs to know Him. Lord, Lord, there You are and just like me, like every good soul, You too couldn't abide by the hincty. Four years' worth of Sundays and Wednesday meetings had drummed that lesson into Anita. God not only likes you, He's not asking you to jump off a bridge and grow wings to prove you love Him back.

Instead of hours long, riddled with biblical passages no one knew, their Sunday prayer meetings were short and to the point. "Dear Father in Heaven, I know You're busy, but so are we. So real quick . . ." And then a fast rattle of babysitting requests, calls for someone to bring by Sister So-and-So's a dessert after dinner on Thursday, an announcement that Brother What's-His-Name was in hospice and would just love it if somebody, anybody, would stop by for ten minutes. Carl's God asked for small things you yourself had thought to do, but really, did you have the time? Would anybody care if you didn't? Because when you thought about it, was knowing God, loving God, worshipping God that easy? Don't tell me God was just a little nudge toward things you had a mind to do anyway. Carl preached to his congregation for six years, "Well, believe it or not, yes, God was the nudge. Yes, HE was." God was finishing off gratefully offered tea and wiping the refuse of bagel crumbs on a napkin while planning to blanket the neighborhood with one question: Have you seen Tyrone Jackson?

Wanda, arm in arm with her version of God; Anita, clutching hard to hers; and Carl's faith somehow bridging the divide, Carl said, "All together, sisters. We're in it all together." He convinced the neighborhood to stop and look and think. "Where were you yesterday, and did you see a boy who looked like this?" Most people wanted to glance, shake their heads at the flyer, and quicken their steps. But Carl drew them up short. The long-honed body language that had kept them isolated on the bus, on the subway, on the sidewalk, even in their homes, cracked and fell away when Carl the reverend spoke as if he were reading Scripture. Who couldn't help but hear his plea? Carl, fearless or stupid, reached out to caress an elbow or pat a shoulder before the eyes could scat away.

"Now, Sister, my name is Reverend Carl Harpon, and I need your help. See here now; take a look. Have you seen this boy?"

MISSING

Have You Seen This Boy?
4'10" Weighing 94 lbs.
Black Hair, Brown Eyes
Last Seen: 10/21/85
Wearing Blue Shorts, Black Shirt
British Knights Red and Blacks
Please Call

At the police station, he wasn't as commanding as Reginald or as tall, but he got the job done. He reminded the police that he, Anita, and Wanda were taxpayers. Pillars of the community. Voters. "I would hate—wouldn't you just hate, Sister Anita—for One Police Plaza to know how you police treat tax-paying, union member mothers. No, I don't need a cup of coffee, but I do think everybody working here needs a little cup of shame." Anita was properly dressed, coiffed, perfumed and unrecognizable from the wild-haired black woman who had landed breathless inside their doors last night at eleven o'clock. "Just in case y'all too busy to make copies, we brought you some flyers."

In 1973 roughly 900,000 people were born in the United States. Reverend Carl kept statistics: 441,000 were boys; 26,460 were birthed in New York State; 13,372 in New York City; 5,782 in Greater Harlem; 1,902 in El Barrio. And of those, 98 black boys were born with the name of Tyrone, Tyrell, Tyrese, and nineteen derivations thereof. Carl, Anita, and Wanda were searching and had embarrassed a police department into helping them, but none of them had a prayer when you ran the numbers.

That same Monday, quiet as it was kept, thirty-six people went missing. Carl's righteousness didn't stand a chance against that kind of statistic. The city was awash in numbers that were growing all the time: 1,487,000 students were enrolled in New York City's public schools. Only statisticians and the nosy mothers on the Parents Board wanted to know how many truants there were in an average year. Carl said that if this city had any shame it would blush at the thousands of kids who skipped school to watch *All My Children*. Never mind the hundreds of children who with the aid of their parents went to watch an afternoon Yankees game. Sure, it's all educational. Sure. The cops had an inkling, but Carl, Anita, and Wanda were completely unaware of the staggering number of kids who played hooky October 21, 1985. Neither the trio nor the police realized just how busy roughly six hundred employees of the New York City Office of Chief Medical Examiner could be on any afternoon.

All the lost, the nameless dead, found their way to a city morgue in each borough. The Office of Chief Medical Examiner was primarily dedicated to and responsible for two things: identifying the dead and connecting them with their families. Teeth and body weight were cataloged as were items of clothing. Black hair. Brown eyes. No distinguishing marks. Ninety-four pounds. Tyrone Jackson was one of those boys—twelve years old and looked it. All the morgue had to go on for identification was a pair of swimming trunks two sizes too small that the dead boy wore as underwear. Written in black permanent marker that had grown faint with age: *Ty*(smear) *J*(smudge).

So much surrounded and obscured his identification. Seventy-one black boys were truant the day Tyrone disappeared. But no one, not the coroner or the police station or the public schools or even Reverend Carl considered what would happen when seven of them whose first name began with *Ty* couldn't be immediately located when the morgue called to confirm their whereabouts. ("Where Tyrone at?")

Standing in line at the medical examiner's at 520 First Avenue, one plump mother peered closely. *Ty* (smudge, smudge) *J* (oh, what the hell does that say?). She still had to squint and wonder if the little bit of a boy laid out on the slab was hers. She joined the other mothers who were shaken from looking at a dead body and declared, "That's not mine. That ain't Tyrell. Why y'all scare me like that for?" At the 110th Street stop, the plump one who thought she would never smile again after she had seen a little boy dead like that saw Anita, Carl, and Wanda, who were working the subway station.

"Sister, my name is Reverend . . ." Carl said.

But this young mother was already reaching for the flyer. She looked at Carl and then again at the flyer, Carl and the flyer. And Anita knew it was bad news.

CHAPTER 5

That all started six days ago and none of it mattered now. It didn't matter where Anita worked or who she was. She had a dead son. Help me, God, because it used to be young people could make a mistake. Somebody passed you something, and instead of drinking a little bit you drank it all. And then a vomity headache. A mistake sure, but one you could live with. Nowadays and, yes, it made Anita feel so old to have such thoughts, but nowadays just one little mistake and you could get killed for it. Or worse. It didn't matter that she paid bills on time (almost always) and went to work and church, that she voted when she remembered to. She had done all she could to raise the best of little boys, but he was dead anyway.

As decent as Anita thought she was, for the past six days it was Wanda who constantly reminded her friend of the little ways to keep going, to be civilized. "You call your mama yet?" she asked.

"I'm going to; I will." In the end it was Wanda who spent all Thursday morning on Anita's couch telling people who needed to know terrible news in a whisper.

By Sunday Anita looked at the sleeveless black dress and thought what she always thought when her hand ran across the garment in her closet: Why, oh why wasn't she one of those women who possessed the extravagance of grief? Everything in her longed for a lit match when she saw her funeral dress. The thought of doing something wild shaped her dreams, but caution always prevailed. Her constant decency behaved like a high school crush she couldn't outgrow. Everybody acted a fool; the eighties demanded it. Everybody but Anita. And Reginald. And Tyrone.

But her son didn't count either, because now she was burying him too. She should be pulling down pots and pans, hurling cassette tapes out the window, but instead she found herself in his empty room making and remaking the bed. She slipped off the covers and sheets, fluffed the pillows, then dressed the bed again and again. All the while her whole mind seemed occupied with the decision of whether to go to work tomorrow. They had told her to take the whole month off, to take care of herself and not worry about it. They'd all be there when she got back and so would her job. Don't worry.

She tried not to think as she headed for the funeral home. But all she wanted to do was hide in her bed. Her mother, who never offered anything, had offered to invite everyone to her house for the funeral dinner, and so had Wanda. Carl even suggested (twice) that they gather everyone at what he called the Institute, his storefront community and political center. But the thought of stepping inside the last place she had felt capable and whole shook her to pieces. How dare she feel that good about getting things done? How dare Carl, in his church suit and double-wide polka-dotted tie, look at her as if she were a decent mother? Sipping coffee and eating bagels as if all would be well? "I don't want to go back there," Anita had said and meant it. Carl reminded her, "God's got this too. He will not abandon us." But hadn't He?

She turned to Him, but He was busy with other people's woe. Carl's soothing and earnestness made nothing in her lie down. That "come on, let's do this" was wonderful when Tyrone was lost, but now that he was found and dead she considered her former preacher's energy inappropriate. He was giving the eulogy. He had asked and been given permission to greet everyone at the door of the funeral home. Anita felt grateful for all his help. She really was. But she hadn't planned to say one word. If anyone hinted that she stand near the podium, she'd pick it up and hurl it down the aisle. Carl and Wanda and her mother could do whatever they wanted. She longed for her bed. Her clean sheets. If she had everyone gather at her mother's, she would have been able to lie down, but sooner or later she would have been asked to get back up.

Before she knew it, she was standing in line with everyone else, filing into the funeral home as if she were just another person who wanted to stop by and pay respects. Folks she had last seen at the Sunday service before their church burned down made up the line. Their faces were familiar, but only a handful of names came to mind. Deacon Dan, I remember you. There was Brother Ezekiel, then an usher whose name wouldn't spring forth. Sister Morning and her daughter Lara, who was lead soprano in the youth choir, were both puffy-eyed. Carl saw Anita behind one of his parishioners and her cousins. "That's the mother; that's the mother" floated out of the crowd. "There she is. There's the mother." They sounded like a flock of birds all with the same call. "Oh Lord, there she is. That's the mother."

Wanda's loud voice: "Stop acting. Sit down somewhere." No one dared to catch Anita's eye. Wanda walked Anita to the front row where she could see Tyrone's coffin draped in lilies. Keisha, a former congregant at the Ethiopian, came to embrace her. "There's Shelia over there. You see her? There's Lizbeth too." They came and kissed her.

Anita tried her best to keep up, but she found her son's profile in the coffin breathtaking. It was surprising how grown he looked. If we had been going to church the last eight months, I bet I wouldn't be so shocked. I'd be one of those mothers who told everybody this was his favorite suit. God, she hoped the mortician had remembered to take off the price tags. She groaned at the thought of her son spending all of eternity with 50% OFF dangling from his jacket sleeve. They did right by him. Everybody has, except for me. Singly and in pairs, people grabbed her hands. "Anita, I'm so sorry."

"I'm so sorry for your loss."

"I'm so—"

"Let her alone, now. We need to sit down."

Wanda steered Anita to her seat, saving her from having to say anything. Shelia and Lizbeth had their kids. How dare they bring their children? Well of course they brought their children. Anita found herself staring again at her son's small, kid-sized coffin. She went over that final bit of news the Chief Medical Examiner's Office had told her: Almost two days he was outside? We were walking all over the neighborhood, and he was lying outside dead? And didn't nobody see? Didn't nobody do something? "Where?" she had asked the man who stood beside Tyrone's gurney.

"Ma'am, he was found out on Second."

"But where? Where exactly?"

"Second between 109th and 110th, ma'am."

"No, where?! On which side of the street?! Where? Closer to 110th or what? In front of which building? Where? Where?" She had screamed because no one had seen her dead son in the street! I hate you! I hate all of you! But what if she too had walked past her murdered son? What would she do with all that hate then? Had she? Walked past Tyrone while he lay curled dead? Or worse, while he lay dying? Her mind fled back to that first morning when she went to Carl's, to her feelings of dignified worry and mothered grief. How at ease she had felt when Carl's and Wanda's faces were so close and concerned, and Carl had stroked her thumb. I was wrong, she thought. Come to find out you can't have a missing son and be a good mother at the same time. A warning sign to every relative and neighbor here. Don't be like her. Don't be like that mother sitting at the front. No, not that one, that one, the lady with the already worn black sleeveless dress and the dead son we're all looking at. Yeah, now you see her, that one right there.

Anita was there all right, with her mother on one side and Shelia on the other. Somehow Wanda got jostled to the end of the row, leaning on flowers that traced the border of the pew. So Anita endured holding hands with two women, but thankfully she couldn't feel their grip. Suddenly everything about her was slack and slouching. Front row, just four feet away from her son's coffin, Anita didn't catch a note the lead soprano sang. The song must have been earnest and true, because though she couldn't hear it, she saw her mother crying.

Her mother hadn't wept in public since 1962, and that was just a rumor. What is that young woman singing? It must be unbearable. She strained to listen, but all she heard was a watery sound growing, cresting, deafening.

INTERLUDE

Secrets are funny. Some are passed along as soon as they are told, while others find a dark cave and stay there. No one talks about the bliss. White folks cluck; the church tsk-tsks; black people shake their heads, but nobody tells about the bliss—not the sort that awaits in another life but bliss right now. Bliss easily gained, like walking through a door. Pfff. Bone-colored smoke. And then fathers are set free from jail; mothers are noted and loved; sisters are supported and surrounded by twinkling lights, and when scores and scores of brown brothers are carted away by the police, it is by the elbow, accompanied by a gentle cooing in the ear. Come back soon. We won't forget you.

There's a reason it's named "crack." Every problem, every hurt tumbles into it. And spellbound, two women watch their pain fall into an abyss. Crack's chasm is so deep they never hear their hurts hit bottom.

With the bliss came the talk about their mothers and their sons and their jobs, oh the jobs—"God can you believe we worked that hard?"—and their lovers. "Where is Tony?" "I don't know." Their talk is both pointed and profound. Giggles punctuate. For both women these are the best conversations they have ever had.

"One and Two!" And somehow that is funny, so funny Wanda stands up on tiptoe and Anita joins her. "I bet you money that's what Carl was thinking about when he seen the both of us that day."

"What day?"

"The day we went looking." Wanda tries to focus on her friend. "You Rosa Parks, and I'm the other one. One and Two! See what I mean?"

"No," and Anita's answer is hilarious. They are standing in Anita's living room. Stomachs are clutched, hands reach for foreheads.

"No, huh?"

"Well, yes. No." Anita loses her balance and collapses onto the couch. Dust agitates and rises. Somebody needs to hoover. Me? The thought makes Anita laugh again.

"Okay, listen. Seriously. Listen. My grandmother was talking to me one time about it, and she said . . ."

"What? What she say?"

"Oh, girl. I forgot." But Wanda hadn't forgotten at all. She just can't remember the words in which to say it. "No, no. Wait. I remember." The blank spot of forgetfulness is shoved aside, and Wanda tells Anita a story she thinks may be apocryphal but believes anyway because her grandmother is not a liar. Back in the day when all the trouble black people were in was because white folks kept fucking with them, a bunch of black dudes decided to do something about it. A lady came to them and told them how she had to sit in the back of the bus. And how fucked was that? Them dudes decided to do something about it, take it to the courts, maybe get all the blacks to rally around it. Okay. But then they went looking to make sure she was cool, and they found out she wasn't. She was like divorced and had some other shady shit going on. So they dropped her. But the idea stayed, and they found Rosa Parks, who was perfect and everything a black woman wanted to be.

"What's that other woman's name?"

"I don't know."

"Wait. Wait. Who's Rosa Parks?"

"You."

That starts another peal of laughter. Wanda beats the couch because she finds it so funny. And Anita, thinking about her dead husband and son, finds it funnier. The laughter dies a little but stutters here and there when Anita asks a question on her mind. "Okay. What's the point of that story again?"

"I'm just saying. When bad stuff happens to us. First, it's got to be real bad, and second it's got to happen to somebody that's a saint. And third . . ." But her thoughts dribble off and Wanda can't think of a third. It doesn't matter. Anita is there to feed her—she's a pro now—and tips the pipe to Wanda's mouth.

CHAPTER 6

Sneaking out the house for the third time that day, Twin felt as if she were the lone somebody who didn't attend Tyrone Jackson's funeral. His murder was front-page news for two days, and even when it moved to the back of the dailies Twin's neighbors wouldn't let their outrage go. "See what they did to that boy?" followed her to the bodega where she bought sandwiches. "You hear about that boy?" came out of the mouths of men playing dominoes and hounded her down the sidewalk. "You think they gone catch somebody?" chased her up the subway stairs at the 116th Street station. The only place those questions could not follow was inside her building with her uncle and cousin. There a bigger question loomed: How was Uncle Manuel going to whoop his niece's ass when she was twice his size and four inches taller than him? Manuel had been gnawing on that problem for more than a week and no solution reared. He was too old to grab her by the neck and bang her head on the living room table. And he couldn't handle her the way he would one of his work-ers who stepped out of line—a bullet in the foot—because goddamn it she was family. But he had to do something. Quick. Twin walking around like she didn't have a bit of sense was going to get them all in trouble. Growing up, he had let her have her way because she was his baby sister's only child. A girl too. When she wanted money for the movies, he handed it over without giving her a chore to earn it. Twin came in and talked lip to him and his son like she owned the place, and not once had he put his foot down. She was a spoiled child who managed to nab the corner piece of the corn bread—all four pieces. Had he told her, Save one for me? No. He let her do it. But it was clear he had been too lenient. She never had to sweat a paycheck, wandered around all times of night doing what? Came home with a bag full of trash that she pawed through. For what? Stupid girl.

Didn't she know what she had exposed them to? Manuel had asked Twin that question the very day she returned home from the precinct. Nobody, *nobody* should call the police. Ever. If someone broke into your car for your radio, lump it. You got robbed? So? You see a knife fight break out? Bitch, you didn't see a thing. That was the scripture of their lives. With calling the police Twin had sinned. And because of it seventy-eight-year-old Manuel was scared.

It had been a while since he had felt the lip-licking fear he experienced now. Not since he lived in Eastman, Georgia. Ever since Twin had come home from the police, Manuel was startled when strangers looked him in the eye as he walked down the street. A Jehovah's Witness knocking on the door made him jump out of his skin. It was like he was being punished. Twin was family, but Manuel couldn't trust her no more. He couldn't bear to eat the breakfasts and dinners Twin prepared. He pushed heaping plates away and trudged to the bodega for a pint of potato salad. And when he wasn't eating food he was hungry for, he tried to make plans to prepare for the moment when inevitably things would go bad. Twice he lifted his mattress, ready to take his secret money to a safe deposit in Jersey, but he was afraid to make the trip lest the police follow him and pull him over. The mailman had always shown up the same time every day, but now when he heard her keys rattle in the vestibule to open the mailbox, Manuel pressed his hand to his chest. Who knew who would show up at the door now that Twin had done what she did?

Eleven years ago Manuel had turned their whole building into an illegal drug one-stop shop. He, his son, and his niece lived on the top two floors; three women he employed part-time boiled and cut up product in the back of the building on the third floor; and Manuel Jr., his son, took in customers in the basement. He had never wanted to get big—take over a whole project building, knock out all the lights, which forced tenants to come and go during daylight. A dozen girls worked in their panties, and brothers watched over them with guns stuffed down their pants. Sooner or later here came the prostitutes looking to give you a taste, and you give them the score. Sooner or later up showed some toughie ready to do battle and take over your territory. Too much work, Manuel had thought, too many ways for things to go wrong. Sure Manuel would shoot a motherfucker in the foot if a dude crossed him, but he didn't like the notion of roughing up some lady just because she wanted to leave her apartment at nine o'clock for a quart of milk. He had been running his business for over a decade, changing and adding product to fit the needs of his clients. But even with that he had been careful. He had rules. No kids. No homeless. He catered to folks who had a habit not an addiction. Folks who needed a little something to get over Wednesday's hump—those were his customers. Uppers, downers, weed, even crack for those who hadn't gone over the edge and lost their jobs. Now all his success was in jeopardy because Twin had called the police. Everybody knew once you let the cops in they didn't leave until somebody was in cuffs.

When Twin walked in the door, Manuel started in as if she had heard all that private worry. "And so you called the police! Like you ain't got a lick of sense."

Twin put her bags on the floor next to the kitchen table. "Hey, Manuel."

"Where you been at? Huh? Roaming? Here and there like you ain't got a care in the world. Must be nice."

Her uncle's ache for fight sat in the air, but Twin just wanted to put the groceries away. She knelt and began to take out bushels of collard greens, a bouquet of parsley from the community garden, a smoked ham hock, whiting from the fish store, a bag of crackling from the Puerto Ricans. Silently she debated whether she should put the pork chops and chicken necks from the Met grocery store in the freezer or place them in the fridge and hope they didn't go bad before she was ready to cook them.

"You hear me talking to you?"

"I hear you." With the collards on the table, she wondered if the green beans were still fresh. I need to get a Crock-Pot. Should she put the ham hock she bought in the fridge or start a simmer on the stove? If she wanted to eat the collard greens tomorrow, she should put them on now. She opened a bag, pulling out the ham hock. The day after, she thought.

Tomorrow felt like fish.

"You not acting like it." Manuel moved closer to her, but the kitchen table separated them. "All this"—he waved his arms over the mound of green on the table—"is because I make a way. Them clothes on your back, I bought."

What to cook and when fractured in Twin's mind. Though she didn't want to, she finally paid attention to her uncle. "I know, Manuel."

"Then what you go and call the police for? What we all gone do if they show up at the door?"

Twin looked into her uncle's jaundiced eyes, taking in his powder-blue polyester jumpsuit. He hadn't dyed his hair in six months; so though snow-white hair grew from his crown, jet-black hair made up most of his fro. He is so old, Twin thought. His arthritic hands were curled close to his chest. She knew those hands that had brought her up were too weak to wring out a towel nowadays. That they were barely strong enough to pull the trigger of a gun. But Twin didn't know how to answer his questions. Her uncle found her behavior odd, but so did she.

Hadn't she been asking herself the same thing? Just what had possessed her to call the police? It wasn't that little boy's shoes. Not really. Or that he was so young he probably hadn't had a wet dream before he was murdered. Maybe it was his baby lashes crawling with bugs. Maybe it was all of it. Or maybe none. She found out after the funeral that she had known his mother; she'd attended the Ethiopian too. But knowing she had a casual acquaintance with the boy's family didn't quite explain her behavior. Maybe I wanted to be good for a minute, and I fucked that up cause I don't have a church to do it in. The thought made her laugh.

"You think that's funny? Bringing the po-po in our lives?" Manuel couldn't tell what he was angrier about, her long blank stare or the chuckle that flew out of her mouth.

"Naw, Manuel, naw."

"You ain't never had to work for na'an dollar." Her uncle walked around the table to stand a foot away from her. Twin winced, watching him hurt himself as he uncurled his hand and pointed a single finger at her. "You the fool who call the police. A grown-ass child who don't appreciate where the money come from." His finger drifted closer. "Money just there easy as you please. And you get to not care one way or the other cause you ain't never been scared that you ain't got the cash to keep the lights on or buy a loaf of bread. But I'm gone fix all that." Manuel's finger touched her chest. Twin barely felt it. "Mind the trap, why don't you? Till I say quit it. Work that midnight shift. Earn your keep."

Twin wouldn't have been so spooked had she seen the trap during the day. But by the time she showed up for the eleven o'clock shift, she only knew the contours of the basement by touch, shadow, and her cousin's say-so. Midnight till dawn she was going to be in charge of selling product to folks who gave a special knock at the door, and for another twenty bucks they could come in and smoke up in their basement. She had peppered her cousin Manuel Jr. with questions over dinner. "Who do I let in?"

"Anybody who gives the knock."

"What's the knock again?"

"Yo, girl, this shit ain't deep. Three knocks, boom, boom. Boom. Then tap, tap. You know?" She didn't.

"And so what? You just let them in and let folks take a seat?"

"Come on, girl. They let you in the movies without paying? You gotta pay for the show before you get entertained." Manuel Jr. tried to watch his cousin's embarrassment and his father's frown at the same time. "Look. Most everybody who knock just gone make the exchange. You got a hand out; they got a hand out—here you go, here you go—and they gone bout their business. But a bunch more gone want to come in for the ride. Feel me?"

"Okay."

"Make sure those nodding motherfuckers don't set shit on fire. And when the sun come up, get they bitch asses outta there. That's it. Do all that and you straight."

"I got you."

"Easy."

"What if shit jump off?" Twin's attempt to sound both wise and curious failed.

"You can't handle it?" her cousin said. Uncle Manuel hadn't said a word during their conversation. He grunted and picked up his empty plate to set in the sink.

"Oh, she gone handle it." Manuel Sr. grabbed his napkin from the table and wiped his clean mouth. He didn't bother to look at his niece or his son. "Shit bet not go wrong, Twin." He left the kitchen. Twin and Manuel Jr. watched him slowly take the stairs to his bedroom.

Twin's plate was empty too, but she didn't move to give herself a second helping of smothered pork chops and green beans. Rather, she waited until she was certain her uncle was beyond hearing their conversation. She leaned across the table and took hold of her cousin's thumb. "For real. What if shit jump off?"

Manuel Jr. dropped the bluster and impatience he had when they all had been eating their pork chops and rice. "Baby. Girl, if it get that bad, I'm gone hear it and I'll come downstairs."

"Okay."

"But it's not gone get that bad. Most folks just stopping by to handle business." He put his free hand over hers. "For real. Shit's just boring. Take *Jet* down there, or maybe a bunch of *Ebony* magazines."

"Can I take the boom box?"

"Naw, girl. No music. If shit jump off, you got to hear it." Manuel Jr. marveled at his older cousin's scared face. He hadn't seen her this unsure and shaken since she was nine years old when her mother had whipped her and locked her in the closet. "You got this."

But his assurances didn't help. Twin picked up their plates from the table and walked over to the kitchen sink. Her back was a knot of worry, and she groped for a question to ask her cousin, one that would give a map to what would happen to her over the next ten hours.

"It get smoky down there?"

"Come on, girl. Throw open the window. None of them like it, but it's our trap, you know?"

Twin turned on the faucet. The hot water loosened her clenched fist and somehow gave her the courage to ask her cousin what she couldn't in front of her uncle.

"You get scared down there?" She respected him enough not to turn around and look him in the eye. He could lie to her back if he wanted to, but she wouldn't force him to fib to her face.

Manuel Jr. stared at the wide expanse of his cousin's back from the table. Black men don't get scared, even when they are. Vulnerable, he looked everywhere. The white linoleum floor needed to be mopped; the embossed tin ceiling was as pretty as it ever was. "Daddy built a closet around the boiler. I close myself up in there sometimes."

Twin squeezed dishwashing liquid onto a sponge. Bubbles erupted. "Cause you were scared?"

"You can't unsee some shit." Manuel walked over to his cousin and rubbed her back.

He felt her trembling but didn't comment on it. She was bigger than he was, but he was taller. "Remember? Remember when we was little and we took baths together? Member that time when I took a dump in the tub and that turd floated up top?" Twin trembled harder, but Manuel didn't look over her shoulder to see if she was laughing or crying. "Shit, you was so scared you scared me. You was out that tub like a shot." Though Twin couldn't see him, Manuel took a step back to demonstrate his point. "Girl, you flew. Like Superman!" He flung his arms over his head.

Twin shook harder and then laughed out loud. She turned off the faucet and wiped her hands slowly on the dish towel. "Fuck that,

I'm Wonder Woman." But when she turned around her cousin had already gone.

Green, blue, red light bulbs swung from the ceiling. Their weak light failed to illuminate the scant furniture Manuel Jr. had placed willy-nilly. Three undressed twin mattresses, a two-cushion couch, and a broken La-Z-Boy were situated just beyond the lights. "You got this," her cousin whispered as he took the steps from the basement at eleven o'clock. From midnight till two in the morning it was just as her cousin had promised—the staccato beat on the door was so constant it provided its own music. Twin, in the space of two hours, learned a new language.

"I need five."

"Give me ten."

"Dime bag."

"A nickel and a touch if I can have it."

Every somebody who knocked on the door refused to meet her eyes and bowed their heads. No one said thank you, but everyone felt compelled to give a final word before they shuffled away. Twin began to believe she was involved in some sort of sacrament where *amen* was replaced with "Okay; all right then." But at two o'clock in the morning the customers and their mood changed. A young woman grabbed Twin's hand and wouldn't let go. She leaned in, her shoulder touching Twin's. "I got the extra. I need to cop."

"Okay." Twin didn't count the large nest of dollar bills in her palm the way her cousin had told her to: "If they look like they got something scary on them, kick they ass to the curb; if they look too tight, say, 'Can't help you'; if they got on too many clothes for the weather, don't let them in." Just before eleven Manuel Jr. had told her a whole list of things to look out for, but she couldn't remember any of it as she let her first customer stalk past her to cop. Instead Twin opened the door like a maître d' and watched the woman walk through green-and-blue light then into darkness. The only thing Twin could see was the sole of the woman's tennis shoe as she lay down on the mattress near the wall. Twin heard or thought she heard rustling. A zipper yawned. Twin's head turned toward the sound; her hand started to close the door, but a familiar knock arrested the action.

"I'm copping, okay?"

Over the next hour they came so quickly she barely had time to run back to the closet and hide the money she'd taken at the door. She tried to run back and forth, but more often than not she was arrested during the journey—halfway to the closet, the special knock called her to the door—and she had to pivot and let in another person. How many, she thought. How many had she let in? That was one of the many things her cousin had instructed her to keep track of. Twenty? Twenty-five? It wasn't just the crowd of people arriving at almost the same time that had her failing to conduct a head count. She knew them. Luis the bodega owner and his wife Linda showed up holding hands. There was the bus driver who ran the Second Avenue route. The checkout lady from the grocery store. If Twin didn't know their names, she knew where they spent their hours during daylight. She startled at the dude who once saw her racing down the subway stairs and had kept the closing doors open with his foot and shoulder. That dude, that cool-ass dude's face, was revealed in the glare of a Bic lighter. These were good people.

Twin thought now was the time to go and get Manuel Jr. if for nothing else but company. She felt lightheaded; the air smelled of chemicals, and while she knew she ought to walk to the other end of the basement and open the window, she didn't want to step over Luis and his wife, who lay sprawled in the middle of the floor. I need to breathe. She snatched open the door and bumped into a woman in a floral dress and a green cardigan. The woman held a black purse with short handles under her arm.

Twin blurted out what was on her mind, "No more."

The woman nodded but pulled out a wad of dollar bills. "But I need to cop." Twin looked down at the woman's hands. She didn't have to take the money to know it wasn't enough.

"That ain't twenty dollars."

"Close."

"It's twenty to come up in here," Twin said, but her eyes roamed over the woman's face. I know you. Like know you, know you. This woman was someone who stood apart from the transactional relationships she'd had with the other customers. Church. You from church. You a sister. Sister . . .

The sister took her purse from beneath her arm, opening the clasp with one hand.

"Jewelry too. It's good stuff. My mama's."

"We ain't a pawnshop."

"I got ten on me. I just need half the time, ma'am. Please." It wasn't just the "ma'am" and the "please" that made Twin let her in. Twin was rummaging around in her mind, searching for this sister's name. She's worn that dress to church, Twin thought, looking at loud purple and yellow daisies splashed over the dress; large white buttons marched down the middle from collar to calf. We did something soft and serious together once upon a time, and you were wearing that dress.

The crowd had changed again while her back was turned. In the dark and trick of red-and-blue light, Twin could make out tips of nipples, the curves of shoulders. Bic lighters flickered on, revealing upturned chins and pipes. It reminded Twin of Christmas lights. Everything dimmed but illuminated. I won't be able to unsee this, she thought, and she couldn't close her eyes because she needed them to see her way to the closet. In a puddle of blue she noticed the bus driver's open fly. The checkout girl's head bobbed up and down on his lap. Luis's and Linda's foreheads touched, their mouths open. So close to kissing but not quite there. That they all were half-dressed made them look more naked. Smoke and dark obscured most of it, but Twin heard a grunt from one of the mattresses. I'm never not going to see this. Twin, bad motherfucker of the neighborhood, shamefully realized she was scandalized. She hugged the wall and didn't stop moving until she stood inside the closet with the boiler. As she sat with her knees curled to her chest, she thought about the time. How long until dawn? How long do they keep this up? She wasn't a prude; Twin had a friendly man in the Bronx and another secret one in Staten Island. So why am I tripping? It's because she knew she would have to see them the next day. Give money to Luis for a bag of chips; pay her fare to catch the bus downtown. Look these folks in the eye and pretend she didn't know the color of their pubic hair. I don't want to face my neighbors. Uncle Manuel was responsible for snatching away his neighbors' dignity. So was Manuel Jr. So am I.

Through the door Twin heard a hand radio. The sound permeated through the door, and Twin prayed for Al Green or LL Cool J to follow and save her from her thoughts. I'll even take country, Lord. Instead a familiar jingle floated out. 1010 WINS. "All News, All the Time." "Oh hell no," Twin said and began to struggle to her feet. "I'm not listening to that shit." She was still on her knees when the sister with just ten dollars and family jewelry opened the closet door.

The green cardigan was gone. Her daisy-covered dress was unbuttoned to the waist. And she was bare chested. Not a bra to be found, but her name came to Twin in a clap—Tillis. Sister Tillis. Their shared moment felt so close that Twin could almost forget all the half-naked people right outside the closet. Sunday. Ten a.m. service. The pastor had preached something reverent and timely. A sermon that felt personal, one that moved everyone. There was a chorus of amens where pews full of hands shot up meaning Twin was not alone. There was a congregation to surround her. Collectively, the Ethiopian was moved by a spirit so holy it could not be fanned away or shouted down. That's where I know you from. I remember. Sister Tillis had turned to her left, crushed into the crook of Twin's neck, and wept. Now this sister fell to her knees in the boiler closet of a trap den. Now like then, Twin stroked her shoulder, feeling equal parts awkward and close.

The only difference was that now Twin's hand glided up and down a naked shoulder.

Yes, Twin thought. Yes, we've done this before.

CHAPTER 7

It took two days for Anita to make a move. Two days and she'd had enough. Enough of Carl. Enough of the seven women who had viewed her son in the morgue. Enough of the former sisters from her church who she hadn't seen in the eight months since their church burned down. Anita found herself in their company at Carl's storefront Institute; she had been told not to go to work this Tuesday because she had buried her son on Sunday, and she couldn't bear to stay inside her apartment. The walk to 125th and First was the lone delight of her day, but that feeling died as soon as she stood in front of Carl's shuttered community center. She stood and waited, swaying to nothing at all. Carl showed up ten minutes later. "Sister. Morning." As he unlocked the gate, he asked, "You want a key so you can get in without me? I got spare keys I can let you have."

This was the second time he had asked. "No. I don't. No . . ." Anita tried to think of something to say, some comforting word, but she was at a loss. Carl was worried about her. He had been since he saw her slack face at the funeral parlor. How long had she been standing outside waiting for him? When he had arrived yesterday at eight o'clock, she had been waiting for him. And today, when he showed a full hour earlier at seven, here she was again.

As he watched her take a seat and stare at nothing in particular, he thought again how he should go to the secondhand furniture shop and maybe pick up a rocking chair or a La-Z-Boy if he could find one cheap enough. Anita had the look of a woman who could stand a nap and would take one if she could only find a comfy chair to do it in. Carl guessed how her nights were spent. How she avoided her bed because the preparation for it—the face washing, the teeth brushing, the donning of a clean nightgown—would only sharpen the sense that she was in her apartment alone. He had grown up with women like Anita, capable women stunned they could be crippled by heartache; he had consoled them when he was the head pastor of the Ethiopian. For four years he had shepherded that flock. Led the lunch power hour Monday through Friday, preached the four services on Sunday. And when his Beloved voiced their unspeakable suffering, he guided and counseled them to a better day. Anita's cawing, overwhelming grief he could handle. It was the seven other mothers who had been brought in to see Tyrone's dead body at the Chief Medical Examiner's Office who were giving him a hell of a time.

One young woman had even followed him home last week. Keisha, a plump, light-skinned twentysomething-year-old with kitty-shaped eyes. She had been the one who had fondled the handout of a lost Tyrone, the one who had told them she had just seen who they were looking for and then burst into tears. Outside his West Harlem apartment on 139th Street, Keisha had waited for him.

"Morning." His hello was heartfelt but did nothing to hide the surprise at finding her outside his door at six o'clock in the morning.

"Hey, Reverend." She was dressed in a gray janitor jumpsuit, but Carl didn't know if she was headed home or just getting ready to go to work. The lack of knowledge was new to Carl.

In the past he knew his flock's every longing and habit. But these seven mothers were different. Until now they had approached him all at once or in sets of twos and threes. That made it impossible for Carl to figure out who they were individually.

"What floor you on?"

"I live on the second."

"That's nice."

"Yeah."

"It's nice over here," Keisha said, fidgeting, looking up and down the tree-lined block. Like a criminal casing a score, she readjusted the strap of her backpack and noted how slowly the reverend walked down the steps of his stoop.

"It is nice."

But then Carl's eyes went all melty. That's what Keisha told the other ladies when she recounted their conversation. "It was like the only thing he wanted in the whole wide world was for me to tell him what was the matter, and even though I hadn't said one important thing yet, his eyes turned all soft, right? And I knew we was going to talk about all my troubles like it was bad weather and not my fault.

"The thing is my momma ain't right no more."

"Sister—"

"Keisha. My name's Keisha Tillis, and we used to go to your church. I mean I didn't really go, but my momma did. Janice. Janice Tillis. Every Sunday and sometimes for Wednesday Bible study. You know my Tyrell just turned thirteen two days ago."

"Keisha. Tell your boy happy birthday."

Carl heard the soft sigh from her nose. "So the thing is, I think my momma's out there." Keisha lifted a heart-shaped chin to the street behind her. "She was gone for about four days, right? And we was looking everywhere for her, you know? Like what you did with Anita and her Tyrone. And I was going to tell you about it, but like my momma is grown up, and Tyrone, I mean Anita's Tyrone, was just a little bit, and I thought, 'I bet Rev. Carl only look up little kids and not grown-ups who have a job and everything.' But I was gone call you and ask anyway. Like, do you look after grown folk too? But then Momma showed up yesterday morning."

Keisha was panting, like she had run the block twice and just caught up with Carl. "We was all really happy. Like *happy* happy.

Me and my boyfriend and Tyrell all live with her at the Washington. And Momma got a man friend too, and even his sorry self showed up when she went missing and was asking where she at, you know?" Carl said nothing. Keisha readjusted her backpack strap, her gaze taking in everything: the snow-white lace curtains on the second floor, the two stone pineapples (or were they pine cones?) perched on the pedestals on either side of the stoop, the maple tree just behind her, gated with wrought iron. It was all so neat and nice. Somebody living here wouldn't want to hear the end of her story.

"What happened?"

"Her eyes was funny when she came home. That's the truth. And she was acting like this was the first time she sat on her own couch. She kept touching everything. It was just weird, right? And she didn't want to tell us where she been at all that time; she just kept saying she needed to be off by herself for a bit. So we all, like, cool, but . . ."

"Keisha, what is it?" Carl was just a stair above her, having heard a story like hers a dozen times over, ready to take her in a kindly embrace if she would let him.

"She took everything. She took it all, and now she gone again. Like the radio, all the silver spoons and stuff, the bill money we keep on the top of the fridge, my grandmomma's good jewelry. Everything."

"Oh, Sister Keisha . . ."

"Just Keisha, all right? And how you s'pose to call the cops on your own momma?" Keisha wasn't crying, not yet, but her cat eyes gleamed. "Cause if they catch her and shit, we the ones who gone have to come up with the bail money. We can't be pressing charges. That's fucked up to call the cops. But we need that shit back. Like she can keep the rings and bracelets, but I want the radio back. I mean, if it was on you, would you call the police or what?"

From the height of the last stair Carl looked at this young woman whose roaming eyes glanced up and down his block. If Anita's son had taught him anything, it was that sometimes the mystery of someone's disappearance made for better sleep. Lord help us all when the lost are found. Looking like a woman caught in an avenue wind, Keisha squinted, her lips held tightly together, but not a tear fell. It was too early in the morning for Carl to think up something dignified and calming. He couldn't even remember a well-placed line from the King, but oh my how he wanted to soothe this young woman.

Her mother was out there, maybe prey for men who hadn't grown chin hair. Because of her mother's absence their apartment turned into a place unfit for a home. Both the preacher and the young mother stood in Harlem morning quiet, wondering just what had happened to Janice. And though Keisha refused to voice as much, she knew all this was her fault. I got me and my son and my boyfriend who is taking too long to become my husband, and maybe Momma looked at all that and took off. I'm taking all these classes so I can be a nurse, but maybe that's not happening fast enough. Down the block a garbage truck rumbled. How could Keisha ask something that shoved all her worry into one question? I can't, she thought, as she glanced at the garbagemen down the street.

"Sister. Keisha."

Oh, Lord, help. Was Keisha's mother ducking inside drug fronts dressed up like bodegas and arcades? Was she sleeping in the Wagner Playground every night, curled under a man's coat on the pitcher's mound? Finding a lost child was one thing; finding a grown woman who had scooted away from her life was another.

Both Keisha and Carl watched the sanitation truck's slow creep down the street. "Keisha. I'll help you look for your momma, but I can't promise you we'll turn up anything."

"Okay. Yeah, I know it."

The garbagemen lifted trash bags over their heads and tossed three days' worth of refuse into the waiting mouth of the truck. The shame that Carl knew more about the sanitation department's weekly habits than the woman who stood before him burned. Carl stewed in their awkward silence and wondered how much he needed to know in order to help her out. Was it possible that Keisha's mother had lost herself on one of those blocks that should always be avoided? That she had turned down the wrong side street and the monsters had snatched her up? East Harlem's complicated geography took a lifetime to learn. And Carl, who had only been living here for five years, didn't have a prayer of figuring out her whereabouts because the old adage is true: to get into trouble you've got to know where it is. "Ain't none of it your fault, Keisha. Not a bit of it," Carl said as he stepped off the last stair.

She had spent the last week or so hanging around the Institute, yet still she startled at Carl's height. Keisha had to look down to catch his eye, Man, you a little thing. "I know that."

"I mean it, Keisha. Nothing you did made your momma get out there." Carl's hands slid up her forearms, glided past her elbows, and came to rest on her shoulders. "My word on it, we'll get her home and make her stay." It was a heavenly promise, one that had Keisha drifting home thinking future thoughts. Oh, Keisha.

Carl began to look into her problems—where on earth was one Janice Tillis hiding herself?—only to find himself surrounded by six other women in similar predicaments. He had the ambition but not the necessary hardened heart to go with it. Not yet, anyway. Carl winced at the ugly details when he heard them. Mothers and fathers and cousins had gone missing or worse never left home at all. Misery sat at their tables like an unwelcome guest, eating up everything these families had and then shamelessly reaching for more.

Carl sighed heavily as he thought about what to say to Keisha if she stopped by today. He had asked around, but no one had seen Keisha's mother. Maybe he'd file a missing person report, but Keisha had already told him she didn't want the police getting involved. As he made a pot of coffee, he tried to think of problems he could solve. He looked back at Anita sitting on the folding chair. A pillow. The least he could do was bring a pillow from home. A footstool too.

As he offered Anita a cup of coffee, women came through his door in twos and threes with their hands full. Seven mothers including Keisha had spent all night or the early morning making their very best: collard and mustard greens studded with ham hocks, blackeyed pea salad, broccoli salad, hoppin John, roasted chicken. They hadn't planned it, but not one of them stepped inside Carl's Institute empty-handed. Anita's arrival yesterday had prompted the bounty. When they first found Carl last week, they had mainly gathered to talk about the shock of seeing Anita's dead son at the morgue. But by the grace of God, day by day, their woe replaced Anita's. They had living black sons, and their worry about them sat up front in their minds. Seven mothers couldn't help themselves. But Anita's arrival yesterday had pulled them up short. How could they have so quickly replaced her grief with their private worry? They tried to express their apologies by stroking her knees, caressing her shoulders. As those mothers pulled up chairs and sucked their teeth every time Anita opened her mouth, she tensed, unable to bear the way they touched her as if she were a relic. She couldn't even manage a grateful smile. It was then they noticed the state of their hands. Empty. The shame that they had forgotten a tradition they were born and raised in sharpened their errands when they left for home.

Today, when they saw her, they were ready. Tupperware filled with their best. Plastic cups and forks. Paper plates. One by one they put in Anita's lap their hard work and talents, recipes that they had wheedled out of their great-aunts. Anita didn't eat a bit, but the food and her presence gunned the conversation. It was a wonderful funeral. Yes, it was. Anita gamely tried to get interested but couldn't raise her voice above a whisper. Talk about the funeral moved to questions about the murder.

"I mean, how is that going?"

"They reach out to you yet?"

"They looking at anybody?"

They stared at Anita's mouth when they asked but turned to Carl for answers. What was the city going to do? And that poor boy was out there damn near two days? What about that? Those seven mothers knew they hadn't birthed angels. You got to fix this, Reverend, cause *my* Tyrone, Tyrese, Tyrell is not going to be left on the sidewalk, you hear me? I mean, the city's working on that, right? You can't let that happen to my kid, Rev. Carl. You working on that, Rev. Carl? His placating "I'm on it" failed to soothe. It could have been any one of their boys; no promise or assurance mollified them. Are they even looking for the killer? I mean, can you believe that? They didn't dwell on whatever bad thing Tyrone might have done that had gotten him killed. More than likely he hadn't done a thing.

So, all right, maybe Tyrone Jackson had forgotten the golden rule—stranger danger—and had been out past dark roaming. Maybe his mother had tried to spare him and herself and never told him about Spanish Harlem's violent infamy. Theirs was a neighborhood where everyone, sooner or later, got shot or stabbed; where running to the bodega for a pound of bologna meant risking being mugged en masse, which was so much better than being robbed alone. Those who lived on these blocks knew the sweet relief Anita must have felt when the medical examiner informed her that her son had not been raped. And while downtown and Staten Island could read about what happened and eagerly set about the business of laying blame at the victim's feet—well, what was he doing out there that time of night? where was his momma?—those recriminations never got off the ground in East Harlem, because, well, fuck, they knew he could have been killed because of the shape of his smile or some crackhead thought they heard a jingle of coins in his pocket. And that poor kid out there for two days, so who cares what he did?

Their recriminations, her grief and their own tightened around Anita. She didn't slap anybody, but God as a witness, her palms itched. Their talk kindled her imagination and treated her to a vision of her son fighting and flailing against a giant of a man. Tyrone had been strangled to death; that's what the medical examiner had told her. How long? she wondered. How long did that take? She remembered the softness of his skin under her fingertips. In a year or two he would have grown taller than her. She was sure of it. His head had already doubled in size in the last six months, making his neck look scrawny by comparison. When would that soft texture of his chin become studded with whiskers? Would it have tickled her cupping hands or scratched?

She stood up from her chair, longing for a touch she would never feel. The women surrounding her stood too. Their anger was palpable, but the emotion covered a hard kernel of fear. They kill us and leave us out there. They kill us and don't even look for who did it. That's why the pleadings for calm, for time, and the heartfelt apologies issued by Carl went nowhere. "Who killed that boy?"

"You on this, Reverend Carl?"

"Yes, Sister."

"Let's move! Shit. I'm ready to find out!"

Carl didn't answer; rather his whole attention was fastened on Anita. Her once slack face was alight. With what? he wondered. Anger? Disdain? Whatever the emotion, she looked at these mothers as if for the first time. It was clear she did not like what she saw.

"Careful," she said. Carl heard Anita and not the cacophonous women around her. Her eyes were quite sane. "You all be careful. Go around asking that kind of question, you never know who you might turn up."

Carl's heart skittered in his chest. Who killed Tyrone and had the audacity to leave him outside for the whole neighborhood to see? "Careful," said the Anita with the sane eyes. "Never know who you might turn up." Maybe all this time he had swallowed her caution whole, and that's why until seven mothers had the audacity to ask, he hadn't given the obvious question hard thought. Who did it? No, no, Carl, scare yourself real good and ask: Do you really want to know who did it? Because maybe it was some made guy in the Genovese family. Or one of Ray's crew. Or the Latin Kings. Even those new to living in El Barrio knew there were certain directions your finger couldn't point. Until right now, no one, not once, put into words the anger that would befall them all if they found the murderer and it turned out to be one of those boys who worked the project hallways for a crew or who ran the Game Room on 110th. What would happen if the guy who dropped a dead Tyrone curbside as trash was one of those men who had tears tattooed on their cheeks, wore red Kangol hats with matching red Nike sneaks? Think about that, Carl, and don't be coy. Was that the question he should have been asking all this time? And if he didn't, what else was he going to do with the authority these seven mothers pressed into his hands? Suddenly New Jersey real estate snared the mind. If he was lucky, fleeing a state away would keep him safe. Who did it? Who killed Tyrone?

"Well, I think we need to get out there," Keisha said, walking to the wide windows at the front of the shop. "Out in the streets." She moved over to the glass door and yanked it open. The crew of women stood up to follow her. "They can't do us like this." No one thought to put the lids on the Tupperware or rinse the dirty dishes. Out there, outside screamed at them to come on. Their percussive anger amazed Carl. He turned his hungry stare inward, thinking and this is what I missed. All of it. The Freedom Rides and *Brown v. Board of Education,* Rosa Parks and Little Rock, the Sit-Ins, the voter registration organizing, the Mississippi Freedom Summer, the Birmingham Campaign, and the Albany Movement. For most of it Carl had lived in a small speck of country in southern Arkansas where racial conflict and the men and women who stood to fight it were spoken about as if it were rumor. He was told stories by his uncles and mother about the struggle—that had been what his mother had called it—since he was toddling along, but he had no personal memory. As they snatched scarves around their necks, Carl stole glances at the women. These were the kind of black women who braced his life. They knew how to read and react to neighborhood gossip, knew how to make a meal from two ham hocks and a packet of mustard. They even knew Carl's move from a small county legend to the city's gossip was a hard one; these women and those from his former church could make any man under the age of seventy-two duck his head and blush when his behavior became outlandish. These smart black women never raised their dresses or voices in public, and yet even the badasses of the neighborhood called them "ma'am." They populated his world, his former church, his life back home in the South, and though he had tried to rectify the predicament throughout his adulthood, he still couldn't call one of these women his friend. Before Tyrone's murder he would pass one on the street and say hello, sure, tremble under some sage, unsolicited advice, yes, but share and eat from the same plate of some wise, sass-talking black woman? Never.

Sometimes Carl felt if he had just one black woman like that in his life he would be set. But now he had seven. The front door of his storefront tinkled open, and three more women entered: Sister Shelia, Sister Morning, and her daughter Lara bringing up the rear. They looked around at the commotion, nodded, and kept on their jackets. Morning had been by his side since he had opened the Institute. Her daughter had sung lead in his choir. And Shelia, Sister Shelia, was close friends with Anita. The newly arrived trio was a sign if only he wanted to read it. He should know that much, shouldn't he? Great men who stood on the precipice of the greatest times knew as much, didn't they? King hadn't felt this muddled anger that didn't know where to land, had he? King hadn't been a scaredy-cat, afraid to holler Where is justice? lest someone point out there is no justice and rain misery on them all. Right?

He wondered. Well before Anita found him, too many of his dreams were populated with men in black suits and pencil ties, each of them carrying a placard that declared: I AM A MAN. But was this it? Were Anita and Tyrone his sign? And who had taken this young boy's life, two days dead and on display on the sidewalk? Carl couldn't help it; he pitted his present circumstance against the Emmett Till murder, the clarifying moment. White folks asked where you were when JFK got shot, but black folks knew their measure from knowing where and when they drew breath when Till was killed by a posse of white cowards. And like everything else Carl had missed that too. Born in 1950, he couldn't even claim a solid memory of the event. Had his mother unexpectedly gathered him in her arms and covered him in an anguished cry? Had his entire family followed the papers and radio until Till's mother cawed out the world's shame with an open casket? What had his people done back then? As a teenager he had asked that question over and over again and heard the same response from his mother and his uncles: "Oh, baby, them was some dark days." Carl had always suspected their piteous words hid the real answer: they had done nothing. His family had heard the news or not and, without missing a beat spent the next day doing what they always did: fixing cars, hunting, and squabbling among themselves. And now, now, these seven mothers along with his three former parishioners told him the confusion and anger he and his neighbors felt might be the most critical moments in black living? When justice had clarity. Really?

"We really do, Reverend." Keisha spoke up. Her words gave him purpose the way nothing else had. "Let's get over there." Ten women clapped hands as they stalked out of his shop and onto the sidewalk.

The police precinct was twenty blocks away and two avenues over. So what? Come on. Fists slammed into palms; Carl led them, then was surrounded, then slipped behind. As they neared the corner, the mothers surrounded Carl once again. He stood shoulder to shoulder with them and felt a curve of breast on his back that touched then retreated. The sensation repeated itself.

No one saw Anita fall back a step, then two, then several. While crossing the street at the corner of 125th and Second Avenue, Anita parted ways with the ten women and her pastor.

She turned down Second Avenue, unable to care about their angry clapping hands.

CHAPTER 8

January 1986

Anita's night was full of bad dreams, though in the morning she could only recall snatches. Tyrone in thigh-high grass, breathing, laughing; every now and again popping up to yell "Boo!" She never managed to see the top of his head, but she kept turning in the direction of the taunt. When had they ever visited a place like this? Not ever. And as she tried to nail down the foliage (Central Park, Udalls Cove?), grass grew. From thighs, to hips, to stomach-high. In the dream, she wasn't worried when her son jumped in a soaring meadow or she couldn't make out the shape of his forehead. All her concern circled around his height. If he were taller, all would be well. Then that dream winked out and was replaced by another. She sat at a table (her own, her mother's, a restaurant?) and lettuce towered on a plate. Or was that collards? Or spinach? Whatever the green, it was uncooked, and she had no fork. Where's the bowl of pot liquor? Where's my fork? And then that dream too was shoved aside. Clothed in a blue silk Sunday dress she did not own, she shook hands with a six-foot-tall baby's head attached to a teddy bear's body. And most worrisome about the dream wasn't the Frankenstein's monster she clasped hands with; it was the texture of his fur. Almost brand-new. A three-month-old baby's head attached to a furry body that had been handled ever so gently. As she shook hands with it like a dignitary, she wondered about its previous owner. What in the . . . ? She woke.

For three months Anita let the phone ring. Why not? She knew for sure it wasn't the cops. Anita may not have followed Carl and those seven mothers to the police station back in October, but her heartache prodded her to go a week later. Alone she walked to the police precinct to ask, "You find out who did it?" Through the late fall and now in the middle of winter since Tyrone was murdered, twice, sometimes three times a week after work, she headed down Third Avenue to speak to the police assigned to her grief. Two detectives and a sergeant.

"Ms. Jackson, we don't have anything yet, but we're looking. Just . . . just go home and we'll call you when we have anything." Sometimes the two detectives directed her to their bosses, but she worked for the U.S. Post Office, so she knew all about the technique of making customers walk a few extra steps and placing some shiny, well-dressed manager in front of them who was skilled at not helping and sending you on your way. So on top of not knowing just where my son dropped dead, I'll never know who killed him either. Because no one wants to know. Not Wanda, who came by three times a week with a plate of food. Not the cops or my friends. Not even Carl. Not really. It's because we live in a neighborhood that makes everybody flinch. The phone's ringing pierced Anita's dark thoughts. Whoever it was trying to talk to her wouldn't give up; her phone bring-bringed once an hour, ten rings at a go, but clearly the person on the other end had no idea how long it took for Anita to get to the phone. She heard the telephone's muted echo for the third time since she had come home from work. They have no idea what they're up against.

· · ·

Since Tyrone's death everything Anita heard had to compete with what Anita called "the roaring." That keening sound of a mother's loss in her head, though she didn't know if everyone who lost a son experienced the same phenomenon because she was too afraid to ask anyone about it. I start talking about it, and they'll put me in the nuthouse. Who knows? Maybe I'm the only one, she thought, since nobody told her they too knew about the wailing or screeching that had become her own private elevator music. It blocked out all language, forcing Anita to dust off her old habit of reading lips. But worse, the sound refused to anchor itself to anything like common sense. Don't look at a black boy who could be twelve years old. Sensible, right? Obvious. Anita would see a cluster of them, a beatbox blaring in one of their hands—"DON'T PUSH ME, CAUSE I'M CLOSE TO THE EDGE"—but before she could command her feet to cross the street, four twelve-year-old boys were upon her, and yet not a peep out of her head. Her mind should have been stuffed with holler. Nope. But let Anita step inside a bodega and look at a bag of popcorn, and the wailing screamed so loudly she staggered. The ringing phone competed against that noise, and the phone lost every time. They should give up. I have.

The phone didn't ring again, but an hour later somebody was at the door. It's probably Reverend Carl or the landlord, Anita thought when she saw the door rattle on its hinges and heard the muffled sound of a knock. "Coming," she said as she saw her door shudder again, this time without the noise of banging. The wailing in her head kicked in and she felt deaf. "Coming, coming." Anita peered through the peephole and saw her friend Shelia, whose son had been best friends with her Tyrone.

"Hey."

"Hey," Anita said when she opened the door wider, peering steadily at her friend's mouth in case she said something Anita couldn't hear. Once upon a time she had really liked Shelia.

The older woman was one of those mothers Anita knew just because their sons were friends, and Anita was glad for the happenstance. For years the two women kiki-ed on the phone after the boys' bedtime, timed their morning walks to work so that they would meet at the food cart to buy an egg and cheese on a roll at the same time, and found excuses to spend Saturdays together doing nothing at all. It was Shelia who Anita told tiny secrets to; those small confessions made the seam of their friendship. "Girl, sometimes Tyrone get on my nerves. I wish I never had kids."

"Me too."

And though that felt like a towering admission, it wasn't. It was just a piqued moment that needed to be given air like a well-earned belch. Shelia's commiserate nod gave the hateful thought the smallness it deserved, and together they threw it away.

As Anita stared at the stout, tallish woman, she wanted to remind Shelia of that special friendship, but her girlfriend wore the expression everyone had when they looked at Anita nowadays. Anita stopped the urge to take her friend's hand. "Well, don't stand there and catch cold. Come in if you want," Anita said, smelling "the talk" on Shelia though she hadn't said anything but hello. Lately everybody wanted to sit Anita down. Her boss had sat her down just this afternoon to have "the talk," and now clearly it was Shelia's turn. But Anita had decided to open her door for a reason. She was spoiling for a fight. Anita wanted to ask her if she knew who killed Tyrone just to see her friend snatch her hands back and look embarrassed. God knows she needed to act ugly to someone who couldn't evict or fire her. Anita walked back toward the kitchen, leaving Shelia to close the door all on her own. "Came to tell me all about it, huh?"

"Girl, come on. It's me." Shelia closed the door behind her and followed Anita to the breakfast table. "If I was hanging with Wanda as much as you are, wouldn't you say something?"

"Might. Might not. We all got kids, right?" A gulf as wide and murky as a river divided the two friends. There were two kinds of mothers—the kind whose children got caught out there, and those whose children were at home.

"Anita." What's the matter with me? Shelia thought. She hadn't stopped by to talk about Wanda. Her mission as told to her by Reverend Carl and the seven mothers whose numbers had grown to thirty-two was clear: Anita needed to come out from her apartment, step away—just for a minute—from her lonely and join them. Testify her tragedy. They had been out there in the streets, agitating the police, their councilmen, their neighbors. But over and over, their pleas and anger were caught up short. "Could the mother step forward? And the mother is . . . Where the little momma at?" Anita's absence cut off what would have been productive conversations. It gave officials a reason to have them escorted to the door. "Sister Shelia, you know her best. You know her Tyrone. Go and talk to her." She couldn't remember which of the mothers had given her that command, but here she was sitting at Anita's table, pretending she didn't notice the grease spots or the smears of food that hadn't been wiped away.

There wasn't enough of Anita to dirty an apartment, but still Shelia found herself breathing carefully through her mouth. She didn't want to, but she took fast glimpses of her friend's living room, her kitchen, the short hallway that led to both bedrooms. Nothing was out of place, not really. A pile of mail towered but then went lopsided on the counter. Breakfast, lunch, and dinner dishes made an interesting sculpture in the sink. Styrofoam cups and plates littered the counter. But that's my house when I don't think anybody is coming over. So why is my stomach roiling?

"Shelia."

"I just wanted to see about you." Shelia thought she ought to make small talk before she leapt into it. She hadn't stopped by her girlfriend's place since Tyrone's murder, a fact that sat bloated and obvious between the two women.

"Well. You saw." Anita didn't bother with opening a window to let out the stifling radiator heat or ask Shelia if she'd like a glass of Kool-Aid. In fact, Anita was so quiet, so inhospitable, Shelia found herself getting mad enough to show it.

"You still live in here?"

"Where else would I be?"

"Well, it just looks like—"

"It looks like what?"

"Anita."

But Anita stood up from the breakfast table, refusing to give

Shelia the small lie of picking up a towel or handling a dish as if suddenly the need to tidy up overwhelmed. Shelia stood up too and stepped away from the kitchen table. Anita didn't say a word but moved toward her friend as if she were sleepwalking, as if she would walk right over her if Shelia didn't get out of the way. With Anita's every step forward Shelia took a step back.

"What you doing?" She wasn't ready to go. Not yet. She still needed to tell Anita that they couldn't fight for her or her son without her being there. Despite feeling uncomfortable, Shelia had plans to tell Anita something righteous. God has a plan for you; come stand with us; this too will pass; quit feeling sorry for yourself and rise up with us. But Shelia couldn't get out any of the words she had prepared. In the face of Anita's awful eyes Shelia's clichés turned mute.

"Just walking. You?"

"Nothing." Shelia tried to laugh, even opened her mouth and everything, but nothing sounding like a chuckle came out. "Quit it."

But Anita continued her dreamy shuffle. Together they floated out of the kitchen and into the living room. The whole procession took so long Shelia had the time to figure out what was bothering her. With the exception of the well-worn path that she trod on— backward no less—nothing in the apartment had been touched. Tyrone's pile of shoes huddled in the living room corner; two of his winter coats were draped over the couch.

And Shelia would later swear she saw his homework and a folder from school casually strewn on the coffee table. Those things alone looked as if they had been fondled. As for the rest, the lightest layer of dust coated everything—the television, the end tables, for God's sake, the wilted plants. There were two trails clearly marked in Anita's apartment. One led to the kitchen, and the other split off and wandered into the short hallway toward the bedrooms. It wasn't natural.

"Wait a minute. I mean it, Anita. I got something to say. Could you just quit it?"

"Quit what?" Anita smiled. It was terrible. She had all her teeth, but her gums were gray, swollen. And the expression that tore at her lips looked more like a gash than a smile you gave a friend, a good friend checking up on you.

Shelia found herself standing outside Anita's front door, embarrassed that she didn't want Anita to touch her. "I was just trying to give you a hug."

Anita quietly swung the apartment door closed.

CHAPTER 9

Anita turned around and followed the well-worn path to her bed-room. Her head ached from all the lipreading she had been forced to do with Shelia. It was bad enough to have to decipher the shape of mouths at work; at home, at least she could let the keening surround her with impunity. That was until Shelia showed up out of nowhere with a look that reminded Anita her house was a mess. At least I have tomorrow off, she thought, pulling off her shoes and settling heavily on her bed. That was the reward given to her by her boss Marvin for sitting down with him yesterday and putting up with his bullshit about God and a plan, and you can get through this. Bullshit. Bullshit. They ought to be glad I'm going to work. Most days anyway.

Anita had gone back to work at the post office, but last month was rife with missed hours, and her punching in at ten o'clock was just as shocking to her as it was to Marvin. You did it; you got here. Late, but you got here. Marvin didn't write her up, but yesterday he sat her down, and it was not like the visit from Shelia. Anita had to sit there and take it. He ended their conversation with words no employee wants to hear, "Anita, you know I like you." What did he want her to say? Should she tell him this neighborhood she had lived in all her adult life was acting like a flasher—its trench coat thrown open, all its privates flapping in public? Suck it; suck it. That every morning she woke up feeling a shame so familiar it felt like family? Or maybe Marvin and Shelia wanted to know that the trail of condolences Anita had been forced to endure since her son's death had exhumed the kind of grief Anita thought she had long buried. Her husband had been a good man. Everyone said so, and Anita agreed, but losing Reginald was a paltry misery compared to this. Each morning Anita was stunned anew to realize she had no idea what to do with her day. Have coffee, then eat breakfast? Or was it the other way around? Get an egg and cheese on a roll from the bodega or start out early and head for the Triple A Diner? Thanks for the day off, Marvin. The possibilities were endless and damning. She tried. She tried so hard to hold on to her options, because the habit shaped like her son could fill a room and knock her down. Half asleep, if she weren't careful, she would find herself already making his lunch and searching gamely for his shoes, and where did that jacket go? She'd be watching the broadcast not for the bad news but for the weather, so she could tell Tyrone to put on a long-sleeved shirt. Her whole apartment was traitorous because it housed her son's comfort.

Had Marvin wanted to know all that? Did her coworkers? Did Shelia? All of them seemed too content to tell her, "I'm so sorry, Anita. I'm so sorry for your loss." How many times did people need to say it? And what should she say in response? She ached to say what was on her mind, but Anita knew she had such ugly thoughts she didn't dare whisper them to herself or dream them in her dreams. Yet there they were: Fuck you, Shelia, your son is alive. Fuck you, Marvin, your wife is at home. And thank God I don't love my mother. Thank You for sparing me that at least. Did her boss really want to hear that?

But Anita hadn't said any of that. She'd sat in her boss's office and stared impassively as he ever so gently insinuated he was going to fire her if she didn't straighten out. "Anita, you know I like you."

"I like you too, Marvin."

"Take the day off tomorrow. And we'll start fresh on Tuesday."

It wasn't her fault. That's what she wanted to tell Marvin. If Shelia hadn't been bold enough to try to scold her in her own home, Anita would have told her the same thing. She couldn't help it. Not any of it. Lord knew she hadn't planned on being late to work almost every day. She didn't want her apartment looking like no one lived there. But these last months she had begun casing her neighborhood like a burglar trying for their first score. The nervousness, the known danger got her lost every time. Anita had gone astray and squinted at street signs on her four-block walk to work. When had her Spanish Harlem turned into this Spanish Harlem? She remembered giving finely detailed descriptions to coworkers who made the commute from the Bronx: the bodegas that carried every want, the African ladies who braided hair on the second floors of buildings that lined Second and Third Avenues, the Puerto Rican restaurants that tempted even those who had just eaten with trays and trays of plantains and pollo arroz right there in the window. Just try to walk past all that without your stomach growling. That she got turned around walking streets she had lived on for fifteen years was so embarrassing it became another secret she never told anyone. Not Marvin or her coworkers or Shelia or Carl or her mother. Like any of that matters, Anita. She slipped off her jeans and panties, then debated whether to get up to put on a nightgown. Why bother? There was no son to be decent for. Sleep didn't come, but Anita slid under the covers.

Anita's mother used to tell her life comes at you in threes. Get hit once, twice, might as well brace for the third, cause Lord knows it's coming. So Anita wasn't shocked at all that before she had a chance to think about brushing her teeth or whether she'd lean out her window to check the Three Kings parade, someone was pounding on her door first thing in the morning. Definitely the landlord, Anita thought, struggling into her bathrobe, or maybe Reverend Carl. First her boss, then Shelia, but leave it to Anita's landlord—because Anita was six days late with the rent—to be her third visitor and thus make the trio.

"Hey!" Wanda shouted when Anita cracked open the door. Anita was so shocked that it wasn't him, she paused. "Bitch, let me in!"

"Sorry. I thought you were—"

"Doing who? Billy Dee? Girl, please." Wanda pushed the door open and walked through. "And I got bagels. My black ass wouldn't even be up, but these damn bells won't let a nigga sleep." As she said it, Anita heard the persistent clang of church bells. "Happy Three Kings Day, right? I swear to God I'm a catch a donkey and eat him for dinner."

"Girl, stop." Leave it to Wanda to be the one to show up, though Wanda's "talk" was so happy Anita forgot to think of her as the third.

"I mean it. Who gone clean up all that horseshit they leave behind; tell me that? And girl, open the fucking window. Hot as hell in here. You want me stripping to my panties?" Wanda laughed and jokingly leered at her friend. Good old Wanda, who Shelia said was a bad influence. Wanda who visited three times a week, so often Anita didn't consider her a guest but family who didn't cluck concern, who didn't look at her floor and think vacuum, who didn't look at her sink of dishes and sigh. "Let's eat. I got cream cheese and everything." Wanda rummaged in Anita's cabinets and set the table as if it were her own.

"You in a good mood."

"Yes, ma'am. First the lawyer called me last night and told me I'm all paid up for now, and then Tony went off and got himself a job." Wanda sat down and began to laugh. "Girl, I got up this morning feeling jinxed as hell, you know. So I told myself, 'Girl, you better gone and do some third thing.' You know that saying good things come in threes? I believe that shit. And I was like, 'I'm gone stop by Anita's. Make her my third good thing.'"

"Tony getting a job is really good, Wanda."

"I know, right?" Wanda leaned over the table and snatched up a poppy seed bagel. She touched the bagel to her forehead, made the sign of the cross, and then offered the bread to her friend.

"Girl. You a mess," Anita said. She laughed then. It sounded weak but heartfelt. The roar, Anita's constant companion, decided to find its fun elsewhere, and she could hear the chime of church bells through the open window amid Wanda's wisecracks. But then Anita went and messed it all up and told Wanda not only what was really on her mind but how she had been spending her days.

"The thing is, as much as I want them to catch the guy, I want to go back to where they found Tyrone."

"Girl, leave that alone." Wanda licked poppy seeds off her fingers.

"I mean it. I just want to stand there again. We went by just the one time. What if when we was looking for him, we passed him by? What if I walked past my own son?"

"That's not true."

"Might be. You don't know. I don't know either." The chiming of the bells grew louder. "I haven't gone again, and I should."

"Girl . . ." Half-eaten bagels curled on the plate, shot with cream cheese here and there.

"I had a dream."

"You did, huh? That one day black boys and white boys, Jews and Gentiles—"

"Stop. I mean it. I had a dream." But Anita was lying, feeling the only way she could say what she wanted was to pretend she had dreamt it all.

"So what was it?"

In fits and starts Anita told Wanda what she was up to. Clutching her bathrobe closer to her, nibbling at a bagel she wasn't hungry for, she got it all out. The thing was, buildings Anita had passed a hundred times on the way to work now behaved like unnurtured plants, rotting around the edges, inexplicably growing black mold. When did that happen? This neighborhood is ugly. "Don't you think so, Wanda?" And what her neighbors did to gussy it up made it uglier still. Puerto Rican flags and the cheap Christmas lights that draped the fire escapes just highlighted how unsightly thirty blocks could be. "In my dreams I get lost, like the streets aren't straight anymore but curl in circles, and I keep wondering, 'Where am I? What's this place over here?' The only place I know where to go is the police department."

Forever ready to curse or cry with anyone nearby, Wanda was

silent as Anita continued to tell what was on her mind. You lying. You so lying, Wanda thought. The blocks to steer clear of—110th, 116th, 103rd—were as familiar to Anita as her own hand. I see you. See you, girl. Wanda didn't know who Anita thought she was lying to—herself or her friend. But one thing was clear as glass: Anita was wandering around looking for trouble. Wanda took a blistering look at her friend and thought Anita was five pounds away from being solicited. Aching for the moment when some dealer hissed at her, "Five-dollar hit, five dollars," Anita would say yes.

"I guess I'm not dreaming at all," Anita continued. "I mean I'm awake when all this happens. And last week I was just wandering around, and I saw a bunch of teddy bears and baby dolls hanging out of an abandoned building." The sight of teddy bears, some the size of first-prize carnival toys, had so startled Anita that even now she shivered in her kitchen chair. She remembered them again, pink, brown, powder-blue teddy bears sitting on fire escapes, leaning out windows, aching for a fall, but wire hangers, butcher's twine, and just plain old rope curved under their arms or lassoed around their necks held them back from their impending splat. They had been there for a while, exposed to cold and snow and rain so long their fur had nappied.

Whoever had put them out there wasn't concerned enough to care for them, though when Anita stood on the other side of the street looking at a building populated with Christmas and birthday wishes, Easter Sunday surprises, and first prizes instead of people, she wondered just what kind of care they would need. Silly thought. Silly woman. Some of the stuffed animals were three feet tall; others were small enough to snuggle with. There were even a couple that held receiving blankets or smaller versions of themselves. All of them looked out with unblinking button eyes. I wonder what they see. The Franklin Court projects carving a skyline? Or maybe the height on which they perched let them look all the way to the World Trade Center. The whole building, dotted with good luck and winnings, looked like a carnival suddenly abandoned.

"What was you doing on that block?" Wanda's anger surprised Anita. "Stay off that block, you hear me?"

"I was lost," Anita said, watching Wanda do what she had never done before: clean. Wanda briskly swept the bagel crumbs into her hands and then clapped the refuse into the trash can. The remaining bagels were shoved back into their brown paper bag, and she threw it all into the refrigerator. Anita felt the thud of the fridge door. "Wanda, what's the matter?" But her friend didn't answer. Instead Wanda snatched up the dishes from the table and flung them hard enough to clatter in the sink. Anita was suddenly reminded about the stories she had heard about Wanda. How if she got mad enough, her anger had no bottom. How she'd hurled a shoe at one of her cousins and didn't miss, and how she once waited in the dark with a knife for Tony who had been late coming home. Anita felt her kitchen was unsteady and overly hot. "I just got lost; that's all."

Wanda stood there for a moment, waiting for Anita to look her in the eye. When she didn't, Wanda marched to the door, yanking it open. She didn't turn around. "Then get found."

CHAPTER 10

Honestly, Wanda was a tattletale. So nobody, *nobody* should've been surprised when she hotfooted to Carl's Institute right after she banged Anita's door shut. Yeah, she laughed with her good friend, but only the blind wouldn't have been startled by Anita's words. That weak laugh Anita gave didn't come close to reaching her eyes. Added to that big grief, Anita was getting lost and taking a good look at blocks she shouldn't ever set foot on. Well, Wanda knew she had to tell somebody who could do something. That was what had Wanda huffing uptown to Carl.

Wanda was so agitated she leapt from "Hey" to telling Carl all of it in one breath. Anita, the bagels, the teddy bears, Daryl's problems, the lawyer's payment, Tony's job: she vomited all the news on Carl's lap. He hadn't even taken his coat off, though he tried.

"Motherfucker, don't get comfortable. Go get her."

"Well, Sister, you don't know if Anita—"

"Fuck that. Who saw her face? You or me? I'm telling you she's going to where Tyrone laid out dead."

"Sister, Sister Shelia told me—"

"Who the preacher? Get over there and figure it out!" Wanda

reached over and helped the reverend put on his coat, going as far as buttoning the top three buttons. "What you looking at me for? Go, go!" And that was how Carl found himself walking alongside the Three Kings parade that Monday.

He loved this parade, even tried to become an official attendant, but clearly he had to know someone who knew someone. This time he strutted down the sidewalk not minding that he wasn't a participant. Wanda and Anita were on his mind. "Go, go," Wanda had told him. "Who saw her face? Who the preacher?" she'd asked, and those two questions managed to lance any good feelings he had about her.

He knew Anita wasn't in good shape. Sister Shelia had danced around the details of her visit when she'd told him and the other mothers what had happened at Anita's apartment. "She doing fine, I think. Told me she was feeling okay and she was thinking about stopping by here soon. I think she needs a little more time. She's always been shy; you know that, Rev." Well, what you mean by soon? You tell her that we need her out there with us? "You know I did. I told her everything we been up to. You know I really think I ought to go back. Maybe in a couple of weeks I'll head back." Shelia had lied to them before she realized it, ashamed to admit she got booted out. She had no intention of returning; even though Anita hadn't laid a hand on her, he figured in a couple of weeks she would grow courage and try again. Like Carl she was ready to move beyond the aw-shucks and fuck-the-police talk. Shelia had watched Carl deal with those who had come back to the Institute and commented on Anita's absence. "Say, Rev., where's the little momma?" Carl's quick answer that Anita was too tore up over Tyrone to come out got sympathetic nods but suspicious eyes.

Carl was lucky Wanda had caught him opening up the storefront with no one around. She gave answer and shape to what Carl had been asking himself since Shelia had told her lie. Where was Anita? What was she doing? Carl had called her a dozen times, but no one picked up the phone. He had even stopped by her apartment building and rung the buzzer. No soap. Wanda had saved him again. Before he brought himself to tell Shelia he knew she was lying; before he had to ask his assistant Morning or the seven mothers who had grown into thirty-two at the Institute what next; before he had to ask Anita's neighbors down the hall or her boss Marvin for help; before he had to go to the police for assistance, Wanda had shown up. Her fast lip sounded oddly chagrined while he put his hat on.

Anita stood in her bathrobe, looking at her front door, and couldn't get her hands and mind around Wanda's anger or Shelia's half-hearted censure or Marvin's embarrassment. All her thoughts circled around what she should wear. Not the funeral dress, but not something flashy either. What was appropriate to wear to the place Tyrone drew his last? Her two church dresses, one red, the other gray? No. It was too cold for her one sundress. Momma, the one person who hadn't called on her, had given her a black dress she loved, but an event had never reared. Anita walked to her bedroom closet to search for it. She didn't plan on stepping and kissing the exact spot where Tyrone had been murdered—nothing in her saw her standing in that spot—but her mind was dressing for the occasion. The roar that had died when Wanda stopped by stayed dead. Nothing, not the bag of popcorn or the bologna sitting out on the counter or the smell of corn chips and baby powder, would revive it. While Anita picked out a slip and bra, she breathed in the smell of farm animals wafting in from the window. Perhaps there was something charmed in waking up to an elephant's trumpet. The hot desire to see where Tyrone was found made her forget to wear her coat.

He saw her a block away. Anita. Carl sighed her name. He saw her in her mother's dress, a dress that shoved his imagination to the fifties, when women looked both proper and good. Alone, on her knees, curbside, as slim as a ribbon, and in that last morning light just as shiny. Oh, she was good-looking. She had the kind of beauty that had stalled her late husband, that had her son say apropos of nothing, "Momma, you so pretty." Anita's beauty now made its final appearance. Carl wasn't the only one who noticed her slow, steady stride to the curb. A group of cameramen searching for the interesting found her at the same time. Too skinny transformed into nicely slim with the click of a camera. Oh, there was no need to make mention, but the press was there. CBS, ABC, NBC local reporters followed the religious procession along with their photographers. A wayward camera lens caught Anita's solemn stride to the curb right in front of the beauty supply shop between 109th and 110th Streets. Her neck wasn't scrawny; it was slight, as were her wrists. Click. A photographer captured both the curiously quiet parade teeming with camels and donkeys and little girls outfitted in purple tulle. Click. Click. But Anita, dressed in black, snatched their attention. Her mother's dress looked a wonder. From the fifties, flared right at the knee, the pageboy collar—all of it reminded the viewer of decades ago: when injustice was crisp with inequality; when "that is wrong" was so obvious it didn't need Walter Cronkite to give commentary.

Anita wasn't thinking about her figure or the photographers, and the roaring that had crowded her days was blessedly silent. All her mind was sharpened, pointing one way: she would never share that girl-can-you-believe-him? smile with some random mother who she'd never become friends with, never share a coffee with, but whose smile nevertheless would carry her for days. Anita looked at the curb right in front of the beauty supply shop and thought about when she spoke not in a din of passion or a fit of anger but slowly, because it would be remembered. Her mother had given her scores of advice about how to raise a child, but Anita had kept and cherished one: "Y'all remember. Just know whatever you say, he'll remember and throw it at you at the worst time. Mind your mouth, baby, cause this little boy gone remember every word you say." Twelve years of careful language: "Stranger danger, little man." "Come on here." "Look at you."

She broke. Her fragile knee bruised the curb. And a donkey's bray marked the occasion. That close. Carl walked up to Anita, who knelt on the curb. Neither of them saw the crowd of photographers who appeared out of nowhere. That close, the two words that both thrilled and announced Carl. That close, a phenomenal experience that followed Carl since he could say the words. The cameras were right there, right in his peripheral view. Anita wasn't thinking of Carl at all, but when his hands floated into her sight, they looked so much like Tyrone's she gasped. Look at you. Baby boy, I missed you so much. Anita's lips as they touched his knuckles were soft and damp. The shutters of the cameras sounded like applause.

Carl's heart beat a dangerous rhythm as he pulled Anita into standing: That close. So close.

That close.

The cameras didn't rise from their perfect angle here, a perfect angle there; the lens of publicity rose no higher than the ground floor of the storefront. Anita and Carl, with camels and elephants and farm animals in the background, made for a compelling story. Click. Click. The photographers created the spectacle of Carl and Anita, memorializing their meeting. Politicians made their way to the curb like sharks to bloody chum. Anita was the only one who didn't have plans.

CHAPTER 11

The next seven days were filled to the rafters with shenanigans and comings and goings. Notoriety lapped up the street curb in a wave for a solid week. This part of East Harlem, peopled by neighbors who'd gone to the funeral, who had stood around and pointed when the cops and paramedics showed and carted away the dead twelve-year-old Tyrone, was all the news. "Where were you and when . . . ?" dotted sidewalk conversation. And those who were absent during that first walk to the precinct or failed to show up to the Three Kings parade on January 6 were worse than shunned; they were forgotten. "You got no story to tell, baby." Most famous or infamous were those who sat around the room-length oblong table in the conference room at the police precinct two days after Carl and Anita's picture graced the papers. Those in attendance had had their sleeves pulled at the grocery store, at the fish market, on the way to the subway, were sought after for more story. "You go?"

"Fuck yeah, I went."

"What happen?"

"Them police ain't got shit, that's what, but they want to roll up like they got something for a bitch."

"Sons of bitches."

"Man, you know it."

But only the men spoke that way, with their arms folded across their chests against late-January cold while spitting carefully between their own two feet. The women—the church ladies from Carl's old congregation, the seven mothers whose sons' names were variations of Tyrone—their memory of the police meeting was cluttered with confusion.

Wasn't there a heavy quiet? What had caused it? They could remember hearing the men sliding out of their coats. The gurgle of coffee as it splashed into Styrofoam cups. But that there was silence couldn't find consensus. The seven mothers contended it wasn't quiet at all. No, no, that whole room was filled with the smell of stale coffee and Brooklyn fast talk. White men in and out of uniform surrounded the table and thus surrounded them; they'd talked a mile a minute while managing to convey nothing at all. Those seated around the table could barely get in a question. Those police were on it. Working night and day. "Do you have a suspect?" "We are working on that." "A witness?" "And that too." Working on it. Working, working, working, but nothing to show for it. They spoke to Anita, who sat at the middle of the table. But she hadn't lifted her head to meet their eyes. Instead she watched both her hands roam. Her middle finger traced the rim of the coffee cup in front of her; her palms lay flat on the table then slid slowly toward her. Fingers and palms died in her lap. Then reborn, they traveled up her chest, pausing on her collar.

Her hands repeated the journey over and over.

Carl, who sat beside her, wondered what was on Anita's mind that had her so fidgety. Was she, like him, trying to find the rhythm of this conversation so that she could pepper in its counterpoint? The whole meeting frustrated him; he wasn't looking for the righteous call-and-response that came to him in the pulpit but its softer cousin that happened when folks were talking. Those pauses existed to let the listener get in a question or a hum of agreement. There were too many of them. Too many cops circling the table. None of them had taken a seat. The arrangement when offered had felt like an act of kindness. "You guys take the chairs. We'll stand." But now, as they paced a circle around the table like a posse, tossing assurances, Carl struggled to figure out who he should keep an eye on. His head swiveled left, then right, left, left, right, left. There was no music to their speech at all.

But that's not the reason Anita neither took part nor took interest in trying to find her conversational place in shaming the detectives or nodding when the police guaranteed them that their top priority was catching the murderer. Along with her hands, her mind was in a traveling mood. Get on the downtown train, then she could transfer to the L at Fourteenth Street or to the J at Chambers Street, get out at the Broadway Junction–East New York station, then walk down Bushwick Avenue. Evergreens Cemetery was on the left. She had called its main office several times but was still unsure of the directions she had been given, since the last time she went out there she had been driven by the funeral home's limo. This morning had been the third time she had written down the instructions, and like before she couldn't read her own shorthand. But this time she was going. The city had given her news that had her searching her closet for her best coat.

A little after nine fifteen, some official called and informed her that the city performed an act of kindness for the murdered. All you had to do was get shot up or cut down or strangled, and New York City would pay to bury you. And well, ain't that nice. All you had to do was suffer a grief you'd wish on no one and the city would say, Sorry about that; here you go. But like all good things there was a catch. The police had to call it a murder. Not just you and your cousin could think your momma was killed. The police and the coroner had to agree. And since, well, that sort of understanding took more than a minute to get to, the singular generosity was always tardy, but here they were now and sorry for the delay. You did keep the receipts, didn't you? Anita didn't know whether to spit or say thank you. She must have said something, since the official voice prattled on as if answering a question. By the time Anita cradled the phone, for the first time since the funeral she had plans.

And they weren't about attending this meeting to watch policemen make excuses.

First, she had to buy a bouquet. Something in season? What grew in the cold? Then she had to go to Evergreen, clean up the grave site if it was dirty, lay flowers. And third, she had to figure out if she should tell anyone seated at this table. That question divided her manners. All of them had been so kind, God knew that to be true, but at a certain point shouldn't she leave them alone? Her neighbors had missed work because of her and Tyrone. Look at them all wasting this late morning. And truth be told, she wasn't sure she could stomach the long trip with those seven mothers in tow. Anita darted a look up and tried to catch the attention of Shelia, who sat on the other side of the table. The older woman avoided looking her way. Shelia had remained close by but unapproachable since her unannounced visit to Anita's apartment.

Still Anita wanted to see the look on somebody's face when she shared such mangy, marvelous burial news. Sister Morning from the Ethiopian, who now was the executive secretary at Carl's Institute, sat next to Shelia taking notes. She would probably say yes, but it meant she would bring along her sullen daughter Lara who sat next to her mother. Her manners were worse than Anita's. The young woman slumped in her chair, nodding gently to music Anita could not hear. Headphones, sweet Jesus. Who sat in an official meeting listening to their Walkman? The old motherly scold in Anita thought, Who mis-raised you?, but she concealed her irritated sigh with a small cough.

And, of course, there was Carl, the man beside her who would say yes, yes, oh yes, but his caveats were too heavy.

Carl would want to bring a news crew and the old congregation. Preach a sermon. No thanks. Wanda? Anita would have to find her first, and she wasn't in the mood to go looking for her friend. But the real reason she kept such news secret was because she wondered if going alone would help her get a handle on her grief. The emotion had become extravagant.

Every day it grew. Crowded out common comforts. She couldn't enjoy *The Price Is Right* or Wanda's dropped-off gift of corn bread. And like she did with anything too expensive, whose purchase so emptied pockets not even lint was left behind, Anita found herself embarrassed by its luxury. It was time to go back to work at the post office and to take Tyrone's clothes to the Goodwill. For the life of her, Anita couldn't get interested in anything at all. East Harlem was filled with women like her. Hardworking, law-abiding, church-going, voting black women who for no reason had what was most dear, most loved, snatched from their hands. Yes, it knocked them down for a time, but somehow those black women made it through. They went to church all day Sunday, got involved volunteering in the community, signed up to be poll workers. They made scrapbooks filled with their dead's funeral programs, clipped out the obituaries, pressed flowers between the covers, made photo collages of pictures and report cards. Everything had to be just right to show the relatives and friends who stopped by; nothing was askew except for their hearts.

Going alone to Evergreen would help her get there. It had been a while since she opened up her window and looked outside. When *was* the last time she rummaged through her wardrobe with the weather in mind? It had been a while since she hoped the corner bodega sold flowers to her liking. Carnations were hardy but common; roses felt inappropriate, but that she was thinking at all shocked her. It had been a while since she had thought, So what then? Would she lay flowers on the ground or should she buy a vase to put them in? What then? Kneel? Pray? Look both ways to see if anyone was looking, then tilt her head to the sky and caw her grief? I guess I'll know when I get there. Afterward—if she could just get through what she knew would be at least an hour commute—she could turn back for home and get started cutting out the articles with Tyrone's murder in them. She could join the ranks of black women who scrabbled through, who said things like "Give it to God" and meant it. Along with pondering the weather and being properly dressed for it, she thought about church. It had been a while since she stepped inside one. And this time it might be easier for Anita to find one that fit her needs since she didn't have to worry about its day care services or after-school programs or the credentials of the sister teaching Sunday school. Anita, so steeped in daydreaming, jumped when she heard applause.

It's the cops surrounding the table who made the noise. But it wasn't the standing ovation she expected. Their hand clapping reminded her of the gesture made when trying to move a band of pigeons out of the way. Shoo. And like city-raised birds her neighbors didn't startle into flight by the noise. Rather, on clumsy feet they rose. No one had even been asked if they cared for a second cup of coffee. Some officer opened the door: "Well, okay, then."

As the police ushered them out, Carl managed to jam in a question. And it embarrassed him that he didn't sound like a preacher surrounded by his flock or a leader galvanized by a cause. He sounded desperate. "Well, when can we come back? Check in?"

"Exactly, right."

"What?" What did that mean? They were still struggling into their coats as they stumbled outside onto the sidewalk. As Carl tried to think of what to say, one by one his people drifted. Anita, alone, tilted her head to the sky. It started to snow.

CHAPTER 12

For the first time in his life Manuel Jr. became a lookout boy. His father normally gave ten-year-old kids on the block five dollars to notice anything in pants that could terrorize. But lately in the mornings Manuel Jr. had begun to sit on the stoop to watch for trouble. The real kind. The sort that wrecked families or brought killing woe right to your doorstep. No, not the unexpected arrival of an undercover detective or a rival drug dealer. All of Manuel Jr.'s attention was pointed in the direction of his cousin Twin. Somebody needed to keep an eye on her. He watched her limp up the trap house stairs at dawn, fall into bed fully clothed, and sleep hard until late afternoon. There were signs when folks got ruined or dirtied up for good, and over the last several days, Manuel Jr. was making sure his cousin didn't have any.

When they struck the signs were clear: eating too much or too little, breathing hard for no good reason or trying not to cry. Staring out the window at nothing at all. Until his father decided to punish Twin by making her mind the trap in their basement, Manuel Jr. had never worried about his cousin. She was bigger than he was. Nobody he knew had the nerve to step up on Twin during her late-night wandering. She knew her way home. But now, now that she was spending all night in the trap, handling the money and the customers, his stomach clenched when he saw her come trudging up the stairs with her head down.

Yesterday she got dressed and walked out the door, only to stand at the corner for ten minutes, then turn back for home. What had she seen in the trap? What had happened? But he knew. Something unmanageable had jumped off in the basement, and his cousin was so tore up she couldn't bear to cross the street and buy groceries. So now, now he had to step up and be a man. All he had to do was ask her about it. Ask Twin what he himself was never asked. You okay? His father never asked him about what went on in the basement under colored lights, but neither did his homeboys when they drank forties and played dominoes on the corner. You all right, man? It wouldn't have mattered that he couldn't talk about it. That most days he didn't think about what he had seen, what he had done in response. He hadn't ever told anybody, nor did he have plans to tell. The point was to be asked. He longed for that act of kindness. Was that what Twin wanted too? Did she want him to rub her shoulder and ask, Are you okay? You want to talk about it?

Once, a long time ago, Manuel Jr. had stood in the living room while the radio blared and his father studied the OTB receipts clutched in his hand. They were making money hand over fist, but the living room was still decorated to his aunt's taste. Avocado-colored paisley wallpaper, all the furniture mustard yellow, the wall-to-wall carpet dyed a color that tried and failed to marry green and yellow. He hated this room: its coloring, the way the furniture's velvety texture reminded him it was best not to touch a thing. But his father, even though he never invited anyone over, adored the opulence.

His son and niece knew it was the only time they could cajole him into conversation or borrow money. He would often turn dreamy and stroke the velvet couch. His father loved spending the afternoons alternating between the television and the eight-track stereo. He seemed to have a personal grudge against quiet, but if Manuel Jr. raised his voice or caught his father just before he made his choice between the best of Elvis and Diana Ross, he'd have a chance of being listened to. Manuel Jr. had waded into a din of song. "Upside down / Boy, you turn me inside out / And round and round / Upside down . . ." He watched his father bob his head to the beat, waiting to be recognized.

Diana's voice trailed off and there was a pause of quiet while the eight-track machine queued up Elvis's "Love Me Tender." Manuel Jr. didn't cough or shuffle his feet to get his father's attention. The past had taught him that nothing but his father's sharp irritation would come from it. Rather Manuel Jr. stood there praying for luck to find him. And it did, in the guise of a car accident crashing just outside the open living room window. His father snatched his head up. "Well, what is it?"

"Nothing. Nothing, Daddy."

But today he was going to do it. March right up to Twin and ask, You steady after what you see going down in the trap? He tried. All day long he gave his level best. He wanted to ask her while they watched television together; after he'd asked, "You want something from the bodega?"; he wanted to throw the question at her back while she cooked dinner or when he offered to clear the table and wash the dishes. Over and over he tried to get out, You want to talk about it? Trying to summon up his courage, Manuel Jr. stared so hard at Twin it caught her attention. "Well, what is it?"

"Nothing, Twin." He walked upstairs to his bedroom, miserable and ashamed. Manuel Jr. suddenly realized why his father and his friends had never asked if something was wrong; that if they really forced him to, he would tell them every scary, unseeable thing that occurred down there in the near dark. They didn't want to know. And neither did he.

Her mind as of late was like her name: twinned. She dreamed of her soon, so soon, runaway, while simultaneously remembering her childhood. When Twin was growing up, everyone got whoopings; in fact ass beatings were a community effort. Get caught doing something untoward meant not only were you smacked by your parents, but the neighbor who saw you do it swatted your bottom too. And if what you pulled was infamous, a random stranger would pop you good based on the rumor they'd heard about your mischiefs. Now, when washing the dishes or taking a shower, everything her mother had whipped her with as a kid crowded her mind. Twin remembered when her mother had spanked her with a wooden spoon. And that time when her uncle's belt in her mother's hand—good God—curled around an eight-year-old Twin like a living thing, snaked around her chest, and then incredibly, impossibly, its buckle snatched Twin in the mouth, giving her a fat lip for two weeks.

Twin pulled clean clothes from her dresser drawer, struggling to remember her childish sins, astonished at how the punishments remained vivid. How old was I? When I was young enough and Momma was strong enough. When my youth and Momma's strength found their equilibrium, so my mother could and did hold me aloft with one hand. Twin remembered when her feet dangled from what felt like miles away from the floor, and her momma had whacked her under the arm with the flat side of a kitchen knife. "Now you get out of here." Her mother let her go, and Twin dropped to the floor. Twin heeded the instruction and fled. "And shut up all that crying! Hear me?" Sniveling, shaking, fat tears rolling down her chin. Oh how she had hated her mother then. Sometimes Twin remembered from her childhood a singular joy: when Manuel Jr. would get a whipping too. Together they would sit on the edge of her bed and compare welts. Eight-year-old Twin, eleven-year-old Manuel Jr., spoke with the cold-blooded logic of serial killers. "I. Hate. Her. So. Much."

"I wish she was dead."

"I'm gone push her in front of the bus and make her dead."

Such thoughts didn't make the bruises heal any faster, but dreaming of their older, tougher selves—adults who could kill a lady dead—soothed. When Twin wasn't thinking of packing a bag and buying a bus ticket, her mind circled around those ass beatings. How getting her butt tore up so thoroughly, Twin never repeated whatever bad thing she had done. In fact, she couldn't remember her childhood misdeeds at all. It was as if her mother had beaten all the sin out of her.

Now at fifty-seven, working the trap filled with a bunch of crack addicts, Twin had to admit her mother had been onto something. Twin pulled on her overalls and then donned a forest-green farmer's jacket. Dressed, she opened her closet door and pulled out the treasure she had recently begun collecting: wooden spoons, a broken yardstick, a brown extension cord, a leather belt her uncle wouldn't miss, a long stretch of rope that Twin tied in knots every three inches, a high-heeled blue leather shoe, a two-foot-long piece of a water hose, a beaded red, yellow, and white jump rope, a yarn mop no one had used in over a decade, a bundle of switches, some stripped of their bark, others with their withering leaves still attached. She was tempted to add a kitchen knife to the bag, but she didn't trust her aim in the dark. Lord knew she didn't want to accidently kill anybody. Afterward she would catch a Greyhound, but before she hopped a bus out of town, she was going to whoop every single fucker who stepped inside the crack house within an inch of their lives.

For days Twin had been forced to wander back and forth between meek and mean. Upstairs under her uncle's glare, she ducked her head when he entered the kitchen and whispered, "Yes, sir," when he asked for seconds at dinner. But downstairs in the basement she put her streetwise reputation to shame. She couldn't stand these people. "Stupid motherfucker." She snatched their money, threw crack vials on the floor for them to pick up, turned away those who came to the door with family heirlooms tucked under their arms. When they tried to talk among themselves, Twin was quick with "Niggas, shut the fuck up." But despite all her downright cussedness, night after night they returned. They stood at the door, five-dollar bills wadded in their hands, already offering sheepish grins before she had said a word.

It wasn't their antics that had Twin clutching a hefty black bag stuffed with ass-whipping weaponry. She had seen too much during her nightly roaming of the street to be spooked by what went down at the trap. Gangsters killing each other; prostitutes selling their wares, teenagers doing nasty, unspeakable things: she had become inured to street life and its shenanigans. Manuel Jr. was wrong on that score; there was nothing she had seen that had turned her head or given her nightmares. No. The problem Twin found herself confounded by was juggling the sight of her customers high and bathed in colored lights in her uncle's trap and then having to deal with them the next day at their jobs. Was she a prude? Twin? She didn't think so, but she also couldn't shake the acute embarrassment she felt when she saw them walking down the street, sitting on the crosstown bus, standing at the checkout counter at the grocery. Her world, formed by the boundaries of Spanish Harlem, had rules. There were the chuckleheads and the citizens, the nasty bitches and the churchgoers, the voters and the lazy. Twin prided herself in knowing who was who, where each and every one of them spent their free time and laid their heads. She knew her neighbors; she knew her neighborhood. Hadn't she spent the last forty years strutting down its streets?

But her uncle's punishment had turned who was supposed to be where and when upside down. The stitching of her private civilization unraveled every time she worked down in the basement. The sister from her old church had stopped by the trap half a dozen times. Still dressed respectably but dirtier each time, the sister would get high, then dreamily want to play church in the dark. Half asleep, she reenacted the last time she had seen Twin in the pews. She reached for Twin's hands, bowed her head into Twin's neck, then began to pray. "Take it, Jesus, amen. I'm with You. Sweet God." More than once, Twin caught herself falling into a prayerful call-and-response. And when Twin tried to shake herself loose, the sister wouldn't let go. "We're not supposed to be doing that here."

Manuel Jr. certainly didn't have this problem. For years he came and went, hanging out with his friends on the corner, going all the way to Brooklyn for a house party. He worked the trap every night and napped in the afternoon. On the rare occasion when he and Twin stepped out together, he nodded and said hello to their neighbors without a stutter. Whatever Twin was feeling, he wasn't. She had spent days thinking of what to make of her feelings. What was she supposed to do? Write some advice column? Ask Dear Abby how to deal with working for her uncle who is a drug dealer? Ask her how to handle people who she hadn't realized are crack addicts during the light of day? How should Twin start conversations with neighbors (the bodega guy, the bus driver) who she had seen all night getting high? Should she mention last night's festivities or pretend she didn't see them at all? Thoughts? Advice?

As much as Twin hated to admit it, those little conversations with her neighbors braced and plumped her casual Wednesdays. She missed them. Gone were the small thrills felt when you went to the fish market only to find all the whiting gone. But don't fret, because Nico, the fishmonger, had set aside three pounds just for you. "Girl, I knew you was coming by. Better smile, now."

Racing for the bus, patting down her pockets, remembering that she'd forgotten to grab a token, and before she could sigh, she saw the bus driver whose name she didn't know and who didn't know hers, cranking open the door. "All right, Ms. Lady. Get on this bus. I know where you going." She would sit at the front where she belonged, and they talked about nothing at all. His wife was having their second baby and union work was good. Twin ought to look into it.

When her talks with her uncle had led to fights, and conversations with her cousin turned carefully caring, she could depend on the back-and-forth with the shopkeepers to always satisfy. No more. She had looked everywhere except at Luis when she'd bought her lunch at the bodega last week. How could she, when all she could think of was the night before when, while Luis stroked his wife's cheek, a man knelt in front of him, head bobbing, earning the Crown Royal sack of nickels that Luis had clutched in his hand? Luis passed Twin her turkey sandwich, chips, and Hi-C. "See you, Twin," he said softly, but the pat of menace in his voice was unmistakable. Twin pocketed her change.

She didn't leave the block after that. She tried. Put on her coat and scarf. Walked all the way to the corner, but her courage fled when the light changed and she could have crossed the street. Never had she been so afraid. Not when that belt buckle popped her in the mouth. Not when her mother hurled an iron at her head and missed. Not when she saw a shoot-out in the middle of the night and ducked behind a car for safety. Sure, her heart raced. She wasn't a fool, but she wasn't scared. This was different. She was afraid of bumping into the bus driver or the cash register lady. She hated that she found herself at a loss for words when conducting regular business. How could she say, Keep the change, when just last night, I saw you half naked and another man sucking your dick, Luis. How was she to decide if she wanted her sandwich on a sub or a roll? She had thought she was too tough, too mean, too old to be steeped in this kind of heartache. And it wasn't that they were her friends. It was worse than that. They were her people.

"But I'm gone beat that ass tonight."

She waited until two in the morning, when the trap had taken in as many customers as it could fit. When the two mattresses were crowded with bodies and she couldn't have walked a path to the door even if she wanted to. But she didn't want to. Twin took a step out of the boiler closet and reached inside her black plastic bag. The two-foot-long water hose felt good in her hand. "So y'all don't want to go? Huh? Want to stick around?" Her arm flung out and down. She wasn't sure who felt the first lash, but almost as one they shook out of their stupor.

"Say, girl, what you doing now?"

Twin pulled her arm back and let the hose fly in the direction of that voice. "I bet y'all won't come back here no more! Bet money on that." She had expected them all to run for the front door, but no one had done so yet. Instead, they crouched low, crab walking away from the lash of the hose, trying to push other people in front of themselves.

"Cut that now! Stop it now!"

Twin dropped the hose, her hand suddenly slick with sweat, and reached again inside the bag. She couldn't pull the belt free. It was caught on the bundle of switches.

"Get her!"

But no one but Luis was brave enough to rush her. His arms were flung wide as if to hug her, and Twin stepped into the embrace. In the closeness, she kicked the bodega owner between his legs and laughed when he crumpled to the floor. Just as she curled a fist, aiming a punch at some grandmother, the crowd pressed in, surrounding her. And down Twin went, thinking this is it; I'm gone now. But that wasn't their intention at all. They just wanted her to stop hitting them. Twin heard quiet whispers. "Cool out, girl." "She all right down there?" "You think she still got the stuff?" Someone's hands snaked out of the pile of bodies and stroked her head, her shoulders. The clumsy, earnest gesture reminded her of when she and Manuel would take turns trying to soothe each other. "Don't cry, T."

"It's gone be okay, Junior. I hate her so much." The soft pats she and her cousin had exchanged never staunched her crying. In fact they had often made them both cry harder.

Not this time, not buried beneath a heap of people. Twin didn't shed a tear.

CHAPTER 13

It wasn't just their disappointment with the police meeting that had them craving to city-stride their way to the subway station. Nor was it the baying call of their lateness to work. Anita was right. Partly. They wanted to get back to their lives because a minor mystery was occurring in their homes. And until they all stood outside the police precinct, talking small talk while Reverend Carl tried to get what was next from the lieutenant, they hadn't realized the phenomenon had infected all their apartments. Its discovery started innocently enough.

"You smell that snow?"

"I had an uncle who claimed that. You can smell it?" It was cold enough to see their breathing, and the seven mothers, along with Sisters Shelia and Morning, marveled at the relative quiet a mid-morning had in their neighborhood.

"Sure."

"I can only smell the rain coming." Shelia tilted her head to the sky to take a sniff. That promising conversation was sidelined when two heartbeats later small snowflakes fell, stinging their faces.

"See there."

They wanted to leave—get to work by eleven so that they could go to lunch and not feel guilty about it—but Carl still stood talking to the officer, trying to convince him to put something, anything, on a calendar.

"How's Kendall doing?"

"Girl, sleeping. That's all he manages to do nowadays."

"Mine too. Can't keep his eyes open."

A mutter of agreement danced among them. "Yours too?" "And yours?" "Yes." "Yes." "Me as well." Until the seven mothers and Shelia, though not Sister Morning, all agreed that their children had come down with a bout of unexpected sleep. Their children had taken to napping anywhere. You couldn't blame them for not noticing. The habit of the days ate up all their attention. When to go to the grocery store, when to put on dinner and thus stave off a night of Chinese takeout that needed to be avoided. Nobody had money for that sort of regular extravagance. It was always time to rush to work, time to rush home. Since they had no church to attend, Sundays meant calls to the South or their parents. Let's finally fix that chair and unstop that sink were one-off chores that punctuated their weekend mornings. It took a collective conversation to realize their children were sleeping, all snug in their beds. Or anyplace at all.

These mothers didn't say it aloud, but when they first noted the sleeping, they were happy. So much quiet. So much time. Mothers and fathers watched the evening news in peace. Nothing interrupted gossipy conversations on the telephone. They wrote out checks for utility bills and walked payments to the mailbox with nary a child's want to stand in their way. On random Tuesdays there was leftover chicken, enough to make a sandwich the next day. No more did they sneak kisses with their spouses; bold as day they kissed mouth on mouth in the kitchen. Everyone had been so happy with the quiet it took all of them walking to the subway to wonder if something was amiss.

"What you think it is?" they asked one another, scared of the answers they had privately come to. These were black mothers living in East Harlem. They bowed to busy work-filled days because that's how you made it through. They felt pride that they had made the time to stand and call out for who had killed Tyrone, a son who looked like their own. But now, walking so slowly to the subway station, careful of the flakes of ice that refused to melt on warm pavement, realizing their children were nodding off, sometimes in the most inconvenient places, they wondered. While they were off minding other people's business, had their children gotten themselves into trouble? Crack was real. Nowadays everywhere they looked, regular people, folks they had grown up with, sisters and brothers they had gone to church with, were getting into trouble. Smoking this, shooting up that. Stealing from loved ones. Not bathing. Smiling and laughing for no good reason. And always nodding, nodding, nodding off. Sleep could catch them at any time. These women had seen the sight with their own eyes. Folks staggered against the side of buildings, and then, ever so carefully, their knees buckled, and they slumped into sleep. Nothing roused them. There were sleeping black beauties all over the neighborhood. Was that the answer to the mystery plaguing their children?

A dozen feet from the stairs of the 110th Street station, they refused to take another step. Finally, Sister Shelia, clutching at her coat, cleared her throat, ready to give voice to their fears. "Maybe our boys done got—"

"I got a grown son, living way out in California," Sister Morning interrupted. "And this one here too," she said, nodding at her daughter Lara, who hadn't heard a word of their conversation. Tinny music floated out of her headphones as she stood several steps away from them all. "My boy when he was that age slept plenty. Boys sleep that much. It's growing is all. They doing it so fast, it wears them out." The seven mothers and Shelia traded dubious glances. But Morning wasn't finished; her final words had a pat of authority that soothed them. "My grandma told me to be on the lookout when my Abraham got that age. And sure enough he slept almost three years."

"Where your people from?"

"Arkansas." Her words didn't convince them entirely, but they got them on the subway and on to work.

Funny how they didn't mention Wanda. Though she was known, they stepped around her name. Since their church had burned down, her comings and goings and all her troubles had struck them as a warning: Careful, or you'll turn up like Wanda. No one blamed her. They hadn't dared. Lord knew what happened to Wanda could happen to them all. Trouble could strike you down like bad weather. Still. One couldn't help but notice Wanda's tipped-over life. She had some kind of boyfriend or maybe common-law husband who just up and vanished one day and left behind a little baby boy. Daryl. And in the beginning he was fat and happy and just as smart as could be. Wasn't that the story? And she had family too but far away; hadn't they heard she was from all the way down in Florida, or maybe close by—the Bronx?—but her people were stuck up and had left Wanda to make it through the best way she could. And she did. She had joined the Ethiopian, dropping off little Daryl at Sunday school and at Wednesday Bible study. She always had a chicken casserole to offer at the Tuesday food swap and complimented the fruit salads they provided.

She was a good neighbor. A good sister. Nobody said different. But about a year ago something went awry. She got a new boyfriend—Joe, Joey, John—whatever his name was. One of those good-looking brothers who never had steady employment but always found pickup work. None of them knew what he did for a living; they only knew where it happened. "Oh, he's working Midtown." "They got him downtown this week." Then all that work disappeared, and he spent most of his time laid up under Wanda. After that she morphed into one of those women. You know. Loud talking. Complaining to whoever sat next to her in the pews, stood next to her in the checkout line, hung out with her on the corner. Wanda, a woman who had been like them—hardworking, churchgoing— suddenly wasn't, and she couldn't wait to tell everyone about it. In the middle of that carrying on, true trouble struck: Daryl had gotten himself into some kind of mix-up with the police. None of these ladies knew the details, but the crumbs of his story certainly made a meal. Daryl had stolen something or maybe attacked somebody. Or, or, or . . . who knew? Whatever, the police wouldn't let him go. And as sorry as everyone was for him, they didn't want Wanda or her boy's latest trouble tumbling into their own lives.

And anyway, weren't they dealing with their own worn-out children? Weren't they standing around in the snow, listening to Sister Morning's parenting advice as if it were sanctified news? Weren't they late getting to work so that they could stand with Anita? They were dealing with murder. They were brave enough to ask the whereabouts of a killer. That took so much courage there was none left to spare. And on top of that, no one had the time. Not really. Plus Wanda had it handled. Didn't she? Hadn't you heard that? The churchwomen stepped inside the subway car, then scattered to their jobs.

So they didn't want to end up like Wanda. Really? Well, good luck. Because in Wanda's mind, these high and mighty and, yes, Jesus, saditty sisters were already there. The only difference was that Wanda didn't need to be soothed by Morning's advice. She knew the cause behind Daryl's sudden sleepiness. Or she thought she did. She had other worries. What was she supposed to do with Daryl's crying? He just couldn't or wouldn't stop. For months now he slept then woke and cried again into sleep. Just this morning at breakfast while those women clustered around the conference table at the police precinct feeling thwarted but righteous, Wanda and her son sat at their kitchen table eating leftover General Tso's chicken. He'd cried all over the broccoli and red sauce. Her son's steady, quiet tears prompted an emotion that came out both brusque and heartfelt. "What's the matter with you?"

"Nothing, Momma."

"Why you crying then?"

"I don't know."

"Can you cut it out then? I mean, what I mean is what's the matter?"

"Nothing, Momma."

It was January now; almost a whole year had passed since the burning of the Ethiopian. Wanda had thought it was bad back then, but these last eleven months showed her how a DA could tilt your life without provocation. Wanda had laughed when she heard the litany of small crimes lodged against Daryl, but she wasn't laughing now. On a whim cops could take her son away, place him in front of a judge who intoned a dollar amount for those petty charges—and every time Wanda met with Carl, she cajoled him into accompanying her on yet another trip to the courthouse, got him to explain to her what exactly the lawyer was doing, bullied him into being the cosigner for her son's bail—every time, she felt Carl's concern for Daryl wane. Who could blame him? Nobody was going to make a name for himself defending her son against nickel-and-dime charges that added to dollars Wanda couldn't afford. What reporter would make sure to bring a cameraman to Daryl's arraignment where his bail was being set? If constantly putting up bail weren't putting her in the poorhouse, Wanda would have thought it was a joke too. No wonder Carl didn't want to fool with her and her son.

If Wanda were so inclined (and she wasn't), she could have pegged Carl's fading interest to the day, October 22, 1985. The day she led Anita by the hand and got Carl to help her. Three months later and Wanda still marveled that her friend's troubles would be a rocket climbing higher, its bright tail mesmerizing a neighborhood, her included. What trouble could hold a candle to Anita's grief? To Tyrone's manner of death? And who would want to lay their tragedy alongside that one? Not even Wanda dared. The days when Daryl was out on bail and she didn't think about him at all were a blessing. And Carl's inability to juggle both women's problems didn't worry her too much; she kept a steady eye on his ambition. Wanda knew her life and her son's well enough to know she needed pity, the currency of the neighborhood. Wanda made sure to seize on it, but she needed Carl.

Just this morning her son's lawyer asked her to come in for a sit-down during her lunch break. That he wouldn't tell her what he wanted on the phone was the beginning of her bad news.

"So I've got good news," her lawyer told her while offering her tea or coffee.

"You do, huh?"

Well, yes. Yes, he did. It should be abundantly clear that the district attorney didn't have the evidence to bring her son's arson case to trial. Isn't that wonderful?

"Uh-huh."

Was Wanda sure she didn't want a cup of coffee? Maybe a bagel? A muffin? Would Wanda like a muffin?

"Naw. I ain't hungry."

That was too bad. Anyway, all this lawyer needed now was a retainer of two thousand dollars, up front, and he could get her son's major indictment dismissed.

"Two what?"

There were a lot of billable hours that he would have to put in to wrap up her son's situation.

"Dollars? Two thousand dollars?"

Yes. Up front. Wanda's payments thus far had been . . . wayward. But certainly she could see with this money the entire episode was about to reach a happy conclusion. Really, Wanda should have a muffin. Or she should at least take a cookie. They were delicious. She left her lawyer's office with three sugar cookies wrapped in a napkin.

And just how was Wanda going to get together two thousand dollars? She certainly didn't ask the lawyer, whose every word and breath cost her money. Instead she created a list of things she absolutely had to do. First she needed to keep a job. Wanda had a job, sure. Stocking groceries at the Met on 106th. But already she had managed to piss off most of her coworkers, and her boss was none too pleased with her taking these two-hour lunches. Maybe I'll let a couple of bills slip. Con Edison. And the telephone bill. My landlord won't come asking for rent money for at least two months. But still, with no more lunches and overtime and a second job and asking family and friends and cashing in on every favor she was owed, and letting her phone and lights get turned off and squeezing out every kindness from every person she knew, even if she learned to cry on cue, she'd still be twelve hundred dollars short. So now what? Now I got to be back at work in ten minutes, or I'll be taking more than a two-hour lunch. Wanda slipped a token into the turnstile and walked down to the platform to wait for an uptown subway. Late or at least not in the time she needed it, the train slid into the station. So maybe I'll work overtime and get the second job and just get the money in six months or so. But thinking of Daryl stopped that line of thought cold. Oh, he was good nowadays. At home on time, "yes, ma'am," "no, ma'am," and all that. But the cops' habit of picking him up whenever they felt like it and then having to spend anywhere from two days to up to a week in jail until his mother could gather up his bail unsettled both their lives. The constant movement into jail and out on bond felt unmoored from what had gotten him into trouble eleven months ago.

Like all children, Daryl couldn't quite understand why he was being punished for something he may have done a lifetime ago. Momma said I'm innocent, but the police don't think that count for nothing. He was an adult now, the Santa judge told him, but he didn't feel like one. Child Services didn't come around; his mother hadn't cooked dinner in months, and no matter how hard he paid attention in class, no matter how kind he was to anybody who would let him be, a patrolman out of nowhere would pluck him from his classroom desk and handcuff him in front of everybody. The rough paws of police officers gave him nightmares. If there was a God, He would bless Daryl, and nobody would ever touch him again. If they would just leave him alone, he would never ask for food, cold or warm.

Wanda couldn't help but notice the tune-up from the police had changed Daryl. He was too quiet. He slept all the time. Cried when he was awake. He never laughed. He almost shook out of his skin when a door banged shut or a dish clattered in the sink. Who wanted a kid like that? Wanda couldn't even enjoy her son's new-found obedience because she knew exactly where it came from.

She thought of Carl. I should be able to count on him for this. He should be good to me, because . . . because he should be good to me. He should help me read this litany of money and woe my lawyer handed to me on the way out the door. Carl could answer all the questions she wanted to put to her lawyer. There was a reason she hadn't approached him yet. She wasn't really sure if Carl would say yes. Don't ask unless you know you gone get the answer you want; this had been her mother's mantra, and Wanda directed her life around those words. Even so, right after work Wanda made it her business to go and see Carl. God help her. She needed that money. I need him bad, she thought as she left work at sundown and walked uptown toward the Institute.

The banner was the same, as was the air of shabbiness, but the sight of the Institute set Wanda's teeth on edge as she pulled its doors open and let in the city's winter. On her walk she had planned her attack. So, if Carl steps to me and looks like he's going to say no way, or he starts up with Anita and all that, I should . . . Well, I'm going to start off with . . . The more she thought about it, the more her plan sounded like how she approached most problems, but louder.

So what? I'll just loud talk him. Wanda took a calming breath, ready to yell, but walked into what she could only describe as an eighth-grade homeroom class. Carl stood at the lectern, and some twenty or so people sat quietly in neatly lined-up chairs. Wanda was so prepared for a chaotic milling about she almost bit her tongue as she held back her holler in the schoolhouse quiet. Everyone looked right at home in the cluttered shabbiness. The new paint job did little to hide the warped wood paneling; leak stains had already begun to reappear on the stucco ceiling. And underneath the layer of smells—Pine-Sol and lemon-scented furniture polish, beef patties and coffee—wafted the unmistakable odor of mildew.

"Okay, so I want us to divide up in threes. Nobody walks alone. And if you think a conversation is bout to turn dangerous, leave. Now another thing: we need delegates for the assembly, congressional, senatorial, and city council districts. Now listen, folks," Carl said, "I want our delegations to number somewhere between five and seven people. I'd really like each team to be at least ten strong. But I understand folks got to work and what all. What I will say is that we ain't gone send out some two-man delegation. You hear me? Keisha is gone head up the city council meeting."

Wanda couldn't figure out what she had walked in on, and she slipped quietly against the wall next to the door. Ah, girl, while you were away.

After the police meeting Carl had sworn he would never again suffer from that brand of humiliation. He hadn't waited until the next planned meeting with his members. Rather he slid notes under their doors or inside broken mailboxes and told them to meet him at the Institute this evening after work. Twenty faithful had shown up. "Police don't want to hunt for the culprit who killed our black son. Fine. Just fine, then. We'll do it ourselves. And I know the trouble we are hunting," Carl told them. "So before we head out, we are going to make a visit with every elected official in our zip code. Let them know what we are about to be up to, let them know the danger we're willing to court. We vote, damn it. This won't stand. Police can't treat us like this."

Wanda felt the start of uncontrollable laughter burbling in her stomach. As if. God, as if.

"Anybody got questions?" he asked.

A brown hand close to the front of the assembly rose.

"Brother Elijah. What you need?"

"These muckety-mucks always want to know what you want to drink. So, I'm just saying up front. Coffee. Black. One sugar."

"Man, what the fuck does that have to do with anything?" someone from the crowd asked.

"Well, I'm telling it. I like my coffee black, one sugar."

Carl chuckled. "Okay. All right now."

Wanda took the moment to push away from the wall and prepared to get herself noticed. But a funny thing happened just as she took a deep breath. Half of the room raised their hands. She couldn't see anyone's face, but she found herself moved to quiet by all those earnest black palms reaching for the ceiling. Wanda didn't want to interrupt with tales of how Daryl was as good as cooked on a platter complete with an apple stuck in his mouth and now the police were making a meal of him. If twenty of her neighbors heard that story, wouldn't they feel lousy? She knew what would happen; all those hands, yearning for answers, would drop back into their laps. Even if she did cut up, what were her neighbors going to do? None of them had the faintest idea who was the true culprit, and they couldn't speak to the legitimacy of the numerous accusations leveled at Daryl.

Carl called on the woman wiggling in her seat, and her question set the tone for the next dozen: "What will happen if it all goes wrong?"

"Brothers. Sisters. I got this." Carl sounded so sure and steady, hands fell into laps and didn't knot in fear. What Carl said was real. Well, I'm real, Wanda thought, and my boy is really in trouble.

As twenty or so of her neighbors milled around the snack table and lined up to have a private word with Carl, Wanda looked to see if Anita had showed up. She was nowhere.

So whatever solutions were being bandied about, Wanda didn't fit in and neither did Anita. That made sense. All her friend wanted was for her son to be alive, and no visit to city hall or political dignitaries would make that so.

Carl stepped away from the knot of people that had formed around him and began to circulate through the assembly. Hands were shaken; pats on the backs were meted out; light hugs that crushed nothing were given. All of it made Wanda want to cry. When was the last time she had wept? Whatever the age, Wanda wasn't going to let her tearless streak end right in front of all these people who looked like friends but spoke about law and justice in a way she had never experienced. She was so busy concentrating on not crying, Carl's hand almost touched her shoulder before she realized it was there. She took a measured step back.

"You busy here," Wanda whispered to him.

"Oh, Sister." He looked at her, and his air of confidence made her feel as harmless as a turkey sandwich. Carl held on to her shoulder and squeezed it tenderly. Wanda sighed. She had no place here—all the talk about city leaders and councilmen and hunting for killers and being voters picked her up like a dirty dog and placed her where she belonged, back outside. "I guess I'll catch you another time." She shrugged out of his embrace and slipped outdoors.

There was always music in East Harlem. In the summers cars blared beats, soaring notes floated out of windows. Even in the middle of a January winter there was song. Quieter, yes. But still, music was there. Women hummed softly. Men clapped their hands for warmth. And of course the dealers hawking their wares provided a certain kind of melody. Walking down Second Avenue, hunched in her coat, Wanda really listened to them for the first time. "Say, baby. You need something? Five dollars, five dollars." She swayed to their haunting tune. It was early evening but dark outside. At least it had stopped snowing. "Five dollars, baby. Ten dollars, yo. Let me get at you." In the right frame of mind no one could say no to that beckoning.

There's a saying that given enough time people can start looking like each other. It's true for a certain set of married folk. You start out your own person, but if you stick around for thirty years or so, all those differences get sandblasted away. Lord knew how it happened, but two people with nothing in common but marriage and time by the end both liked the color blue and action movies. They finished each other's sentences. And when one half of that kind of couple sees a small, cherished thing, they smile at the bauble before them but also at the thought of delight on their spouse's face when they tell them all about it. That phenomenon is true for friends too. Two people can like the same things and get mad in the same way because the undying admiration for each other shapes their manner. Wanda just watched her feet as they marched down the sidewalk, her purchase clutched in her hand. Her feet knew where they wanted to go.

Arriving at her destination, she gave a knock on the door that was loud and bold. But her face sat on the edge of a crumble. More than twenty years of not shedding a tear was about to end its winning streak, and all Wanda could hope for was to be indoors when it happened. Anita opened her door wearing four T-shirts and a skirt with green jogging pants underneath. Wanda didn't ask Anita why she was dressed like a hoodlum. She knew. Searching around for something clean and warm, Anita had found nothing but summer clothes. Her face looked helpless. Hopeless.

"Hey."

"Hey."

Look; look there. Their eyes met and the two women traded smiles that looked like homecoming. Wanda and Anita. Unmistakable. They looked like sisters.

CHAPTER 14

Seven days after Wanda was shooed out of the Institute like a cherished but unruly pet, they caught him. Carl and the members of the Institute had been searching, asking the neighborhood about whereabouts, looking gangsters dead in the mouth, but collectively they were so steeped in their dreaming the capture caught them unaware. Some of them dreamt of their sudden courage; others dreamt of an afterward where justice had been meted out and they were singular victors.

This was not the kind of dreaming you woke up to, bathed in something light and soft. Anita and Wanda and Carl, the seven mothers, the former members of the Ethiopian, and the police were plagued with walking visions that wore track shoes. Their dreams hollered ready, set, go. And then after seven days of all that, the culprit was caught and it shocked them all.

They got over the surprise quickly enough. Secretly they always knew it was him. Hadn't they been in his shop, once, twice, at least three times? Weren't they suspicious when he dropped his perfunctory courtesy the second he realized they weren't there to make a purchase? He hadn't let them put up the missing boy poster when Tyrone went lost and refused again when they asked him to put up a Crime Stoppers poster. He didn't want any trouble, he'd told them. How much trouble could he have gotten into when every shop for ten blocks had one taped to its window? That alone should have made them realize he was telling on himself. His beauty supply shop on Second Avenue, between 109th and 110th, was right smack in the middle of the block. Tyrone had been murdered and found on the corner. They should have been looking at him as the culprit since last fall.

Listen, everyone knew innocent until proven guilty, but this motherfucker looked guilty. Everybody knew him, or at least all the women did. Wo Ren, the beauty supply shop owner, who told bad jokes in broken English. "How you make seven even number? Take *s* out! Hahaha!" He stood in the aisles and watched them deliberate on whether they should buy Palmer's or Jergens lotion. Palmer's worked better, didn't it? But Jergens smelled like their childhood. And when they took too long (in his mind), he asked in a voice brimming with menace, "Can I help you?" Not one woman—there were no male customers—said what was really on her mind: Back the fuck up and let me compare prices and decide which nail polish color to buy, if you please. Sometimes they allowed their annoyance to show with a nose flare. And did that get him to leave them alone? No. Instead, he made pointed comments no one asked for and then laughed. "That not your hair! Hahaha! $7.95! Hahaha!" See, motherfucker; that's not even funny.

He was exactly who they thought he would be. Not even in the country for five years, not even speaking good English, a Chinese man who bullied them when they bought his merchandise. "You buy that? You buy?" He was an asshole. And an entire neighborhood put up with his rudeness because where else were they going to go? Why was his store open when everything else was closed? The obvious answer: that he timed his store hours to the beauty shop a block away, was scoffed at. Sure. Bullshit. Like black ladies couldn't buy what they needed—hair grease, relaxers, extensions—the day before like everybody else. Like he needed the money and thus shaped his business hours to his clientele's. Those bad jokes he told that gave him bellyaches came back to haunt him. Of course he killed that kid; he doesn't even say thank you when he takes your money.

While the men in the neighborhood expressed surprise—"Get the fuck out of here. That guy?"—the women felt vindicated. They hadn't poked at it much, but the women who lived within a ten-block radius of his shop all hated him. He knew all the things they wanted to keep secret: who had good hair and who was sporting a Jheri curl and tried to pass off the hairdo as a natural. He knew who bought Wave Nouveau and who dyed their hair surreptitiously in their bathrooms. He knew who bought his fake gold earrings and lied and said, "No, they're real; I bought them at the pawnshop." He knew all their undercover business. Now they knew his.

Because their search of almost seven days discovered nothing, they posed questions that revealed damning answers. Why hadn't anybody called? Didn't somebody owe them that much? They had had one or two meetings with city councilmen, had been promised that they would be kept in the loop. The phone tree lit up. Keisha called Shelia who called Morning and on and on, until all the ladies were talking on three-way. They filled in the gaps of information with personal speculation. "I went by there two days ago, and he kicked me out when I said I wanted to put a poster up. He was acting funky."

"Funky? More like he was acting guilty."

"Cause he was."

"Right?"

"You get a call from somebody?"

"Naw, ain't nobody called me."

"You?"

"I bet they called Reverend Carl."

"Sister Morning, you called Reverend Carl on the three-way?"

"Twice now. Nobody picking up over there." And there was the rub and source of frustration. The conversation circled the happiness in catching him, but the undercurrent of displeasure was clear. None of them had a hand in making it happen. None of them knew what really happened. They had found out this surprising news the way everyone else found out: on television. Had a witness come forward? Was that what happened? Where was Carl?

And where was Anita?

INTERLUDE

They should have been prey. Two women prowling outside in the middle of the night surrounded by young men who peddle and trade trouble, Anita and Wanda should have been easy pickings. But Wanda and her lost-and-found nature keep them hidden. She knows all about alleys that curve into dead ends, the quiet spaces of community gardens that some well-meaning man locks up. Still, there's nothing to it. A jiggle here, a grunt there, and then two women slip inside a space meant just for them. They duck into some nook or wall space that feels as safe and secret as a dollhouse. Anita and Wanda cannot wait, just cannot wait, to get inside Anita's apartment and taste bliss. Both of them agree Anita's place is the best. Its couch is the softest. The tub is a treasure where they get high and slip and slide. Outside is good too, but dangerous. And while both women love the remembering and the forgetting they dart in and out of, they both know the safest place to feel it is in the confines of Anita's apartment.

How much time passes before they become bold? Before they become unafraid of what is outside? Two months. Spring is sharp now. Even children who think it's funny to pluck new leaves from branches can't stymie their growth. There is so much to see. Wanda and Anita roam the blocks; they are sixteen-year-old trouble in thirty-year-old bodies. "Hey, man." A coquettish cry is ruined by the state of their mouths; the smoke they need to snuggle close to bliss makes canker sores on their tongues. Wanda's sore is the size of a dime; Anita's a nickel. Still they have all their teeth. And when they smile at men they shouldn't, the men smile back and don't grab their crotches.

At night, in small spaces during the day, the talk comes. "What about my son?"

"Who?"

"See? See! Daryl, that's who. He's alive so he don't count?"

"Nobody said that." This time they can't wait to go home to Anita's, and they slip inside an empty lot on 110th.

"I don't punch in at the post office so I don't count?"

"Girl, stop it." Anita hears her friend's anger but is more intrigued by the dirt that scatters every time she takes a breath in the empty lot.

"And through all that, I stayed true. Everybody hopping up and down over Tyrone, who's DEAD! And Daryl still in the system. Every time we come up for a court date, they set up a new bail, and he got to spend at least a week in jail while I scrape the money together and sort it all out. I gotta go tomorrow. I gotta get on a bus and do all that tomorrow to visit him in Rikers."

"Wanda, I didn't—"

"That's right; you didn't know cause you never fucking asked, Anita." Wanda is heaving. "Everybody gave a shit about you! The whole city turned on for you! You so decent and law-abiding you might as well be white." It is the ugliest thing Wanda can think to say, and it stings just as it is meant to.

"Fine."

"Find what?"

"Nothing. Just fine. Be that way." Their silence is awkward, tightening around both friends like an ill-fitting dress.

"I gotta go, Anita. See you, girl." Wanda stands, but she has nothing to pick up, and she feels the absence of the gesture. They are standing in the middle of a lot filled with things folks don't want—old toys and furniture, tires and broken refrigerators—stacked and threatening to fall. If this were a movie, Wanda would have a coat to throw over her shoulder or a purse to tuck under her arm. But she has come empty-handed, and she is leaving the same way.

"Well . . . well, wait. How is Daryl? Like is he okay and everything?"

"You ask now?"

"Well, yeah. How's he doing, you know?"

Wanda tries to hold on to the blister of anger she feels, but Anita's pitiful face pops the emotion. It is the last real fight they have. Anita asks about Daryl all the time now, and Wanda's answer is unwavering: "All right, I guess." She is not keeping secrets, but Wanda fails to tell Anita about her sober days when she accompanies Daryl to the courthouse. No one wants to know about Daryl's slick, sweaty hand that holds his mother's. His darting eyes that manage to still and find Wanda's face as they haul him away. There is so much about those days she wants to forget, and if she tells Anita, she will remember forever. No. No. It is better to forget all that and have deep conversations that swim nowhere and hurt no one.

"I never thought it would be this hard."

"Hmm, what?"

"To be alive. It shouldn't be this hard just to be alive . . ." Anita's smile is dreamy, but that thought burrows deep. Success is difficult, and being decent takes a kind of daily maintenance that can make anybody wonder if it is worth it. Anita isn't talking about being some big shot or sending your kid to college or going away for vacation. She means the simple act of drawing breath, of watching your chest rise and fall. It is harder than she ever imagined. Maybe when you're old. But everybody knows that; when your body becomes the biology lecture you finally pay attention to. But this. Anita is just thirty-six. And has a whole life to live.

. . .

That was the start of it. The beginning is when they use Anita's apartment as a place to dream, and sleep is so close and comes so fast they think of their pillows as best friends. Then the middle comes, and they have to change, but the transformation happens so quickly they don't notice it. Wanda, so close to the edge, begins to use pawnshops like a bank. Suddenly they never have enough money. And Anita, sweet Anita, who never has been any trouble to anybody, becomes what she had never been: in the know. She knows which stores have video cameras that actually work and aren't dummies perched in the corner like toy owls made to scare the pigeons. She knows no good reason her apartment building isn't on the slow crawl to becoming a crack house. Maybe she is the start.

Anita becomes one of many who sneak into storefronts late at night. She is now the kind of woman who frequents candy shops and botany stores that after hours put up their wares or shove them into corners and then hot, damp linoleum floors bow under couples slowly grinding, panting, real sex paling to the slippery grappling done by youth under the spell of a steady thump sounding out of stolen speakers. She doesn't belong here, but here she is, looking for a drug dealer who promises he will be perched in a corner. As she waits for him to give her the signal to approach, she grows sober and frowns at her condition. Who she was steps out from its hiding place. She listens to the thump of music and thinks all that bumping and grinding is trouble just waiting to happen. Anita sees some girl in spandex and shoulder pads try to pull out of her partner's embrace: "Stop it. Let go." Her frantic, moving mouth is unheeded and unheard under the blast of music, the crush of bodies leaving no room to budge. Anita doesn't move to save her but wonders which building will she trudge home to, her bra in tatters. Am I on the way to becoming one of those girls?

"Bitch, you want this?" her dealer shouts in her ear. Anita doesn't flinch and slides a twenty-dollar bill into his hand.

PART TWO

CHAPTER 15

In 1985, after it was all done and done, and the church had burned down to its foundation, the black women who had attended the Ethiopian were tempted to tell stories of their time there if anyone had cared to listen. They all had a taste to say aloud what they had done there, how they had praised His name, when dependence on each other felt like a fairy tale. Once upon a time in 1979 there was an all-wooden church called the Ethiopian United Federated Church of Christ in East Harlem. The original church had been built by a group of black lumber foremen who were not only wood-carvers by trade but idolized English woodwork. Those men had dreamt of Devonshire paneling in walnut, Lancashire woodwork in Renaissance oak for the pews, but their reverence was tempered by financial constraints, forcing them to use compressed pine shavings for decorative wainscoting.

The women of the Ethiopian didn't know this history but still marveled at the effort and skill, all in brown hues. They loved that the poor acoustics swallowed their words and kept their secrets secret. This house of worship—where men and women and children prayed and laughed while walking and staring at etchings unable to withstand time—encouraged their faith. The engraved double hammer beamed roof along with the mahogany pulpit hinted at greatness. For a while—six years to the day—this church was home, a place that became so familiar they could navigate the aisles in the dark. Some of them discovered the building's secrets: sisters discovered the exact spot to sit in the pews at sunset to see sunlight refracting in such a way that in the large wooden relief of the Virgin and Child Mary's praying hands shaded baby Jesus's face. One by one, two by two, sometimes in threes, black women found this respite. Or maybe the new pastor had found these sisters. Or maybe these black women with husbands and boyfriends in tow and the new preacher all found each other at the same time. It didn't matter. Once upon a time for six years the black women and children of East Harlem under the roof of the Ethiopian rose in praise. Sanctified and whole.

Whose boy was it who at seven years old shook the tambourine, then leapt into the aisle? Was he yours, Sister Shelia? Or yours, Sister Anita? Young women and old men huddled around the raised stage, gasping at the pastor's ability to jump two feet in the air. Joy and sorrow on wanton display. Carl Harpon was a believer. He believed in the Lord. He believed in his flock. His thought and purpose were clear: *There is none as holy as the Lord: for there is none beside Thee: neither is there any rock like our God.*

The story these women knew best was a story in which none of them appeared. But they loved hearing about it because it held struggle and a touch of deviousness. Best of all, by the end of the tale these black women were the happily ever after. They were the good news that finally arrived. They loved the story about how the deacons traveled to the South and found Reverend Carl in middle-of-nowhere Arkansas and convinced him to follow them back to East Harlem with nothing but a Bible and the suit he wore. So he arrived to tend a congregation of twenty-seven, and God as a witness, fifteen of them would be dead in less than three years from old age. Twenty-seven people, not including the twelve deacons, and a six-hundred-dollar church endowment. From the vantage point of the pulpit there didn't seem to be a cousin, an out-of-town guest, or even a wayward teenager who needed to be punished for being caught with a joint among them. Just a recent widow and octogenarian couples who shared oxygen tanks. Afterward, when Harpon asked if any of the flock had grandchildren, the embarrassed deacons shrugged and admitted they didn't know. It was the smallest congregation in Harlem when Reverend Carl was asked to lead it. But he set to work, bringing his brand of country savvy to the Ethiopian and performing the formidable task of guiding Harlem's sheep back into the EUFCC fold.

"Put your pride in your pocket," he told them. "I'm going to sign us up for food stamps." Carl used the vouchers to buy breakfast muffins and coffee for the morning commuters who walked by the church. "Let me fill your stomach now, and come by on Sunday so I can fill your soul." For months while pouring Minute Maid and Sanka, Carl learned who had a hard time keeping up with their rent, which women had children out of wedlock, and who was able to keep a steady job. And the black people living in Spanish Harlem liked Carl, not simply because he showed an interest in their lives and remembered their squabbles but also because he seemed to be as poor as they were. Every day he stood behind his long cardboard table in some outlandish suit, always in dire need of a shave, without shame.

Then Matilda "Twin" Johnson arrived and turned it around, or rather Carl's decision to invite Twin did. What was needed, he decided, was a show. A kind of production the entire neighborhood could know in advance would be guaranteed entertainment. "Who's the crazy in the neighborhood?" Carl asked the deacons one Wednesday.

"Excuse me, Reverend?"

"You know, crazy. You telling me ain't not one soul in ten blocks of here ain't crazy as a peach orchard boar?"

"One of those Southern sayings again, Reverend?"

"Yeah. But we got one, don't we, Deacon Dan?"

"I'm Deacon Rueben, Reverend. Her name is Matilda Johnson. She's four blocks south."

"All right, then." Carl walked to the door, grabbing his hat.

"You know, as deacons, we try not to attract that sort of . . . element to the church."

Carl didn't bother to answer him as he struggled into his coat and opened the door.

Deacon Rueben called Carl back. "People in the community call her Twin, Reverend. And be careful."

He found her just off Lexington Avenue, squatting on the steps of a failing brownstone she owned, with a rather long, heavy stick on her right side and more than a dozen empty Tab cans to her left. She was unafraid of the gangbangers, didn't shudder when crackheads tried to approach her for money, and despite her size she could run after (and more often than not catch up with) some smart-aleck teenage boy, all the while hurling empty Tab cans with amazing accuracy.

Without introduction, Carl said, "You mean old bitch, come on to church."

"I got bad habits. Been kicked out of six churches." Though she had never come by the Ethiopian for breakfast, she knew about Harpon, the new pastor who seemed to be handing out goodwill as if it were free. Carl rocked on his heels, then carefully spat between his feet. "Yep. Six."

"Well it's never too late to get religion."

"That's what you say now." She smirked at him, and without being told he realized she had heard this very statement before. In all likelihood half a score of previous reverends full of ambition had stood just where he was standing now, asking would she come and grace their church in order to increase attendance. And when her mischief became too much to bear, when the very congregation her presence had helped build couldn't tolerate the humiliation, they had cast her aside. His offer shamed him. She was the local freak show simply because her antics mirrored the God she knew—a violent, sophistic, and relentless deity who could never be appeased. Galling though it was to realize, his very original idea was in fact an imitation of what every brand-new pastor had done; still he knew he had to have her. So he lied. "We got a soup kitchen on Tuesdays and

Wednesdays and eggs, bacon, and grits for breakfast on Saturdays, Sundays, and Mondays."

"Where this place at?"

"Church, Twin." He reached out and shook her hand, promising himself that he would never ask her to leave, no matter what she pulled. "It's not a place; it's a church. And I welcome you to it, Sister Twin."

The next morning Carl made sure to tell those on the way to the subway that Sister Matilda "Twin" Johnson would be attending Sunday services. The news reached the entire neighborhood before the end of the morning rush hour. As tempted as his potential congregants were to see just what Twin would pull, thirty-three teenagers braved entering the Ethiopian that Sunday. Shoulder to shoulder, they filled the back three pews while Twin sat alone in the middle of the church.

"Morning, beloved."

Those who had come to see Twin giggled into their hands.

"I can't hear you. I said morning, beloved."

"Morning, Reverend Harpon."

"Just call me Reverend Carl. I see this Sunday we got new faces. Now just stand on up one by one and introduce yourselves." Quickly he scribbled their last names in the margins of his Bible. "I got a message for you today, brothers and sisters. I know some of you have come out today not for the Lord but for a show."

The boys in the back of the church snatched off their baseball caps and settled into an embarrassed silence.

"I know it. What will she do today? Maybe even some of you thinking, 'I'm gone have some news for my mama when I get home; I'm gone have something to tell my friends at the schoolyard tomorrow.' So I got a message for them that are thinking that way. I got something for you to go home with."

"Tell it to us."

"I want each and every one of you to pick up your Bible. That's right; pick it up from your lap and hold it close to your heart." The sound of rustling paper and purse zippers creeping open filled the Ethiopian. "All of God's ways are right between these covers, beloved."

"Amen."

"Now I want you to close your eyes while I give you the rest of this message today. I see some eyes in the back. I said close them eyes." He waited until the few left did what he instructed. "There is the destruction of the wicked found in this Good Book. And the righteous being tried."

"Yes, Lord."

"And with all that: the love of the Lord and our Savior, the praises to His name . . ."

"Yes, Jesus."

"His sometimes harsh judgments, and yet the glory found therein . . ."

"You tell it."

"But I got a hard message for you today, beloved." He paused for a moment, letting the silence pervade throughout. "Sometimes you got to put down the Book."

"Ooh." Every eye opened, baffled.

"Oh, yes, beloved; I said it. Sometimes you got to put it down and walk another path. Sometimes you got to put up your dukes. You got to fight your way out of a corner, and the Good Word can't help you then."

The young boys in back slapped their caps against their thighs and guffawed. "I know that's right."

"Sometimes we got to fight our way through and then we look at ourselves, raggedy as sin, and we think, 'I ain't stepping to the Lord and His Word, flashing my secrets. I won't be telling the Lord about this beatdown I had to hand out.' We get so big, so full of ourselves, that we all walk around thinking, 'I don't need no Book. Not that book no ways.'"

"Make it plain."

"I know there are those of us who think, 'This book here can't help me get no job, can't help me with my Section 8 housing. This book won't help me shake off the hard times I'm going through. Gospels don't mention being black in America in the eighties nowhere.' And that's the truth! So, I want you to do this for me. Put it down." Both those in the front and back pews continued to stall, waiting for him to take back what he'd just said. "You heard me, beloved. This beautiful Book and all its stories and all its goodness and all its wisdom . . ."

"Amen."

"Put it down. Take it away from your hands, like you trying to take it away from your life. I want you to put down the Book right now. Stand up, beloved. Take a step back." The very old in the front pews reached for their canes and unsteadily stood. Without the equilibrium of sight, they swayed. "You feel it now, don't you? Right now, right here, you longing to get that Book back in your hands. Imagine your life without the story of Christ, without the guidance of the Lord. Got a little hollow feeling in your stomach, don't ya?"

"Yes."

"Hold that feeling, beloved." And then the moment they had been waiting for, despite Carl's chastising, arrived. Sister Twin, sitting in a sea of empty pews, jumped up and hurled her Bible at the pastor's head. Carl too had been expecting that moment and calmly ducked. It flew past his ear and landed with a thud upon the stage. Except for Twin's heavy breathing, the church had suddenly gone silent. Carl stood up and straightened his tie. "And sometimes you got to pick the Good Book up. Let's all turn to Samuel chapter two, verses one through ten. Sister Twin, look like you got to come up here and get yours."

From that Sunday until all their dreams went up in flames, Twin could be counted on to tear at her clothes, hop on top of the pews, and march back and forth while bellowing the lyrics to "Oh Happy Day." She hurled her Bible and extra songbooks at the congregation, and her aim was deadly. If the Spirit so moved her, she dove headfirst, fists flying into the deacons' pit. Every month at least one of the twelve church officers had a swollen jaw.

And while Twin provided the entertainment, Reverend Carl Harpon made sure the same spell he had spun in Brightstar, Arkansas, was being woven in Harlem. Carl's brand of religion called for an almost overwhelming love of the Lord tempered by practicality. Simply put, it was in the community's best interest that they attend regular services at the Ethiopian United Federated Church of Christ. He found affordable yet competent lawyers to represent their sons in court, helped them out of countless problems with their landlords. He had even helped one family figure out the intricacies of a mortgage application to buy a brownstone on 138th Street and St. Nicholas Avenue. It took four years for the Ethiopian to grow tenfold. Now it had 275 regular congregants, and that number swelled to 350 on Easter Sunday and at the midnight service on Christmas Eve.

Carl started a homeless outreach program. For those willing to be baptized in the kiddie pool graciously donated by Brother Elijah, breakfast or lunch was available directly after the religious rite was performed. And for those either from another denomination or unwilling to be baptized, a buffet dinner was provided. So Reverend Harpon was busy. From dawn till night some aspect of church business concerned him. And his hard work, his love of the Lord, paid rewards.

That was the beginning of their Ethiopian story, and the black women's arrival in twos and threes was the happy ending. Twin had been there, carrying on and crying out, but so were they. Depending on one another as if such a thing would last. Volunteering when before they were always busy. Willing to cook a little extra for their neighbors. Stepping out of their apartment doors clad in their best selves. And oh, how they sang. That's the story these women wanted to tell. Don't you remember when we sang and sang? That choir director, Sister Morning, tore it up. The lyrics to "How Excellent" reminded them that He was and they were too.

And so what that Morning's daughter Lara just so happened to be the lead soprano? Her voice led to leaping, standing up, and crying out what had been bottled up in their chests for at least a week. Every Sunday Lara's singing song rose to the rafters, battled the poor acoustics, and won out. The hymns her mother chose for the morning and afternoon services didn't matter—"This Morning When I Rose" or "Go Down, Moses"—the emotion in Lara's voice brought them to tears.

She's got it; she's gone make it even though this congregation would be hard-pressed to describe what the *it* was.

In this house, in here, they sang and they were family. The honorific of "Sister" stated the familial claim: "Sister, could you . . . ?" "Sister, would you . . . ?" "Sister, won't you . . . ?" and the chorus of women cried amens that sounded like yes. And the Ethiopian cradled their dreams. The youth choir was better than good, and the constant invitations to fellow churches around the country—as far as Missouri—proved it. They were raising children who knew the city better than they did. Of course there was Reverend Carl, the small, slim pastor who glided among them all, who banked arguments before they could reach a shouting shore, who told them, "Come on in, stay, stay," and meant it, who told them to pay attention at work and bring back helpful news if they happened to hear any. All that good intention and safety crescendoed into a moment that left them all homeless. Who would have guessed that shrouded in that sort of kindness they failed to see the damage it would cause until it was too late.

Sister Shelia and Reverend Carl walked away from the locked-up Ethiopian to the corner. She nodded along to Carl's musing: What's next? How can we grow? But their back-and-forth missed a familiar beat that followed Shelia wherever she went. The sister noted the absence.

"Oh, shoot. I left my purse in the Sunday school classroom." Before she could roll out the litany of reasons as to why she really needed her purse, Carl had already handed over the keys. "Are you sure?"

"Sure, I am." Shelia, trustworthy and trusted—she had a best friend who made the claim—held her head high. She was tempted to milk the moment, have Carl affirm over and over that she was worthy enough to be trusted with a whole church, but Reverend Carl was running late, having promised a sick visit and a dinner plate to a family. That's where that sort of kindness began, but it didn't end there. Sister Anita had forgotten her family Bible under a pew and was given the keys to unlock the church. Sister Keisha was given keys because she wanted a moment of quiet and couldn't find one anywhere but the church. Even Twin was given a silver four-sided key, because—"Why you want to know why? You giving it or not?" They never revealed to one another that Reverend Carl had a habit of passing out keys to the kingdom, but in a span of six months most of them had a copy on their key ring.

So when six years of a fairy tale went up in smoke, they didn't know who was at fault. But they all worried, because the police always found someone—innocent or not—to blame.

CHAPTER 16

Every Thursday night the church was barren. Carl had decided long ago that everything needed a day of rest, even the Ethiopian, so no programs were ever planned for that evening. So there was no one around when the wooden floor in the broom closet blackened and flared a sullen red. No one was there to hear a church burning, which sounded like a bunch of starving children who at last were given a meal: heavy breathing and munching. That hungry sound deafened.

Along with the noise came its flame. Starting on the floor, making quick work of the straw brooms and a dirty mop, it wandered to the nearest wall. From there the destructive heat behaved like tourists and jubilation. What could be found in the space where twelve men shared two offices with six cubicles in each room? Fire found the spot where women instructed children to learn the kindest moments in biblical stories.

Nothing can remain secret in a fire. The place where brothers gathered and worried about their next job was revealed in light and flame. Beyond the carpeted rooms and hallways in the back of the church, fire roared through the congregation hall of the Ethiopian. The hymnals and communal Bibles delivered sudden flash fire. The medley of humble wood, covered in decades of lacquer, kept it going. Solemnly, fire walked intricate paths along the side aisles, stroking the pews and arching and falling as it flared up against the relief of the Last Supper.

The fire was a pyrologist's dream. The secrets of a patchwork wooden church were revealed in an uncontrollable blaze. It ate the deacons' offices in a gulp, but as if ashamed it could grow so large, it turned into a flame that split in two, making quick work of the side panels that weren't solid birch but compressed wood shavings. Fire behaved as paint thinner would in some places, eating away at the thick coating of shellac, and exposed the pine pews to the flames. A blaze blistered down the aisles, leaping into every pew. The walls began to groan, unable to withstand the heat. And sixty-eight-year-old varnish acting as an accelerant helped the ungovernable flame burn through the interior partitions with relish. Shouts of discordant music rang out as the organ surrendered to the inferno.

There should have been nothing left; nothing able to escape as the EUFCC's supporting beams buckled and the entire structure crashed into a smoldering heap. But the new baptismal pool with its walls of limestone and treated brick was uncharred, miraculously untouched.

CHAPTER 17

The church was burning, but Lara, the lead soprano of the Ethiopian youth choir, didn't cry about it. Her mother shed enough tears for everyone in their apartment. Lara's mother was one of those women who hoarded her secrets but wanted to know all of yours, so Lara figured her mother's tears came on and kept coming because she secretly knew what would happen to them all now that someone had set fire to the Ethiopian. They saw the church's flames on the news but smelled them through the window. For days a good bit of East Harlem smelled like a smokehouse. The odor saturated their clothes, seasoned their meals, and the only tears Lara shed were caused by the lingering smolder stinging her eyes. Still she didn't cry. But neither did she sing.

And Lara Taylor could sing. Even in a neighborhood crowded to the rafters with talented youth, her voice stunned listeners, brought them to unexpected weeping or barks of laughter if the lyrics dictated it. But being so good at one thing made her careless with everything else. Lara could have been an A student, but her schoolroom boredom doomed her to nothing but C's. "You have so much promise," her teachers had told her. "All you have to do is apply yourself." Her quiet nature kept her from saying what was on her mind: I know my promise and show it every Sunday and during the week at choir practice. A year ago what to do with her potential had bothered her. Should she go off to college? Or sing in a nightclub? Or find somebody who had a studio and would let her cut a record? Or just get a job doing something or other? But those questions had died.

A month after she received her diploma her mother looked at her daughter's eighteen-year-old self and told her what she had only hinted at since graduation. "Girl, you need to get out there and find some work. You can't just lay up under me." Lara's mother had handed her a copy of *The Village Voice* opened to the Help Wanted section. Circled in red ink were jobs she thought suitable.

"Like right now?" Lara was in her nightshirt and still in bed. She sat up slightly and looked over at her alarm clock: 6:37 a.m. The newspaper crinkled lightly in her hand, and she rubbed her eye with the other one.

"Yes, now. Get dressed. I left a stack of subway tokens on the coffee table for you." Lara's mother turned around and headed for the bedroom door. "And I made oatmeal."

That was a year ago and she still hadn't found a job, though every morning she left the house with copies of *The Village Voice* and the *Amsterdam News* tucked under her arm. Their classified sections, duly marked up to highlight the appropriate and aspirational, hid Lara's lack of drive to find employment. Every early evening she returned home and faced her mother's questions.

"How'd it go today?"

"Nothing yet, Momma."

Morning sighed through her nose. Lara's mother wasn't frustrated. Not yet. She wasn't even resigned. The sound was made just to accompany the chore of folding clothes or stirring the last stir of the oxtail stew. At her age and almost a lifetime living in East Harlem, Morning still had an absolute faith in luck. In fact Lara suspected her mother put more stock in good fortune than she did in the Almighty.

"You just got to stay out there, Lara. Luck will find you."

"Okay, Momma." Lara hadn't put down her purse or taken off her jacket before her mother started her familiar evening conversation. Nothing stopped the litany. Whether cleaning the kitchen or putting the finishing touches on dinner, Morning would begin talking as soon as she heard the front door open. The early-evening conversation had begun to sound like a sermon, with Lara as the sole congregant.

"Lord knows black folk need luck for anything to move our way."

Lara hung her purse and jacket on the coatrack near the door. Her back faced her mother, but still she answered. "I know."

"I ever tell you how I got to New York?" She had. Lately almost every day. "Luck. Nothing but. I should be in Florida. That was the plan. I had the money for it and was all packed up to go. Got myself turned around, and look out, I was in Little Rock. Fore I could figure out which way was up, I was almost in Harlem. That was luck, plain and simple."

Lara's keys clattered on the coffee table.

"If I wanted to, I could scare you to death and tell you just how hateful Lake County is."

"I know, Momma." She sat on the couch, giving herself permission to grunt, then proceeded to take off her shoes.

"Oh, baby, you don't know a thing. All Florida good for is picking oranges and chewing black folk clean to the bone. That's it. You probably wouldn't have been born at all if my momma's plans would have gone through. But that's good luck for you. Stay out there. Keep looking."

And Lara did. Every morning she rode the train all the way to Brooklyn, crossed the platform, then rode it back to East Harlem. Holding on to the subway strap, watching her feet almost lift off the ground as she moved with the masses, Lara listened and loved the syncopated life of the city. There was a music to the subway doors banging open—once, twice, three times—against the frame. "Step in. Step in," the conductor called out, the language so garbled that the only thing you could understand was the beat. Hundreds of commuters shuffled out the open doors of the train; hundreds more replaced them.

She watched as her fellow commuters pulled out paperbacks and neatly folded newspapers. Though she wasn't a tourist, Lara had the look of one. Her eyes roamed and marveled at the scrawled graffiti; she silently mouthed what she thought they meant. The amateurs were easily discernible—MIKEY LOVE M; FUCK REAGAN—but the graffiti made by the professionals revealed nothing but their beauty. Bright sunset-orange spray paint moved to yellow, morphed to blue. R, Z, K? A man's initials, a gang's name, a code, a plea? This young woman didn't know but thought it all lovely. She swayed with the hurtling train and wondered which would she rather be, understood or admired. Both.

That's what Lara wanted to tell her mother when asked how her day went. And how she felt as she watched the day go by. How she longed to strut on the subway, but there was no room for it. Only her hand gripping the strap had space to wave along with the sway of the train. But this young woman's mind was full of long-legged thoughts. She imagined herself not inside the subway car but standing out on the platform as the train barreled toward the station, its breeze lifting her skirt and showing off a pretty knee. And as the subway slowed, she turned and walked with it, as if steel and rail were alive and aware of her movement. Someone sneezed behind her and startled her back to the present. But diving once again into her daydreams was better than easy; it was effortless. In her dreams she's singing. Not at church, but here and right now, in front of everyone, like the doo-wop guys who got on the train and surprised people into paying attention. In her dream it's, How'd it go today? Oh, Momma, today I almost had the courage to join in and sing "Under the Boardwalk." Did you now? Almost. Almost. I was about to, but then one of them, the one whose face went beyond pretty and leapt right into beautiful, looked me in the eye and winked. So, almost. The wink stole my voice.

Disconcerted but quiet, Lara then leaned over to read the news in a man's hands—"Two Held as Slavers, 'Dead' Woman Alive in N.J. Hosp . . ."—imagining herself in the paper, but she couldn't complete the headline. "Black Woman Does . . ." "Harlem Resident Dares . . ." Such thoughts, while sharp, were incomplete. The doo-wop crew doffed their hats, smiling when passengers threw quarters into their felt fedoras. The train moving uptown was as quiet as church. There must be hundreds of us all inside here, she thought.

Suddenly she wanted every passenger in the car to pay attention to her and begin applauding, hands clapping and congratulating the sounds her voice hadn't uttered. Her eyes gleamed as she tilted her head and read the bottom of the white guy's paper: "Gunman Shoots Two Outside Bronx Bar." Tomorrow if I see the doo-wop guys, I will be brave, and I will hum.

She never found the courage. Instead, most days Lara watched the Westchester-bound depart at Forty-Second Steet. For a moment the train emptied, and in that five-beat space, the strut this young woman had longed for let loose. And a one, and a two, and a three, and a four. Her stride was tentative but carefree. It was her mother's walk. The one that made men hiss and stroke their crotch when they saw it. Come here, girl, and break my heart. Her gait, by comparison, looked like a little girl's in a grown woman's pumps, but she didn't stop until she reached the end of the subway car and grabbed the strap. Three women—perfect strangers—filed past her and put her stride to shame. Their legs were synchronized like a chorus line, and they took a seat as one. All three women had their heads buried in books; they had no idea the show they'd just put on. Lara wasn't the only one to notice. People all around her smiled privately to themselves, hiding their appreciation in their hands, in their newspapers, in their coat sleeves. She watched them, her face as still as a carving. That was all Lara wanted. To have an admiring crowd look at her that way as long as it took to take a seat.

The inability to join the city's singing followed Lara all the way home, and as the subway hurtled uptown, Lara Taylor remembered her mother's voice. A snatch of a song, low and full of scat, surrounded the cooking of eggs. Her mother Morning happy. The church they went to was the cause of it. For a year, all day every day, a stunning city full of song kept her quiet, but Lara turned daring during choir practice and Sunday services. She taught her singing sisters how to do the cabbage patch, the snake, the prep—"All together now! You second sopranos, go this way. You tenors, go the other way. And then shake your shimmy. Shake it, babies," Lara instructed them, remembering the doo-wop guys dancing two-step, then dip and turn. Morning shook her head at the antics, slightly embarrassed, but she couldn't help but feel swollen pride when Lara mingled gospel with R&B. And when the congregation caught the Spirit—"Yes, Jesus. Amen, God"—and the praise and exultation turned pointed—"Sing, Whitney! Sing it, little Whitney!"—Morning's conducting arms didn't shake, but her toes clenched.

A year of that. Well, almost a year. The oldest congregants clucked their disapproval, but the rest of the church leapt to their feet and taught these youngsters how to really do the Charleston. And when young boys floated to the aisle and danced the moonwalk, Reverend Carl took off his jacket and gave it a go. These last few months, right in the middle of a hard winter, Lara's apartment was warmed with praise. During the early evening story about luck and its importance, Morning interrupted herself to ask her daughter what songs should be added to Sunday's choral program. "I'm liking that Shirley Caesar. How about you?"

"I can learn her real quick."

"And I'm thinking we should head to Newark this summer. Sing with that congregation. What you think?" Lara marveled that she hadn't yanked authority out of Morning's hands; her mother seemed to be giving it to her, piece by piece. Lara needed the subway to instigate her dreams, but her mother, Sunday after Sunday, before and after practice, had started having dreams of her own. Maybe she could sit back once in a while, let Lara take over the choir every now and again. Who knows? In a year or two, Lara could become the director. Morning put a platter of fried catfish along with hush puppies on the dinner table. She beamed at her daughter. "After we eat, teach me how to do that dance named after that ugly doll."

"Okay, Momma."

But for the last three days, when everything she ate in their apartment tasted like barbecue and there was no need to salt the food because her mother's tears flavored the meal, Lara was plagued with the question: What now? She hadn't wondered about that for almost a year. So what now? Should I sing at a nightclub? Or try to find some type of job? Or cut an album?

It was Sunday, and she went through the familiar motions of the morning half awake. A sleepy hand rummaged through her sock drawer for sheer stockings. Yawning, she reached inside her closet and took out her blue church dress and choir robe. Her body was already in the middle of getting ready to go to church before her mind caught up with it. The cold water from the tub faucet splashed over her toes. I should let Tracy sing a solo. Stop hogging the whole thing. Lara smiled. She could clearly imagine the young sister's delight at the invitation. The water was just right. Her mind was already headlong in this Sunday's choir program. Tracy's shy, proud smile. The other little sisters' frowns of disappointment. Don't worry. You'll get there. You'll have your turn. Lara turned the shower on; the warm water woke her up.

She didn't have to be awake at seven in the morning. There was nothing to get dressed for. She would tell Tracy nothing. Her momma was probably still asleep. The question "What now?" clanged around her head. Maybe she could make a mixtape. She saw guys who sold their songs out of the trunks of their cars, but—her shoulders slumped in the shower—she didn't have a car; she took the train.

The revelations she had seen and sought on the subway were revealed in her church. And without the Ethiopian, now what? If I can't show or teach what I see out in the world, now what? Finally, though three days late, she cried. All that time she'd been hiding from her mother what she was really up to felt silly. The water from the showerhead washed away her tears before she could taste their salt. She braced both hands against the bathtub tiles, her neck bowed, her back a curve of grief.

They weren't the silent tears her mother shed, but rather the kind that held the accompaniment of sound. The way children cried until they were taught they were too big for all that. Shut up that crying. You hear me? Cut it out. Grown-up tears came with a stack of manners; do it quietly, silently, and if you couldn't manage that, cover your mouth. Lara wasn't a grown-up yet. She wailed. Helplessly. She cawed, standing under the warmth of the shower. With the help of the acoustics in the bathroom, it was hard to tell the difference between sobbing and singing. They sounded the same. "Oooo. Oooo."

CHAPTER 18

After the fire the children of the Ethiopian scattered. They searched their neighborhood first for purpose, then for fun, but without that sanctified destination, they were everywhere: in the bodegas, on the playground, in the library, watching betting men play dominoes, loitering on steps and corners, wandering hallways and doorways. The locksmith on 112th did brisk business. A generation of latchkey kids was born in the space of weeks. Parents made copies of apartment keys and gave stern instructions: "Just stay at the playground till I come and get you. You hear? Don't make me look for you."

"Yes, ma'am." The children did not hear the fear in their mothers' voices, only the ferocity.

"Because I swear, if . . ." Their mothers failed to finish the sentence; there was no need. The threat and dread were clear. Still. Someone, anyone, tell a bunch of children aged nine to nineteen to stay still and keep that way. Good luck.

One would think Lara, being nineteen with a set of keys she'd had for years, would have had a better time of it. But she felt more homeless than the younger congregants of the Ethiopian. It was one thing to stare at the rare subway passenger who openly cried on the way to their destination; it was another to become one of them. She couldn't bear to get on the subway, ride the train to Brooklyn and back, and watch the singing of her city.

After her first Sunday of nowhere to go, Lara went to sleep thinking either her determination or her mother would wake her up first thing in the morning. But that Monday nothing but morning sunshine roused her from bed. Her mother hadn't bothered to shake her awake and put the classifieds in her hands. Lara had left the window slightly open to cool down their overly heated apartment, and a cold, sharp breeze woke her. As she got dressed, she noticed the quiet. Had her mother already left? Lara pulled a white undershirt over her head and could hear the heavy tread of the neighbor's feet upstairs. Across the hall she could just make out the 1010 WINS radio broadcast. Done dressing, Lara walked softly down the short hall and thought her mother had probably headed up to the church site to finally bear witness to the Ethiopian's burnt ruins.

But Morning hadn't left the apartment to find out what could be salvaged from the church's remains. She sat at their small kitchen table with her back facing Lara.

"Momma?"

Morning turned her head, and Lara saw her mother's profile of grief.

"I think ... I think I'm going to head out. Look for ... I guess. Just for a bit."

Her mother said nothing, and Lara backed out of the kitchen and into the living room.

"I won't be long. Promise."

Lara didn't give herself time to put on her coat. With her keys clutched in her hands, she left the apartment. Outside, her coat over her arm, she realized she had forgotten to take her hat and a pair of gloves. She didn't go back upstairs. Instead, she began to wander the neighborhood the way the rest of the scattered Ethiopian children did. Her walking took her west, since east of East Harlem was off-limits to black people. The city said Jefferson Park was open to everybody, but the neighborhood Italians who lounged near the place had other ideas. They patrolled Pleasant Avenue, scowling at any black somebody who dared to walk on their block.

Lara drifted up Second Avenue to 125th Street, but by the time she passed the Furniture Warehouse, she was almost trotting. Not because she had somewhere to go but because of the cold. Winter sliced through her green woolen coat. She huffed into her collar for more warmth. The February weather dictated the strut of her gait; she lengthened her stride, but she couldn't brake her wondering mind. Thoughts of where to and what for surrounded her. It wasn't as if she hadn't known she loved the Ethiopian. She had always known that. The fault lay in her confidence that her church would last. Nothing lasted in this city. Not a thing. Store owners, beloved teachers—if you turned your back for a minute, they vanished. Your favorite shoe store turned into a wig shop, then a bank. Her neighborhood's constant transformation had no rhyme or reason, but somehow she had thought the Ethiopian was different. That its all-wooden structure would always be there to welcome them and let her sing within its confines.

She had never walked her neighborhood at this time of day, after the morning commute but before any of the shops had opened. Everything shuttered and almost, almost quiet. Where was everybody? Lara's rushing across Fifth Avenue didn't stop her from shivering with cold. The tips of her ears hurt. The stoops were empty of people, and when she looked at the avenue skyline, she was struck by how many windows were boarded up. Windows bricked over as if whoever left had no intention of ever returning. Had her neighborhood always been like this? Or had it all happened while she had been riding the train, marveling at other parts of the city? The House of Style wasn't open, and neither was the discount store, but Lara wasn't in the mood to window-shop anyway. She needed to figure out her what for. But besides the pressing need to buy a hat and scarf what decision to make about anything remained beyond her reach. If she had stayed at the apartment and asked Morning, her mother would have told her to join another church. That that was the only way to really start over. But even Lara knew no one was that lucky. Where? La Sinagoga? She didn't even speak the language, never mind being asked to sing in their choir. All the other black churches in their neighborhood already had established choirs. It was one thing to be welcomed as a visitor; she'd be treated with suspicion if she wanted to stay.

When she stood in front of it, Lara didn't kick herself because she didn't want to look crazy in front of strangers. The Apollo. Her mind may have been full of questions, but her hurried stride knew exactly where to go for answers. The Apollo. The answer came so easily she almost laughed at how she had wasted a year traveling to Brooklyn and back, getting misty-eyed over doo-wop acts. All their names rolled out in front of her mind's eye: Ella Fitzgerald, Pearl Bailey, Sarah Vaughan. Women younger than Lara was right now had stood on that stage and made their fame. Like everyone who lived in Harlem, she knew the Apollo's history, but sketchily. A long time ago two Jewish cats opened up its doors to everyone. And everyone came. The Apollo. Every Wednesday night at seven thirty the talented and the brave tried their luck. The winner was awarded money. And even if you lost over and over again, you still could become rich and famous. Don't believe it? Ask Luther Vandross. Sandman, the "executioner," wouldn't get near her with his broom, she told herself. Standing outside in the February cold, she could already hear the applause, feel the slick smoothness of the tree of hope beneath her hands.

But was she too late? She had heard a rumor that the Apollo only had auditions a couple times a year. Had she missed it? Or worse, would she have to wait for six months until they announced an open call? Lara walked close to the building. Compared to her lonely walk here, the front of the theater bustled with people. Two men had set up a table laden with gloves, hats, scarves, and incense. More than a couple of folks surrounded them, haggling down the price of their wares. But even more were like Lara, stalling to look up at the marquee or walking inside the lobby of the place. "Excuse me. Excuse me." Lara moved through the small throng to find out if bad luck had leapt from the burning of her church to the open audition times for Amateur Night. She read the announcement inside the glass display case. And even though she knew her mother still sat at home, that she probably hadn't stood up from the kitchen table, Lara heard her mother's voice: "Lord knows black folk need luck for anything to move our way."

Yes. And yes.

Lara practically flew to Lehman Music Company for sheet music. She had three days to prepare: to pick a dress, to get a pair of shoes, to figure out her hairstyle and makeup, to find a song. During the walk back to her apartment, Lara hummed every tune that came to mind, but she already knew the song she wanted to sing.

Lara had told her mother to meet her on the corner of 125th and Adam Clayton Powell Jr. Boulevard a little bit before ten o'clock because she didn't want to listen to her mother reminding her to project her voice, don't slouch, God's got you, and all we need is some luck. Lara needed the quiet of a walk alone. But when she arrived on the corner, she realized her mistake. The line to get inside the Apollo at nine forty-five in the morning turned the corner and went on for a block. By the time Lara had reached the back of the line, she was six blocks away from where she had told her mother to meet her. But that wasn't what sank her heart.

As she walked toward the back of the line, she heard her song. Her song sung by better voices. Little Whitneys everywhere. Little Whitneys who hummed with a country twang, Whitneys who clutched violin cases or clarinets. Lara passed by a little Whitney whose instrument was so large its case was on wheels. What was in there? A harp? A tuba?

Lara needed her mother. She now couldn't sing the song she had chosen, and Morning would know what to do. Twice she was tempted to leave the line and walk up to where she had told her mother to wait for her. She didn't want to lose her spot. Would the family behind her hold her place? Lara turned around to ask, but their closed expressions stopped her from trying it. At ten o'clock sharp the line moved. Somehow she expected the procession to be reminiscent of the step and wait of a grocery line. Instead everyone in the line moved at the beat of a slow march, one measured step after another. To Lara it felt as if they zoomed along. Momma, be there, please.

She wasn't. Lara rubbernecked and couldn't find her mother anywhere. The line moved quicker, and Lara stood just inside the lobby. Should I get out of the line and wait for her? Should I try to find a pay phone and call the house? Something awful must have happened to her mother because there was no way she would have just not shown up. And while Lara tried to figure out what to do, seasoned hands directed her this way and that, put an index card in her hands, and told her instructions. She followed their directions, half listening, trying to figure out what else she could sing, still torn about whether to stay in line or get out of it and find her mother. She stood in a white room with no windows. How did I get here?

"Anybody with you? Any family?" said the only man seated. He smiled. Lara had never seen him before, but she heard tenderness in his question.

"No." Was that what her voice sounded like? That breathless?

"Well, all right. That's all right. Let's get your information." He stood up from his chair, holding out his hand.

"I . . . I . . . Okay."

"I'm Billy, and you?" She couldn't force her name out of her mouth. Billy took her information card from her sweaty hand. "And you're Lara. Look at you." Lara had never been around someone this kind, this tenderhearted. He sounded as if he wanted to hold her hand all day or at least give her a hug, and his eyes matched the emotion. "We're going to get started, okay?"

"Okay."

Billy sat back in his chair. "Just look into the camera and do your thing. Ninety seconds."

That was when she noticed the other two people in the room. A slim black woman in a light blue dress held a clipboard. And a man in khakis stood behind a video camera that sat on a tripod.

"I'm going to be on camera?" Lara's heart lurched. Had they told her that?

"It's all right. Just look at me."

She couldn't sing the Whitney song; there had been too many little Whitneys. She wished again for her mother.

"Let's get started."

"'And I am telling—'"

"Thank you!" Billy's voice cut into the beginning of Lara's song. His expression of gratitude sounded like a goodbye. "Thank you. Thank you for your song." That had not been ninety seconds, had it? He was out of his chair, standing next to her, cradling her elbow. "We've got your information card, so we know how to find you. Thank you, again."

Lara stood outside the audition room as the family who had stood behind her all morning was ushered in before she could say, You're welcome.

PART THREE

CHAPTER 19

They all thought it was true because Wanda sounded so convincing. Just as spring arrived in East Harlem, po-po came and arrested her son Daryl for burning down the church. Wanda told everyone who stopped to listen, walking and talking to those who refused to pause. Did they all know the police had thrown every charge they could think of and the kitchen sink at her son? Auto stripping in the third degree—"We don't own a car; he never even been in a cab." Criminal facilitation in the fourth degree—"What the fuck is that?" Criminal possession of stolen property in the fifth degree, loitering for the purpose of engaging in prostitution offense, and on and on it went. When Wanda came to the end of it all, they all had the same question: "Well, what about the fire? If he really did it, why didn't they charge him on that?" But Wanda had an answer for that too. "Cause he didn't do it; that's why." Her circuitous logic made sense to them. Everyone knew if the police wanted to get you, you were got. Everyone had a story like Wanda's, though no one had told so many people.

"You hear about Wanda and her kid?"

"Girl, she done told me about it twice. And that's just today."

They wondered about that, her constant telling, but Wanda wasn't just telling folks for the sake of telling. She was rehearsing. Gathering up private strength because she needed to go get help, and she didn't want to ask. All she could do was hope that Carl would treat her the way he had when she was his congregant and he was her pastor.

Two years ago Carl had seen her in the Ethiopian church's hallway wearing an unmistakable look of trouble. Curvaceous in a bright purple dress a size too small, Wanda was a supple, dark black woman with two dimples in her cheeks and one in her chin. Even now she turned heads. And though he couldn't hear the seductive hiss of her rubbing thighs over the conversations of his other parishioners, he imagined the sound.

"Reverend." Wanda had taken his hands in her own, her saucer eyes slits.

"Sister Wanda, morning."

"I need to talk to you."

Her slack face said it all. If Wanda had been such a good mother, how could Daryl have gotten into trouble this bad? Wanda let go of Carl's hands to cup her fingers to either elbow, then rubbed her forearms warm, then readjusted the strap of her purse. So much movement; anything to avoid staring at the compassion radiating from Carl's eyes that she translated into pity. Their conversation in the hallway, full of whispers, paused and stuttered as people walked by calling good morning and thank you for the service. Most of his congregation carried their best efforts to the potluck that would start at one o'clock, but Carl didn't ask Wanda to speak up. He knew all her words even though he couldn't hear most of what she said. When he had first gone to seminary, he sought divine grace, and his time preaching in the South had given that grace shape—he could mend a gate or talk a sheriff out of arresting some wayward teenager better than anyone. But here in New York standing in front of Wanda, steeped in East Harlem's misery, Carl had honed his ministry's message: "Brothers and sisters, we will not ask for God's help; we are not worthy. Amen, Sister Wanda, we will not ask for His guidance. God is busy. But we plead with You, Lord, for strength. Jesus Lord, give us the strength to endure the test of time. Give us the strength to live through what is surely overwhelming. Amen."

Wanda listened to the start of his advice and clutched her elbows, trying not to cry as Carl stole snatches of his Job sermon and fed them to her. And in return she told him all about Daryl's backpack full of G.I. Joes and the police and a department store that wanted to set an example. She stopped whispering and stepped into his arms. "Thank you, Rev. Carl."

"And you know you are welcome."

Wanda needed that advice and grace again. When she found Carl at an empty storefront on 125th Street and told him the story she had told everyone, he had one question. "Why do you think they're trying to pin the fire on him?"

"They keep asking about it. Not straight out, but they circle it. You know? What was you doing that Thursday night? How long have you been going to that church? You like the preacher running it?"

"What he tell them?"

"The truth. But that don't help any. They pick him up at school or when they see him walking home. And every time they put a new charge on him. Yesterday they picked him up on the corner and hit us with endangering the welfare of a vulnerable elderly person in the first degree. We don't even know somebody black and over the age of sixty." Wanda wasn't sure when she started to cry, but she wept in earnest now. And not just because her son was in trouble. For the life of her she couldn't see an end to what the police were putting them through.

"It's okay. It's okay." Carl said, holding her. "I've got you."

"Thank you. Thank you."

That was the last time Wanda sounded grateful, or at least it seemed that way to Carl. By the end of May and six more "arrests," to Carl's ear Wanda sounded like a weary public defender. When she had asked for Carl's help in mounting her son's defense, he thought she was clever. If her son really had burned down the Ethiopian, would she have had the nerve to ask somebody like Carl for help? So see there? Her son was just as innocent as a lamb headed off to slaughter. Carl's presence at the bail hearing had stunned the presiding judge, and he set the bail so low even a kid with a paper route could have covered it. But all of that was back in March, and though they had yet to charge Daryl with arson and the young boy was out on bail, by the month of May Wanda needed to be in two places at once: at work and at the courthouse; at work and at the bail bondsman's; at work and at the lawyer's. "They got me here; they got me there," Wanda told the reverend as she helped him unfold chairs at the Institute. "I can't even sit down and eat a sandwich."

"Well, Sister, these things take time, and—"

"Fuck that. What you gone do about it?" She banged another chair open.

She had been a good woman; she was a good woman. Carl knew that, but Wanda could try any man, even a man of God. It was as if she counted his words, and when Carl said more than seven off she went with some sidelong comment. Nothing quieted her, not even the heavy sighs or the "Well, Sister." Even when he was pleading her son's case in front of the judge, she loud talked him. Carl was from the South; he grew up with women with a fast lip, but swear to God Wanda would have had them bowing their heads. He hated himself when he thought like this, but the fact was it had been a very long time since she had remembered her place and his. Yes, yes, at this point she knew the penal system better than he did, but did she have to remind every correction officer they talked to? When he felt most uncharitable, most ungodly, he thought Wanda didn't need his help anymore; she just wanted a sidekick. Lord, Carl just wanted Wanda and her son and their fiery problems to go away. Walking past the beauty supply shop he found himself longing, out-and-out longing to have lived a hundred years ago when the preacher was the lone somebody who could decipher the world, the Word, and the words. Enough. That's enough. He took a deep breath and did what he always did when Wanda's antics got the better of him. Carl thought of her son.

Little boy like that getting in all that trouble. If this hadn't landed him in jail, something else would have, Carl thought shamefully. How Daryl's skinny neck held up that big head was beyond him. Bet that birth was what made Wanda bowlegged. His dry chuckle surprised him. At least I can laugh. That's something. With the exception of tomorrow's schedule (open up the Institute; buy a bagel for Morning Taylor, the only active member of his neighborhood center; help the Rodriguezes with their Section 8 forms), he didn't have a thought or a plan. Wanda was right. A sick clutch grabbed him in the stomach and his throat tightened. She may have not been nice about it, but Wanda was right. The police wanted Daryl. Carl couldn't even tell himself the standard empty rhetoric—that they'd set him loose once they figured out he hadn't done anything. So think of something. Anything. But Carl couldn't help but dwell on what he knew to be true. Something was bound to change, but neither he nor Wanda would be its cause.

Yet when the change occurred, it looked the way all Daryl's previous arrests had looked. The final school bell rang, Daryl looked both ways (though there was no street to cross), and then out of nowhere, or like magic, a patrol car prowled beside him, moving no faster than a fifteen-year-old's gait. And like always, Daryl thought to run. The candy store on the corner sprang to mind, but so did home. "Come on, kid. Get in the car." If he put up a fuss, they'd put him in handcuffs. After the third arrest, Daryl Smitheus Morgan didn't put up a fuss. Instead he looked for friends to lock eyes with. Where was Tyrone? Or Kendall? Or even Lucy, who was in fourth grade and was let out of school an hour earlier? And where, *where* was his mother? He scanned the crowd, but she was not there; neither was Reverend Carl. Daryl's head swiveled this way and then that. "Come on, Daryl."

"Yeah, all right," Daryl said, his body a perfect posture of cool. The other children who were not his friends did their best not to stare. And just in case the other kids didn't get it, he added, "Don't rush me, fool."

Like always they took him to the Tombs. Maybe if Daryl weren't sharing commode privileges with twenty-seven other new inmates, he too would have wondered when things with the police would undergo a sudden change. But the thin steel partition reached only to his waist when standing, preventing such contemplative thoughts. Anyway, his mind was on more pressing matters. How the fuck did they charge him with welfare fraud in the third degree? And criminal sale of a firearm to a minor? His reaction when hearing the charges against him had been the same as the last time: a soft chuckle that just wouldn't quit. "All that, Pop-o?"

When asked to sign away his Miranda rights and attest to his typed three-page confession, he did so eagerly. It had been his experience that cops and the judges they sent you to were nicer when you just said, "Yes, yes, yes, sir." Every once in a while some newbie who had just made detective wanted to have a why, but before it could get out of hand the lieutenant would tap him on the shoulder and tell the officer's punk ass to go get some coffee; he'd wrap this up. Then the professionals got back to the job: "You just sign this, Daryl, we'll take care of you." So what that this time the police were trading looks that reminded him of his mother's you-in-trouble expression when she discovered he had drunk the last of the orange juice? Daryl flipped to the final page and scrawled his signature, adding his middle name to his familiar autograph; the sheer heft of the typed confession seemed to call for it. Smitheus, nice. He liked that his cursive *S*'s lower half bulged like a full stomach. Sure that a pat on the head and harmless advice were forthcoming, Daryl pushed back from the table and dipped his chin.

The interrogation room was crowded: three detectives, a lieutenant, and a fat-bellied sergeant kept flickering in and out. So many to walk him through a process he knew blind was a first, but Daryl hadn't spooked. His bowed head remembered the original tender squeeze of his nape after his first arrest at thirteen years old—how he had fallen in love with blue-uniform authority. He'd chuckled along with his friends as they traded tales of escape, but when his turn came to spin stories of criminal exploits, he told the unvarnished truth, "Man, my ass always get caught," and tried his fighting best not to look satisfied. He wasn't quite sure why his buddies spent all their spare time figuring out how to dodge the man. Confess, and you could have the police eating out of your hand. Cops gave sage advice, and judges who looked like Santa Claus punished you with probation and anger-management classes, where the hour-long meetings were punctuated with milk and cookies.

Every so often Child Services would show up at your apartment, and some nice lady with a librarian's skirt made his mother straighten up the house and make meat loaf and green beans and smile and laugh for no reason at all. Daryl loved everything about it. He loved the strangers who came to the house; he loved his momma, who would cook and clean like it was Thanksgiving when they had those visitors over; and he loved most of all the judgmental Santa and the police officers who tried to show him the way. All those soft-spoken platitudes were worth the jackknife fear that accompanied the all-in-good-fun decision to push some old lady down the subway stairs. "Hey, kid, try to keep out of trouble" was always followed by "First sign the confession, Daryl," then by some wife's homemade bounty. Meat loaf sandwiches, cold pasta, chicken soup. "You gotta be good, kid," and Daryl was, or he really tried.

A month, sometimes three, would pass without incident. Home by sundown, perfect attendance at school, listen to the teachers and his mother, do his homework. It wasn't as if the latest officer's homily had slipped Daryl's mind; he just had a strong urge to hear it again. That and the pat on the head and the homemade food. But this time, nothing.

"All right, up, up. Get this kid processed." The detective hauled him to his feet and roughly handed him over to the uniformed cop waiting outside the interrogation room. They led him back to the cell crowded with twenty-some-odd men. What had he done to make them withhold the sage comfort? Daryl slid inside the partitioned bathroom to think about what he had done wrong. The sudden addition of his middle name? Did they think he was putting on airs? Too much? His middle name, dignified, contradicted his desire for fatherly reprimand. I should have left it out. Smitheus. He touched his scrawny neck and longed for the rough paw gently shaking it, then the rewarmed soup with nice crusty bread.

"Bust up outta there, fool." A fellow inmate banged on the

steel partition. Daryl, who hadn't been using the bathroom, quickly slipped out, sheepishly grinning.

"Sorry bout that." He wandered over to a clear wall, rubbing his empty belly. When was he going to get his bologna sandwich? Motherfucker hungry, yo. Lunch never showed, and neither did dinner. Ten hours later an officer stood at the gate.

"Morgan! Daryl Smitheus!"

Finally. He hopped up dreaming, ready to eat slabs of roast turkey and tomatoes so ripe they looked fit to burst.

CHAPTER 20

On the other hand, Wanda never dreamt of hot meals. Until now her son had perennially returned home from his tangles with the justice system looking hangdog, waxing rhapsodic about beef stew and chicken pot pie, and she had invariably clocked him on the head and rolled her eyes, saying, "Get your dumb ass in here." Lord help her noodlehead son. Why Daryl seemed so inept at thievery and all things bad news confounded her. You'd think the more he did it, the better he'd get. But no. His habit of getting into trouble meant some judge every six months droned a solution: Child Services should show up at their door once a month unannounced, and both women (Wanda and the agent) should make small talk that forced Wanda to talk about a home life she kept secret from everyone, including herself. And meanwhile (and there always was something or other lurking in the fucking meanwhile), Wanda had to worry if the mess in her apartment had legal ramifications. If it wasn't Child Services, it was anger-management classes or parental-responsibilities meetings whose upshot Wanda could have muttered in her sleep: Keep your house and child clean; pat his head and not his bottom; breathe, parents! And most important, positive reinforcement! Yeah, like that's helped so far.

This last arrest was the worst, because for the first time the courts were debating whether to try her son as an adult. As if anybody could look at my kid and think he was a grown-up. Bad luck just seemed to follow him. Couldn't even swipe a candy bar without getting caught. Wanda sighed as she dropped a token on the Q100 bus and shared a small, commensurate smile with a few familiar faces on her way to Rikers to put a couple of dollars on his commissary tab and give her son the lowdown on his lawyer (you know, the one your cousin used who got him out in six months with time served and five years' probation), to soothe him with what could only be called quasi-legalese: "You in jail not prison, and they've pushed off your arraignment date twice. And I went to the courthouse; the DA is talking about setting bail. You know that's a sign. They don't think it's you or something. If it was airtight, they wouldn't be talking about letting me put up bail." She had the speech down pat, but when she walked into the visiting room, she barely recognized him.

Busted lip, swollen right eye; God help me, he'll never lose that limp. The studied expression of motherly scold dropped, and Wanda wondered what in the hell had happened. Nobody she knew had gotten the much-rumored police "tune-up." Every neighbor over the age of sixteen had been through Rikers—some families had the poor misfortune of living in a building that went the slow slide from respectable working poor into a crack den, and when the police decided to "clean house" (everyone got a sardonic chuckle from the term), drug dealer and innocent bystander alike got thrown in the police wagon and spent a night in jail. It took two days to sort out the confusion. But this? Her son had a lump on the side of his head the size of a walnut. "What happened? Baby, what happened?" He could barely speak. "Mama" was all he said over and over again. That he couldn't cry because it would hurt too much moved her into action. I mean, did somebody die or something? I mean, okay, it was a church and all; you know I'm just as religious as anybody, but beat up my boy? Who saw him do it? Just tell me that?

Wanda looked all over the neighborhood for Carl but couldn't find him. So she went to the deacons to ask for mercy. Found them in a well-furnished trailer across from a newly paved parking lot and a gleaming new Ethiopian church well on its way to completion. Powers that be had convinced the tire shop to move its business elsewhere. And that power hadn't stopped. The small businesses that surrounded the church had been razed, and a cleared block waited for the deacons to erect their aspirations. All four sides of the new church were finished, but its interior was empty. Mountains of gravel waited to be moved. The twelve didn't bother to trot out Deacon Dan; Deacon Rueben would suffice. "Ma'am, who are we to question police procedure?"

She had come prepared. For what exactly she wasn't sure, but she clutched the bail bondsman's contract, Daryl birth's certificate, and last month's Con Edison bill when she faced them. Proof she loved her son.

Deacon Rueben delicately sniffed his fingernails to display his contempt. "I'm never one to blame the parents, but really, madam." The droll reprimand shamed her off the wooden stairs and onto the sidewalk. Maybe they were stuck up because they hadn't seen hide nor hair of her since the church fire, and now here she was with her hand out. But so what? Didn't these fools know how hard it was . . . Wanda stopped her spiraling train of thought. Think. Think, girl. So what next? And Wanda realized that the sight of her son had so shook her, she had no next, no backup plan if the deacons couldn't be cajoled into aiding her. Without clout or a platform she was powerless to help her son, and she knew it. So. What now? Her empty stomach answered the question with a small growl. It shamed her. How you think about food at a time like this? she berated herself. But the ordinariness of her life rolled in—thoughts of veal Parmesan sandwiches, her hair appointment, a trip to the post office for money orders to pay the bills—settled her stuttering heart. A Wednesday like any other moved her around, and Daryl out of sight yet certainly not out of mind, receded to an incessant mutter accompanying errands that just couldn't wait.

The corner bodega heard the first of it. A meatball hero, a bag of chips, and an orange soda, the entire purchase surrounded by rhetorical questions spoken aloud: "And then they took him, you know? Snatched him up then beat him down when I bet he ain't done a bit of wrong. Daryl got a alibi; Thursdays he's home with me. But did anybody ever ask? Sth. Sons of bitches." Luis and several lunch customers clucked their sympathies.

When she reached the post office, Wanda cut in front of everyone in line and practically shouted, "Where Anita at?" Her friend looked up from a pile of mail she was feeding the sorter, her pleasant smile frozen with embarrassment. Like everyone in the neighborhood, Anita knew of Daryl's troubles.

"Marvin, can I take a fifteen-minute break?"

She didn't need to be told a thing, but Anita listened and draped an arm around her friend as they leaned together against the wall of Hellgate Post Office. Wanda looked up at Anita with her why-me eyes and let loose. The accusation, the police tune-up, Carl's disappearance, the deacons, the bail money—all of it, everything, tumbled out. Anita interrupted her friend's story with small sympathies— "All right, now. We'll take care of it"—but really there was only one question Anita wanted to ask: Did he do it? Did he? The two women had been friends forever, so Anita knew all about Daryl and his perpetual troubles. If she hadn't known Wanda so well, Daryl would have been just the kind of little boy Anita kept Tyrone away from. Anita looked down at her watch, noting she had seven minutes left of her break. "It's going to be okay."

"No, it ain't."

"Wanda—"

"They got a list of charges against him long as Scripture. Even if we can get out from under the arson charge, they can put him in Spofford until he's eighteen. I just—I don't know what . . . You can't take a longer break?"

"Girl, no. I got to ask Marvin to let me off early to go and get Tyrone from school. I'm sorry."

"Naw. It's all right."

"I'm going to do my best—"

"Don't worry about it. Gone back in. It's okay." Wanda gave Anita a shaky smile and held her hand to lead her back to the front doors of Hellgate.

"Wanda . . . I'll see if I can get my momma to take care of Tyrone, and I'll come round tonight. All right?"

"Yeah."

"I mean it. I'll call my momma right now."

But Wanda noticed Anita didn't promise. She couldn't. Too many things would have to go just as planned. And only the foolish or the young counted on things to happen as intended. Anita would have to call her mother; her mother would have to pick up the phone and say and mean, Yes, I'll pick up my grandson. Tyrone would have to be exactly where he should be—sitting on the steps of his school—and not playing pickup ball or hearing some final advice from a teacher.

Anita couldn't promise a thing, but boy she wanted to. Her friend's head on her shoulder, Wanda's tears wetting her starched uniform shoved Anita into rare emotions. She knew exactly how Wanda felt, trying to be in three places at once and failing on all counts. When her husband died, she'd had to lift that weight all on her own. Be a good mommy, a good daddy, a good provider, with no time to spare for grief. Nobody could juggle it all. Anita said none of that. Rather, she dredged up Christian charity and told Wanda, "If I can stop by tonight, I will." She kissed Wanda on the forehead and ducked back inside. That Daryl could have been the culprit . . . Sth. All those after-school programs burning down along with the Ethiopian. Did you do that? Really? Boy, we ought to let you go to the devil.

"I know it," Wanda said, and got back in line to buy her money orders. She tried so hard to let Anita's soothing words calm her, but before Wanda could stop herself, the post office line received an earful. Laden with checks for grandmothers in Mexico, toy trains for cousins in Puerto Rico, Century 21 apparel for nieces in North Carolina, neighbors fondled their giving and offered up shy amens as Wanda's mutter grew into a normal speaking voice: "Beat him so bad my stomach turned." But it was later that evening, sitting in the beauty-shop chair, the Revlon relaxer tingling her scalp, when she'd fully cut loose, the conversational tone she'd managed to hold most of the day climbing to a shout: "I'd like to see them try to raise a boy, a son, alone. My momma down south, most my kin out west. Daryl daddy dead since he was three. And, yes, he died of a fucking heart attack. In his bed. All right. Didn't sling drugs; didn't beat me up; didn't run around; at home every fucking night. We was married. Okay? I got a fucking ring and a wedding dress in my closet to prove that shit."

"Girl, stop it."

"Naw, for real. Cause I definitely need to say this shit. Cause everybody, the judge, the deacons, the DA, the Rikers officers, the fucking police feel like they can whoop up on my boy. And y'all ass too."

"Aww, girl."

"Mm-hmm. Somebody gave him up. And it must have been more than one of you. Just one and the po-po woulda come by and asked me where he been at. Bunch of y'all put Daryl in this mix. That's why they just picked him up." Her head steeping in lye made her shiver. "My only son, and a bitch like me can't do shit about it." She braced herself on the arms of the chair and an acute jab of pain leapt from her scalp, traveling the length of her arm. "Wash this shit out of my head." She was through, had talked herself hoarse, and was so disgusted with the ladies' half-hearted denials she left the beauty shop with rollers still in her hair. Jesus, what next? Her son was still in jail with nothing but an "It's gone be all right" to soothe him. Wanda thought she was different, but like most black mothers with their backs against the wall, only the thought of vacuuming the rugs made her brave enough to venture back home. All that complaining and pleading was for naught, but she could straighten out her life if she put her whole back and mind to it. No deacon could tell her that her life was a mess when she had a broom in her hand. With a mission on her mind Wanda opened her door, almost glad when Anita didn't show up. Straightening out the apartment morphed into spring cleaning in the middle of a hot summer: dusting her scant furniture, wiping down the sideboards, sweeping the floors, cleaning out the refrigerator. At midnight her two-bedroom apartment mocked just how much her life was in disarray. But she welcomed the bone-tiredness. Her head dangling over the edge of her bed, Wanda mulled over her choices and was drifting off to sleep when she realized even with Carl's help there was no end in sight of her troubles.

PART FOUR

CHAPTER 21

Tyrone Jackson fled down Second Avenue, his ragged breathing growing harsher in his ears, and hastily snaked past hot dog vendors and men wearing straw fedoras clustered around domino tables—"Darme veinte, chico"—forgetting a lifetime of rules drummed into him by church, school, and his momma. "Don't draw attention to yourself, boy." "Always yell 'fire'; never help." "Look for the taxis; they ain't looking for you." "Stranger danger, little man."

Private recollections mingled with sweat when a sharp wind barreling down the avenue evaporated both. Tyrone Jackson's labored breathing acted as white noise, muting the sound of his own voice—"I'm a scaredy-cat; I'm a scaredy-cat." Who wanted to recall the look of rage and disappointment on his friends' faces when he froze? He just couldn't, all right?

He looked behind him and didn't even see a speck of his friend Lucy, the only one who understood. But she was safe. Nothing would happen to Lucy who was ten and flat-chested, whose lisp made old ladies grin and turned men leer-free. She's safe. He just knew it. Tyrone would have bet money if he had any: 116th, -15th, -14th Streets, he didn't check for eastbound traffic and was almost clipped by a Sysco truck headed for Harlem River Drive. Running, stumbling, catching his stride, Tyrone moved farther south: 113th, -12th, -11th. Pleadings, advice, admonishments, practical information, memory—all shredded away as he fled in a blur of knees, feet, and elbows.

Wait a second, Tyrone. Wait. What in the hell are you running away from? And what got you into this mess? Back up. As Tyrone mimicked a Carl Lewis hundred-yard dash, just what had gotten him into all this trouble came into focus. All those books. Visions of limestone pillars, twenty-foot ceilings, and air-conditioning units sprang into view. The place was guarded by a legion of librarians who held the dubious honor of being courageous enough to manhandle the indigent they found huddled by the front doors every morning. Man, they touched those druggies like they were family. Ew. Get them niggas up. Nothing shocked. Nothing. And therein lay their secret weapon. The head librarian, Lady Mary Warren, would wait patiently while some homeless guy pissed against the limestone: "No, no. By all means, finish." Some bold dude, bladder full of Colt 45, refused to wither underneath her contemptuous stare, and yes, well, finished beside the brick. "Lovely. And if you could walk to the curb and stay there, many thanks." He never returned. None of them did. The fact that they were treated like humans kept them a block away. Had the city not done such a fine job of producing homelessness, after six months no one would have dared sleep on those library steps, blocking the passage of fourth graders who lined up ready to learn the Dewey decimal system. Tyrone had been one of them. Shepherded inside the double doors of the Aguilar Library, he'd stalled and gaped at the graceful hanging gallery with the cast-iron railing and pressed-glass floor, but it was the books that awed and titillated.

Heaps and heaps of them piled up, aged pages threatening to crumble within their bindings. Their very antiquity screamed respect. Oh, yeah, give me some of that. Tyrone was that kid who fantasized about books the way other children coveted candy and G.I. Joes. Was there anything better than that new paper smell? Sure there was. That old paper smell. Tyrone had loved the Choose Your Own

Adventure series, and this vivid fall Tyrone had certainly found one: You stand surrounded by three friends who want you to help rob some stranger. Will you A) clip some guy twice your size and pass his wallet off to your friend Daryl who needs the cash, or B) run for dear life back to PS 083 and slip into seventh-period history? B, motherfucker!

It hadn't started this way. Not that long ago, *Where the Wild Things Are* and *Marvin K. Mooney*, rhythmic, simple prose had soothed a complicated five-year-old; *Curious George* and *One Fish, Two Fish, Red Fish, Blue Fish* had felt like a righteous path to morality. But by eight? Man. Damn. *The Girl with the Silver Eyes, Charlie and the Chocolate Factory* excited just as long as the plot endured. Tyrone closed the book covers and lingering dreams died. His mother sent him to the 110th Street library saying, "Get something else," but suddenly nothing worked. Science fiction disappointed; journeys where young children found gardens and thus adventures bored. When he was ten, the head librarian had found him crouched in the aisle, a look of disdain clearly etched between his brows, and she made a fateful (ain't it the way?) decision. "Tired?"

Tyrone looked up; the head librarian was childless; even a ten-year-old could see that without knowing the particulars. She stood over Tyrone Jackson, sized up his dismissive smirk, and spoke to him as she would her hot dog vendor. "Bored, huh?"

Tyrone perked. But taking her in, he checked his pleasure: the Filene's Basement skirt, the linebacker shoulder pads lifting a hand-me-down silk blouse. Penny loafers—snort, jeez—with nickels tucked into the slots. Tool. Fake. Maybe even bitch, but he kept his face studiously blank because she was tall. Real tall. Like motherfucker-I'll-jack-you-up big. Six feet? Maybe six foot two? So what if her jacket cuff rested at her elbow? Look at her sideways, and he was liable to get a beatdown. Tyrone mustered his courage. "Maybe."

She smirked back, marching down the aisle away from him. "You coming or what?" she said, not bothering to turn around. Stranger danger was for eggheads, and though Tyrone's bulbous forehead had earned him the taunt, he unfolded his lanky frame from the floor.

"Yeah, I guess." Before he could properly dust off his pants and give the librarian's back a sufficiently sullen stare, Lady Mary had left the book-lined corridor. Nervous (his mother's voice in his head bleated the constant refrain "Didn't I say stranger danger?") and now curious, he followed Lady Mary's heavy scent of Primo! perfume and bubble gum. Past the periodicals, the romance section (four rows wide), popular fiction, Tyrone dropped his ponderous saunter, shed a quick shuffle, and then broke into a power walk in an effort to keep up. Lady Mary stopped abruptly, and Tyrone slowed to a halt, keeping the respectful distance of three feet between them.

As such, he couldn't see the name of the aisle where she stood. Finally she turned to him, but Tyrone, his mother's admonishment of "stranger danger" a bludgeon now, refused to move closer.

Lady Mary allowed herself to look impatient. "Think I'll bite?"

"Man . . . I mean, lady, please." But the sly bluster did little to hide his mother's inner scold, and despite ten years of city living, which meant on most days he sounded like he was twenty-four with a record, he was still a kid. How many times had he heard his mother and her girlfriend Wanda sucking teeth about some snatched baby? Or worse some little kid Lucy's age who came to school after a trip down south with a swollen mouth and punched-out eyes? Whatever had happened, a slap or a slip or something, that kid had looked so broken that girls gave wide passage and boys refused to tease. Schoolyard bravado failed (Man, some dude try to touch me, wop, wham, boom!). Tyrone gingerly touched his suddenly hot neck.

"Scared?" Lady Mary said with such sympathy Tyrone manned up. He crept closer to her, to the mystery lane she guarded.

"Tsk. Nah, man." And he wasn't. Her murmur, brimming with kindness, dashed his fears. His mind wasn't on the aisle she had led him to or even on her, for that matter. His mother's voice had been banked and quieted. No, Tyrone Jackson crept toward Lady Mary's powerful stench of perfume and Big Red, thinking about one thing (well, two, actually): his face and its arrangement. Suddenly that seemed paramount. Whatever was around the corner, he had to prepare his face not to show shock or pleasure or disappointment. Like all adults, Lady Mary Warren was testing him, and hopefully his face, a study of passivity, passed. A small reveal of joy or sorrow meant weeks, maybe months, of self-inflicted shame. A ten-year-old city boy knew this much: whatever a kid wanted, grown folks sooner or later took. Especially if it was the adult hand who offered it in the first place. Pat a head, puppy, or baby, and it was gentle, Gentle, GENTLE, and even when instructions were followed exactly (the hand never settled, just hovered), you were ordered to quit it. Never squeal, never sigh, never let your hands uncontrollably grasp, and your average adult was liable to let you hold it, smell it, lick it, pet it, or have it for a good hour more than their instincts told them. So Tyrone, his gaze fixed on the head librarian's shoulder, sought to settle his face into a disinterested facade. This small triumph allowed him to walk to the mouth of the aisle and read the brown plastic placard hanging from the ceiling.

Classic Literature

The mask slipped. Why bother keeping it fastened, since Tyrone hadn't the foggiest what the label signified. He wandered in a couple of feet, taking in impenetrable spines: Austen, Balzac, Brontë, Chekhov, Conrad, Dostoyevsky. Names that read like exotic locales or suspicious fruit. Unpronounceable, they kept their secrets hidden in plain sight. Two people placing their names on the same book— Miguel de Cervantes, *Don Quixote,* Gustave Flaubert, *Madame Bovary*—told him nothing. What was between the slip of pages: sex, drugs, death? If books offered in the children's section were so obvious they might as well have called him stupid, this puzzling aisle pushed aside all pretense and named him just that: Dummy. Hey, dummy, leave.

Years of praising commentary—"Tyrone has such potential"— was a lie. What he knew to be titles refused to guide. Tolstoy's *War and Peace.* Well, which was it? And whose war, and what peace? Tyrone's ten years of defensiveness reared its shy head. Calling me a dummy, like I don't know shit. Like I even want to know. "I mean, so?" But his sarcastic question was for his benefit alone. Lady Mary Warren had already left, and Tyrone couldn't go after her lest she think he needed her help (which he did) or was confused (which he was). Tyrone couldn't even leave the aisle since he was sure Lady Mary stood somewhere nearby, ready to crow that Mr. Smarty-Pants over here just got his head handed to him by a bunch of books. Tyrone crouched suddenly in the middle of the aisle, then inexplicably stood up again. Fuck. Fuck shit, fuck shit. His repertoire of curse words was now exhausted.

Maybe the inauspicious beginning should have warned him off. But he closed his eyes and randomly plucked a title off the shelf. Two years later and he couldn't remember the name of the book he checked out (*Gulliver's Travels*) or its premise, but whatever he tucked under his arm made his momma forget to whoop him when he came home late. He remembered her feminine cooing: stroke and coo, stroke, stroke, coo. He had no idea his mother's hand could feel like that on his head. After bedtime he heard her on the phone with one of her girlfriends, giddiness and pride in her voice. "Girl, check this. Tyrone comes home from the library with a book as thick as my head." Pause. Laughter. "Fuck you." More laughter. "What? Hold on." From under the covers he saw a strip of light, then heard his mother's rummaging hand in his backpack. The bedroom door squealed closed. "*Gulliver's Travels*. Ain't seen this since eleventh grade. Didn't read it then." The conversation quieted but was marked with sighs of pleasure, like his mother had found ice cream and gumdrops and a rent-controlled apartment. Or better it was as if his daddy walked through the door like a miracle. As the phone call came to a close, unadulterated joy joined the giddiness, the pride, and something else. Ah, yes, triumph.

Tyrone's mother had won something, and he didn't know what it was. Funny enough, neither did she. "I know, I know. He's ten," she said loud enough to wake him if he had been asleep.

Click.

His mornings were now plates of cheese rice and scrambled eggs with sausage, old-fashioned oatmeal with raisins and brown sugar. Third helpings were not asked for; they were offered. Imaginary lint plucked, scatterings of dirt dusted from his shirt, and weekly laundry done without a grumble.

. . .

Anita called on a good girlfriend to do her hair, and she took the money saved from grocery shopping with coupons and spent it on trips to the zoo and the Brooklyn and Queens botanical gardens for Tyrone. And throughout it all, stroke and coo, coo and stroke. Tyrone didn't have to tell Anita about a book's plot; momma and son discussed the mood. And Anita thought this was what college must be like. Second helpings and conversations that made you feel fit to burst.

My son. Almost eleven. Man.

It had been a good two years. Parent-teacher conference meetings where the only side defended was his; his mother sounding out of sync with the rest of the neighborhood parents: "Ain't no bad kids, just bad mommas. Look at my boy." Along with the giddy pride and triumph came a dollop of arrogance. Crack babies, boys younger than Tyrone who had moved from lookout boys to drug cutters, children who led bogeyman lives, terrifying a neighborhood—Anita looked at them all with contempt: "I remember when that kid was three." A two-year lifetime and his mother had slid from protective to careless with the greatest of ease.

Why bother hiding Tyrone under the bed or calling the neighbors when sundown arrived and not her son, when Cervantes would shield her child in a way she never could? She knew mommas who locked bedroom doors and inspected butt cracks; who checked, then rechecked, then got second opinions on homework; who made home-cooked meals after a ten-hour workday; who scored perfect attendance for PTA and parent-teacher conference meetings and school-sponsored block parties. "Wash your hands now," "Get a belt for those pants," "Hold your head up, son," "Didn't you hear me?," "Stranger danger, little bit," all for naught. The city had eaten up their children. Ten-year-olds roamed the sidewalks looking for and finding trouble, and grown men's stomachs rolled when some teeth-sucking twelve-year-old girl hustled across their path. The cluck-clucking from the newspapers and politicians paled in comparison to the fretting done after lights-out. Try living in this fucking hell called El Barrio for a month. Then you'd know. Their fear shamed them. Despite the perpetual "watch out," all Anita's friends' kids had been swirled inside the city's sucking soup. Brenda's baby girl had turned eleven in May and had been missing since January. Gloria's boy was doping up in the bathrooms at school. Wanda, her good friend, for a while her best girlfriend, had a son whose trouble arrived more often than trash pickup. And Henrietta's little girl (what was she fourteen, maybe fifteen?) was slapping her momma. It had gotten so bad all Anita could muster was a "Lord, help the day" and tremble.

But Tyrone. Her Tyrone. Her best best. Her best little man was exceptional. The comment section in the report cards told her so. Hemingway and Kipling clapping a delicious rhythm against his thigh kept him safe. So she let Tyrone run wild and rule their roost. Certainly mommas running the show was no kind of guarantee. And wouldn't you know it: Tyrone's brand of wildness meant staying out until the library closed, which in a bankrupt city meant well before sunset. At dinnertime he tried out eighteenth-century manners and called her "my dear" and said "of course, madam."

Thrilling wasn't the word. Anita wasn't sure how she felt. But whatever the emotion that scattered her heart and made her dive for kisses under Tyrone's eleven-year-old chin in their apartment it worked. It piqued dinner conversation, kept grades high, made work—first working the postal window, then the mail sorter, then as assistant associate manager—bearable.

Listening to his mother's happy hum kept Tyrone well within the lines of his mother's sense of decorum. Anita was wrong. It wasn't the pile of library books that kept her little man safe. It was her happiness. Rolling praise, constant interest, her good little boy lapped it up. He would never do anything to derail the clucking, giddy pride. But now, two years later, proverbial chickens were roosting.

CHAPTER 22

Tyrone had a tight circle of friends now. Kendall and Lucy weren't so bad, but the third was Daryl, who had the vacant stare of a two-year-old. And his stupid-ass momma, Wanda. God. How many Sunday mornings had she spent with that woman? Oh, Anita, be nice. You like Wanda. She makes you laugh. It wasn't Anita's fault that she sometimes forgot just how good Wanda could be. Wanda's good-turned-sour son could put an ungovernable yawn in their friendship. Only Anita's memory of Daryl at six years old, when he was manageable and kind, permitted him continued access to her apartment. Anita longed for an adult version of her conversations with Tyrone, discussions where grown folk moved from God and faithlessness to single motherhood to sex, all of it riddled with creative cursing. Wanda wouldn't do it and Tyrone wasn't allowed to.

"You having a good time, Momma?"

"Know it." That was such a blatant lie he and his mother would dissolve into laughter. No harm. Until a twelve-year-old Tyrone made ruinous plans to help his friend Daryl, it was a good life if one didn't think about the loneliness of single parenthood. Unless. Luck. And a plan. Anita had neither. But her son. Well. Who knew?

Those books, thumping an alluring beat, promised not only good manners but a road map. A lawyer, maybe? Or a doctor? Definitely college, sugar bear, cause Lord knows you're smart enough. When Tyrone took their high-minded talk to his knuckleheaded friends, she balked; what did those num-nums know about higher education? What did they know about Anita's dreams of Tyrone becoming a lawyer? A judge? The president? But Tyrone wasn't chatting about bachelor's degrees; he needed money. More, Daryl needed money. His book life and real life agreed on one thing: unless you had it, your existence was destined to become complicated. Dickens hadn't taken him to some fantastical place; the stories just made him more acutely aware of his bleak surroundings.

Tyrone had just turned twelve when he decided to pull his head out of the books long enough to take a good hard look at their lives. They were okay. But Daryl's life was crumbling. His friend was in trouble. Big trouble. For no reason at all, a bunch of cops thought Daryl had torched the church they all used to go to. Daryl, Lucy, Kendall, and Tyrone would be walking down a street minding their own business, and cops would pull up to the curb and put Daryl inside the car. He'd be gone for two, three, five days. Now when they all hung out, Daryl would shake for no reason. "What's the matter?" And when he told them, "I'm innocent," Tyrone's solution seemed obvious. Money. Lots of money. Daryl needed money for the courts, money for the lawyer. The next time he got pinched, they all knew what would happen: days and days in Rikers, and them cops would give him a beatdown. Daryl needed the money to set bail right now. Everyone knew if you had enough money folks couldn't just fuck with you.

Tyrone's towers of books all led him to the same conclusion: when one and one just didn't add up, the hero had to set out. For the first time Tyrone wanted to talk about money with his mother— maybe he could help out, get a paper route, work for Luis the bodega owner—but Anita heard something else when Tyrone tried to persuade. He hadn't mentioned Daryl's troubles, just their own, but her long-held faith in him began to crack under his pleadings. Her nights were filled with tortured dreams where Tyrone was a lookout boy or worse dealing rock.

Her son was old enough to be insulted. "Nobody talking bout that, Momma." He wasn't thinking of trouble. Really. He just wanted to talk to his friends about how they could make some extra cash. And she let him. As long as it was in her apartment. Not at Lucy's. Not at Kendall's. And definitely not at Daryl's house. "Okay, okay." In the beginning those plans—"just talk, Momma, just playing around"—sounded exactly as they should: like the ruminations of a little boy with too much mind and time.

"I could help you, Momma. I'm no baby." In the face of such innocence, Anita had nothing to say. Lucy and Kendall and sometimes Daryl spoke about being pirates and building race cars. What about him going to college and being a judge? How was he going to do that and get around to unearthing gold in the Amazon? "Momma, don't say that. When we get together, we just talk. Like it's going to happen, but probably won't."

"So you think being a lawyer and winning the lottery the same thing? You not going to college now?"

"Nah, Momma. But I might not be a judge. I might be something else."

She should have known.

"We just trying to make a little cash, that's all." That's what Tyrone had consoled her with, and it had been such a long time since he had caused her any trouble, she felt horrible for doubting him. Still she noticed the sure slide from fanciful to practical. Weeks passed and his plans sounded less and less like the high plot of novels.

"What y'all talking about in there?"

"Nothing, Momma. Like selling candy on the subway."

Anita didn't bother to shoo away her worry. "I don't know."

"That's why we get together and talk about it."

When Anita was alone, her Saturdays were spent going through bills—what should get paid first, light or telephone; what could she set aside for Tyrone; maybe she could get together enough money for some sort of summer camp—and she listened to childish ponderings with half an ear.

"We should stage a lottery and rig it so we win."

"We should get drafted in the NBA."

"Daryl, you're not even six feet and you're fifteen already. Give it up."

"We should sell candy."

"Psych."

"We should make a movie and charge double to get in."

"We could tell Luis to hire us at the bodega."

"We could collect cans."

"Ain't no money there, kid."

"We could sell candy."

"Lucy."

"We should put together a singing group. No, a dance group. No, a singing, dancing, acting group. On the subway."

"We should sell candy."

"Psych."

"Shut up, Lucy."

"I said psych."

"So why you keep bringing up that candy shit if it's a psych?"

Tyrone was right. Just talk. Harmless. But the conversations got quieter. Daryl mouthed his fears, repeating the litany of criminal charges: mischief in the fourth degree, criminal possession of a controlled substance in the seventh degree, possession of burglar's tools in the second degree, criminal possession of marijuana in the fourth degree, criminal nuisance in the second degree, failing to respond to an appearance ticket, burglary in the third degree, disseminating indecent material to minors in the first degree. His friends heard every word, and even Tyrone struggled to understand what it all meant. "I just got out yesterday. The cops are messing with me. They won't let me stay at Spofford. Talking bout how I'm a grown-up. Life. They talking about me going away for life. We have to do something. And fast."

.   .   .

Anita could barely hear them. "What y'all doing in there?" But most of her mind was on trying for a third time to get a Sears card, and if she got it, then she could buy all Tyrone's clothes for the coming school year, and then maybe she'd set aside some money, put her son in an after-school program, or start a college savings account. "You hear me? What you doing? I said."

"Just talking, Momma." But now the talk had dwindled to a whisper and would abruptly stop when she walked into the living room. Those upturned, angelic expressions and Lucy shyly asking for Kool-Aid should have made Anita break up their planning sessions. But her boss squinting at her hours at the post office, the shame of not being able to give Tyrone thirds for dinner, and the oppression of knowing a good life but not being able to quite afford it made her negligent. So busy trying to keep her family's head above financial water, and maybe a little bit more—that was always the tease—Anita didn't hear Daryl's dumb idea at all.

"We should steal it, man."

The plan was so simple, so stupid, that instead of throwing it in the rightful bin with Lucy's idea of selling candy, Tyrone, Kendall, and, yes, even Lucy perked and nodded.

Sst. Anita. Girl, you hear this? Anita? But Tyrone's mother couldn't hear the criminal turn of her son's conversation. Her mind was on the Museum of Natural History summer program she could enroll Tyrone in, if only she had a bit more money. Either she didn't pay NYNEX or she needed to skirt around her landlord for a couple of weeks till she received her next paycheck. Her numerical ruminations drowned out their plotting. Had she heard though. Lord. There was nothing more chilling than listening to a twelve-year-old calmly discussing how to knock a man out then pluck his wallet.

That's what she would do: pay twenty-five dollars down on the phone bill, everything but fifty dollars on the rent, and tell her landlord Charles to lump it. She'd pay him ten or so dollars a week until she was caught up. And then she would have enough left over that she could have Tyrone somewhere from three till five, and she could stop asking to leave early from work. Anita pushed away the mountain of debt and desire heaped on the table. Papers folded in three: bills, coupons, advertisements that promised not just a good life but a great one if you would pay $19.95 in ten monthly installments. Still for thirty days at least she could forget that this inedible pile of bills was the biggest thing that would grace her table. Not even the Thanksgiving turkey would curve such a heap. Anita thought to put it all in her bill bag, a reused plastic sack from the Met, but changed her mind. It would be better if she was forced to move it twice a day, once for breakfast, then again at supper. It would sharpen her desperation, though by now the feeling of where the money was going to come from was pointed enough to splice a strand of hair. Heaving a sigh, she thought, that'll work. Charles knows I'm good for it. And next month, I'll have Tyrone somewhere, and I'll open a college account for him.

She began to mold the misshapen paperwork when she noticed the quiet. The silence felt so complete, she thought Tyrone and his friends had skipped without telling her. Four o'clock in the afternoon, they could have booked and gotten into anything—drugs and pimping, slapping old ladies, God knows what. Didn't Tyrone know about that crazy-ass nigger who snatched up kids in broad daylight? Didn't he know Twin Johnson would clock him in the head if he looked at her wrong? And now look a-here, she thought as she scooted back from the kitchen table and took three steps to the living room and thus the front door.

But they were there. Tyrone, Kendall, Lucy, even Daryl, who straddled the arm of her couch. Just like she left them. The tail end of their planning still ripe in the air, just down to who should they pick. And Tyrone, her sweet thing, her best best, had sprung the idea that they should choose someone old who maybe owned a business in the neighborhood. Oh, and a man. Definitely a man. You could beat down a man and not feel bad about it.

"What you all doing?" Anita stood on the door saddle, trying to calm her breathing.

"Nothing, Momma. Just talking."

Some old maternal instinct reared. He was lying. She didn't

know what to be shocked by, the lie itself (which meant trouble) or that her son had the gumption to tell one.

"Uh-huh." Talking my ass. She had no idea why she was so sure, but the certainty that he was fibbing didn't slip. Oh my God, he's lying. To me. Only her pride in what sort of mother she was kept her from raising her hand. "Talk, huh?"

"Yeah."

Her suspicions crystallized. Lying little ass. Which was the first time Anita even thought a curse word about Tyrone. "Still?" Both she and the question arched. Her mouth settled into a grim line, and her left brow rose.

"Yeah, Momma. Just talking, still."

Her gaze swept the living room, not just Tyrone, Kendall, and Lucy crossed-legged on the floor, but the threadbare rug they sat on. Not just Daryl, straddling the couch arm, but the furniture that was so worn it was beyond cleaning. The television was a hand-me-down from her grandmother; worthless knickknacks cluttered her leaning display cabinet. Two ceramic pigs. One Salt Lake City snow globe. Two china dolls with movable eyes, both gifted to her by her great-aunt. In fact if anyone felt compelled to stand back and take it all in, the tilting four-shelved cabinet looked like the longings of a dozen people. Cousins and aunties and grandmothers all trying to get Anita to fix her mind on something beyond her son, paying bills, and putting food on the table. Good luck with that, ladies. Anita's shoulders ached from the weariness of city living. By 1985 New York City had emptied like a toilet, leaving behind smears of sticky shit. Anita and her best best (till he started lying like a rug) were thought of by the media and well-meaning politicians as dung. And what remained? Anita, her boy, and a handful of girlfriends. Oh they always knew somebody who knew somebody who cut this lady's hair who had moved to Weehawken and was making a go of it. A backyard and a car, growing zucchini when they felt like it, but Anita didn't know a soul. Not even a nobody who was making minimum wage but somehow managed to set up shop in Leonia. It was an ignorance that stung. She had thought Tyrone's library jaunts would protect and keep him safe until college, but no. He was sitting on the same toilet she was. And now here he was lying—badly. Anita's mouth watered, and she ached to cross the room, lift a gifted trinket, and bash it into Tyrone's head.

Lucy and Kendall sat on the rug, unmoving. They saw as plainly as Tyrone his mother's anger, her shame, and a touch of hatred. Tyrone's place was supposed to be different. An apartment where drunken fathers didn't leer in doorways, dicks limp with mouths jutting out at kids. A place where you could ask for Kool-Aid and not be felt up while you stood at the refrigerator. How many times had they come over to Tyrone's house and his momma asked them if they wanted a sandwich like she meant it? But now her face was reminiscent of the reckless anger they saw in the adults who lived in their homes. And even if she didn't hit them, even if she somehow managed to quell her rage and not pick up that hefty ceramic pig sitting on the shelf and hurl it at their heads, the look on her face said she could. If that kind of parental anger had a scent, she reeked of it. She smelled like their apartments. Like boiling ham hocks, weeks-old laundry, and an ancient waft of hate all hidden by heated ivy plants that crawled in the windows. Now Tyrone's apartment was just like the homes of their other friends whose kitchens they avoided because they never knew which way the mothers would fly. Upside her kid's head or yours if you were close enough. The familiar sour air invaded, and they took a real look at where they were gathered. Daryl was the first to summon the courage to speak.

"We going, Ms. Anita."

"Uh-huh."

Lucy, Kendall, and Daryl gave her a wide berth until they stood in front of the door, then booked. Tyrone slid his hands into his back pockets and rocked on his heels, hamstrings taut, the way he had seen Kendall posture when his mother was two seconds away from clobbering him. Anita locked all four locks on the front door.

"What you doing, Momma?" The earnest question threw her for a moment but failed to clear the haze of rage circling her head. "We was just talking."

"Uh-huh."

He hadn't admitted to anything. And she wasn't smart enough to string him out and along, catch him lying the way she had seen other mothers do. She had witnessed the circling interrogation that began softly enough, lulling the kid into a sense of security, then pow! Got ya, motherfucker. I thought you said you went to the store. Standing by the bolted door, Anita knew that sort of interrogative talent was worse than atrophied in her; it had never existed.

In fact had she left well enough alone, their plan would not have gelled. Her entrance, catching them mid-act, made the thieving plot the final thing on their minds, an arrested moment that followed them to bed, bedeviled their dreams, and became the first thoughts of a brand-new day.

A deep, heavy silence settled between mother and son, and though she would have denied it, she aped the movements of the children who had just departed. With a slow, almost blind grop-ing, she felt her way to the kitchen. She was frightened by her rag-ing impulse, and worse she was scared to death of the lie Tyrone wouldn't confess. They talked about everything. Really and truly, they did. How many times had she told her girlfriends her little son couldn't even hold water? So whatever he was holding on to was bad news. Anita edged away from him, hewing close to the perimeter of the room. First the door, then the wall, skirting the credenza, pat-ting a welcome to it along the way, then finally, gratefully escaping through the open doorway to the kitchen, leaving Tyrone alone with a cliff-hanger's heart.

As stunned as he was that his momma really meant to tear his ass up (and oh, yes, yes, Tyrone, that almost ass whooping would have been the stuff of legend), he stood in the middle of the living room stupefied by his pounding heart. Now he knew what Kendall, Lucy, and Daryl had been talking about when they said stuff like "Man, she looked like she was gone kill me." He had finally experienced it for himself. The look. A stare of such glittering hatred that had she lifted her hand the strike would have cleaved him in two. No novel's climax had come close. Tolstoy and Dickens and Twain had nothing on his momma. Jeez, Momma. All cause of one little lie? We probably won't go through with it anyway. But then he recalled the look on Daryl's face when he talked about what happened to him when he spent nights in jail. No. Maybe they will do it. This is what it must feel like to be Huck, to be Anna. Your heart bucking so fiercely you were sure at any moment you'd lift off the ground. Tyrone woefully thought, God, I'm never going to be this scared again.

CHAPTER 23

Lara tried and tried not to get angry because she wasn't quite sure where to place the feeling: at her mother's feet, which seemed right because she'd failed to show up the one time Lara needed her; at the long line of talent, who had clearly made a winning impression before she had sung a note at the Apollo audition; at her own voice, which had gone high and warbly with nerves; or at the fucking arsonist who had burned down the one place she thought of as her sanctified home. Day after day she placed blame and mounted evidence. The only change in her thoughts was who was the culprit, because for Lara there was one constant: surely some inequity had befallen her family, her church, her neighborhood. Too many bad things had piled up to think otherwise. And so, like every black woman everywhere who had bad luck show up out of nowhere and close the door on their dreams, Lara adapted.

She picked the Fastrada beauty school, the one all the way downtown off Union Square, because nobody would know she attended it. All she wanted to do was learn how to dye hair and figure out where to place her anger. You would think after eight months Lara would have let the emotion go, but try as she might she couldn't. Anger tore her out of bed in the morning, wore her out, and then knocked her into sleep. She gave her mother the silent treatment and only grudgingly muttered, "Pass the salt," through clenched teeth.

Maybe that was the problem. That was where the blame lay. Not once had her mother taken her aside and asked what was the matter. You don't seem like yourself, baby. What's going on with you? But Morning hadn't asked her daughter what made her slam doors and suck teeth. The older woman hummed during her daughter's silent treatment, passed salt and dinner rolls without comment. Where were you? The question sat on Lara's tongue at the breakfast table, so heavy she couldn't swallow her mother's oatmeal. Whether or not she should ask her mother where she had been that day was a question Lara couldn't help but pick like a scab. It would certainly prompt a confrontation, but Lara wanted her mother to confess her whereabouts. That way no matter where the inevitable argument led them, Lara could always say, You started this. Meanwhile, Lara's scowling, slamming, sullen hints got her nowhere.

Worst of all her mother would sometimes look downright smug, and Lara couldn't shake the prick that she wasn't the reason for her mother's happiness. Only twice had Morning's contentment shattered. Once at the end of spring, when out of nowhere her mother came home and muttered all evening, "He's gone," and then a second time, "I can't find him." Find who? the young woman thought, although she knew the answer: Reverend Carl. A nice enough preacher, she thought, but there was something too eager in his smile, and the earnest way he asked, "How are you doing?" scared her.

Lara didn't try to have these worrying conversations with her mother. She just wanted to finish school and get her beauty license. She wanted girls like her sisters at church to tip their heads into her hands and know they would sit up clean and beautiful. She wanted boys like the brothers in high school to tilt their heads and let her edge up their napes. If she couldn't sing and be famous, then she would become their caretaker. And that meant knowing the details of beauty. Then her mother wouldn't be running after some preacher who everyone would think was a runt if he weren't running a church.

If this young woman knew beauty well enough, she could hold it up to her mother and say, See? Look at it. Look at me.

Those thoughts hounded Lara all day long. At Fastrada she thought about how to shape beauty and how to curtail her anger. The school taught bright young women to coif loveliness, to give perms, relaxers, and Jheri curls, to trim split ends or cut a style. But there wasn't a seminar that taught people how to make conversation. And because she was still mad at her mother, she couldn't practice talking with clients at home. Somehow you should just know. Lara, nineteen years old and ready (for who knew what), looked at her colleagues caress sudsy hair and whisper secrets. "Girl, I know it." "Mmm, me too." Hush-hush and murmurs circled customer and beautician. Her jealousy choked on their ease. Women as young as her voiced success. Maybe Lara would get over her natural shyness and practice on one of the girls at school tomorrow.

But that notion never gained ground, because her tomorrows were filled with dreaming, with questions topped with a dollop of anger. Most mornings and afternoons Lara lurched along with the train and thought about why she had switched songs. Why did she choose that *Dreamgirls* song at the last moment? She hadn't practiced it. Scared of showing off the little Whitney she knew she was, she'd chosen a tune that had been played on Hot 97 on a loop for over a year. And when there was no answer to why she did what she did, her mind shoved the question aside. On the train or while she silently practiced haircuts on mannequin heads named Destiny and Keith, or when she traveled to school and back looking at where her feet fell, she daydreamed she was talking to her mother again.

On walks home Lara's daydreaming led her to moments that never happened in real life: her mother draped an arm over her shoulders, her curiosity curling around her daughter—Lara's doings, her whereabouts cradled them both. Morning wanted to know the texture of Lara's desire, much in the way a lover wanted to know the suppleness of a beloved's skin. In Lara's fantasy, the two of them were in the kitchen, then on the sidewalk, then back inside their church (in her dreams the Ethiopian was spared from fire), and together mother and daughter practiced dance moves—the electric slide, the cabbage patch—laughing themselves silly at their antics. But Lara's anger wouldn't let go, following her even into her dreams. She watched herself list her complaints about her colleagues and her teachers, how certain hair-care products made her nose crinkle, and she saw her mother's eyes go flat. Every privately made belief ended in the same way: her mother scowling and asking, When will you be out of the house?

"Hey! Hello!" Lara blinked out of her reverie and took her part in a conversation she had once a week. Wo Ren, the Chinese guy who owned the beauty supply shop on Second Avenue between 109th and 110th Streets, gave her weekly discounts on the hair products she bought for school. She stopped by so frequently he didn't rush her out of the store or follow her down the aisles. She liked him. He was as short and slim as she was. They shared the same awkward manner. And he was the only person she pitied. The way his jokes toppled in the telling made her shake her head, but she knew he told them in order to practice his English. Otherwise his stabs at conversation were wayward. When he taught her how to say hello in Chinese, they laughed so hard at her pronunciation he gifted her with another joke: "What did the math book say to the other math book? Boy, do we have problems."

Lara left the beauty supply store with a plastic shopping bag full of combs and brushes, applicator bottles, butterfly clamps, a Styrofoam head, and a practice hand for manicures. Her mind was filled with the price of wigs; when she should schedule to take her beauty license test; her mother's contentment with her persistent silence; whether she should let one of her peers give her a Jheri curl or just keep pressing her hair, something she could manage alone in her kitchen; and should she audition again for Amateur Night at the Apollo. She was embarrassed to try a second time even though she was sure no one would remember her. Lara had been so busy going to school and being mad at her mother she hadn't carved out a moment to pick a song, let alone practice it. What could she have accomplished had she set her mind to it? But she hadn't, and now she had to make the decision with her church gone, steeped in anger, aching to sing.

And how had her voice startled and strained like that? She, who had sung in front of a congregation since she was five? That's what Lara thought as she strode down the sidewalk. This time would be different. Eight months of beauty school had taught her how to apply makeup. A touch of blue eye shadow? A hint of blush? Should I go out and buy sandal high heels despite October weather, or wear patent leather Mary Janes to look younger than my nineteen years? That's what she hadn't appreciated the last time she went to audition. It wasn't just about what you could do; it was also about how you were seen. And Lara, who had grown up feeling comfortably invisible in the city (with the exception of her role as lead of the youth choir), had stumbled because she had no experience with perfect strangers paying her rapt attention.

Lara swung her bag of beauty supplies from her shoulder, where it had begun to hurt, to her chest; the smooth Styrofoam head peeked out, tilting forward. Everything jagged settled to the bottom. The sharp teeth of the rattail combs, the double dip piks, and the seven-row styling brushes pricked her stomach. Damn it. She was so close to home and didn't want to set down the entire bag and readjust her purchases.

"You want a taste?" It's funny how in a city full of noise, you always knew when someone was talking just to you. The spiky end of the rattail comb pierced through the plastic bag; Lara felt its tip scratch her rib. "You hear me, girl? Five dollars; don't take no change." Did it break the skin? Was that a light sweat or blood dampening her shirt? "Yo, girl!" He was behind her, and she spun around, her face a cloud of irritation. Through the bag the sharp teeth of the pik dug into her chest.

"Leave me the fuck alone. All right?"

"Bitch, what you say?"

What *did* I just say? she thought, snapping her head up from the contents of her bag. She didn't look at the man in front of her but at the two boys who stood up from their slouching against the apartment building.

"What's up?" one of them asked, but already she was scrambling away, tripping over her own two feet and trying to hold on to her purchases while pulling away from the prick of the combs and brushes. The mannequin head tumbled out of her arms. Lara ran, leaving its serene face to rock back and forth on the sidewalk.

It wasn't that bad; he wasn't that mad, Lara told herself over and over again. She pulled the kitchen phone with its long extension cord to her bedroom and called friends she hadn't spoken to in six months. Too rattled to bother with niceties or excuses, she leapt into the telling: how it wasn't her fault that she had done the unthinkable and had turned on a crack dealer in broad daylight and told him to fuck off.

"You said it like that?"

She'd called Tracy, a second soprano who did solos in their choir once upon a time.

"I don't . . . I mean, I don't think I said it just like that. I mean, I said leave me alone or something like that."

"Well, what he look like when you said it?"

"I don't know. I was watching the two dudes behind him."

"What colors were they wearing?"

"I can't—I don't remember."

And then Tracy called Joyce, who called Martha, and so on and so on, until they had created a daisy chain of three-way calls. The conversation, filled with "Girl, where you been?" and "I was just thinking about you," circled around one crucial point:

Lara, did you actually say the word "fuck"?

"I don't know, maybe. I just told him, you know, gone now." Had he been trailing her? Hissing, whispering loud enough for her and the entire block to hear, "Come on, bitch, you know you want it," but she hadn't really paid attention, because of those damn combs. Why? Why had she turned on him and spoken to him the way you would to any young man who jerked you out of your reverie for no good reason? But her friends wouldn't let it lie. Which was it? Did you say "fuck alone" or not? Her answer came out shrill and full of tears: "I don't know, I don't know."

"Who you say it to? Ray's crew or the Latin Kings or who?"

"I don't know . . ." Lara was almost faint with confusion. She couldn't remember exactly who she cursed out or what he was wearing or the exact particulars of the altercation; she just remembered her anger and her mother and her own voice thin and scared at the audition. But she couldn't tell them that, which in turn made Tracy and her other friends search for even more detail.

"Did he throw up a hand sign when you told him to get away?"

"Did he say something back?"

"Maybe whatever you said wasn't all that bad if he didn't say something back."

But Lara couldn't or wouldn't remember what, if anything, was said after she told the man to back off.

"Look, I know you struggling, but you can't be turning on a motherfucker like that."

"I know. I just didn't—"

"What street were you on?"

"110th. Right past the Game Room."

"Girl."

"Girl."

"Go back and tell me exactly what you said."

Lara knew what she had done was serious, but the cluster of her friends sounding so nervous made her want to withdraw her confession. She had bigger problems. Her anger, pointed and righteous at the moment she'd worked her neck and cursed him out good, had curdled. You don't point the finger at the bad guys; you don't give them lip when they take up a block and make bakery shops into drug fronts. You find another way home and buy bagels elsewhere. Because who knew what those men would do? The hardworking of El Barrio were beginning to suspect even the gangbangers didn't know what they'd do. When exactly did your anger, your fear at a slight, mean it was time to cut a bitch? The Game Room crew, the Supreme Team, had no idea. Shit, baby, I'll tell you when I get there.

Lara. Jesus, Lara. What did you do? She wasn't the only one. Lately that unexpected anger that didn't know its limits had infected everyone. Somebody looked at you wrong, clobber the motherfucker. Can't trust Granny; that old ho might have a knife. Little kids will swarm your ass and beat you down just cause. And the gangs? The John Johns, the Vigilantes, the Preacher Crew, the Bronson Gang? Those motherfuckers do nightmares, girl. And even when you knew they were the reason your mother came home humming show tunes and acting sixteen, you keep your head down. Lara had broken the neighborhood rules. She knew it. So did her friends. Their fear for her, for themselves, was a moving, touchable thing taking all the air out of their conversation and made for shallow breathing.

Her friends—and they were her friends—suggested that they meet up and figure out something. That was bad. Lara and Tracy and Martha and Joyce hadn't seen one another in months. And even though they lived in the same neighborhood, in the last eight months they hadn't even bumped into each other on the subway. And then what? That's why Lara was worried and needed to get off the phone. Then what? Most of them grew up in Spanish Harlem, and they all knew to keep safe it was best to keep to yourself. Sure, they said hello to folks in the street, and of course they went to their grandmommas' for Sunday dinner, but what exactly could a bunch of former choir girls do? Lara's problem was large and dangerous.

And now because of Lara's runaway mouth, because she had forgotten just what neighborhood she lived in, because she had the gall to think of her anger and heartache first, they were all talking on three-way about whether they could do something and be brave. To scatter would be easier, safer, but they were church sisters, even though they didn't have a church, and didn't that mean something? No one made mention of it, but Lara could feel their friendship, a lifetime in the making, shredding. She said to no one and everyone, "I'm sorry, okay? I'm so sorry."

Everyone on the phone agreed: strength in numbers. Maybe Lara wouldn't have to go seven blocks out of her way to get to the subway station for the rest of her life. If she showed up somewhere with everybody she knew, maybe, just maybe, she would be allowed to get mad and not get jacked up because of it. With luck she wouldn't have to spend the remainder of her days with girlfriends who had to be brave enough to be seen with her.

CHAPTER 24

Oh, Tyrone. A mere month later and that gut-wrenched episode when his momma was about to beat his ass to dust was a waltz compared to what he was now feeling. Flying down Second Avenue, his head and heart roared. And it wasn't his friends' look of pain as they crumpled to the sidewalk that had him wondering if the blaring sound came from the street or his chest. It was the books. All those stupid books that he had lost himself in for years. Books that had convinced him he knew the inner workings of another man's soul. Anita, his mother, was right to be worried. He and his friends had spent almost a month planning their great heist. And who did they ask to pick the mark they would rob? Tyrone, that's who. The smartest one in the bunch. He was flattered and ready to advise. After Anita's anger had thrown them out of her apartment, they began to meet just after school before Anita could run home from work.

Not that it would make Anita feel any better, but they did try other things before they settled on stealing. A couple of times a week Lucy, Tyrone, Kendall, and Daryl rode the length of the 6 train, singing for money. They were good. Anita's record collection kept them that way. "Tomorrow," "Mr. Pitiful," Sam Cooke's "You Send Me," sung in three-part harmony and loud enough to hush any potential conversation. They didn't know it, but Tyrone's near-cracking soprano saturated with stage fright filled their paper cup. His voice quivered throughout the melodies, and still he managed to hammer out the beat with a spare token on the subway seat. Even the heartless weren't able to get off at their stop without putting a nickel in Lucy's rattling cup. At the end of each ride, they finished the recital with a song they made up:

> *A penny, a quarter, a dollar, food stamps*
> *Anything, anything, anything, hah!*
> *Anything, anything, anything, hah!*

But crooning their hearts out meant ten dollars for the effort. And what kind of money was that? Certainly not enough for bail. In their meetings before Anita got home, Daryl said he could feel it coming. "It's gonna happen, man." The cops would drop by his apartment or his school to take him back to jail. He knew because days before they pinched him, his nights were filled with bad dreams. Lucy's eyes were saucers.

"What you dream about?"

"Fucked-up shit. You don't want to know." He didn't say it the way a storyteller would, with the more, more, tell me more hidden in the tone. Daryl meant it. No one wanted to hear about hands touching and squeezing tight, too tight; Santa Claus judges with red eyes growing teeth and gobbling him up. He liked his friends too much to give them details.

"What we do next?" Kendall asked.

"We steal it."

"No," Tyrone said. "First we plan."

For a week they scoured the city looking for prey. And how perfect they all felt when they found a mark right in their own neighborhood. This little old man who owned a locksmith shop. A little nobody who, even if he cried out, nobody would jump and run to his rescue, because he was the lone white man on the block who never said hello to anyone and never gave out candy for Halloween. Every other store owner did that. Even the drug dealers. He was the one. Some little old guy who shuffled everywhere and never looked up when he walked down the sidewalk. In a neighborhood where every door had six locks and everyone left as soon as they could, this guy must be carrying around a mint. Unlike the other store owners who stayed open late hours to catch kids with the munchies and working folk trudging home, this little man closed up shop around four o'clock. As if daylight would keep him safe. As if no one noticed the bulging bank envelope he tucked in his pants as he locked up. Tyrone, little bookish Tyrone, devised the great robbery. Lucy would be the lookout, Daryl would sit on his chest, Kendall would grab his legs, and Tyrone would lift the dough.

They decided to case him for a week. Tyrone found out that the old man went to the bank on Mondays. Kendall watched him in the mornings before school; Lucy took the afternoon shift and Daryl would help. He was an old man who like most working New Yorkers had steady habits. "And, Tyrone, what you gone do?" "Nothing. I'm the plan." He wondered if the old man was Italian or Irish or Jewish—"Who fucking cares, man? Let's lift this motherfucker." But Tyrone cared; maybe he could whisper something scary in the old guy's native tongue as they mugged him. "You sound like Lucy, man. Let's just do this." The arrangements were at once so simple and yet so nicely complicated for a bunch of preteens (Daryl being the glaring exception), it was destined to go off without a hitch.

In their plans this little old man was supposed to fold and cower. He didn't. Daryl did his part and sat on the guy's head. Kendall tried to hold his feet once, twice, and the third time was the charm; he had the man's ankles in a clutch. Lucy was looking and looking, her neck swiveling back and forth. "Hurry. Hurry." They tried to roll him like a rug. "Take his wallet, fool." "Take it." "Get it." Lucy, Kendall, and Daryl were shouting at Tyrone. But Tyrone couldn't move.

When Daryl punched the guy, Tyrone at last saw what he had only read about in books: despair. He had always wondered what it looked like, and now he knew. All of them froze, and that was all the old man needed. He shook off Daryl and kicked Kendall—hard—in the chest. Like birds they startled into the air. "Fuck! Fuck!" Should they try to clobber the man to the ground again? Their plans had never thought of that. And then Tyrone ran, away from the anger snarled on the ground, away from the despair he saw scrawled on an old man's face. Run, Tyrone. Run. He did. Someone shouted, "Come back here, motherfucker! You promised! I'm gonna kill you, bitch!" Tyrone didn't know who said it. It came from the throat of one of his friends. That was enough to know. He turned, grabbed Lucy, and ran. Two blocks later, Lucy's hand had slipped from his own, but Tyrone kept going. His legs were lead, but still he had one clear thudding thought: home, home.

He had less than an hour to figure it all out. Less time than he spent in social studies to wonder and solve where to put his shame and fear and excitement. In forty-five minutes his mother would be home, and so should he. His friends would know where he fled to. He was one of those kids who could be depended on to be where he was supposed to be. And for Tyrone that was one of three places: home, school, or the library. And tomorrow? Tomorrow he would have to face his friends. They'd come by and ask, What the fuck was that? How come you didn't snatch that dude's bank envelope? Tyrone. Tyrone? What the fuck? So now what? The fear, excitement, and shame he should be folding away jumped in his chest. So now I leave. And go where? his conscience asked. Outside. Just stay outside. Nobody would guess he would be out of doors.

Tyrone found a brick wall and leaned on it. Six o'clock sundown came and wrapped around him. Just how it had all gone wrong, why he froze when he had the easiest part of the score swirled in his head. I'm not a punk ass. I'm not. As he watched an early sunset, Tyrone thought about how all the books he'd read had let him down. In real life you don't plot; you don't find an old man with a bag of money, a man nobody paid attention to. You don't plan. You just do. You wait for night and snatch at the first thing you see. That's what I'm going to do. That's why I'm out here. Hours passed. If he could find somebody to rob, then he would be able to face his friends when they showed up. I'll do it. Knock somebody down and give the proceeds to Daryl.

Tyrone didn't know it, but his victim was riding uptown on the train. She had her mother's coloring (midnight black) and height (five foot two), though there was something long-legged about her. If anyone were watching they'd notice she moved the way a newborn does: unsteadily, with a bright-eyed fear that a fall was just a step away. That she was respectable made her invisible—calf-length skirts and dresses, the relaxed hair. She looked at no one; her shoes held her complete attention. A sly hiss of admiration floated toward her; her flinch was so small it was barely seen. To those who didn't know her, who had never heard her sing, she could be mistaken for a nothing, a former latchkey kid whose solitude had followed her into adulthood.

The sun vanished, and an October night with winter's teeth arrived. Tyrone shivered in his thin jacket but still refused to go home where he belonged. Maybe his friends would have forgiven him or laughed at his stage fright when he'd stood under a thieving spotlight. He could imagine Kendall slapping his thighs, pointing and sniggering: This little nigga spooked. You wet your pants? Kendall was a good friend, kind enough to soothe Tyrone's shame with a bout of giggles. But not Daryl. He remembered the despair of the old man's face. Tyrone hadn't realized he had been staring at the same expression for weeks. Daryl looked like that all the time.

The plan was to walk in twos or threes. Lara and Tracy, Lara and Martha, Lara and Joyce and Martha. But nobody was available that first Monday. "I can do next week," Tracy had told her. So, Lara stood on the platform at Union Square, wondering how to get back home. The 6 train pulled in, and she stood on the threshold of the subway doors, torn with indecision. The conductor coughed out garbled instructions that died away, only to say next in an irritated voice: "Step in. Move all the way into the car. There's a train directly behind us. Step in." She removed her sliver of a heel out of the doorway. The voice was for everyone. The subway door cranked closed after she removed her foot, and she began to read the graffiti that covered the subway car like wallpaper. People's hopes and taunts were everywhere the eye could land. She studied spray paint that looked Arabic and translated the words into English. BECKY LOVES JESUS. EASTSIDE HOMEBOYS.

Tyrone stood well beyond the bug-smeared streetlamp, and even if he were to stand beneath it, no one would have been able to see him in its light. He tried so hard not to think of anything. But like most people, he was unable to wander too far from who he was. His mother was at home now and worried sick; she probably had called his school and his friends. But Tyrone couldn't think about all that. His mind was on bigger things. He tried as best he could to just think about the now, Now, NOW courage he needed to yank on some lady's purse hard enough to snap the strap and then run for dear life. But his mind wouldn't cooperate. Instead his back warmed the building brick, and he remembered a story he once read at the library about a young man who finds a very special ring. It is made of gold or brass, or silver. And the young man slips the ring on his pinkie finger. Nice. A man of my rank and family should own a ring such as this, he thinks. He is but a shepherd; he has never owned any jewelry of any kind, and yet he thinks this. The man decides to keep the ring. Yet he is nervous and frightened that he is keeping what he knows is not his. He fiddles with the ring, all jittery, and when he turns the jewelry, poof, he disappears. And then the man, who was never very good, but certainly no one would call him bad, did every criminal thing he could think of. I want to be that man, Tyrone thought. Pressing his back harder against the building. I bet everyone in New York wants to own a ring like the shepherd's. I bet you can buy one at your corner bodega for a dollar.

Lara couldn't figure out if it was a sign of good luck or not when the doo-wop guys entered her car at Fifty-Ninth Street. Either way she couldn't stand their crooning anymore and got off at Ninety-Sixth Street. Maybe I'll walk up Second Avenue. The streetlights sputtered on, and Lara squinted into the near darkness on the look-out for dealers who might be watching her passing on the corner, hawking their wares without bothering to use a sotto voce. But no one tried to get her turned on or tuned out. All she had to do was get home tonight. Her tomorrows would be filled with her friends. Friends who were quick to comfort her and to figure out how to accompany her hither and yon until this all blew over, and Lara tried hard not to bristle at their payment in criticism. How could Lara be the only person in her family who had never seen the inside of a jail? Who didn't know whether cop cars still had bucket seats? She had never been arrested. Really, not even once? Not even a pat down? Jesus, girl, where have you been?

There were no peekaboo panties in Lara's closet. Her friends promised to stand and walk with her as soon as they could, but perversely they all looked down on her for needing protection. "But, girl, you were the lead of the choir," Tracy finally said, as if singing a song meant she had lived the lyrics. How had they looked up to her for so long? Lara thought about all that her girlfriends had said and turned up Second Avenue, walking faster and faster.

Tyrone watched working adults stride home. He was looking for a shape of shoulders and a loneliness even children could see. Someone small. He saw more grown people in those six hours than he had seen in a year. Searching for his mark, he noticed how adults could look at everything and nothing at the same time. How the hips of mothers acted as a third arm. He knew only his teachers, Lady Mary and the librarians, his mother and her friends, but outside all the grown people seemed to know each other. They muttered hello and paired off unexpectedly. He even thought he saw his mother, but he chalked the sight up to his longing. His momma leaving their house this time of night, wearing sweats and that ratty shirt she wore to bed? Outside? Never.

Lara walked up the avenue, passing the Franklin Court projects. Her head was down, pondering the shape of her shoes. Steeped in her dreaming, all her thoughts were about tomorrow, when she'd prove to her sisters she was worth looking up to. I may not have been arrested, but my voice led us all. Do you remember when the Ethiopian still stood and I taught you all the cabbage patch? Do you all remember when everyone thought I would be the next Whitney Houston? I didn't have to be in trouble to be worthy then. All my bad news was being turned away at the Apollo. I won't tell you a thing, and my momma won't ask me about it. That alone makes me fierce. I don't need anything else. I study beauty downtown. And I will bring it back to you all. The next motherfucker who steps to me will get a beatdown. I can't even say what I will do. Don't fuck with me, bitch. Tracy and Martha and Joyce will walk with me and shiver in fear. I'm that kind of bad bitch.

It was a little after ten, and he was ready now. Tyrone's heart thundered, but he knew it would; he had already experienced a loud heart earlier in the day; he was ready for it and there it was. Thump, thump. It drowned out city noise. Thump, thump. He could only hear himself. Thump, thump. Everyone decent was inside now. Only the stragglers remained. No one minded him; he was almost invisible as he draped himself against the building. Lara was no more than a whisper as she rounded the corner. How old is she? Tyrone thought. Seventeen, twenty-nine; who cares? She walked and cowered at the same time; that's what was important. She's invisible, but so am I. Go, go, go.

They grappled in silence. The purse strap wouldn't give, though Tyrone pulled and pulled. Down they went. Together. His little nobody, his perfect victim, turned out to be a crazy strong monster whose grip Tyrone couldn't shake loose. Lara Taylor, Morning's forgotten child, squeezed and squeezed, bursting with adrenaline. He sees me. My God. He sees me.

Tyrone was croaking something, her hands still taut around his neck. She leaned close to listen.

"Okay. Sorry. Okay."

PART FIVE

CHAPTER 25

January 1986

Upon hearing the news, Wanda thought at last there was something to help her snap out of it. When she saw that Chinese guy's face on the evening news, she thought finally she too would be swept away by the tide of righteousness that had crashed onto her neighbors in a wave. But nothing. The bad guy got caught; it was all anybody could talk about, but Wanda felt uninterested. She even suspected she was jealous but didn't want to admit it to herself. Still in the teeth of winter, Wanda shivered in front of Anita's apartment building and mapped out yet again just how she'd landed where she stood. Was it when October had showed up and Wanda's bad news had been clobbered by Tyrone's death? What could Wanda complain about when her best friend's son had been murdered and was in the ground? Daryl was in trouble, but at least he was breathing. In the moments when Wanda couldn't help but think about her own tragedy instead of her friend's, she remembered the shivery fear she had felt eleven months ago when she first stood beside her son in front of the judge, her fear melting as she uttered the same excuses again and again, arraignment after arraignment.

She remembered seeking out Carl's help when Daryl was arrested after their church burned down. Wanda had found her old pastor unpacking his belongings on an empty floor in a brownstone. Luis, the bodega owner, and a heavyset girlfriend from the beauty shop who Wanda was still on speaking terms with decided to come along. As soon as Reverend Carl opened his front door, they all began speaking at once, "What you gone do about Daryl, Rev.?" "What did they want from him, a confession?"

"Brother. Sister . . . Sisters." Given the circumstances, Carl thought he handled introductions fairly well. He clucked sympathy when Wanda's girlfriend muttered, "How you been?" but the bulky woman's effort at small talk made the conversation that much more awkward.

"It done got real bad." Wanda draped herself over the diminutive reverend. "I ain't seen him this time. They won't let him have visitors."

"All right, now. Take it easy." Carl's small hands found her back and gave short strokes of comfort.

Wanda made a grab for the handkerchief Carl offered. "I don't know if he gone make it. Goddamn cops trying to beat the why out of him and he ain't got it, you know? And he keep trying. They knock him over the head, and my boy try to get out a reason why he did it, but ain't shit he say make sense. Cause he didn't do nothing. So they pop him again."

Carl reached up and caressed her shoulder, leading Wanda away from her two friends to his brand-new bedroom. "Give us a minute, will ya?"

Once they were alone, Wanda told him the whole story. Stripped of the much-rumored broken legs and a missing eye, Daryl's treatment at Rikers sounded all the more pitiful. There wasn't a legion of police working over Daryl, just two detectives—one black (don't say it, Sister) one white, both young, equipped with nothing more than the belts holding up their pants and wedding bands. "Married men whoop your boy?"

"Daryl tell me fore they go upside his head, the black one tell him what his wife making for dinner."

"Sweet Jesus." The acute pang of guilt that had eluded him for a week and a half suddenly appeared, throbbing, wince-worthy, and made itself at home. He tried to slow his breathing at the bleak news.

"What you gone do bout Daryl?"

Carl stood, forcing the next words. "Come on by tomorrow. I'll have something planned by then." Before she could ask, Like what?, he pulled her up and away from his bed where she sat, snaking his small arm around her waist, and led her out to his front stoop.

Suspicious, Wanda parked her hand on Carl's closing door. He wouldn't be able to shut it without giving the wood a real shove. "You okay? You got this?"

"Sister, yes. Yes." Carl couldn't help but blurt out his lack of direction, "What are we gone to do?"

Having heard the question so often as of late, she decided not to deride the one person who was supposed to have the answers. "You and me gone fix this shit. That's what we gone do."

Wanda had thought it was bad in the beginning, but nowadays she wondered: Where was that woman, that hustle-and-go black lady who talked smack to pastors and police and judges too? Where had she gone? She remembered when her hip worked like a third arm, capable of opening and shutting doors. Lately Wanda missed her: the woman she used to be; the one who was quick to laugh and gossip; the mother who cursed out other people's children when they felt sorry for themselves; the woman who held down three part-time jobs and was on the lookout for a fourth. With luck, one day she would land steady employment that came with health insurance. She had been as shocked as anybody to realize her hustle and busyness weren't endless. Vast, yes, but finite. And Daryl's trouble had used it up. Running off to court and trying to soothe her son's fear, working a second shift at the grocery store and trying to get to the lawyer's office before it closed, cutting out coupons while making breakfast in the morning and trying to get Daryl to stop crying before she joined him—all of that made her tired. Blasphemous to even think it. Black women did not get tired. They weren't allowed. To voice such a condition was met with immediate admonishment. You call yourself tired, huh? And when did you get the kind of money that allowed you to get so sleepy? Guess you want to take a nap now? No one turned down a third job even if you couldn't find the time to fit it in your schedule during the day. You didn't ask about the night shift? Don't be lazy; find a way. The hale call "Working hard or hardly working?" was rhetorical; black women knew the right answer.

Right now she needed an echo of that woman full of hustle and go. She trembled, shivering all over and not from the cold. I can't wait any longer, she thought, and pressed Anita's bell. When her friend buzzed her in, Wanda pulled as hard as she could at the door.

Anita stood just outside her apartment as Wanda mounted the steps. "That you, girl?"

"Who else?" Wanda watched Anita fidget in her doorway. Both women smiled, both nervous but for different reasons: Anita because she wondered why Wanda hadn't plucked the vial and aluminum packet from her purse, a grin of victory scrawled across her face, and Wanda because this was the first time she had failed at some streetwise action she thought herself capable of and she wasn't quite sure how Anita would take the news. Their conversation started soft, plucking around the edges of politeness, asking questions they both knew the answers to but out of obligation were asked anyway. They fell back into the life they used to lead as church ladies. All they were missing were the hats.

"Let me get your coat. You want a coffee?"

"Girl, yes. It's cold as all get-out out there."

"Sugar?"

"Hmm. I'm surprised I caught you; thought you'd be at work."

"I still got sick days. Might as well use them." Anita went to the kitchen and turned on the coffeemaker. Wanda took a seat on the couch. "What about you? Thought you'd be at the grocery store."

"That piece-of-shit job don't pay enough for me to mind it. I'm looking for something else. Maybe I can sit down for a change."

"Yeah?" Anita called out while pouring Wanda a cup.

"Maybe I'll take up something at night."

Anita walked into the living room with the cup of coffee, complete with the useless saucer underneath. They both felt amiss. Unless they confessed to each other what they really wanted to talk about, the conversation would soon move to talk about their mothers or even worse their children. Anita noticed her friend perched at the edge of the couch, her whole body poised to take off in a run. And when Anita passed the cup and saucer to Wanda, the ripples didn't stop. The hot liquid splashed into the saucer.

Anita didn't take a seat, nor did she look at her friend. All her attention was fastened to the brown rippling in the cup. "Well?"

"It's a story. You should sit down for it." Everyone knew this story. Everyone except Wanda, who told it, and Anita, who listened. The guy, that guy Wanda bumped into, who was so kind and understanding. While talking to Anita, Wanda also relived it: How she heard the singing from the street and fell into its song. Just a taste, her dealer had offered. Put a kind of freedom in her hand. The first time she took a hit, she flinched from the heat of the glass bowl. The smoke that curled at the bottom of the bowl banked complaint. Doubt. Loathing. But it fulfilled its promise: peace and quiet.

No more thoughts about Tyrone's death and Daryl's troubles, Wanda's little bit of dwindling money and Anita's grief—all vanished because that guy gave them—for free no less—that hit, that gift. And when Wanda went and accidently on purpose found him again, before she could tell him why she had sought him out, he put bliss and forgetfulness in her hand. For free! And he had said, "Come by anytime, baby. Anytime at all."

"So, I went back. We both agreed that that last time was going to be the last time, since you were going back to work. But I didn't know you still had sick days, and I need to get out there and get me some real work that won't keep me on my feet all day. But then I got to thinking, maybe I'd stop by and get us one more hit. You know?"

"Okay."

"This brother was trying to get rent out of me! All I was trying to do was get a hit before I start looking for work for real, cause you know once you start a new job they're not going to let you step out every time you want to. And he just came at me like insurance and car payments. I ain't got the money for that. You and me both can't come up with the money he's asking for."

"So what now?" Anita reached out and took back the shivering cup of coffee Wanda hadn't sipped.

"We got to go on a mission," Wanda said, letting the declaration linger. Wanda still wanted to trade secrets, talk about sit-down work that might even require wearing a skirt, and most of all convince her friend to head out one more time to cop a score, but looking into Anita's face, she realized she didn't need to. It had been three days since Wanda had last seen Anita, and both women hurt all over. Her stomach cramped, but nothing she ate or drank soothed. She couldn't hold a thought, and all the little details of her day—make breakfast, get the laundry, go to work, see to Daryl—felt both overwhelming and inconsequential. "We got to find somebody, cause, girl, I'm on a mission."

Anita placed the cup and saucer on her dusty coffee table, then rose. "Me too."

They weren't so in need of a fix that they forgot their coats. Their hats, yes, gloves and scarves, yes, but they remembered their coats. Both women tucked in their heads when the January winter bit them with cold outside. "Which way?" Anita asked, her whisper warming Wanda's ear.

"Let's head to 110th," Wanda shouted back. When they reached the front of the Game Room, they learned another lesson of the streets—a lesson they thought only applied to the real citizens of the neighborhood, those who worked jobs and went to church and voted—no strangers allowed. That knowledge shocked them. Wanda's rehearsed "Hey" was met with an arched brow and an "I don't know you, baby."

Their anonymity made drug dealers sneer. "You think I'm a bodega or something? You ain't my customer."

"Back up, bitches." Two men stood shoulder to shoulder, beginning to scowl at them, but then decided Anita and Wanda weren't worth the stress. "Get the fuck out of here, smelling like po-po."

The two ladies slunk away, too shocked at the accusation of being narcs to be angry.

In a neighborhood it's funny how you can finally meet people you've known all your life. Every day you go to the bodega and get chips and a drink, say hello and thank you to the guy behind the counter, but it's not until you bump into that dude on the subway that you find out his name is Luis; he's got six kids and a wife, and he lives two blocks away from you. Forever trapped within commercial transactions, Wanda and Anita were those neighbors—there were folks they only knew from the grocery store or the playground. The only place they saw the bus driver was on the bus. They wandered the blocks, looking to score, asking anyone who seemed idle for directions, the very question marking them as suspicious. But when some lady looking high and happy pointed a shaking finger and said, "Two blocks up, middle of the block. It's in the basement," they thought their luck had changed.

They hadn't seen her in almost a year, but Anita and Wanda knew her. It wasn't as if they could have mistaken her for anyone else. Taller than most men, almost six feet, a short neat fro with a touch of gray hair growing from her scalp, she stood in the doorway of a basement apartment. She was the woman they had spent hours gossiping about after Sunday services. "Girl, did you see how she knocked Shelia's hat off?"

"Think she did it on purpose?"

"Come on now; course she did."

Then they laughed, Shelia too, despite the fact that the brim of her new hat had cracked in two. Twin, the scary delight of their Sundays and Wednesday Bible classes. The woman whose antics shored up their own dignity. Almost all the sisters at the Ethiopian were poor and working; they sometimes needed to borrow money from friends or in-laws, but everyone knew they were saner than

Twin. Without the church's vaulted ceiling to place her to scale, she looked even larger than they remembered. She didn't have to, but she bowed her head to poke it out the door. "What?"

"Hey! Remember us? You look good, girl." Wary but pleased, Wanda stepped closer, her mind filled with potential discounts or better, maybe a free hit for old time's sake. She smiled, and Anita joined her in the expression.

"I know you." Twin seemed startled with the recognition. And angry. "The fuck? Get the fuck outta here." Her open hand swung at Wanda and landed. "Get the fuck to church! Hear me?"

The two women stumbled back and away, up the three steps, onto the sidewalk. They ran, elbows pumping, certain she was right behind them. Both women had the same thought. Twin had to know; they knew she did: There was no church. Not one that was theirs, anyway. It had burned down.

CHAPTER 26

It was February and cold, and Carl's thoughts sharpened on a word. One word that grew arms and legs and held on tight: "time." He didn't have much of it. Or at least not enough time to do it all. The last planning meeting came back to him in a rush. Drug-free school zones, more police presence, fixing with Child Services, streamlining the welfare and food stamps process; all that took time. Two or three years of hard work at least. A year if he was lucky, and then every city office would have to bow to his pleasure. How could he do all that and save Anita too? He had heard the rumors: someone had seen her in front of the Game Room, underdressed considering the weather but looking happy despite the cold. "She's out there in these streets" was whispered. "Wanda too." His murmured calls to take up a collection were greeted with half-hearted agreement. They all knew the truth. Not one person they knew who had been turned out had come back from it. Sure there were stories that folks stayed clean for six months, but inevitably they went right back to it. Grateful, good people who fell prey to crack would take the money given and spend it all on a score. There was no time for all that. Carl could have had all the time in the world and an army of the like-minded, and still nothing would have worked, or at least nothing had worked thus far. The thought frightened him. There was no way he and his would make a dent in all that trouble. He and his members didn't talk about the fact that Anita's solution for her grief made them all failures. To think about it too much would make all their meetings with so much promise shameful. Put your shoulder to dreams that could come to life if you worked hard enough—that was the only way to honor her little boy and his murder. That and rant about the asshole who put him in the ground. Carl remembered all those eager hands raised, his members' suggestions that seemed just the thing to beat a path to a better life. He was afraid he couldn't give that to them. He smiled sadly. None of that would make a difference for Anita and Wanda. Helping those two for now felt hopeless, but maybe he had the strength and luck to straighten out the lives of his neighbors. The thought made him square his shoulders and head to Morning's place. They needed to get to work. The two of them would turn to the Institute with renewed vigor.

For a season all through spring relationships Carl had let atrophy he massaged back to life, and he and Morning manned the phones, wheedled and begged for five minutes, just five minutes of meeting time. Wednesday. That's the day they told everyone who would bother to listen. Morning and Carl spent the month of June trying to put together the big city hall meeting they had planned for back in February. Wednesday, July 2. "Can you be there?" Carl asked his ninety members. "Can I count on you?" he asked city councilmen whose schedules loved nothing more than a four-day weekend, and with the Fourth of July falling on a Friday, they couldn't find a reason to take the whole week off, but man did they want to. "Can we get together at ten?" "Oh, I don't know."

Carl and Morning and the seven mothers and the ninety-some-odd families called and set up appointments with every agency they could think of: New York City Department of Citywide Administrative Services, New York City Department of Finance ("Could we stop by at ten thirty?"), New York Public

Service Commission, Office of the New York City Public Advocate ("Maybe we could catch you at eleven? Just for a minute?"). They had no idea if they needed to see the rest of the agencies: the Office of the New York City Comptroller, the New York County Clerk, the Department of Buildings, the Offices of the Inspector General but they scheduled to see them anyway. Just in case. If everything went their way, they'd have the entire city on their side by afternoon rush hour. The Manhattan Municipal Building wouldn't know what hit it. Giddy hope wrapped Carl, Morning, and ninety families in its caul. By July when they all saw Carl's Wednesday schedule, they giggled.

"This shit's jumping off tomorrow, man. I can't wait to get in them cops' faces and be like, 'Yo, Strawberry is killing it. Little Darling is a pussy.' Po-po still walking that pavement know that." A young man who had been brought along by his grandmother offered that suggestion and was immediately told to shut his mouth, but the teenager's fondest wish was soon joined by others. Sure they still wanted those drug-free zones, and cops tipping their hats to them while helping little DeShawn play stickball titillated. But these last weeks of planning allowed them to plump their real desires. If they were going all the way downtown to hand over a list of demands, shouldn't it read exactly the way they wanted? A real bank in the neighborhood would be nice, and how about some free checking to go with that? And why not ask for one of those street markets to set up shop for a couple of days during the summer? Wouldn't that be nice? Free pre-K and day care, so they wouldn't have to scramble so hard just to get to work. Not that they didn't appreciate the whole drug-free zone idea, but there was so much more they needed. They didn't want to turn into a bunch of saditty blacks, but if we worked this right, we could walk to work unafraid; we could sit on stoops all night long in the summer if we felt like it; we could let our kids go outside and play and not be worried that the neighborhood would snatch up what we have tried so hard to keep safe. "So don't you think we ought to ask for things we really want, Reverend? Don't you?"

Carl looked at the small dais at the back of the assembly and sighed. As he reached the podium, he raised his hands for quiet and got it. First of all, he wanted to assure everybody—now listen here— he hadn't given up. No, sir. "But you got to be practical minded about all this. You can't lay down all this on these kind of people at one time. They'll spook. Now they know about Tyrone. And they know about Wo Ren. That was just on the news a couple of months back, but the rest of it, the drug-free zones and cops walking the beat and the free day care and all that, well, that's got to wait."

"Wait for what?"

"Yeah, Rev. What we waiting for?"

The Institute was crowded; even with the air conditioner work- ing full blast, the place felt muggy. That was what Carl thought as he felt sweat collect in his shirt's collar. He reached in the podium's cubbyhole for the document he had been hiding from them for weeks. What he wanted them to affirm and sign barely filled one page. According to the paper in his hands, their Grand Purpose was to express the utter outrage at the manner of death and subsequent treatment of Tyrone Jackson's body. The members of the Institute for Galvanizing and Organizing True Christians of Harlem and Associates ask that the city hold town hall meetings dealing with the identification of persons who have perished on the streets of New York. Item one: blah, blah, blah. Item two: blah, blah. What the fuck? These suggestions were so mealymouthed he hoped no one would ask him to read them aloud. He twirled the words he had written around in his hands like a baton, desperately wanting to pass off the task of asking for signatures to someone else.

"It's about the timing. Maybe the timing ain't really right." But that wasn't the truth. Carl was scared. What if we fail? What if I do? They were going to fail because of him—he didn't possess the soaring rhetoric of Jesse; he had lied all his life about his height. His members didn't rush him, but everyone gathered closer to the small stage as if suddenly they couldn't hear him under the white roar of the air conditioner. More than a few balked. Their mouths had been set for a better life, and they would be damned if Rev. Carl started talking about some jive-ass bullshit. Fuck the timing. We want some shit right the fuck now: You hear this? No CPT for the police and no CPT for you, motherfucker. We want our shit now. The time is now! You said that shit back in January. Yeah. Remember that? His people pressed closer and closer. Carl's back touched the wall of the Institute. En masse they moved away from him and were quiet. Someone in the back, someone Carl couldn't see, bit back a sob. Her strangled cry summed up what everyone felt.

"All right, folks. All right. I hear you. Sign the petition. That's what we are giving them. And hear me: don't forget, nine thirty sharp. No CPT, people. You hear me?" Carl didn't quite shout, but the room was so hushed it sounded like it.

"Yes, Reverend. Amen."

But the crowd, hot and crushed, was filled with fear. People looked at their watches, out the window, at the floor as they passed around Carl's paltry document and wrote their John Hancocks. Someone with a sick sense of humor scribbled a large *X* on the third blank page meant for signatures. They looked everywhere except at each other.

"Let us pray," Carl began. "Guide us, Jesus."

"Amen."

"Let them hear us, O Lord. Let them understand us."

"Amen, Reverend."

"Let them fear us."

"Yes. Yes."

"In Jesus's name . . ."

"Amen."

CHAPTER 27

At nine thirty sharp they gathered. The ninety families had promised, pinkie promised, they would show on time, but fear dwindled their crowd to sixty-seven people. Sixty-seven folks who believed in Carl. Sixty-seven people who believed the fairy tale, dredged up their faith in God and Carl, and showed up at nine thirty were enough. Their number, their smell—a heady mixture of Ivory soap, industrial cleaning solvent, and Tuff's deodorant—crowded around Carl. He felt their deference. People on the way to somewhere else stalled in front of the sixty-seven, wondering what was about to happen, until meetings that could not wait pulled them away. Clad in their work clothes, janitor overalls, mailroom blues, nurse's aide jumpers, they stood out and gathered stares. Yeah, well, we're here. They marched toward forty stories of civic power.

Sixty-seven neighbors tried not to gasp when lofty arches greeted them just inside. And even though the receptionists were nice enough and the politicians weren't called away for last-minute, but ever-so-important, meetings, Carl knew when he and his were being snowed.

Though they were just sixty-seven folks, a fraction of what they thought there would be, political handlers saw Carl's people and immediately decided most of them would have to stay downstairs in the lobby. "But we told you how many we would be." A very nice woman in a sand-colored business suit clucked her sympathy, then clapped her hand on Carl's shoulder. "I'm sure you did. Interns."

Not wanting to embarrass themselves and draw straws or count off, Carl and his people looked at each other and broke themselves not quite in half. Twenty or so followed Carl to the elevators, while the rest, including Morning, waited behind.

The assistants made sure to be on the phone when their chins directed them to their bosses' offices. Suit-clad men cupping their hands over a phone's receiver, their faces a study of constant harassment. "Down the hall and to your left. I'm sorry; could you hold just one more moment? No, sir, your other left. Yes, the public advocate will see you now. One moment, please. Your third left." Once there, crowded around massive mahogany desks teeming with stature and power, Carl and his now tiny delegation solemnly placed the crinkled sheaf of signatures in influential hands, ready to sit down and start negotiations, only to be slowly but firmly shooed from the office. "Oh, no need to take a seat; I know why you are here." The borough president, the city councilwoman, the comptroller leapt from their chairs and yes-yessed the twenty or so with "Yes, I've heard about what is happening to your young Tyrone. Such. A. Shame." Not even Carl corrected their mistake. Important men and women worked Carl's small delegation as if it were a crowd, passing out election buttons and literature, patting and caressing shoulders, nodding sagely, copping the perfect attitude of power listening while interrupting every fifth word.

"Mr. President, thank you for—"

"Actually, it's Mr. Borough President, but let's not stand on formalities. This situation is such a tragedy. I want to let you know that I've put in a call to the police."

"Well, that's not really the—"

"And of course both this troubled young man and his mother are in my prayers."

"We appreciate that, but Tyrone—"

"Now what we have to do is wait."

"Wait for what? We want—"

"And I really do wish I could give you more time today, but I'm afraid my secretary has me overscheduled."

"Tyrone was murdered, Mr. Borough President. We are here to—"

"Goodness. Goodness. Have Martha pencil you in for another appointment. I want you all to know that I am very concerned about this situation, and as soon as I hear back from the authorities, you'll hear back from me. That's a promise."

And then the shooing began. Once up and talking, the politicos never sat, and so neither did Carl and his cohorts. Only Elijah, good old Elijah, managing to keep his train of thought, threw in current news about the Mets and said what he had always dreamt.

"Say, man, Strawberry's on fire, but Knight won the game. And listen here, can a brother get a cup of coffee? Black, one sugar."

The look of sweet relief on the borough president's face assured them he too was a Mets fan. That he directed Carl's group to the break room should have made the members of the Institute suspicious. All twenty sipped from Styrofoam cups, whispering their plans to speak at least a paragraph of grievances. "These motherfuckers don't let you get a word in, hear me?" "Shh." But as they drained the last of their lukewarm cups of joe, found their way back to the third left, and headed again for the borough president's office, they realized they had been had. Apparently the powerful and political operated on the snooze-you-lose rule. The borough president was gone for the day, and no he wasn't avoiding anyone or anything, thank you very much; he merely thought all of you had left. And of course he'll see you again at his earliest convenience. Well, he's busy then; he's got game tickets that day, and then too; no he's on committee then; no, no, no good. Why don't you call in a month from now, we'll see what we can do? Carl was tempted to yell, but even he saw what an exercise in futility that would be. This would be the last time anyone asked for coffee.

They all turned to go. Quiet. Chastened. And that was probably why they all heard the borough president's office door locking. It sounded like a gunshot. Elijah, the brother who had asked for the coffee, flinched. Two, three others began to duck and caught themselves. All of them turned around sharply, glaring at the door. Carl looked at his people again and noticed how ashamed they looked for startling at such an innocent sound.

"That's it. Let's go."

But that wasn't it. Hadn't they all let Carl convince them to keep quiet with what they really wanted? Carl took away their dreams; the borough president's callousness told them to wake the fuck up, and now the locking door sound, ricocheting around their heads, was the final signal to get up on out of there.

Really? They took the stairs, and their grievances echoed on the steps. What did he think we was gone do, kick in the door? That motherfucker didn't even know Tyrone was dead, that Wo Ren had been the cause, and that their lives weren't the better for it. The justice they had sought ended up being denied. So how do we get our justice? That's what we wanted to talk to him about. By the time they hit the ground floor, their angry faces made strangers give them a wide berth. Reverend, we gone take this? Don't tell me we gone take this. After studying the rage of his twenty-member delegation and the confusion of the forty-seven they had left below, Carl made a decision. "Let's go to city hall. We talking to the mayor."

"Now?"

"Now."

It was a short trip, just a couple of blocks, but long enough for the twenty to tell the forty the lowdown of what had happened. Elijah was rubbing his shoulder as if he had been hit. Maybe it was the look of righteous indignation on Carl's face or his stride or how confident he sounded when he said the word "now," but they really all thought they were going to curse out the mayor any minute now. Their cluttered march out of the municipal building drew stares; their mutters made those headed to Century 21 pause. By the time they were one block away from city hall, they had grown a raggedy tail of tourists and businessmen taking a late lunch.

"What's going on?"

"Fuck this. We're taking it to the mayor."

Carl's group sounded so strident, so confident, that those inclined to slow down and gawk at a traffic accident let their curiosity prod them to follow a bunch of black people who in normal circumstances would be handing them the mail or pouring their coffee. What do you think they're up to? But Carl's members didn't bother to answer. Their collective sneer said it all: Back the fuck up; these motherfuckers gone to hear us. You feel me? City hall came into view; mile-high stairs met power in the shape of a building. But this time Carl's people didn't gasp; they were not impressed; they were imagining just how tight they would have to pull the mayor's tie. Till it felt like a noose. "I'm gone tell this motherfucker something."

Sixty-seven people didn't even get past the security guards. The whole day was a bust, and the shape of their shoulders showed it. They had shown up looking like walking violence, and no way were the security guards going to let them pass. All together they walked back outside and drifted down the grand stairs. Everybody but Carl, who stood stuck on the third step from the top. He watched as those crazy enough to believe in him drifted away, and before he could stop himself, he was shouting, his voice loud enough to stop and turn those who had followed, big enough to stall passersby. "Wait! Wait!" Now that he had all their attention, he realized this was not his perfect day. It couldn't be. This was the day he'd watched his members eat a bowl of shame and there was nothing he could do about it. This was the day he convinced his people to settle for less because their own were scrawled out over a police blotter. Even when you hacked away at your ambition and made it reasonable, look what happened. Still, out it came. The speech that had been on his mind forever and had no words. The distance between Carl and the crowd captured the moment. No reaching arm could touch him, but his voice carried.

"So what did he say?"

"You just had to be there, man."

"Man, what the fuck?"

"I mean it was about this beat. How we all grooving to this one beat."

"What's the beat? Snap it out."

"Shit, man, you just had to be there. It's like thump, thump; thump, thump. Like that."

The sixty-some-odd members carried away the essence of Carl's speech, and so did the hundred or so who paused for ten minutes to hear a speech that seemed to explain their lives.

Nobody could recall the exact words. But there was a rhythm. A go-to beat they all knew. And no matter who, they all danced to it. Nobody spat you in the eye anymore—you know what I'm saying?—but they all knew that sound. Thump, thump, it was the rhythm of our country.

Thump, thump; it's the door locking. You flinch or you don't hear it at all, and still that's the dance; that's the music. Thump, thump. The sound of opportunity closing for no good reason. Thump, thump. That's the sound of your luck running out, your dreams crumbling. Thump, thump. That's what you snap your fingers to, cause dreaming the symphony of a better life ain't nothing but trouble. Thump, thump; start small and stay that way. And for all y'all who think I'm about to jump into some riff, forget it. There is no riff. There is no way. There is no space for your voice. There is no vote. There are no dreams. There is only room for the beat. It blares out of our cars and apartments. Thump, thump. And we all move to it because we can't help ourselves. Carl spoke without waiting for a call-and-response to kick in and walked away from his people and the strangers gathered around them before anyone could think to applaud.

Thump, thump.

CHAPTER 28

It took a minute, but Wanda reclaimed her label as the lady in the know. She bought the hits and sometimes even bargained. "Two for one, motherfucker." The two weren't pros yet, but already they'd developed a code: "You coming over? You ready?"

"I'm on a mission."

"Me too."

It's still the middle, and strange as it is, the color seals it. Anita, whose skin color never turned heads or raised eyebrows, is the perfect thief. The two women never speak about just how close Wanda straddles color infamy. Not quite blue black, but the Italians on Pleasant Avenue scowl at her when she buys bread from their bakeries. Anita skirts all that. Brown. Beautiful brown. Her skin is the exact color of a paper bag. Covered in an invisible brown, she pillages Macy's and bodegas and grocery stores with impunity. Half-gallon bottles of Tide are plucked and tucked inside her dead son's backpack, along with socks, gloves, cassette tapes, ties, and underwear. Joy in a bottle. Sometimes bold as day, she grabs two bottles of Tide for each hand and walks right out the sliding front door. No one stops her. They think her stalk is meant for the cash register. Tide, the scent of the best of homes. The smell of warmed underwear during winter and summers full of sugarcane and dill pickles wafts out her thieving bag. Tide is money.

They sell their bounty to barber and beauty shops. They don't look like crackheads yet. Wanda and Anita look like two women down on their luck. It is in the middle, when they still have Anita's widow money coming and she still hasn't been fired—Marvin, her boss, turns a cheek and turns it again—when they have one, two, even three days of sobriety that they learn the most about themselves and the city where they live.

"I like to sleep."

"I like my dreams."

"I don't like my mother. At all."

"Me either."

"No one sees me, and I don't like that."

"Everyone sees me, and I don't like that."

"I miss my son, and he is drawing breath."

"I miss my son, and he is gone forever."

Then crack finds its bliss. Anita's heartbeat slows, thuh-dum, thuh-dum; it piques and sharpens and sings, Ty-rone, Ty-rone.

"I do believe when we all get together: trouble."

"What 'we all'? Blacks? Women?"

"Oh, anybody at all. Just folks. When folks get together, here come trouble."

"You live in the city and say such a thing."

"Girl, I know it." The two women spoon on Anita's mattress. It has no sheets. They speak into each other's hair.

"They made a shadow, you know."

"Girl, hush."

"No, really. You ever see one of them seagulls up close? One of them big like a laundry basket flew right over the sun, and for a second, not a tree around, I was in the dark. It happened then. I know, Wanda. Right then somebody cut my boy down." Anita snuggles closer to Wanda's back; her face contorts as if to dredge up tears, but nothing comes. She is dry-eyed. Worse, she is happy. A warmth steals over her shoulders.

"Hush."

"I bet he fought. All the way down, I bet he fought like the devil. But twelve ain't so big."

"They still tiny when they twelve. Even Daryl was little, little when he was twelve."

"Shit he little now."

"Shut the fuck up."

"Sure he was. Basketball." Anita snorts and buries her hands in Wanda's nest of hair.

"Little nigger needs to get into golf."

Sooner than they think, they are asking for little loans. Just a little bit of money to tide them over, just a couple of dollars till next Monday. "Just ten dollars will do me. Come on. Help me out, now."

"You used to be good," Anita's mother said as she reached into her purse to hand over a few dollars.

"Still am."

When she's sober, Anita can hear the neighborhood whispers trailing in her wake. "Girl, ain't that—?"

"Stop it. Ain't that Anita?"

"Oh Lord Jesus, there she go."

It's rare when Anita goes outside grounded, which is what she calls her brief moments of clarity. When she's clean, she marvels at her thinning hands as they rove over her rib cage. She feels as if she were flying before, and now with bird feet she ruts around for edible scraps. She doesn't like it. Bliss beckons.

She and Wanda figure out how the city is divided and how it directs its troubled citizenry: NO LOITERING; BATHROOM FOR CUS-TOMERS ONLY; NO SHIRTS, NO SHOES, NO SERVICE; NO SKATES; NO BASKETBALL; NO PLAYING MUSIC. Before the bliss they wondered who in the world those signs were meant for. Now they know: for them. Women who roam the streets with thunderhead hair, who smile for no reason at all, who grab their crotches in broad daylight. It's not just the cops; regular people look at them and shout, "Can't you read the sign?"

They have left the nadir of the middle. Now they are at the beginning of the end. They just don't know it. Street people know them now and try to tell them to be careful. People the two women don't know at all try to give them the score of what can happen now that they are out of doors. When they were inside, they left their houses when they should and came home when they should, listened to other mothers and fathers who worked and stayed away from the windows and huddled their children indoors when dusk arrived. When you are inside, you don't have to see the trouble; its rumor is enough to make you tremble and make you good. But outside, outside stories have shape and heft. Despite the dreaminess crack offers, Wanda and Anita listen to saucer-eyed stories that until now they have only heard the edges of gossip about.

"Stay off that block."

Both women know that, Wanda especially, but one day in July they find out why.

"They haul women in there. On that block in that building with all the teddy bears hanging out the windows, they take women inside and ten, twelve men try to fuck them at the same time."

"No."

"One time they pushed a little boy to try to fuck this woman they were all fucking at the same time. She was on her hands and knees, and she was shivering like a dog, and them boys said, 'Fuck her,' but the boy didn't know how cause he was eight years old. So he put his little thing in her mouth, and everybody was shouting, and he got so scared he peed in her mouth."

"Then what happened?"

"Then she puked, and all them boys jumped on her and beat her down. Then she disappeared."

Wanda is high but suspicious. Even Anita shakes her head with doubt. "No way. I don't believe you. How you know this?"

"I was next."

CHAPTER 29

they are told to stay away. but like birds looking for just a crumb of this, a speck of that, they circle and peer at the building. august sun is fierce. they long for shade. but. but. bliss is there. so is shadow and cool. just inside. the teddy bears leaning out every window tell them, come on, come in, come see.

everything falls apart. bosses shout and mean, go home and don't come back. wanda and anita tuck in their wings and wobble away. marvin is an asshole. i hated that place. every day i hated that place. me too. i hate my boss. what is his name. i can't remember.

stay away. do you hear me. stay away. shoo. shoo. okay. they try so hard, but the bliss and the teddy bears say, come on, come in, come see. no. no. they are bold. they walk out of stores with goods in their hands and no one says stop. no one wants to touch them. strut, strut down the street. they trade their bounty. they find their bliss. for days, like birds, they are aloft. as big as two women in the sky. swathed in bone smoke, wanda and anita dream mighty dreams. tyrone touches and touches. he is soft and kind. daryl jumps up and down. he is unafraid. his hands are dry. love you, momma. love you, momma. these days do not last. where is my bliss? where is it? come in, come on, come see. they go. unafraid, they are searching. where is my bliss? where is it? wanda looks at anita. we are on a mission. come in, come on, come see. i don't know. no. you know. i will go first. close your eyes.

the smoke men are waiting. waiting. they are laughing. the sound does not touch their eyes. wanda does not shiver. her eyes are like the button eyes of the teddy bears who greet them and say, come on, come in, come see. her eyes are dead. she kneels. they circle her.

i am next.

they push her. down. down. wanda does not fight. she doesn't shudder. her eyes are open. close your eyes, wanda. the men who are smoke circle wanda. closer. closer. they come in. they come on. they come see. they come. closer. close.

i am next.

wanda makes no sound. not even pfft, ooof, umph, ahh. she is so still, a man of smoke raises his hand and strikes her. stop being dead. be alive.

i am next.

she is scared and not scared. she is waiting. she is next. i am next.

light carves the room. my turn.

and they rise off of her like smoke. the mountain comes, fighting. the smoke men are scared and disappear, poof. like that. the mountain makes the light. she is the light. she is the mountain. open your eyes, girl. my eyes are open. and the mountain turns, looking for me. she finds me. what you doing here. you get on up. i am next. next for an ass kicking. get up. hear me.

i see the mountain and she comes for me. i have not shivered. i shake now. hard. i say, umph. ow. where we going? somewhere, the mountain says. get up, fool. and i am up. i want to be out of this place. there is light. outside. ha. ha. i can laugh again. i give my button eyes back. take them. the mountain is here. she carves the light. ha. ha. the mountain is soft. as gentle as a mother and all for me. there is light, and me and anita and the mountain are in the light. where we going? somewhere safe. you shut up now. i am talking.

they are up now. three women, one as big as a mountain carries the other two. anita's head lolls back and forth. well? what is love for? i think. i think. shut up. i am talking. love is interested, and well, God isn't interested in none of us, not one little bit. He looked at us long and hard and then left us at the zoo where we belong, or better, at the grocery store, where every edible thing under the sun is right there on the shelves, and it is not until we eat, eat, eat, tight stomachs now that we realize someone is missing and it is Him. He left us, y'all, and He's been gone for a while.

okay.

okay.

twin?

shut up, girl. the mountain tucks each woman underneath her arms. do you know what love is for? the question is urgent, spoken as if asking for directions to the train. well, do you?

anita, thin light, snuggles against the mountain that for all her bigness is soft. no, she murmurs. who knows that? bliss slips, and anita chafes at the philosopher's question. wanda wakes; her bliss is gone and she hurts everywhere. it is day and two women are stunned by a goose-egg sun that greets them as they step outside. it is so hot. too hot. heat won't bury the question what is love for? that is impor-tant, wanda thinks. anita thinks the same.

do you? do you know what love is for? the two women ask the mountain. the mountain sets two women on their feet. oww. they wobble.

"No," Twin says. "I don't know what love is. That's why I asked. Get on outta here."

CHAPTER 30

Time is an odd thing. Really. Stare at a clock for a while and you'll see. Things that transpire in moments can feel like weeks. Weeks and weeks of desperately pursuing some desired thing can feel like seconds. Months and months when the moon directs the river tides and city children crane their necks at the stars only to see nothing at all, can feel like no time at all. Don't believe it? Ask Morning or Anita and Wanda. They would be able to tell you how July gathered itself like a woman in a full skirt and leapt three months in the air. They would tell you that before any of them could say, Well, well, look at the time, they all landed in October.

Ask Carl. Go on; ask him. For him time had moved so quickly he got whiplash.

In July he got a week. A week that passed faster than a minute. A week where he went full chicken and then called up his own courage. A week of famed clamor and fawning pats on the back. A week of instant friends who even during first introductions Carl knew he could never depend on, but nevertheless he found himself loving the attention they paid him. "That shit you said downtown was gold, man. Like fifty-cents-a-pop gold." Men whose height and weight he envied looked up to him.

"Sell it, huh?"

"Hell, yeah. I can set you up. Make that paper."

"We've got membership dues—"

"That shit don't work. Everybody know that."

"Well, now . . ."

"You write up that thump, thump; I'll press the record."

"You think so?"

"Brother man, brother man. I heard you had white folks clapping to the beat. Hell yeah, we can make that money."

Doubtful of the scheme and the tissue-thin business card the young man pressed in his palm, Carl still couldn't help but preen underneath his newest closest friend's warm gaze. Carl had had no idea how good it would feel to have his honorific stripped and replaced with the caressing call of "brother." It was a great week, the best week, full of learning complicated handshakes and knowing nods. When the press came around, he felt for the first time the kind of fame he read about in history books, the sort he had seen on the news during his childhood. A press he had fantasized about leapt out of his dreams and hounded him as he went about his day. They all wanted to know about his speech, the speech that no one wrote down. White people who belonged in Midtown walked with him down East Harlem sidewalks or waited for him as he stepped out of his brownstone in the morning or became the surprise! as he unzipped at a pizzeria's urinal. When that glory of a week came to a close, three months of high fives and hour-long interviews took their turn. Three months of hard work and promises kept. Carl had told his people back in July that what they wanted—the free pre-K, a benign stepped-up police presence, farmers' markets, and stickball games that didn't devolve into gang-related mayhem—was on the way, but at the start of July they had to keep their dreams manageable. That was then. Now dreams of good living strutted about like a flasher exposing his privates. Calls were returned; meetings were scheduled and attended. Those seven mothers heard the news and nodded. What we dreamt may come to life. Idle talk about the baseball season morphed into talk about politics, and somehow having both conservations made sense. For three months the very mention of Carl's name opened back doors and pulled out seats. Heady stuff. It all seemed so quick and easy that Carl and his followers found themselves wondering what else to ask for. Cause the pre-K thing was going to happen, and so were heaps of tomatoes and zucchini on Saturdays that would put grocery prices to shame. What next? What next? The question shaped seventy-two families' comings and goings from the Institute. You know what we really need? A job training center, a place we can learn all about computers. A twenty-four-hour methadone clinic stocked with clean needles and no questions asked. Six months ago such suggestions loaded with largesse would have been laughed at. Now with summer toddling into fall, with Carl's name and cause opening every door, and fuck Wo Ren, hear me, folks nodded and added to the list of things to accomplish the stuff of their dreams. To have jobs where they could sit down and wear ties, employment where they had paid vacations and the money to actually go somewhere. Florida, maybe? Or visit their people in Georgia? Seventy-two families spoke about their dreams aloud, and Carl was there, encouraging them to say more. "Any day now," he would murmur as he listened to their longings. The start of October arrived and so did the cherry on top: Deborah Sutter from Channel 7 found him at the Institute.

"This is just the kind of tragedy that needs the city's attention, understand." Two Manhattan phone books stacked on the floor acted as a crudely made curb, and the prop allowed Reverend Carl to rest an elbow on his thigh and hitch up a pant leg revealing a twin-kling green dress sock. He wore his burgundy pimp suit, so muted from years of dry cleaning it seemed respectable.

"Hmm . . . Do you have any words for the police?" the reporter asked, furiously scribbling in her notebook.

"Heal this community. Walk these blocks; check in on not just the ailing but the well. Take care of the little ones. See to the working mothers, and yes, Lord bless it, working fathers need a helping hand too."

"And what about the Asian man who murdered Tyrone? Do you have any words for him?"

Only Carl noticed how he stalled over the question. One part of Carl wanted to say, Thank You for putting me in front of this reporter; another wanted to point out, Look what You did to Sister Anita, to Sister Wanda. Neither thought he could say, since both damned him. He couldn't even speak the obvious: Tyrone's murderer was a means to something greater. "I think . . . I think while he spends his time in solitude, he ought to turn to Christ. The anger that caused him to put hands on Tyrone, choke the life from our son, he ought to lay down. Most days, my mind turns to Tyrone, but I also pray for . . ."

"Wo Ren."

"Yes, I pray for . . . Wo Ren. Every day I pray for him."

Deborah Sutter may not have known why Carl stalled before responding, but his awkwardness while answering her question about Wo Ren was apparent. His propped leg wobbled. Don't push, at least not now, Ms. Sutter thought as she watched him. Put him at ease, until you pounce.

"So, you're praying for Wo Ren. I hope you're also saying a little prayer for the Mets? Do you think they'll win the World Series?"

"Hah. Anything could happen. I'll say a little prayer for them too. Lord, let the Mets win."

"People are saying they have a real shot. Darryl Strawberry is incredible on the field, and the curse of the Bambino—"

"I don't think the Lord dabbles in curses. His is a higher justice. What will be, will be."

"Hmm. Speaking of justice, I'd like to talk to you about what people are calling your 'thump, thump' speech. Do you have any thoughts about that moment?"

"Oh, yes. Oh, yes, Sister." The two, reverend and reporter, weren't having a conversation or an interview; they were holding a séance, though who weaved what sorcery was the question. Whoever was graced with the witchcraft, those gathered around them heard private talk that had stumbled into the public, and such murmurings not only needed night but also candlelight. The stacked phone books allowed Carl to cop and keep a pose, and when his head dipped toward Deborah's shoulder, it looked as though he whispered against her pale neck. And Deborah Sutter, reporter, instead of reeling back, which was what any white woman would have done south of East Ninety-Sixth Street, curved her body into a caress that didn't touch. "I spoke the people's mind."

"Hmm . . . yes. But what exactly did you say?" The two swayed together, rhythmic, synchronized as if music played.

"That only God knows how He wants to handle me. That I pray He moves me in profound ways." Carl whispered his answer, but the members of the Institute, those who had followed him and heard the speech, surrounded Carl and Ms. Sutter, eating up the sighing words. Only the knowledge that this was an interview and not a congregant confessing kept seventy-two families from kneeling in prayer.

"Yes, well, could you give me just a little part of the 'thump, thump' speech you delivered on the steps of city hall? That is, if you can remember? Our viewers would be grateful."

Carl reached out and grabbed Deborah's wrist. His two fingers found her pulse. It was throbbing. "Thump, thump, my Sister. Thump, thump."

CHAPTER 31

When Carl left Deborah Sutter's clutches, he wondered just how he found himself sleeping with Morning Taylor, a woman almost twenty years his senior. He could have found another woman. Maybe. She was sexy, yes. And she seemed to possess that black woman age retardant. She'd look thirty until she was eighty-five years old. But that wasn't it either. The answer stood in front of him as clear as sunrise. She loved him, and she loved his cause.

That night in Morning's arms he felt powerful. As he held her, Morning laughed. Hers wasn't the tittering of a teenager: when Morning laughed, her whole body joined in on the fun. Carl held on. His stomach tried to match hers in its heaving, and as he arched toward her, he marveled at how interesting an elbow could be. Their affair had been shocking for both of them. From the sidelines she watched the circle of the media tighten around her lover whose specialness had been her secret. Morning was proud, yes. But fearful too. She hadn't felt this emotion in such a long time she couldn't place it. For a moment Morning thought she had been overcome by a kind of kink. That was mother love, Morning. Don't you know? Handcuffs and lollipops and Vaseline competed with the desire to inspect his underarms and pull his toes, smell his breath. I want him. Maybe forever.

Their postcoital conversation hinted at a future. Nobody is in love like this, Carl thought while he watched Morning's bushy hair kindle in the dawn light. Her body stretched out of her bedroom window, and suddenly he knew why he loved her. He reveled in the stories they told each other. Her love for Carl didn't feel like resignation. Morning didn't treat him as if he were a limping, lisping child whose faltering she could do nothing about, whose speech had endured years of correction, but she would love him anyway. His previous lovers treated Carl like winning a first, second, or even third prize. A ribbon for effort. But with Morning, sex was so good it made a man want to write a bad check, and their conversations gave him a hard-on. Their talk often skipped from the practical, to the profane, to the profound. Carl watched her head swivel right then left out the window. I'm falling in love with you. I really am. The emotion prompted him to tell her another secret. And he felt blessed when Morning didn't laugh.

"Back in April, I thought I was gone get stabbed."

"What?"

This would be their last morning confessional. Maybe that was why Carl told her.

"For real?" Morning stared at the sunrise intently, but her mind was on the short man twisted underneath her covers.

"Yeah. I thought I would be assassinated."

"Get out of here."

"No, it's true." Carl had wanted it to happen because that would be the final stamp of an important man, and when April 4 came and went without incident, Carl had hidden his disappointment. He ached for a knife-wielding (could it please be a woman, preferably weak-wristed) somebody to come along and pierce him into stardom. That's what he'd wanted. Those were his dreams. He should have become a great man on April 4. Everything in him dreamt of that.

"You dream of dying?"

No. No. Not at all; not at all. Carl just wanted the sort of overwhelming success that included ticker-tape parades, dinner and photographs with the president, congressional talks about a federal holiday in his honor.

"All that?"

Carl knew how silly it all sounded, but he couldn't stop the shape of his dreams.

"Okay," Morning said, and offered him such a sad smile he asked her what was the matter. "Nothing."

"Don't nobody look that sad when nothing's the matter."

She didn't say what was on her mind—that in all the time she knew him April 4 was never important, that he was talking about someone else's life and not his own—but what she said was close. "It's just, you know all about a great life, and I just wondered if you know anything at all about a decent one."

"What?"

"I mean what if you are just meant to be a good man? And that's it. Ain't nobody gone stab you. And maybe you grow the Institute one person at a time; maybe you help the folks around the neighborhood, and ain't nobody ever gone give you a ribbon for it."

Carl felt as if she had cursed him out. "So you want me to be a nobody." He sat up in her bed and reached for his shirt. He felt his semen drying on his thigh.

"Being good and decent ain't being a nobody." As Morning spoke, she leaned out of the window. It was their first fight, but because it was all said in a murmur, neither realized they were arguing. Morning, feeling deep in a mother's love, just wanted Carl to be a good man the way mothers have hopes for their children. An October wind tingled, and she stepped away from the pane. She felt naked. The bathrobe draped over her bed called to her, and she shrugged inside of it. "I'm just trying to say—"

"I hear you." Carl buttoned up his shirt and picked his pants off the floor. As he left, the smile he gave Morning was apologetic.

"Carl?"

"Ever think maybe I could be a good man and a great man too?"

The door closed before Morning had a chance to answer.

Later Morning would think about this moment again. Did she

push the door closed, or did Carl pull it shut? For now Morning's mind was filled with thoughts of decency and Carl's with greatness. Neither realized how what happened in the meantime could dash dreams. The city swirled around them and made news that had nothing to do with them. All around them, folks got up in the morning and made mischief. Got up and fucked up the day. Carl and Morning had forgotten the power of meanwhile. Meanwhile, people fucked and killed and cheated on each other. Meanwhile, thirty-six men stretched and trained for a game. Who wanted to hear about a mother's love and a preacher's regret when men with names that sounded like candy or good things to eat could slide into third and bring thousands to their feet? Hanker for a good or great life all you want, Carl and Morning, but meanwhile thirty-six men who trashed hotels, snorted cocaine, beat up patrons in bars, but could hit a ball that far, could snatch the attention of a city and leave you with nothing.

CHAPTER 32

Roger Clemens. One minute he was pitching a no-hitter; the next minute he was tied. In the Sox bullpen, that's Al Nipper chatting with him.

This time there were no klieg lights or calls to the press. This time the police worked quietly and stayed quiet. A bunch of some-bodies called the tip line numbers sowing doubt, dropping hints at the end of July, and while they may have been tempted to chalk it up as a prank, the indictment of Wo Ren (oh, yeah, remember him?) had begun fraying the moment they arrested him. The span of his hands didn't match the photograph of bruises around Tyrone's neck. He was in Flushing arguing with a grocer and two customers at the estimated time of death. It took a while to get the story. But slowly, where Wo Ren was on the night of Tyrone's murder came out. For three months they watched and noted Lara's habits. Where she was during what time of day the cops knew.

Three outs away.

. . .

The three cops who knocked on Morning's door were irritated. They were missing the game of their lives, and they knew it. The police captain made the call: Round her up at night. We don't want a circus. That game six of the World Series was happening while he meted out instructions was just icing on the cake. Fix this fuckup; arrest the right goddamn person. The captain didn't say that, but that was what he meant when he sent out his three best men for the arrest. Make it happen, and keep it neat and quiet. The bosses always want it all. Let's just get this over with, they muttered to themselves as they stomped up the staircase. The handcuffs were out. Two of the officers stroked their holstered guns and were prepared to gain entrance with the battering ram they brought along. There was no need for any of it. Their distracted knock opened the door because Morning thought Carl had come back to either finish their argument or eat her bean stew in apology.

Ball one.

Her arched brow kept the police from barging in. "Can I help you?"

"Ma'am, we have an arrest warrant for Lara Taylor. Is she home?"

Boggs, two singles, ground-out hit into a force play, and walked intentionally; he's two for four.
Fouled away.
One ball, one strike.

It didn't take long for Morning to call him. She knew she had to, lest Carl hear from somebody else first. As she dialed, she prepared herself for every shade of rage, and as the phone rang, she wondered about her own lack of emotions. Why wasn't she surprised? Or angry? Or sad? Maybe it was the quiet relief on her daughter's face as they handcuffed her that kept at bay every emotion Morning might have felt. She wasn't even sure she felt numb.

"Hello?"

"Hey. You should take a seat. Police came and got Lara."

.　.　.

So a home run and a double in the tenth inning. And the batter now, Marty Barrett. Marty Barrett lined out to center, two singles to left, and two walks.

In there. Ball one.

So Carl was wrong. And his wrongness couldn't even cloak itself in opinion. Like: Well, see, we thought it was that Chinese guy because . . . Or: If you look at this a certain kind of way, you'd see . . . Carl's stomach flipped and folded when he heard Morning's news. There was nothing to save him. All year Carl had been pointing the finger at the wrong man. He was wrong. A wrong with no wiggle room. He had built a political platform on that Chinese guy. He had been so sure. Folks frequented the Institute because finally they got the guy who did it, and Carl had helped. God. He was wrong, so wrong. While he listened to Morning's whispers, he knew he was the first to know. But for how long? Was being this wrong supposed to hurt his stomach this much? And when folk found out, wouldn't they wonder when Carl knew? Soon. Too soon, everyone would know he was wrong. Carl cooked dinner, and for the first time his appetite fled. The thought of putting food in his mouth made him choke. He had bigger things to think about, and food got in the way. When was the last time Carl prayed? Not before the congregation or at the start of family dinner appeals, but the kind of prayer he counseled his parishioners to do—solitary, in a dark place, the holy beseeching done on one's knees. "Don't look for His word; God ain't talking to you. Don't look for a sign, the Lord is not a charlatan; He don't do tricks." In all these years he had never taken his own advice: "Ask for peace—not world peace or even peace in your family. Ask for your own. Pray to the Lord for calm. And sit in the dark, holy, on your knees; praise Him in the quiet until the Lord Jesus sees fit to see you." I should listen to myself more often.

.　.　.

"O" in one. Backman deep at second. One ball, one strike.

Boggs at second, two out in the tenth, a run over. Red Sox four, Mets three.

The problem, he thought simply, was women. Yes, the problem was certainly women. When was the last time he had heard a story of how a murder transpired without a mother or girlfriend there to offer "See, what you don't understand is . . ." They were always there with an excuse. "He wasn't like that with me . . ." Carl needed a man . . . a friend. Oh to be brave enough to call that tall young man who had looked up to him. Carl didn't bother to find his tissue-paper business card. He knew better. Besides the deacons he couldn't recall the last serious conversation he had had with a man. He had followers and a lover, a God, even enemies, but not a friend. A man could get into a whole heap of trouble when he was friendless; Carl, testify. God is a wordless counsel, and lovers tell you what you want to hear. But only a friend can sometimes rise to the occasion and let you know you're fucking up, willing to be shunned while you crawl to the inevitable truth.

One ball, one strike.
Ball two.
Three in one. On deck, Bill Buckner.

Until the arrival of the deacons Carl couldn't let it go: every decision he made had been fraught with indecision, but the deacons had been the first lucky thing that had fallen his way. Didn't ask; they just came. He realized he had put up with their constant, subtle berating because they had wanted him—no, no, scratch that—they needed him . . . and now without them he wondered if he had spent this year rootless. Carl had quickly conquered the Ethiopian flock's mundane problems, most of their challenges tamable with a few phone calls to the welfare office. But the deacons? Mealymouthed, self-righteous, they curled their stiff necks, and under a mountain of multisyllabic verbiage said please, please, please. And who delivered?

Who put flesh on their skeletal numbers at the Ethiopian? Just who bought that drum set? Being untethered from the deacons' constant need had made Carl reckless. Maybe even dangerous. Look at what he had become when he didn't have twelve men standing behind him.

And it's hit into center base. Dykstra charging, here comes Boggs: he will score. The throw backed up by Aguilera goes to second. And it is five to three Red Sox, and what a big run that was.

He should have been able to right himself earlier or at least take a cold look at just what he thought he was doing. When was the last time he'd knocked at Anita's door? Where were Wanda and her son? Those two women, what were they up to?

One and one.
The Oil Can, at least for the moment, looks like he has tomorrow off.
One and one.

Instead of taking care of Anita or at least finding out how she was doing, instead of helping Daryl or at least not being ashamed of his mother's antics, instead of examining his own heart, Carl had basked in adulation when reporters appeared on his doorstep, when an entire neighborhood waited on him to roll up the gates at the Institute. Shame on you, Carl. You deserve this torrent of bad news, cause Lord knows you did it: you did the worst thing and forgot about Wanda and then let trouble land on a fifteen-year-old black kid. You knew Anita was in a bad way. You tried to get Shelia to carry the load. You didn't do a thing to stop it.

So, the Mets, thirty-nine times they came from behind to win, battling to stay alive.

Who did he have to share that realization with? Nobody. Not his congregants, not Morning, and not the seven mothers who, while keeping the Institute's buffet table full, gave him the kind of information that did nothing but knock him down. Their spoonfuls of encouragement didn't make bad news easier to swallow.

Fifty-five thousand and seventy-eight here at Shea, and they have really been put through the wringer.
One ball, one strike.
Ball two.

He was waiting for the urge of prayer to steal upon him. Morning had called and given him the bare facts, and he couldn't ask for more. So maybe when Morning went to bed, he could speak aloud the thoughts clanging in his head. I was so close. Morning said good night, and Carl waited and waited, staring at the living room wall clock that seemed to hang forever at eleven. Everything in Carl wanted those two tines of time to close together like praying hands and declare at least that the day was over. Give me midnight. Please.

And it's gonna go to the backstop. Here comes Mitchell to score the tying run, and Ray Knight is at second base.
Three and two to Mookie Wilson. And he pops it in the air. Foul off to the right and coming over, he will not have a play. That was a wild pitch.
Five–five in a delirious tenth inning.
Line-drive foul.

But time would not clasp its hands. It just sat there, hanging suspended, forever. Once again Carl was alone and betrayed and so angry he felt snatched off his feet with it. I was wrong, and soon, too soon, everyone will know. For months and months, I said, Look here, look at this bad man, Wo Ren; look at our plight! And I should have been pointing another way. I was wrong and wronged. It was an anger that felt better than righteousness because it was an anger that was holy. And then Carl realized God knew anger too; God *was* anger.

·   ·   ·

So the winning run is at second base, with two outs. Three and two to Mookie Wilson.

Carl did not pray. His thoughts were too sinful. God was just a man who had fooled him and fooled him good. All those years when he had preached and believed that God was friendly and practical. Hah. For too long Carl believed the Beloved was a forgiving God who would not direct His fury at His shepherd. Who for a moment, just a moment, let his righteousness lead him into making the mistake of telling a lie without realizing it. Hah. Carl had thought God was Someone who wanted you as much as you wanted Him. No. Carl knew better now. God was there all right. He existed to run the long con. And the reason He could get away with it all was that, unlike you, God had all the time in the world.

Little roller up along first, behind the bag! It gets through Buckner! Here comes Knight, and the Mets win!

CHAPTER 33

Not much in East Harlem was quietly kept. Buildings studding the neighborhood's sixteen-block area were surrounded by an incessant roar. And while Carl didn't make a peep, and Morning didn't say a word, and the police who'd quietly handcuffed a young woman were more interested in listening to a baseball game, it still got out that Lara Taylor, Morning's daughter, had been arrested for Tyrone's murder.

"They got that bitch dead to rights."

"Oh, don't you say it."

"Hand to God, baby. I hear she's saying she did it."

"Uh-uh."

"Truth. Truth."

"Cause why?"

"Like I know."

"Like you know."

"He was just a little bit."

By the time Carl rolled up the gates at the Institute in the rain on Sunday morning, there was a line of members waiting to file in. They listened. No one folded their arms or jutted out their lips or muttered "bullshit" under their breath. In complete silence, Carl was allowed to plead his case. He didn't know a thing about Morning's daughter. Really. You could have knocked him over with a feather when he heard, God's truth. "And can I say, Lord, let me say, I'm making a difference"—he knew he was—"and I'm making it better. Y'all know this. Know this, my flock, I never loved anybody more than you. Let's sort this out, y'all hear me? I never would have held on to this kind of secret and unraveled all our work. You can still trust me."

When Morning arrived, the crowd parted a path for her. She stood next to Carl, her head hanging.

"Tell them, Morning. Tell them."

"Reverend Carl didn't know nothing about this. Till yesterday I didn't know either." More than a hundred people didn't bother to nod. "She's a good girl. I don't know what got into her."

But Morning looked guilty, as did Carl. Those two may not have known that Lara had done the killing, but look at those two. They knew something.

"All right, now." Elijah of kiddie pool fame stepped to the podium and took Carl's elbow, hitching his chin for Morning to follow. "We hear you. But we got to talk now."

"Brother—"

"Don't you worry none, Reverend Carl. We'll call you."

Everyone waited until the front door gently shut to let loose, everyone except for the seven young mothers, who held hands and bit their lips. What the fuck? And this asshole thinks we believe that shit? The grousing that they had kept bottled during Carl's explanation uncorked. What Morning had done was worse than getting in trouble herself. That they could take. Who hadn't been in the wrong place at the wrong time or let themselves lip off when they should have kept quiet? But this? She was the mother, and she should have known. And having known, she had let them all stand on the shoulders of righteousness for months, almost a year, when she knew all along the shaky ground on which they stood. And the timing. What the fuck, man? Carl wasn't the only one having the great week that dribbled into three months of doors opening and places at the table.

The "thump, thump" speech left them all feeling capable. They had purpose. These last three months had been spent thinking anew about a police presence for the neighborhood, about free pre-K classes for their little ones, about farmers' markets during the weekend. Plans that seemed crazy six months ago felt possible. They too had gotten pats on the back when they returned from downtown. Good job, everybody had told them. What else y'all gone do?

This secret of hers spat on all that. Didn't Morning know better? They (and it was obvious who the "they" were; there was no need to name names; you know who you are) never saw one of us; they only saw all of us. And if the very people who had worked right alongside Morning and Carl for almost a year thought there was no way in the world those two didn't know who the real murderer was, what would the rest of the neighborhood say about these members when the truth got out? What would the entire city think? Elijah and his companions had no trouble imagining that everyone would think they had known the truth all along and kept it a secret. God, Morning. Goddamn it, Carl. The things they had allowed themselves to say about that Chinese guy. Oh, they had given him what's the what. Bet money there would be folks thinking they lied about that man so they could steal his business. And no matter what surfaced, they would never live this down.

Morning had given the nebulous "they" yet another reason to close the upwardly mobile door. The members of the Institute could already hear what would be said over the dinner table: It just goes to show those people can't be trusted. Followed by an obvious, yet dreaded, absolute statement: I told you so. Who did she think she was? Maybe they could convince their neighbors they too had been duped.

But outside the hood? Morning's daughter handed every human resource department manager a reason not to give their spic-and-span boys and girls a job. The members of the Institute could see it already, their children clad in their Sunday best, humiliated when applying for a janitorial position or a job sorting the mail in some Midtown building. "Look, I'm sorry ... there's nothing available right now." The normal progression of a job interview thwarted, no need to take a seat; let's make this quick. The professional smile revealed nothing, no condescension or pity, but everyone involved knew exactly what had happened. "If some girl seemingly well respected, certainly well dressed, was up to no good . . . well, then you know the rest of them are trouble." Just when we had convinced ourselves we deserved a certain kind of life. Now even the respectful would be suspect. Hands rose and fell; muttering climbed to shouting. In their own way they tried to forgive Morning and her trespass. Look, look, okay; we got kids too. Morning knew, certainly, but she was just trying to do right with her own. But Carl? They kept their real ire for Carl.

Elijah stepped to the podium, and when he mentioned the reverend's name, hissing engulfed him. "All right now. Calm down."

"Calm down? Those two were tied at the hip; when Carl started a sentence, Morning finished it. If she were twenty years younger, I'd think they were fucking."

"Come on now, people."

"No, seriously. Elijah, you've seen them together. Most days you can't tell if she wants to eat him or change his diaper. And now. Now? He wants to say he knew nothing about it? She's been at his elbow for over a year, and he doesn't know a thing? Does anybody believe that? Show of hands. Anybody? He knew; Carl knew. And he fucked us all. Just when we were so close to getting shit done."

At the podium Elijah was shouting now. "All right, people. All right. But what are we going to do about it?"

They do the expected: they vote. A bloodless repudiation took place on a rainy Sunday morning. So many hands lifted into the air no one bothered to count them. Only the seven mothers traded looks and stuck their hands in their pockets. As for the rest, "We want him out. This is our place." Seventy-two families were so mad about the Monday they would all have to face they let the difficulties of kicking the man who held the lease and paid the bills fall to the wayside. Next week let's talk about putting Con Edison in our name. Now? Right the fuck now, let's pick someone to go over and ask Carl for a set of keys. In their own way they had sifted through the evidence. "First off, him and Morning thick as stew, and that's God's truth," one member offered, but that tie wasn't tight enough for some. Yes, they had heard the rumors, but Carl's affair with Morning was gossip that had never gotten off the ground. There was no eyewitness to hand holding or heavy petting; no one had seen a breathless exit from Carl's office. So no one's saying hanky-panky, but everyone agreed: I tell you what, if it was my daughter that kilt that boy, as much time as I hang my hat round here y'all better believe the reverend would have known about it.

"Let's pray." And then for the first time, without Carl, they sanctified the place. No one, not even Elijah, whose kiddie pool hunkered in the corner and who acted as ringleader during the meeting, tried to lead the prayer. Murmurs of prayer lifted, then steadied. The assembly felt hushed, since unlike at any other gathering, they were praying to acknowledge their confusion, and their call to Christ huddled close to directionless. Seventy-two families stood, heads bowed in the Institute, their voices not quite silent, asking the Almighty to answer questions that had whipped them up and wiped them out: Sweet Lord, praise His name, what are we going to do about Carl? What are we going to do about us?

The expelled two walked in the rain quietly knowing they would part ways at Second Avenue. "Well, what do you think we should do?" Carl asked. Morning tensed at the "we." Her mind was on their togetherness and the rain coiffing her hair into a fro. All that mother love she thought she felt for Carl melted when she recalled the heat of her neighbors' stares. She now understood why she loved being a mistress: there was nothing to claim; there was no responsibility beyond the reach of your own fingers. She squirmed underneath the glare of seventy-two families. Like it was my fault. But if she loved Carl as much as she thought, if Lara was hers and no one else's, who besides Morning was responsible? The question pinned her. Now I have to carry what a wife should, what a mother should, and I don't want to. Oh, Lara, what have you done?

"You got a friend to talk to about all this?"
"A friend? I ain't got nobody to talk to about this kind of stuff."
Morning shouldn't have been surprised at Carl's assertion, but

still she stumbled over her own two feet when she heard his answer. She pretended to look straight ahead but stole sidelong looks at him. When had she stopped rattling with desire? He was hers. How Morning longed for the unexplained hang-ups, the knowing looks; a sudden change in weight signifying the competition between his neighbors and mistress had begun? That kind of love, that kind of desire Morning knew all about. But this? Morning felt lost and worn out even though it wasn't noon. She would have preferred a show-down. An event complete with hurling pots and pans and a call to the police. Those steps she knew by heart. But the guilt she felt about Lara, her daughter, and about Carl was quite new. The should-haves curled around her steps. She should have been a better mother; she should have been a better lover. Morning didn't like it.

When they reached the corner of Second Avenue, Morning turned to Carl. He looked worse than helpless. Pelted in rain, he looked as if he were weeping. Maybe he was. And Carl looked scared. "Listen; I can't talk to you now. But I will later. I mean it; hear me? I just need to think about it. You too. We both need to sleep on all this. Maybe we can have some good dreams." Morning crossed the street before he could answer.

CHAPTER 34

Turned out everyone needed the night—a whole night, full of stormy weather—to gather and collect themselves, to brace for what surely would be a hard, hard Monday. But Monday was tomorrow. Tonight rumor raced around a neighborhood. Twelve men heard about Lara and her arrest, and though they smiled and felt vindicated, no one laughed. They had told him. They had said, "Carl, don't get involved in politics. Nothing good comes from trying to be like the NAACP, tangling with the whole wide world." But did he listen? No. For an entire year Carl hinted blame at the wrong man. And the hint, the finger-pointing, was so loaded it convinced an entire neighborhood. Hadn't they told him not to point a finger at all? So they smiled at life's comeuppance, but they didn't laugh. They spent the night rubbing bellies and trading loaded stares. That's enough.

Tonight, Anita and Wanda huddled under blankets for warmth and held on to each other. We are friends, they thought. The best kind of friends. Tonight, Morning went home and fingered her hair and thought about bail money and bad luck, but such thoughts didn't slam her into a wall and knock her out. She knew she had to call Carl in the morning for help. She hoped he would give it.

Tonight was a night of reprieve. Soaked in his jacket, Carl opened the door but felt too tired to take it off. He debated whether to take a shower or get in the tub. Unable to come to a decision, he listened to the soft patter of the rain dripping off his jacket onto the floor. The persistent tapping soothed him. No, wait, that was the door. With wet hands he turned the knob without checking the peephole. All seven mothers stood at his threshold, shaking out their umbrellas. "Sisters."

When Keisha took Carl's wet hands and a deep breath, Carl braced himself.

"They say you got to go, Rev. But listen," Keisha said and wouldn't let go of his hands. "Listen, okay."

"All right."

"We voted. I mean you just got outvoted."

"I understand."

"No, wait. What I mean is none of us did. Right?" Keisha looked around, and the mothers nodded. "We didn't raise our hands. Elijah wanted to come get the keys, but we told him we'd do it cause we wanted to tell you . . ." Whatever she had prepared to say faltered, but just before she began to cry, the mothers rallied and leapt to scolding.

"Look at you, soaking wet."

"Catch a cold like that."

They wrestled him out of his jacket, stroked his cheeks while clucking concern.

"Take off your socks."

By the time he put on a new shirt and one of the mothers put a towel in his hands, Keisha found her courage. "Just listen. You have to be good now. I don't know what you're thinking, but I'll say this: There is a time when a man has to stand up. This is your time, Rev. Everyone says Morning's daughter killed that young man. That may be. Still. She needs a lawyer. She needs bail. She needs help. You are that help." She held his hand, tight. The younger women clustered around his chair. "You helped Anita because of her son. You should help Sister Morning because her daughter needs that help."

"Sister Keisha, you just—"

"I just what? I just don't understand how much help you can give? I don't understand how you can be a leader when your members think you were in on it with Tyrone's murderer? And you're wondering how you can lead anybody if there's no one following?" Her stroking of Carl's hand was heavenly. "My momma came back."

Carl straightened in his chair, startled. "Did she?"

"For a minute anyway," Keisha said, shrugging.

"Keisha, I'm so sorry."

"Don't be. I needed that minute. I got her to eat half a sandwich. I kissed her on the forehead and everything. Felt like Christmas." Carl didn't know quite what to say. "I think you have to stand up for Morning, and you have to stand with Lara. You made the Institute to help everyone in this neighborhood." Keisha took a shaky breath. She had practiced in the mirror what she would say to Carl, but looking him in the eye when she said it was harder than she thought it would be. "If rumors are right, she's guilty. So what? So she doesn't need a lawyer anymore?" Carl nodded and wondered how long Keisha would hold his hand. The mothers stood above him, stroking his shoulders. "We live here, Rev. All of us. We live in this neighborhood. And you built the Institute here. It's not just a place for the innocent. You help Lara. She needs the help. Okay?"

"Okay."

"No. Say it. Say it all."

"I'm going to wake up, and first thing in the morning, I'll help Morning. And I'm going to help Lara too."

"As best you can?"

"Best I can."

Keisha didn't let go. She pulled him up out of his chair.

CHAPTER 35

Manuel Jr. didn't knock on his cousin's door before he opened it. "Yo, girl, you can't be beating up the customers." His delivery sounded casual because he had been practicing the sentence for months. He looked down at Twin lying on the bed.

"Who told you that?" His cousin sat up and tucked a pillow behind her head.

"Everybody telling it. Folks saying you had an arsenal in a gunnysack." Manuel Jr. walked further into the room, feeling uncomfortable that he stood while she lay.

"You don't even know what 'arsenal' means, Junior," Twin said, yawning.

"I know everybody said you had a bunch of weapons."

"I didn't have a gun. If somebody said that, they straight up lying on me."

"Truth?"

"For real."

He stretched then up on his tippy-toes and threw his arms up over his head. "Still, you can't go around clobbering everybody who come to the trap." Everything in Manuel wanted to open and close drawers, look under her rugs, search her closet to find what exactly she was using to beat ass with, but doing it would have gotten him popped in the head. He buttoned his nervous energy and sat on the bed next to his cousin.

"So?"

"So, stop doing it."

"Whatever, man."

"Look, you know me. I'm not gone say shit. But keep it up, and he gone find out. Both of us gone get it. You for acting up and me for not telling him. And God knows what Daddy'll think up to get back at us. Then what you gone do?" Manuel Jr. stood up from the bed and walked to the open door. Twin wasn't going to insult her cousin by stating the obvious: don't tattle.

"All right."

"You want me to take over a little bit? I can do it a couple days a week. Or maybe I can keep you company?"

Twin looked out her window; she didn't want her cousin to see how grateful she felt for the offer. She also heard his invitation; if she wanted, she could tell him why what was happening at the trap disturbed her so. Tempting. What she wanted to say was both complicated and simple. It's not that they were her neighbors, that she was frightened to go to the corner bodega and buy lunch from Luis and feel his leer touch her skin. No, there was worse. Did Manuel know that she had prayed with some of them? Long ago on Sundays women would gather, and she had pulled at their arms, snatched off their hats to encourage them to know joy.

It was the only place they were allowed to shout and cry, love the Lord in any way they saw fit. Those were the women getting high. They were the ones buying crack. And when their off-and-on visits turned into stopping by every day, when they offered Twin stolen goods—cans of Café Bustelo and Similac, bottles of Tide—"I'll give you anything, anything"—only then did her uncle allow her to run them off. Would Manuel laugh if she told him all that? Would she? Instead, she scoffed. "Then who gone get in trouble?"

"You won't tell, and I ain't either. Plus Daddy sleep like the dead. I can't do it all the time. But when it gets too tight—"

"I said all right."

He left, closing the door behind him.

Twin knew her cousin was right. If she kept it up, her uncle would find out and then something dangerous would roll up. She'd thought her uncle would have forgiven her for calling the police about Tyrone after a couple of weeks and allow her to return to her regular life, but it had been almost a year now, and his need to punish her hadn't waned. The longer she managed the trap, the more he thought she should stay. At the dinner table while making breakfast she appeared unaffected, unwilling to give him the satisfaction of knowing how much the whole thing bothered her, but the effort it took to push away the flash of anger and violence when she was minding the trap made her feel fourteen again: thin and incomplete. Nothing but knees and elbows. Anyone at any time at all could push her around then.

"Got so a man can't even drive around. Feeling up your privates like they own them," her uncle told her as he pulled his chair to the table for dinner. Twin slid him his plate of steak and roasted potatoes, saying nothing. She had learned at least that much. A question or comment added a month or two to her time in the trap. "This well done?"

"Yeah."

"Cause I ain't eating steak with pink in it." He stabbed the beef. Juiceless and gray through and through. "And there you go calling them! Know what happened to me today? Police pulled me over. Was I speeding? No. Tinted windows. That's why."

"You wasn't driving the hoopty?" her cousin asked as he sat down.

Twin's face had no expression, but maybe the blankness of her look set him off. Her uncle narrowed his jaundiced eyes and hissed, "Shut up, Junior. Can't a man drive around in what he want?"

"Sorry, Daddy."

"Think it's funny. I'll teach you a lesson." Manuel Sr. didn't look at her, but she knew who he was talking to while cutting up his steak into bite-sized pieces. "I was at this before all them young cats. You hear me? I got connections don't nobody know about. Now here you come calling po-po. Like that ain't nothing. I run a business. I keep it clean. You need it every now and again, I got you. See you on the weekend, I got you. But if you gotta everyday habit? If you stopping by breakfast, lunch, dinner, and snacks too? Aw, nah. I don't need that kind of mess," her uncle told them, though he didn't look up from his plate. "I run it respectable. You hear me talking to you?"

"I hear it," she whispered.

"Let me see your license. Let me see your insurance. Get out the car, hands on the hood. I'm seventy-eight years old and slowing traffic." Manuel Sr. cut up the roasted potatoes to match the pieces of steak. "Folks staring at me, and here I'm looking as helpless as a grandpa." His voice never rose to a shout, but Twin and Junior could hear the muttering menace. This was what their uncle sounded like when he was thinking up something awful. Tending the trap was punishment; her uncle had her humiliation on his mind. The cousins may not have known the details of his impending cruelty, but its shape was sharp enough that it could be seen seated at the lone empty chair. It all used to be so clear. Good people did good things, and bad people were white folks. Nowadays that was all mixed up. Because Lord as a witness, her uncle was a bad guy, and she was the one serving him dinner.

Still he didn't look up from his food, mumbling and stabbing gray steak and potatoes.

"Know what I think? You needing a taste of that; that's what. How you feel if you was the one in panties? Huh?"

Manuel and Twin traded looks that spoke paragraphs.

"You in panties. That'll teach you. Spend a day or two cooking crack with the ladies."

When her cousin lifted his brow, she softly nodded her thanks, knowing Manuel would save her.

. . .

Back outside, roaming while Manuel Jr. took her shift, felt like coming home. More, she found out stunning news: she had been missed. Gone for so long folks raised a hand in welcome. "I thought you got clipped."

"You do time?"

"Hell naw," Twin said, shrugging.

"Girl, where you been at?"

"Please." But she basked in her return to the streets. Owners of bodegas, shoe stores, and restaurants left their registers and clapped her on the back. The surprise and hellos were so heartfelt Twin felt brave. Her Spanish rusty, scant and mostly wrong, she bothered with it anyway: "Yo, ése! Qué pasa?" They called her crazy lady in response but smiled all the same.

Along with the "how are you"s came the news. Had she heard; did she know? Yeah that little man she had found dead, everything about that done gone sideways. She listened wide-eyed, and when rumor sharp enough to draw blood was met with skepticism, the folks telling it ended their stories with "That's what I heard."

"The momma of that killed boy tried breaking into some church on First Avenue."

"Like trying to steal or what?"

"No, baby, it was like she rolled up at Sunday service."

"Come on."

"That's what I heard. The momma and her friend getting so high ain't nobody even bothered to tell her the truth about the little sister who really did it. I'm telling you it's bad out here."

"Ain't nobody bad out here. Just us," Twin said as she finished the last of her beer, stepping away from the curb ready to vanish. She didn't want to hear any more.

Was it true? Twin wouldn't have believed any of it, except she had taken Anita and Wanda out of that hellhole months ago. And she had told them to get to church. She wasn't the one who turned them out, but her ready excuse lacked conviction. The thought that she ought to do something, make a way for someone, felt directionless. Do what? For who? Go back to the trap, relieve her cousin who had gifted her a night off, and do what exactly? Her mind so fixed on roaming, she startled when she realized she was back home in her bedroom.

The closet door—it had become Twin's habit to tug on the knob every time she went past it—opened with the politest burp. Well, now. She stood at its dark opening. Twin searched the dark for the thin string that attached to the light above. She found it and tugged. A blue light bulb cast a moody glow as if she lived in a jazz café. The calm pulsating light bathed clothes from Twin's one year working in an office. Gray A-line skirts with fitted jackets to match, tan trench coats, and silk scarves sat neatly on shelves. In the seventies all she wanted to do was move out, get work, rent in Brooklyn, maybe Queens. She had taken a typing class. Eighty words a minute.

Despite the sharp smell of mothballs that almost overwhelmed Twin, she had arranged the closet like it was meant to be used. Twin smiled and remembered those years when she was in a terrific rush to gain respectability. This closet held the real promise. The memories of when she was slim and good-looking were vivid. The dry cleaner's bags wrapped up a year of ambition. I just wanted to get somewhere. Mood lighting revealed a way, and her hand grabbed a belt hanging from a hanger. She hadn't worn it since 1972, and when she slipped the thin velvet around her waist, the space that separated the buckle from the first belt hole was laughable. My, my. Everything she wore was in her dresser drawer, but all that she wanted was in this closet. What was I running to? Her answer felt both sudden and complete: Here. Always here; I just wanted it to be a little better. Cause ain't no bad folks. Just us. Twin laughed. Happy that she didn't feel ashamed, not one little bit, that she still kept secrets. She hadn't told her cousin she had been lifting money the entire time she worked the trap. She had stolen her uncle's coin first out of spite, but over time she thought she might take enough to make plans, to fulfill some unnamed desire.

She closed the door gently so she could open it again when she wanted to. I just wanted here to be a little better. I need to start something. Even if it means not doing everything. She slipped her hand to the back of the closet, grabbing the bag of money she had been tucking away.

Crumpled fives and dirty tens, dollar bills, some of which had scrawled on them: *Happy birthday! Good luck!* Her plastic bag was full of money.

It was all she needed.

CHAPTER 36

Television and three radios tuned to two different stations blared out of the apartment next door, but Morning's place was quiet. Her neighbor stopped by for a visit and wouldn't leave for the better part of the afternoon: "How are you? How are you doing?" Morning thought about her answer. Answers were important.

"I don't know." She meant it. Since Saturday night Morning was unable to talk above a whisper on the phone. It felt as if everyone she had ever known decided to call. They spoke about Lara as if she had passed away. Do you remember when she sang? She was our little Whitney. Neighbors wanted information, and Morning had none to give them. She tiptoed around her apartment, unable to trade poignant gazes with anyone. She tried to remember something kind, decent about Lara. But her anger and shame swept away her memories. Wait. Wait; here was something: Remember when she tried out for the Apollo? And Lord I wasn't there. The phone rang again.

"Hello?"

The caller didn't bother with pleasantries and assumed Morning would know her by the sound of their voice: "Morning, why did she do this?" Oh, baby. That was a question that blanketed the neighborhood. Scores of unsuspecting mothers and friends fielded that question all day long, and never came up with anything that satisfied. Too many families were asking that of children and grown folks who up until then had never been a bit of trouble, who seemed to shoulder their personal burdens without a peep. Why y'all do this?

"I don't know. I really don't." Morning cradled the phone to her ear and wondered if she was responsible for Lara's transgression. I should have paid more attention. I should have seen this coming. "Listen, I've got to go and get dressed."

Carl had called early that morning and said he would stop by and take her downtown to the courthouse. And though Morning would add what money she could, he would take care of the bail and bring a lawyer. "I've got this," he said. His list of instructions was so brief and curt Morning felt as if she were hanging up the phone before she picked it up. She dressed for church; her Sunday best felt like the only appropriate thing to wear. Any minute now Carl would arrive and take her away. In the meantime she stood at her front door clutching her hands. Spatters of past conversations floated to the surface, but Morning shook her head before those memories could take shape and heft.

"You're late," Morning remembered saying to Lara.

"Mama, I'm sorry. Classes went late and—"

"Never mind, girl."

To not remember the exact details of her daughter seemed safest. Otherwise Morning would have to claim her. Otherwise this irrational thing Lara had done would make a bit of sense, and she didn't want that.

When is he getting here? she thought. Maybe I didn't love her enough—I was too busy being proud of her. She thought again about the mother love she was sure she'd felt for Carl, a love that melted so quickly when scrutinized by the members of the Institute. Morning snorted. I could have known love, shown love if only if only if only. She pillaged her thoughts for the last time she had told Lara she loved her. Even if Lara doing what she did wasn't my fault, it's my fault.

When Carl knocked softly, Morning startled. She walked two

steps to the door, trembling and cautious. The sound of his rap felt like the start of a family outing. Waiting, wanting to be thrilled, but ready for disappointment, Morning stepped closer. Six locks tumbled open in her hand. Carl was there, dressed in a suit Morning hadn't seen since he preached at the Ethiopian: pale green with blue lapels. His smile was the way it had always been, slightly apologetic but beckoning. His eyes, however, were those of a stranger. "Let's go."

CHAPTER 37

These two ladies. Lord Jesus. They may not know what love is, but they think they know what they have been saved from. For now anyway. Wanda had been evicted and didn't know it until she tried the key in her lock and some strange man answered her front door with a knife in his hand. She didn't bother to say sorry or what happened to my things. That's okay. There was room enough for three in Anita's apartment. Daryl, who was served his mother's eviction papers from the landlord, was fetched from a friend's house and slept on the couch.

Two mothers took turns watching him through the night. His chest's rise and fall helped them not flee the apartment and find bliss. Nothing else worked. Not the rehab group sessions or neighborhood women's scolding. Not even the kind words the two women traded back and forth.

"You can do this."

"So can you."

Their smiles were shaky and thin. Both women knew bliss and delight were right outside the door, calling, calling for them. Only

Daryl's open sleeping mouth kept them from turning the locks. That, and the lawyer showing up out of nowhere to play Santa Claus. "Your son's okay now. He's in the clear. Sign here. And here." Wanda wanted to whoop and holler; she tried to remember pertinent questions but had forgotten how. Even small pleasures bared their teeth and took a bite out of them. Sandwiches made by some Good Samaritan turned their stomachs. Clothes washed in Tide, smelling like home and good news, itched. They spent three months aching for the bliss.

When they had the courage to go outside, women they knew clucked over them. "Give it to God," these women they knew from church or their former jobs told them. "Pray it to Jesus." They had, and Christ had heard their prayers and given them bliss and made them happy when nothing else did. There was no need to tell this to the women they knew. It would be cruel to break hearts on purpose.

Inevitably, Wanda and Anita wandered back inside. These two women were forgetful. Standing with hung heads as women they knew tried to shame them, they forgot what they wanted outside in the first place. They forgot the courageous thing that had told them, go on; go on now. It didn't matter. Let's go back in. They have all night to watch Daryl curled in blankets. They have from dusk till dawn to look over him and wait for some dream to make him smile. When the son woke, he returned the favor. At breakfast, at lunch, at dinner, he fed them soup. Tomato, chicken noodle, and minestrone marked the time of day. As both women watched a monstrous spoon filled with nourishment float toward them, they thought about the women they used to be. They used to be women with one eye on right now and the other on Christmas or someone's birthday or an anniversary. Do you remember when we thought that far ahead? Remember when thinking like that was a pleasure? The group sessions told them "one day at a time," but even that was too much. Future thoughts, even ones that contemplated today's sundown, were dangerous. Anita and Wanda were smart enough not to think that far in advance. Instead they listened to their son, "One more bite." Daryl's instruction sounded like wise advice and seemed safest.

Some days they couldn't manage that. But they tried to. Every day. "One more bite, Momma." The puddle of tomato soup was enormous, but Wanda swallowed it all.

"Come on, Ms. Anita. One more bite." Anita tried as best she could but gagged all the same. She traded a knowing look with Wanda. And as they held each other's gazes, their thoughts were twinned: does he know how hard this is? no, not one little bit. there is bliss outside. we know where it is. we know the secret places. yes. but to get there we have to talk to the women we knew. seven mothers with grieving, soothing hands. we have to let them shame us. bitches. no. no. no more. inside is enough. all we have left is looking homeless in our own clothes. all we have is watching daryl at night.

Anita's eyes focused on the hand holding the spoonful of tomato soup. "Just one more bite, Ms. Anita." She went for it. Was surprised she could taste its salt. She smiled.

"That's good soup, Daryl." The hopefulness in her voice perked Wanda. She clutched her dress, which was as roomy as a robe. A shard of clarity pierced her.

"Oh my God. Ain't we supposed to be at court today? Lord Jesus, what about your case?"

Daryl's feeding hand was steady. He had answered this question over and over again. His mother's bouts of clarity came and went, and these last three months it had been his job to manage them. The first time when he told his two mothers the complete truth—that Ms. Anita's widow's check had started up again and went straight to the landlord; that the ladies they didn't like to talk to outside stopped by with bags of canned soup and loaves of bread; that Twin, that crazy lady who looked like she wanted to hit him, set it all up and made sure everything happened the way it should—his two mothers laughed and laughed and slapped their thighs.

"It's all right, Momma. Have another bite." Wanda was obedient and opened her mouth.

"But, Daryl, when do we have to go back to court? What if they pick you up?" Her mouthful of soup mangled her worry. Even when the ladies his mothers didn't like forgot to drop off food, Daryl went to the soup kitchen and got enough supplies to last a week.

Anita and Wanda didn't eat much. They spent their days crying and laughing for hours on end. They dressed each other in the clothes they found in Anita's closet. "Girl, this funeral dress is cute." "I love these blue pants." They shivered like dogs in the rain. As long as they stayed away from the window, Daryl didn't worry. When they leaned their heads out the window and heard things Daryl could not, his stomach hurt. Their heads swiveled like hungry birds, and they murmured to themselves, "No. No. You hear that? Shh. No. Did you hear that?" They only acted like that, looking through the curtains and fondling the locks, when Daryl explained to them why he wasn't in trouble anymore.

"Eat your soup, Momma." His steady hand offered another spoonful. The last time he had told them the entire truth, his mothers trembled for days. Even when he thought about it again, he didn't know why. Why was it so hard to hear that Ms. Twin came to their house, a garbage bag in hand, and its contents set their lives aright? Twin wouldn't take a seat and squatted on the living room floor. Take this, hold that; her directions were curt and scared the shit out of the sixteen-year-old. But everything she gave him they needed. An orange knit cap for Anita and one for Wanda too. Orange sneakers for the both of them. Twin dug deep into the bag and hauled out a stack of money. Old fives and tens were bound together with a rubber band.

"This for your lawyer. Get it to him. Hear me?"

"I don't know—"

"You don't know where he at?" Twin sat on the living room rug, packing away all the knit caps and shoes she had heaped on the floor. "You even know his name?"

"Yeah—"

"Get it to him." Every scrap of orange was back inside the bag. "You," Twin said, and looked so mean Daryl thought she was going to raise a fist. "You take care of those two. Hear me?"

"Yes, ma'am."

For three months Daryl had done the best he could. At night he pretended to sleep and dream while watching through a slit of lashes while his mother and Ms. Anita doted on him. Their gazes were safe and waiting. Sometimes he smiled for no reason at all and was rewarded by a blaze of love so fierce he was tempted to pretend to wake up. He wondered, not for the first time, what kind of truth he could tell his mothers that would let him not pretend anymore to be asleep. In the middle of the night, he wanted to open his eyes and meet their stares. The bowl of soup was endless, and he dipped into it once again. Sweet boy, that Daryl. Who told you to give up? Keep trying.

"Lord, I have to call that lawyer. Jesus."

"Momma."

"Where am I gone get that money from?"

"Momma."

"What? What is it?" Wanda's questions sounded harried, as if she were trying to do three things at once, but she only had to accomplish eating a bowl of tomato soup. Daryl didn't mention that. He was sixteen years old, but one night soon he would not pretend to be asleep, and his mothers would see the eyes of an old man. He might even tell them his plans to find a job. Bagging groceries on the weekend would help out. Maybe when he turned eighteen he'd get lucky and land some union job. For now, he thought about the truth and how to pare it down to its core.

"Twin took care of it."

Wanda didn't shiver when she listened to news she had heard a dozen times. She didn't take off to the window. She didn't even share a long look with Anita. "Oh."

"One more bite."

CHAPTER 38

The judge had a microphone but didn't need it. "How do you plead?"

"Guilty." When Lara said it, the press packed in the courtroom sighed collectively, splintering into three. The smallest group careened toward Lara murmuring questions, but in such a quiet space their voices carried.

"Order! Order!"

The small group of reporters leaning toward Lara hushed immediately. They would have given anything to hear the secrets Lara's lawyer poured in her ear. What was he saying? Whatever it was, he grabbed Lara's elbow hard to make his point. The look on his face was seductive, and the look on Lara's . . . Shh. Hush now. Lara was not thinking about their questions or her lawyer's squeeze; the quiet and murmur in the court encouraged her to think of answers. What response did she have for her mother's pleading eyes? All this had happened because some dangerous dude interrupted my daydream, and this one time I said what was on my mind. And that wouldn't have happened, Momma, if you would have showed up at the audition and helped me make a choice when I was surrounded by all those little Whitneys. Whitneys who were better than Whitney.

Whitneys with cellos and harps. And here I was thinking I was the only little Whitney out there.

The quiet of the court with its soaring ceiling and wood paneling prodded Lara to think up answers. Funny how it was everyone's fault but her own. That's not the answer, Lara thought, as the judge called out her docket number and listed her charges. The small group of reporters still staring at Lara needed a spot of quiet to decipher her expression. Did she look angry or sad or tired or resigned? Maybe her expression was a combination of all four emotions.

Was there a word for that? Her lawyer stroked her arm now, but Lara's eyes drifted. They landed on the small cluster of family and friends. Her mother and Carl tried to meet her stare but couldn't. Lara noticed they held hands. The best the two could do was look at the shape of her forehead.

The largest press group turned to Carl and Morning, their pens and notebooks raised. The writing utensils looked as sharp as blades. No one could shush their questions because their voices never rose above a whisper. Did you know? Did you? Did you? What did you know, and when did you know it? Have you apologized to that Chinese guy? What was his name? Can you even remember that? How long have you known Lara was the perpetrator? Do the members of your organization feel betrayed? How could you—? When did you—? Did you know—? Their questions crescendoed, but no one raised their voice. Carl couldn't possibly answer them all at once.

"I said order! I want order!" The judge's instruction pointed to the spirit of the court, but everyone else adhered to its letter. Who was shouting? No one.

Answers are in this place, Lara thought. It looked and sounded like her church that had burned down: high ceilings, wood paneling—even the quiet that carpeted the proceedings felt like the beginning of Sunday services. She turned her head away from the judge to catch her mother's eye. Her mother caught it. During all the commotion Morning had prepared a speech for the reporters. One that covered the plight of the working poor, the responsibility of the middle class, how practical problems must necessarily be solved by godly means. And we need to take care of our children.

Listen to them. Ask them how their day went and want to know the answer. She had spent too much time with Carl. Too easily her worries about Lara spread into fears about mothers and children and who would help us make it through. Ah, but faced with the enormity of her media debut, Morning's nerves got the best of her, and the only words she was able to softly stutter were "She didn't mean it."

The judge took a breath and spoke into a microphone she hadn't used since it was introduced fifteen years ago. "Order! Or I'll clear this courtroom!" Everyone quieted. Lara's lawyer patted her shoulder. And he was smiling.

"You're pleading guilty?" the judge asked.

"No, ma'am. I plead not guilty." The change in plea produced another burp of muttering, but court officers pulled out handcuffs. They meant business: a certain decorum would be kept. And everybody shut up. Still, as Lara was led away, the reporters pressed forward for a crumb.

"Why'd you do it?"

And Lara, shackled between two bailiffs, paused to ponder the question. A flurry of answers came to her. Because my mother didn't love me; because my mother's milk was: you get or get got. Because years on the subway and walking the city learned you. Trust nothing. These little niggers in the hood have a gang of bad news backing them, and unless you were willing to let fists fly, you were a chump, a mark. Hear this: you cut or get cut.

So he was twelve and little. So? So what? I'm little too. So I did it because everything I ever loved my mother bought on layaway. Everything I wanted was taken away from me three months later. I did it because I wanted to sing, and before I got out a note, I was shown the door. And he was so nice about it. I did it because being decent was for suckers. You don't know that? Living Midtown, West Side, Staten Island hasn't taught you that yet? Come stay where I live and learn the lesson: being violent isn't the last option; it's the first, if you want to make it. You try to be good, and a whole neighborhood will bury you. You want to be remembered? You want to be important? Then you've got to know how to put a hand on a bitch.

And on top of all that, I wasn't the little Whitney everybody told me I was.

But all those answers felt paltry. They were all true but still didn't answer a thing. So. So what do I say? Whose voice should I answer with? Every suggestion—my mother's Southern drawl, Reverend Carl's fiery shout, Wo Ren's Chinese cadence with a joke as a cherry on top, Ted Koppel's, Tyrone's last gurgled cry—Lara ultimately discarded them all and was left with nothing but the sound of her own voice, not her singing voice which had held so much promise, but her speaking one, which she hadn't realized she had. Quiet, husky, sorry, and shy, her plaintive answer held a note of music and questioned everything, "Momma?"

Her words stalled the press; the thousand and one questions they had for Carl died on the tongue. What more could be said? they all thought. Why bother with questions? No one heard Morning's lamenting question, "Lord, what have I done?"—not even Carl who stood right beside her.

If they all moved, they could catch good spots at the ticker-tape parade. Now *there* was a story. This one was wrapped up. Even the few reporters drifting alongside knew Carl would be gone by tomorrow. Besides, two months from now real injustice would happen across town. At Howard Beach white men with bats would chase an innocent black man into oncoming traffic. And when the city heard the news, six million people would point fingers and say, That's wrong. No one would think of Carl. Look how he botched this. Who could trust Carl with a real injustice? Despite his speeches and big smile and small victories, no one would say, Go get Reverend Carl and let him speak for us. There was a better man out there, one with weight and flash and from Brooklyn.

Carl stepped outside the courthouse with Morning at his elbow, not bothering to wonder how in the world Twin had found him all the way downtown. He only thought: Do I deserve this because I have no idea where Anita is? Where are Wanda and her son? Twin crossed the street holding her own stage, and though Carl thought the milk crate she stood on would crack under her weight, it seemed steady. So did she. And wouldn't you know it, that was when a lone cameraman showed. Clicking, clicking away at what should always be hidden. Carl's face with a mournful Morning at his side wouldn't be the picture that summed up Tyrone's murder; not even Anita kneeling curbside would be remembered. The cameraman, uninterested in Carl, wanted to snap pictures of the preparations for tomorrow's ticker-tape parade for the Mets' win. He swung his lens toward Twin standing on a milk crate with an orange beret in her hand and made her famous.

The mountain takes a breath, and spilled confetti floats around her; it cannot wait for tomorrow. The radio announcer who calls the game and swears there isn't a breeze is wrong. Dots of winning paper swirl and eddy around Twin, and Carl cannot only feel the wind; he can see the shape of it. It snakes along the sidewalk, and like the success it signifies, it skids along then reaches for the sky, crawling up the mountain's milk crate, circling her knees, up, up, higher. I am everything good; I am all that is right and fair in the world, those little scraps of paper seem to say.

Twin doesn't need one big breath; she needs several. She heaves and heaves, and Carl thinks the mountain will topple. Despite the distance she is looking Carl in the eye, and suddenly Carl knows exactly what she is going to say. Twin, his mountain, will shout about justice and time, and how even when you think what is right and true is running alongside you, it's never quite that way. She will howl that justice happens behind your back, or it takes place so far in the future that you can't see a speck of it. And even when you think there's no justice at all, you're wrong. Justice travels the long arc and leaves folks like Carl with only its name to say. It is not your time, Carl, justice is telling him. And because your church burned down, you are never going to see me. You'll only know me as rumor. That's your justice. That is what you deserve. Justice is religion, and you didn't keep the faith. Anita and Tyrone and Wanda and Daryl are your fault. Now, take that. Carl prepares himself to hear the accusation, to understand its truth.

Twin, our mountain, tilts her head back and hollers, "Our vote don't count!" Her voice is as big as she is, bigger. Her cry for the moment mutes the erupting cheer happening all around them. And the photographer captures Twin's rage and hurt. From a certain angle her expression is quite beautiful. One face, then two, then a dozen more appear in skyscraper windows. From up on high people hear the mountain. She roars again, "Our vote don't count!"

A NOTE ABOUT THE AUTHOR

April Reynolds teaches at Sarah Lawrence College and is the author of the novel *Knee-Deep in Wonder,* which won the Zora Neale Hurston/Richard Wright Foundation Award and PEN America's Beyond Margins Award. She cowrote *The Red Rooster Cookbook* with Marcus Samuelsson. A former resident of East Harlem, she now lives in Astoria, Queens.

A NOTE ON THE TYPE

This book was set in a modern adaptation of a type designed by the first William Caslon (1692–1766). The Caslon face, an artistic, easily read type, has enjoyed more than two centuries of popularity in our own country. It is of interest to note that the first copies of the Declaration of Independence and the first paper currency distributed to the citizens of the newborn nation were printed in this typeface.

Composed by North Market Street Graphics,
Lancaster, Pennsylvania

Designed by Soonyoung Kwon